5 — 3/25 $2.00

HUNTER'S TRAIL

By Melissa F. Olson

Scarlett Bernard novels

Dead Spots
Trail of Dead
Hunter's Trail

HUNTER'S TRAIL

A SCARLETT BERNARD NOVEL

MELISSA F. OLSON

47NORTH

This is a work of fiction. Names, characters, organizations, places, events, and incidents are either products of the author's imagination or are used fictitiously.

Published by 47North, Seattle

www.apub.com

ISBN-10: 147782412X
ISBN-13: 9781477824122

Cover design by Gene Mollica Studio, LLC

Library of Congress Control Number: 2014932572

Printed in the United States of America

For Chad, who saved me and never knew.

Prologue

Remus arrived at the park while the sun was still high and parked in the lot for the Kings Canyon Lodge, now closed for winter. His old pickup looked forlorn in the abandoned lot, a dingy little boat on a sea of white snow. Remus got out his snowshoes and gear and began trekking east, cutting north into the wilderness as soon as he was certain no one was watching. The main road through the park had closed three days earlier on account of a blizzard, and was not expected to reopen for another week at least. Christmas was only a few days away, and between the weather and the holiday, park security had relaxed to the point of near desertion. Even so, Remus kept the Nikon close to hand, in a separate bag slung across his chest. If the rangers did find him, he would play the part of an ignorant hiker, an amateur photographer with no concept of personal safety. Once upon a time, Remus marveled, shaking his head to himself, he had even been that person.

It had taken forty-four years to find his purpose, but now he knew his place in the world, the true calling that pulled him farther north with each shuffle of his snowshoes. The only thing that mattered was protecting the wolves. He talked to himself on the hike, mumbling through the long string of affirmations and pledges that had propelled him through the last few months of preparation.

He paused to rest at the foot of one of the enormous sequoias, squinting up to admire its thick trunk in the fading sunlight. His breath crystallized in the air, and he took a long moment to appreciate the quiet, so different from his parents' neighborhood in Los Angeles. Then the sound of shifting snow drew his attention downward. A white-tailed jackrabbit bounded closer, pausing to stare at him from a few yards away.

Remus was delighted. "Why, hello, baby," he crooned, squatting a little. "I'm headed in that direction too. Can we walk together?"

The hare gazed at him for another moment, its empty black eyes only mildly curious about the intruder. Then it twitched a hind leg and flashed back the way it had come, its white tail disappearing in an instant. "Fine, then," Remus muttered angrily. "I'll make bigger friends, and we'll come back and eat you."

He followed the compass north for another two hours, until the last trace of sunlight had vanished and the moon had risen, low and fat on the horizon. It was well below freezing now, the trees heavy with snow that hadn't quite completed the journey to the forest floor. Remus found the spot where a long, winding line of same-sized trees formed a sort of natural entrance to the thickest part of the woods, and he dropped his pack. He squatted down and unzipped the main compartment with cold fingers, pulling out a brand-new camping lantern and a little collapsible tripod. He turned on the lantern first, using the light to set up the tripod and the Nikon on a flat, stable stretch of embedded rock, with the camera's lens facing toward him. When he was satisfied with the positioning, he angled the lantern to get as much light on his face as possible and turned on the camera, thumbing the switch to the "Record Video" setting. Knees creaking, he settled back on his butt, smoothed down his hair, and began.

"My name is Remus. This video is either scientific evidence or my last will and testament, depending on how the night goes." He gave the camera a big winning smile before continuing. "On the night of December twenty-third, I have come to Kings Canyon

National Park, where I hope to be bitten . . . by a *werewolf*." He paused for dramatic effect. "I have heard that the nearest pack sometimes visits the northernmost stretches of this park during the winter, and that one bite can change a man into a werewolf himself. It is my life's mission to protect and celebrate these magnificent wild creatures, and I feel the best way to truly understand their needs is to become one with them."

Remus sipped from his water bottle, enjoying the sounds of the woods around him. He imagined an audience for the video, an awestruck congregation of his fellow eco-warriors and activists. Putting down the bottle, he turned to face the camera again. "This is the fourth month in a row that I have traveled to Kings Canyon. So far I have seen little sign of wolf activity, but I have high hopes for this fateful night. It is a busy time for the world of *men*," he said with distaste, "and the snow makes the trek difficult for the two-legged. Hopefully—" Remus stopped short, listening. He forgot to keep the low dramatic tones in his voice, which came out high and excited as he continued, "Did you hear that? I swear, it almost sounded like a—"

The second time there was no mistaking it: a long, deadly-sweet howl that was snatched up by the wind and braided through the tree line. The acoustics were confusing, and Remus couldn't pinpoint the direction the howl originated from. The sound wasn't quite what he'd expected, either. It didn't seem wild and noble, like on his recordings. It seemed . . . terrifying. For the first time since he'd concocted this plan, Remus felt a thin edge of fear slicing through his excitement.

He struggled to smile broadly at the camera. "That was quick," he exclaimed shakily, and rummaged in his pack for his digital recorder and the cattle prod. "This was recorded from a pack of wolves in Idaho," he told the camera as he hit the "Play" button on the recorder. A territory howl came blasting out, loud enough to make Remus feel smug about the extra money he'd taken from his dad for the upscale equipment. He played three full minutes of howling, grinning stupidly before hitting the "Stop" button. "Now let's see if they respond," he said to the camera. He made a show of looking toward the forest entrance, but it was fully dark now and the brightness of the camp lantern had destroyed his night vision. The silence was eerie, and he realized that somehow the park had gotten even quieter. *What—*

The attack came from behind. A hundred fifty pounds of predator slammed into Remus, teeth locking down hard on the back of his neck. Remus let out a squeak and scrambled for the cattle prod, knocking over the tripod. He dimly heard the crash of his camera hitting the rock but—oh shit, his neck hurt—and felt the wolf shaking its head, worrying at Remus's spinal cord. *For God's sake* . . . His fingers finally latched on to the cattle prod, and Remus reversed the foot-long weapon so the tip was toward him, shoving it backward under his armpit until he felt it make contact with the wolf. Remus pulled the trigger and felt a buzz of secondary electricity hit his neck, but by then everything was getting dark, and Remus felt a brief surge of noble pride. He would die, but for his cause.

For the wolves.

Chapter 1

"Seaweed!" Molly marveled for the third time, rubbing the sheet of paper-thin nori. "Can you believe it's made of *seaweed*, Scarlett?"

I squirmed around on my utility stool so I could face her. The "Make Your Own Sushi Rolls" class was being held in the science lab of a private community college, the kind of room with shelves of beakers and those two-person tables with little gas nozzles. Molly and the rest of the class perched easily on the metal stools, but I was at a weird angle because I was using a second stool to prop up my knee brace. "I know I grew up in a small town," I said drily, "but I was aware of seaweed as an ingredient in sushi, yes."

She gave me a good-natured swat on the arm. "Don't ruin this for me," she said with a shark-wide smile, tossing back her copper-colored bob. There was a tinge of warning in her voice.

"Yes, ma'am," I said, trying to work up some enthusiasm. Molly, I should mention, is my landlady and roommate. Oh, and when she's not around me, she's also a vampire. I'm a null, a human who negates all the magic in a certain area around me. Vampires who get close to me become human again and age just like anyone else, which is what Molly wants more than anything. She was only seventeen when she was turned, which isn't nearly as old now as it was in 1905. In exchange for a very generous break on the rent, I'm supposed to hang out with Molly and help her get older.

Unfortunately, she'd recently decided that she wanted to define "hang out" as "take a 'Make Your Own Sushi' class together." Vampires can't eat people food, so Molly wanted to try some exotic new tastes while she was temporarily human. And for a traditional gal from Victorian Great Britain, it doesn't get a lot more exotic than sushi rolls. I wasn't about to point out to Molly that sushi had been around for a while and that the rest of Los Angeles had progressed a hundred steps down the evolutionary line of exotic food trends. I was afraid she would make me eat offal or something.

"Ladies," said the instructor, approaching the table that Molly and I were sharing. "Everything all right here?" He had introduced himself as Hoshi ("rhymes with Yoshi") and was a short Japanese man with a mild accent, a gleaming black buzz cut, and a tendency to overshare. He'd opened the class by explaining that he was teaching for some extra money because his American wife was expecting their unplanned third child. Because that's something you tell complete strangers.

"You bet!" Molly chirped, beaming at him. "I can't believe it's seaweed!"

Hoshi cut his eyes over to me very briefly, unsure if Molly was putting him on. "She's new to sushi," I said gravely.

His eyes widened, as if now *I* was putting him on. Which was fair. "Right," he said, a little suspiciously, and then he turned his attention to the rest of the class. "Let's begin our first rolls, everyone," he called, weaving through the tables to the front of the room, where he'd laid out his own supplies on the instructor's desk.

He began walking us through making a simple cucumber roll, and I concentrated on his instructions. I rolled the rice and cucumber up in the nori, pressed down along the edges to make it stick together, and glanced over at my struggling roommate. Molly's hands weren't used to the motions of food preparation, and she had none of her usual vampire grace in my presence, so her lopsided roll fell apart over and over, until each attempt began to resemble a Charlie Chaplin sketch. When she began furtively wiping sticky rice off her hands with the dangly tail of her cashmere cardigan, glancing around to make sure no one had seen her, I couldn't help snickering.

"Good thing I wore my play clothes," Molly said seriously, and my snicker turned into a full-on laugh. In all the time I've known Molly, I have never seen her wear an item of clothing that costs less than a tank of gas, and her "play clothes"—cashmere sweater, designer T-shirt with a picture of a T. rex failing at a push-up, and jeans that looked soft enough to make baby asses jealous—were no exception. She looked up from her sweater, amused.

"What?" I asked, picking up a knife and cutting my long tube of sushi roll into slices.

"Scarlett Bernard," Molly said, her voice low and joyous. "If I didn't know better, I'd say you were actually having a good time."

"Me? What? I am not," I said immediately. Because I'm mature.

"Pants on fire!" Molly crowed, her voice now officially too loud. Hoshi paused in his instructions to send us a questioning look.

"She's kidding, sir," I called helpfully. "My pants are not actually on fire." Giving us a stern frown, Hoshi went back to his lesson, and I said out of the side of my mouth, "Are you suggesting I shouldn't be having fun?" Because frankly, the thought had occurred to me.

"Of course not. I just haven't seen you look happy in . . ." She trailed off, and then finished awkwardly, "You know. A while."

I did know. I'd spent the last few days huddled in bed, alternately icing my knee and staring guiltily at the ceiling. And before that . . . well, Molly was right; it was good to be out. "Thanks for this, Molls," I said quietly.

Molly flashed a smile—and then frowned down at my perfect sushi roll. Arching a smug eyebrow, I popped a piece of the roll into my mouth. It's a rare day when I'm better at something than she is.

"Seriously, how is yours staying together?" she demanded.

"It's all in the wrist," I said around a mouthful of rice. Molly apparently had missed that particular idiom, because she examined her own wrists with new interest, and I almost choked on a bite of cucumber.

Then my cell phone buzzed in my pocket and I jumped, knocking my cane from where I'd propped it against the table. It clattered loudly to the floor, and the middle-aged lesbian couple at the next table glared at me. I shrugged in a "what're you gonna do" kind of way and leaned back so I could dig the cell out of my jacket, which I'd tossed on the empty table behind ours. The caller ID said it was Will, the head of the Los Angeles werewolf pack. I frowned.

My job is cleaning up crime scenes for the three Old World parties in Los Angeles—the vampires, the werewolves, and the witches—and I'm on retainer, so in theory, any of them could call me anytime. But I hadn't had any work calls since my injury, and frankly, Will was the last person I'd expect to call me for any other reason.

The phone buzzed a second time, and Hoshi paused in his explanation to glare at me. I was tempted to turn the phone off and put it back in my pocket, but that went against years of habit—and besides, Will wouldn't call unless he absolutely had to. And by the time I hobbled out to the hall with my cane, I'd miss him. There was nothing to do but answer. "Sorry, Hoshi, but I'm an obstetrician," I lied. "I have to take this." The instructor's face relaxed into a forgiving nod, and the couple next to me went back to their own rolls. I held the phone to my ear. "This is Dr. Bernard," I said serenely. Molly grinned without looking up from her sushi.

Will didn't even mention the fake title, which told me right away that things were serious. "You need to get to my house right now," he said, his voice urgent.

I blinked in surprise. He was calling me into a crime scene? "For . . . working things?" I said stupidly. No, Scarlett, he's got an emergency grape-juice stain. I glanced down at my swollen knee, which looked barely restrained by the metal-and-Velcro brace. "Will, I'm not exactly fit for duty yet. Is it . . . really minor?" I asked hopefully.

"No," he said shortly. "It's a disaster. *At my house*." My face must have changed, because Molly's own eyes widened in alarm. A weight I hadn't known I'd dropped settled itself back into place on my shoulders.

My employers and I don't discuss crime scenes over the phone, for obvious reasons, but we also don't bother using a lot of code words to describe the situations. Codes are difficult to remember, and ultimately, knowing in advance what I need to clean up won't make me get there any faster. They send me to a location, I get there as fast as I can, and I use whatever I have in my van, the White Whale.

One of the few codes we *do* have, however, is "disaster." If Will was using it now, that meant that somewhere in his house there was a dead human body.

Chapter 2

"Scarlett?" Molly said uncertainly. She had put a hand out like she was spotting me, and I realized I had swayed a little bit on my stool. I grabbed the edge of the lab table for balance and told myself to get my shit together. It wasn't like this was my first dead body.

"Hang on a second, Will," I said into the phone. Without hanging up I put the phone in my hoodie pocket and looked at Molly, tilting my head toward the door. She nodded and began gathering our jackets and her purse. Technically Molly could have stayed, since it was after sunset, but she wouldn't have been able to taste anything without me anyway. She handed me my cane, and we walked—well, Molly walked, I did more of a weird pirate shuffle with the cane—out to the hallway. "Good luck!" Hoshi said gaily, probably glad to be rid of the two of us. Didn't blame him at all.

As soon as the door closed behind us I put the phone back up to my ear. "I'll come," I said to Will. I raised my eyebrows a tiny bit at Molly, mouthing *Will you help?* at her. She nodded an affirmation. "Molly's driving," I added, sending her a grateful look.

"Fine," Will said impatiently. "I won't be here; you'll have to clean up without me. I was just stopping home for a second to grab some papers. I was lucky I noticed it on the doorstep."

"Wait . . . you're leaving?" I asked, genuinely confused. I'd expected Will to be angry with me, but I didn't think he'd actually blow me off, not with a dead body.

"Yes," he said shortly. "Esmé's watching the bar, and she has to pick up her kids." I had met Esmé, a short, pretty werewolf in her mid-thirties who had gotten married young, had kids young—and then had been turned into a werewolf when she and her husband were attacked during a camping trip to Canada. Her husband hadn't survived, but Esmé had made it through the change, and suddenly found herself a thirty-year-old widow with three kids and never enough money. With Will's office manager, Caroline, dead and his bartender, Eli, in hiding, I understood why Esmé was picking up shifts at his bar, Hair of the Dog.

But not why the bar needed to be open. "Couldn't you just put up your *Closed for Private Party* sign?" I asked. I'd seen it a couple of times when Will had emergency pack business.

"Health inspector's coming tonight. Too late to reschedule." His voice was coming out as a growl now, his words in terse short sentences. This was not a good sign. Will's control is excellent. If he was struggling to keep it together . . . he was either really upset, or the body was in really bad shape, and the smell of it was pushing at his self-restraint. Or both.

I kept my voice calm and careful. "Is anyone else at your place?" Will's place served as the pack's home base; all the werewolves spent a lot of time there. I'd been there myself twice, both times to clean up blood after werewolf fights.

"No. House is empty. I'll leave the front door open."

"Okay, I'm on it," I said. Will just grunted and hung up. I looked at the phone, shaking my head. Shit. I glanced up at Molly, who was patiently holding out my jacket.

Only a week earlier, my psychotic ex-mentor, Olivia, had been running amok in LA. Olivia had a thing for controlling people, and I was the toy she wanted most for her collection. So she'd come after me and mine, hoping to break me down in every way she could. Olivia had sent cookies laced with wolfberry to Hair of the Dog, where my friend Caroline and my sometimes-friend-with-benefits Eli both worked. Caroline and Eli were werewolves, and giving them wolfberry is basically like giving a regular human a truckload of PCP and a bunch of stabby weapons.

I hadn't been with them when they were poisoned, but I'd seen the fallout. Caroline had died that night, shot with silver by Will when he couldn't keep her from attacking the poor humans who'd been at the bar. Eli had lost control so completely that he'd killed two people. Plagued by guilt, he'd begged Will to shoot him too, but I wouldn't let him. Instead, I'd done something I was not supposed to be able to do: I'd focused my power outward and changed Eli back into a human. Permanently.

It seemed like a good idea at the time, honest.

I'd passed out afterward, possibly from changing him, or possibly as a result of the confrontation with Olivia, when she'd poisoned me with illegal chemotherapy drugs and made me fight an enormous man-shaped clay demon. What can I say, we had some issues. At any rate, it sent me into . . . well, a bit of a coma.

When I woke up a few days later, I'd felt the vertigo before I even opened my eyes, a nauseous sensation as though someone had scrambled gravity within the boundaries of my own skin. It took me a few attempts just to open my eyes because pulling up my eyelids was like trying to hold up the bottom of a curtain with a stick. When my eyes finally focused, I saw a bunch of medical supplies on a little table next to me. The table and the wallpaper behind it were familiar, and after a moment I put together that I was in my own bed, in my own bedroom at Molly's house.

Will was in a folding chair next to my bed, bent over a cell phone. He looked terrible. Which was startling in itself, because werewolves don't really look terrible. There are many downsides to being a werewolf, but one of the few advantages is that the werewolves practically hum with good health. They have a high metabolism and natural athleticism, and they don't get sick or suffer minor ailments like pimples or cold sores. Most of them don't even have bad hair days; they're that healthy. When they're in my presence, some of that sheen dulls a little, but they still look like the picture of wellness.

But Will looked as terrible as I'd ever seen any werewolf look. His tan dress pants and Hair of the Dog polo shirt looked slept-in, and his unremarkably brown hair was greasy and sticking out in weird directions. There were new hollows under his eyes, and even sitting in a chair, he looked like he was struggling to stay upright.

I must have shifted or something, because he looked up from the phone. "You're awake," he noted.

"Will," I mumbled. The vertigo had eased a little bit, but trying to put words together was like trying to do magnetic poetry upside down. "What happened to you?" I managed.

"The pack," he said heavily. "The pack is falling apart."

I don't know what I was expecting him to say, but that wasn't it. "Why?"

Will looked at me patiently for a moment, but when I didn't speak, he sighed and said, "Because you cured Eli."

It came back to me then, in a rush: the witch murders, the mentor-turned-vampire, the scarred witch in the white lab coat. Her pet golem. And Eli.

I had changed Eli back into a human.

Despite the disorientation, I tried to sit up, flailing my arms backward and ramming my head forward like a spastic turtle. "Stop!" Will ordered, and although he looked like shit and he was human in my presence, there was such command in his voice that

I froze. "I've had a doctor taking care of you, but she's on a food break," Will said, more quietly. "Don't do any damage to yourself while she's gone."

For the first time, I noticed the IV and catheter that were attached to my body. Awkward. The IV stung where I had tugged at it during my daring attempt to flail around. I felt so strange, like my head was tired and sober but my body was on spring break in Cabo. "S'wrong with me?" I mumbled.

"You had a grand mal seizure after you cured Eli," Will said matter-of-factly. "You hit your head on the metal bars of the cot and got a mild concussion. You also twisted your knee and tore a ligament or something. The doctor can fill you in when she gets back."

I leaned back and took a deep breath, trying to calm down. *Cured*. I had never attached what I could do to that word before; it seemed absurd, cartoonish.

But . . . wasn't that exactly what I had done?

"I wanted to help him . . . I thought I was . . ." My voice broke, and my mouth was suddenly too dry to swallow.

"I'm fairly certain you weren't thinking much at all," Will said frankly. I started to protest, and Will held up a hand. "Look, I understand why you did it. I saw Eli fall apart too. But now he's had to leave, Caroline's dead, and there are rumors flying in the pack. You have no idea how you've changed things."

I winced. Will regarded me sadly, and for a minute his expression was *exactly* like the look on my father's face when I'd been suspended for liberating a few dozen frogs from the high school science lab. "I have to get back," he said, "but I need you to understand something, okay?" I gave him my best nod, and he continued with careful enunciation, "You can't tell anyone."

I blanched. "About Eli?"

"Eli, what you can do, that night at the bar, none of it. I'll do my best to keep the pack together, and hopefully it'll blow over soon."

I thought of Jesse Cruz, the LAPD detective who'd partnered with me on the witch murder case—who had kissed me after I'd shot Olivia. Oh, God. He must be worried out of his mind. "Jesse . . . ," I began.

"Detective Cruz has been taken care of," Will interrupted. He saw my jaw hit my lap and immediately shook his head in tired bemusement. "Sorry, bad phrasing. We didn't kill him. Dashiell pressed his mind to think you're in the UK for a bit. We didn't know how else to handle him until you woke up."

I relaxed. I had sent my brother, Jack, to the UK to visit another null when Olivia was running amok. Jack must have returned to LA by now, but Jesse didn't know that.

Will stood up. "I've got to get back."

"Will, wait," I protested. I had a hundred questions. Who was the doctor? How did I get to Molly's? Who already knew what? And for the love of God, who had changed my clothes while I was unconscious? But I settled for simply, "Where's Eli?"

"Hidden," Will answered. "I'm keeping him in the city until we know for sure that it's permanent. There's still the chance that the wolf magic will seep back in." There was a note of hope in his voice, which told me just how bad things were. Eli had been tortured by guilt over killing those people when he was on wolfberry. And apart from that, he had hated being a werewolf, which is like constantly fighting a battle for your own identity. Will should have been at least a little happy for him, like a cancer patient whose chemo buddy goes into remission. The fact that the alpha was actually *hoping* the werewolf magic would come back was a very bad sign.

Will moved toward the door. "Can I see him?" I asked, trying to get the words out quickly before he could disappear.

He paused. "You can talk to him on the phone, if you want to," Will said gently, "but you should really think about whether or not that's a good idea."

"Why?"

He gave me another one of those sorrowful, knowing looks, like I was being dense on purpose and it was making him sad. "Because he's *free* now, Scarlett. Give him a little time to adjust, figure out what he wants. Maybe something good can still come out of this mess."

Guilt sagged down on me like a new layer of pain as I realized he was right. Eli was no longer chained to magic or the pack; he could do whatever he wanted. And he deserved a chance to be human without me pulling him back into all the crazy.

So I'd stayed away from Eli. And now there was a dead body at Will's to get rid of. It seemed like a pretty clear sign that I'd done the right thing.

As Molly and I walked out to the van, I glanced over at my roommate, who had a self-satisfied smile on her lips like she'd won a bet.

"What?" I asked.

"See?" she said smugly. "Now aren't you glad I wore my play clothes?"

Chapter 3

I tossed Molly the keys when we got to the White Whale. I'd managed to maneuver it to class myself by throwing my hurt leg over Molly's lap in the passenger seat and driving with my left foot. It was awkward, and I had to go slowly, but I prefer to drive when I go somewhere with Molly. Whether she's in my radius or not, Molly drives like a lot of vampires: as though she would definitely survive a catastrophic car accident. At any rate, letting the vampire Danica Patrick behind the wheel now would ensure that we got there as fast as possible.

The LA night was cool, and I shivered in my hoodie and light jacket. My insides actually felt contracted, like they'd been squeezed by a giant fist. Still dazed by the phone conversation with Will, I climbed into the passenger seat without a word. Molly was looking at me, brow furrowed. "You okay?" she asked.

"Yes. Well, no," I answered. My knee ached with a thick, swollen intensity that I'd gotten used to working around . . . as long as I was taking four ibuprofen at all times. That wasn't what was worrying me right now, but I wasn't in the mood to explain human anxiety to Molly again. "I'm fine. Just go." She shrugged and backed the van out of the parking spot at twenty miles an hour. The tires screeched and the odor of burned rubber wafted into the van. I winced and managed not to comment.

I instructed Molly to get on PCH toward Pacific Palisades. I braced myself against the armrests, thinking about the call. Someone had dumped a body on the alpha werewolf's doorstep? That was pretty damned bold—and also eight shades of crazy. Who would do that? The full moon was still a week away, which made it unlikely that one of the werewolves had changed and killed someone. Technically most of the werewolves were powerful enough to change between full moons, but Will discouraged it as much as he could. Even if one of them had mauled someone to death, I couldn't see them doing it at Will's house.

I supposed it was possible that one werewolf had killed another. A vampire is always a vampire, and witches are comparatively ordinary people with the ability to channel magic, but werewolves have a rough time of it. The magic that forces them to change into wolves once a month never lets them truly relax; instead, it itches away at their psyches, keeping them on guard and antsy like recovering alcoholics at an open bar. That's why the pack members get into fights so often. The problem with that theory, though, was that it's insanely difficult to kill a werewolf— one of the other benefits of their condition.

My thoughts spun around and around like that, testing and rejecting scenarios, until I realized Molly had been asking me a question. "Hmm? What?" I asked.

"I said, this must be a long commute for Will, to get to the dog food place."

I smiled briefly. I'd never heard anyone call Will's bar "the dog food place," but then again, the vampires aren't exactly known for their respectfulness toward other Old World factions.

The stoplight a quarter mile in front of us turned yellow, and Molly stomped on the gas pedal. I grabbed the passenger seat's "oh shit" handle, my fingers tightening until the knuckles glowed white. "I guess he probably works unusual hours," Molly said thoughtfully, oblivious to my panic. I took a few deep breaths, distracting myself by imagining what we would do if Molly got us pulled over. As a vampire she could press a cop's mind and get us off without a ticket, but I'd have to get at least ten feet away from her first, and didn't cops get really upset if you got out of the car?

It was almost eight by the time we wound up Temescal Canyon Road toward Will's street. The alpha werewolf of Los Angeles lived in the last house on a little dead-end street off the canyon road. It was an ideal location for the pack because Will's property backed up to Temescal Canyon Park, which closed every day at sunset. Once a month, all the werewolves in LA drove up to Will's place, hiked deep into the park, and changed together as a pack when the moon rose.

We turned onto Will's street and cruised past Will's next-door neighbor, who was only a hundred yards away from the alpha's property. Will had planted a thicket of carefully chosen shrubs to insulate sound between the two houses. The small lot across the street from Will's was empty—in fact, I was pretty sure he owned it, because I'd seen him use it for overflow parking when his driveway was full.

I made Molly take the time to turn the van around in the empty lot so we could back it into Will's driveway. This was one of the useful tips I had learned from Olivia: when you're dealing with a complete dead body, always back in. It means less exposure, and you can get away faster if there's trouble.

We climbed out of the Whale at the same time, and Molly rounded the nose of the van to walk next to me. I took a second to glance around, checking for witnesses. We were still well within LA County, but the combination of the empty lot and the next-door shrubs made it seem like we were in the middle of nowhere. The smog still dimmed out the stars up here, but the expanse of city lights below made it seem like the night sky had just relocated a little lower. Looking at it too long was disorienting.

It was also *quiet* this far into the mountains. My hometown of Esperanza had also been quiet compared to the city, but not like this. There was an eerie stillness in the air, like we were inside a bubble of silence that covered the city below us, and if we so much as breathed wrong, it could burst. "What *is* that?" Molly whispered, looking around. There was no reason to whisper, but I understood the impulse. The sudden quiet was like being in a church or library. "Why does it feel like something's about to shatter?"

I shrugged. "I think that's just nature," I said. I tried to keep my voice normal, but I was a little creeped out too. Someone had taken a big risk, driving way out here in this quiet just to dump a corpse on Will's doorstep. One flat tire, suspicious neighbor, or broken taillight could have blown the whole thing.

I leaned on the cane to pivot, hobbling around the van to open the back door. I grabbed my black duffel bag of tools and supplies, slinging the strap over my head to wear it across my body. Molly watched me closely as we moved toward the house, probably expecting me to keel over. In her defense, I'd fallen down several times in her house while my equilibrium was returning.

Will's driveway terminated into a small one-vehicle carport, which was empty, since Will had gone back to work. From the outside, there was nothing at all memorable about Will's house. It was a small white split-level with a narrow wooden walkway, sort of like a boardwalk, that started next to the carport and ran around the corner of the house to the front door. Most of the homes we'd driven past made a point to exploit every possible opportunity for a big picture window, but Will's had only a couple teeny bedroom windows visible from the front. However, I knew that the back of the house made up for them with an enormous window that was nearly the size of the whole living room wall. If you were inside the house, it seemed like you were in a cave that looked out over acres of wilderness—the perfect den.

Will had left several exterior lights on for Molly and me, which I very much appreciated as we made our way up the long boardwalk. The last time I was at Will's, I could have sworn there was an extra large welcome mat out here, an ugly green thing that said *Please Wipe Your Paws*. Now it was missing. When we were about five feet from the door I paused, switching the cane to my left hand and pulling a heavy-duty penlight out of the duffel with my right. The penlight's beam was the width of my thumb, and I ran it around the wood at my feet. Sure enough, I could make out a rectangle of darker, less worn wood where the welcome mat must have been only an hour or two ago. I looked for blood and spotted a number of red smears just outside of the rectangle. Whoever dumped the body must have dropped it right on the damned welcome mat.

I glanced back at Molly, who was still scanning the darkness surrounding the house. She was a little flushed. Molly had gone on one other job with me, but that had just been cleaning up a few chicken carcasses after one of the werewolves had decided he felt like chicken that night. A dead body was a different ball game. "Nervous?" I asked.

She smiled ruefully. "A little bit. I've never really spent much time away from big cities. This"—she gestured at the trees nearest the house—"is kind of scary."

Of course. Molly the vampire didn't even flinch at disposing of a corpse, but put some trees around her and it's like she's in a dogfight.

Well. Maybe that was a poor choice of words. "Nah," I said laconically, leaning on the cane again as I poked along beside her. "Scary is what's *inside*."

Then I reached forward and turned the doorknob, giving it a gentle push. The door swung inward with a loud, theatrical *creeeeeeeeeeeak* that would have made Vincent Price crap his pants. I glanced at Molly, who didn't even miss a beat as she drawled,

"Good *eve*ning," in a fakey Dracula voice. We both chortled nervously.

"He's *gotta* leave it that way on purpose, right?" I said, smiling a little. I stepped into the pristine rectangle of darker wood where I knew I wouldn't get any blood on me and thumbed the penlight off. I put it back in my bag and leaned forward to reach around the doorway, feeling for a light switch. "I mean, how hard would it be to get some WD-40 and just . . ." My voice trailed off as I clicked the light switch. I felt the smile fall off my face.

Chapter 4

"We need to get inside," I said quietly, moving forward. "Don't step in the blood." Molly crowded into the entryway behind me so we could get the door closed and I took a good look at what was on the floor.

It was small, first of all. You hear the words "human body," you kind of expect it to be the same size you are, or at least pretty close. But from the chest to the knees, most of the . . . meat . . . was missing. The woman—it was obvious from her face and hair, if not her body—was lying mostly on her back, but bent just a little to one side like she was trying to curl up in a protective ball. She'd been wearing some sort of lavender top, so shredded and bloodied now that the visible purple material wouldn't have covered the strap of my duffel bag. I was guessing she'd worn jeans on the bottom, but only because the denim waistband was more or less intact. He hadn't taken her pants off her. I noticed a corner of the welcome mat beneath the body. Will had just hauled the whole thing inside, which was good. It'd probably protected his hardwood floor, at least a little.

Long experience with crime scene cleanup had taught me to automatically hold my breath when I first arrived somewhere, but I let it out now, and inhaled the scent of damp, drying blood. No rot, which I'd smelled before, or any other bodily fluids, which meant . . . I gagged a little. It meant she'd been killed recently, and whoever killed her had likely eaten her bowels.

Unable to look at the gore any longer, I moved my gaze toward her face. It was untouched, without even a droplet of blood. Given the circumstances, that seemed a little sick. She had been a little plain, with sunken eyes and a spray of freckles across a hooked nose. Her expression was flat—not peaceful, or terrified, or shocked. She just looked *dead*, her blue eyes staring sightlessly in the general direction of nothing. She had blonde hair cut in a chin-length bob with artistically shaded highlights. One lock of hair had fallen across the bridge of her nose, and I suppressed the urge to smooth it aside for her.

I checked Molly's face to see how she was coping. The vampire looked sad. "She was so young," Molly said softly, shaking her head. The woman looked older than me, maybe around thirty, but I suppose that's young to a vampire. Molly looked up and caught me staring at her. "What?" she said self-consciously.

"You've . . . I mean, you know . . ."

"Killed people? Yes. Never on purpose, though," Molly contended, a sudden fierceness in her voice. She hadn't looked up from the corpse since we got inside. "And *not* like this. This woman died hard."

I nodded. Vampires are built to be lethal, of course, but they usually don't kill when they feed. Most of the time they press their victim's mind to forget what's happening as they take a little bit of blood, and everybody walks away happy. Newer vampires, however, have to . . . practice before they figure out how to control themselves. And even if the victim does die, he or she usually goes quite happily, still under the vampire's thrall. This kind of brutalization wasn't their style.

Molly finally tore her gaze away from the body to look at me. "Who would *do* this?" she asked, her voice breaking. She was human, in my presence, which meant that the natural detachment vampires develop wasn't really influencing her.

"A werewolf," I said quietly. "I think this was a werewolf." It was a guess, based on the tearing at the edges of the wounds. But I'd seen werewolf bites before, and besides, the body had been dumped at Will's house. It wasn't exactly a stretch.

"We should get started," I said absently. I needed to destroy all evidence that a crime had been committed here, and the clock was ticking. "I'll do the worst stuff, I just need you to help with lifting." I bent at the waist and unzipped one of the duffel's pockets, pulling out surgical gloves. I handed a pair to Molly and pulled on my own. When mine were secure, I reached into the duffel's main compartment for a box of megathick Hefty garbage bags.

It's awkward, snapping a garbage bag open when you're wearing gloves, but I've gotten the hang of it over the years. I do have a few actual body bags, which seem more respectful, but they're also harder to get, and frankly, the total mass of these remains didn't justify using one. Holding onto Molly's hand, I lowered myself to the floor, crouching awkwardly on my left leg so my braced right knee could stay extended, and began to tilt the body sideways. Then I abruptly froze. "Oh, shit," I said softly.

Molly peered over my shoulder. "Is that what I think it is?"

"Yes." I chewed my lip for a second, considering.

"Scarlett?" Molly said. "What are you thinking? You have that look."

"What look?"

"You know." She mimed an exaggerated, scheming expression and stroked an imaginary goatee. "Like you're about to do something you're not supposed to."

I sighed. "Because I am." Dropping the garbage bag, I dug through the main compartment of the duffel again until I found what I wanted: a nylon camera case. I unzipped it and pulled out an inexpensive digital camera, which thankfully powered up despite months of nonuse.

"You're taking *pictures*?" Molly said doubtfully. "Is that wise?"

"Probably not." I said, and snapped a wide shot. I couldn't blame her for asking—my whole job is based on destroying or hiding evidence, not creating more.

Molly sighed. "I hope you know what you're doing."

Still in the awkward crouch, I sort of half duckwalked around the body with my weight on my good leg, trying to get another angle. "So do I."

When I'd finished taking photos and returned the camera to my duffel, I opened the garbage bag again and worked a hand under the body's intact calves, lifting the bare feet into the bag. I fought my revulsion—her body wasn't even cold yet. The smell of gore was worse now that I was down by the body, and I tried to concentrate on breathing through my mouth. When the feet were in, I had Molly hold the bag so I could work one hand under the shoulders and one under the torso, sliding the body into the bag. I had no leverage, and it was tough to balance on half a crouch, but it didn't really matter because the thing was just so *light* compared to most corpses. The whole body weighed maybe sixty pounds. I was able to slide it in by moving my hands along the body like I was feeding out a length of rope.

The worst part was the perfect head, which came dragging along after the body like an overloaded caboose. "Stop," Molly hissed abruptly, and I froze, with only the head still outside the bag. She reached down without speaking and closed the dead woman's eyes, then muttered something as she crossed herself. I'd never seen any kind of religious behavior from her before, but I slid the head into the bag without comment. I can't imagine that the Catholic Church endorses vampires, but I do understand that some habits die hard.

One of the woman's hands had strayed and was still outside of the bag, so I gritted my teeth and took hold of it. Her fingernails were torn and shredded, her fingers streaked with blood. She'd fought, then. The struggle would have been messy, and the area just outside the door had been fairly clean, aside from a few blood smears. So she'd been disemboweled somewhere nearby, or maybe in a vehicle. I tucked the hand in the bag as gently as I could.

When the body was all the way in, I picked up both ends of the mat and lifted it off the floor, trying not to wring any of the blood out. Molly held the bag open and I carefully put the mat inside, on top of the dead woman. I think Molly and I were both relieved when I tightened the thick drawstring so we could no longer see the remains.

"What now?" she asked. "Do we clean up the rest?"

"Not exactly," I said, eyeing the floor. The mat had done a good job of soaking up most of the blood, but there were a few scuffs and smears of blood that had tracked onto the hardwood. I wiped up what I could with paper towels, which I shoved in the garbage bag before knotting it tightly. Then I pulled a small spray bottle out of my bag and uncapped it.

"What is that?" Molly said curiously.

"Mostly oxygen bleach, and a few other chemicals. Olivia's recipe," I answered absently. My thoughts were racing. I'd seen a lot of gross stuff since I started this job, but this . . . this was more like a message. No—a taunt. It wasn't just food, that was for sure.

I carefully sprayed each and every one of the blood spots on the floor, coating the wood with the stuff. Then I stepped back outside and sprayed every one of those smears too, tossing the spray bottle into the duffel bag. The whole process took less than a minute. I gathered the loose upper end of the bag and flipped it in a quick knot. "Let's go."

"Don't you wanna . . . won't that damage the wood?"

I shrugged. "Yes. But that's Will's problem. We leave the solution on, so it can fully break down the blood's composition. He'll probably end up getting new floors anyway, but even if he doesn't, nobody will be able to prove that this was blood or extract DNA."

She nodded thoughtfully. "I was just thinking of that time at the dog park, where you made it seem like nothing had ever happened."

I zipped up my duffel bag and hefted it back onto my shoulder. "My job is to destroy evidence of a crime above anything else. If bloodstains were the only thing here, I'd stay and work on them, but the priority is getting rid of the body. For all we know, the killer may have called the cops and tipped them off already."

"Oh," Molly said, checking her watch. We'd probably been inside for five minutes, though it felt like longer.

"Are you going to be able to carry that?" I said, looking at the garbage bag.

"Sure," Molly said easily, but her face sank into a frown as she lifted the weight. "Damn, that's heavy," she complained. "Maybe you should get ahead of me." I knew what she meant. If Molly left my null radius, she'd have vampire strength again. Sixty pounds would seem like nothing.

But I shook my head. "There's a lot of blood soaked into her clothes, and a lot on that doormat. You think your control is good enough to ignore that?" The smell of that much blood would likely be overpowering for a vampire. Molly probably wouldn't actually go after the remains—vampires prefer their food fresh—but she'd become suddenly, uncontrollably hungry. She would zoom off to find herself a "donor," and I'd be left alone with a body I couldn't carry.

"The bag is closed," she scoffed, but looked a little dubious.

"It could rupture. Or you could drop it, or it could snag on something. I'm not risking it," I said firmly. *You can't be too careful* is my working mantra. "We'll just go slow."

"Fine," Molly conceded. We made our way slowly back down the wooden walkway toward the Whale. I hobbled along with the cane, the duffel smacking into the back of my good leg with each step, and Molly kept trying and failing to carry the bag while holding it a little bit away from her body. It was too heavy, though, so she tried dragging it along behind her until I objected, fearing she'd tear a hole in the plastic. After a few steps she gave a long-suffering sigh and lifted the bag onto her back like the world's most disturbing Santa Claus. "Ugh," she said, wrinkling her nose in disgust. "I can feel her knees digging into my back."

"No, you can't."

"Can too," she insisted, and we bickered cheerfully for a few more steps. And then we rounded the corner of the house and found four werewolves sitting on my van.

Chapter 5

I froze, which is the third dumbest thing you can do in the presence of werewolves, right after dumping a bucket of meat juice over your head or running away. Molly cursed as she bumped into my back, but fell silent as she must have seen the werewolves. Two of them, both males, were sprawled on *top* of my damned van, leaning back with their legs dangling like they were working on their tans. The last and biggest male and a single female were half leaning, half sitting on the back bumper. I knew the female all too well: Anastasia, the bartender from Hair of the Dog, whose girlfriend, Lydia, had been bitten by another wolf infected with wolfberry. Anastasia was black, with wiry arms and a very short Afro, and her eyes were darkened with rage. She was leaning on the Whale's back bumper, with a thickly built Latino man beside her. All four of them had that rangy, lean, wild-eyed look that seems to haunt all of the werewolves outside of my radius.

"That's her," Anastasia announced, pointing a finger at my chest. "She's the one with the cure."

There was a moment of terrible, pregnant stillness. Then Molly laughed out loud, a short, surprised guffaw that broke the silence and somehow gave me permission to start breathing again.

"Cure for what?" Molly said, laughter still in her voice. "Bitchiness? I know you've got it in spades, poor thing, but I don't think my girl can help you."

Still outside my radius, Anastasia growled, a low, terrifying buzz that started deep in her chest. Then she said simply, "Miguel."

Instantly, the Latino werewolf next to her pushed off the van and trotted gracefully toward us, head erect. He wasn't all that tall, maybe right around six feet, but he gave off a sense of hugeness, of *menace*, thanks to broad shoulders that looked like they'd been dipped repeatedly in several layers of muscle like candle wax. He hit my radius and faltered a little, as expressions of confusion, relief, and anger flew across his face. Then he marched forward, without the gracefulness, and stepped all the way into my personal space, so his hot breath billowed in my face. He smelled of pickles and grease. "Tell us about the cure," he demanded. His voice was appropriately low. And appropriately terrifying.

Unconsciously, I touched the pocket where I usually keep my handheld Taser. But it was sitting on my dresser charger at Molly's house, waiting for when I went back to work. Fuck fuckity fuck. I took a deep breath through my mouth, meeting Miguel's eyes. Then I took a slow, deliberate step backward without looking away. I wanted to get him out of my face, but without making it look like I was fleeing. "I don't have a cure," I said softly. "I'm sorry. I wish I did."

His nostrils flared as he automatically tried to sniff at my body chemistry for a lie, but he was human at the moment, and he snarled with frustration.

"Cure for what?" Molly asked again, looking from Miguel to me. This time her voice was low and serious.

I spoke to Molly without looking away from Miguel. "Anastasia thinks I have a cure for werewolf magic. Apparently she's convinced these folks as well."

"That's insane," Molly said pleasantly. "There's no cure."

"Try telling them that."

Molly put the bag down and stepped between me and the huge Miguel, getting into his personal space just as he'd gotten into mine. "There's no cure," she said, her voice calm and reasonable. "Back off."

I felt a surge of severe fondness for Molly.

"Ana?" Miguel called without turning. Anastasia snarled in frustration and pushed off the van as well. While she was walking, I reached behind me and locked my fingers around the top of the garbage bag. I had no idea what to do here. In a second, they were going to start asking questions about the bag, and I doubted that Will would want his wolves to know about the body on his doorstep. He'd said that the pack was already a mess, and this would only make things worse. At the same time I was feeling the urgency to move, to get rid of the bag, like a physical pressure on my back. Having a dead body with you is very, very bad.

Think, Scarlett.

Ana stepped up beside Miguel, and I felt the pulse of additional werewolf magic in my radius. "Don't lie to us," she snapped at me. "I saw you go into the bar that night, and then Eli disappeared."

"Did anyone check the doghouse?" Molly asked innocently.

"Molly," I said reproachfully. "Not helpful."

Miguel was not amused. He wrapped a meaty hand around Molly's neck and lifted, which I had thought was something people only did in movies. She made a gurgling sound, clutching at the big man's hand as her feet left the ground. She aimed a kick at his groin, but Miguel expected it and turned his body sideways. The kick hit his thigh, and he didn't so much as grunt.

Molly's eyes were wide, and there was suddenly a look on her face I'd never seen before—terror. Molly's keen interest in humanity had always been one of my favorite things about her. She genuinely wants to know what modern humans experience, and she wants to feel those things too—hence the sushi class. But part of being human is being physically vulnerable, and neither of us had ever wanted her to experience that. What Miguel was doing wouldn't leave lasting physical damage, not once she got out of my radius, but I doubted she would forget what it felt like to be victimized.

My fingers tightened on the cane. I could hit him with it and he'd drop Molly, but if we started a fight in human form we weren't going to win.

Think *faster*, Scarlett.

"Let's all calm down," I said, trying to make my voice sound reasonable. "How old are you, Miguel?" I asked. "You look maybe forty, but you're a lot older than that, right?" When someone from the Old World is in my radius, I get a general sense of their power, the amount of magic that clings to them. For the werewolves, that magic determines their strength, speed, and healing abilities, which translates loosely into the pack's structure—most powerful at the top, least powerful at the bottom. Miguel was huge and scary-looking, but he seemed about as powerful as he did smart.

His eyes flicked warily toward me, and the arm holding Molly wavered a little. He was strong, but he was still close enough to me to be human, and holding a hundred and twenty pounds straight in the air would make anyone's arm tired after a while. "I'm sixty-two," he huffed.

Werewolves age more slowly than humans, at about half the speed. "You've been a wolf for a while, then. But you're not all that powerful. So you're a follower." I tilted my head at Anastasia. "I don't know what she's been telling you, but you're backing the wrong horse, Miguel. That nice young woman you're terrorizing is a vampire." His eyes went wide, and I pushed on. "Anyone who violates the Old World peace is going to answer to Dashiell, and if you think Anastasia's strong enough to protect you . . ." I shook my head emphatically. "You haven't been paying attention."

Miguel looked uncertainly from me to Anastasia, and then lowered Molly back to the ground. She coughed, holding her neck, breathing in panicked gasps. "Miguel," Anastasia snapped, but they were in my radius, and the nice thing about being a null is that you have home-court advantage wherever you go. The wolf pack instincts that drove Miguel to obey his superior didn't apply when he was a human. Ana flashed teeth at him, but he simply stood there, arms folded across his chest.

"You said we were here for the abomination," he reminded her, nodding at me. "Not to fuck around with vampires."

Abomination. That was a new one. Not to mention an awfully big word to come out of Miguel's mouth. I would have laughed if he hadn't been quite so big and pee-your-pants scary. It sounded like they were considering applying some violence, so before anyone else could speak, I jumped in. "Look, you guys, this is ridiculous. I'm sorry that Eli hasn't been around, and I know that's thrown everyone off—"

Anastasia's glare turned on me so quickly and furiously that I would have instinctively stepped away from her if I could step easily. "Do *not*," she snapped, "pretend to know about our pack. Eli is our beta. Do you have any idea what that is?"

I blinked. "Uh, the beta's the second in command. Will's second."

She threw up her arms in frustration. "You ignorant little brat. Do you really think that's all he is?"

"What do you mean?" I asked warily.

"The beta also takes care of the cubs," Anastasia declared. "He helps them integrate into the pack, find their control."

Lydia. I'd changed Eli to a human, and now he wasn't around to help Lydia. No wonder Ana was pissed off. If Eli's absence was caused by something common and understandable, they would have been told, and someone else would move up in the pack hierarchy. But Will hadn't been able to explain, and—

"What's in the bag?"

I looked up, startled by the new voice. It was one of the two werewolves on the van's roof. He was a slender black man with a shaved head and sharp slanted cheekbones. It was forty degrees outside, but he wore jeans and a gray ribbed tank top that showed off wiry arms.

Anastasia turned her body sideways, so she could look at him without turning her back to me. The man slid neatly off the van and onto the paved driveway. The second his sneakers hit pavement, the other wolf slithered down after him, flanking his side as he approached us. As he got closer I realized that his arms were covered in thin crisscrossing scars. One of them traveled diagonally down his shoulder to disappear under his shirt. He must have gotten them before he was changed, or he'd been in a lot of fights against silver knives, which can leave scars. Interesting. I wondered if werewolves got pack nicknames. His would definitely be Scarms.

He hit my radius and stumbled a little—he'd obviously never been near a null, because it took him longer than most to recover his balance. I used the beat to gauge his strength, with mixed results. Scarms was definitely more powerful than Miguel, but what I could do wasn't precise enough to get an answer to how he compared to Anastasia. They were pretty close.

Then he was only a foot away from me. After a couple of seconds, Scarms repeated himself. "What's in the bag?" I didn't answer. Without being told, the wolf behind Scarms left his side and flowed past us, entering and then leaving my radius, toward the front door. He was a short, barrel-shaped guy who had probably been chubby before he'd been changed. He had those tight, artificial-looking curls that usually signified a perm, but his must have been natural. When werewolves change back and forth, they lose things like perms and tattoos and piercings. He bent down and examined the bleach-covered blood smears. "Blood here, I think," he said to either Anastasia or Scarms. "But there's bleach all over it; I can't smell anything."

He pulled out a key ring—goddammit, of *course* all the wolves had keys to Will's house—and opened the front door. "Same here," he called. He disappeared into the house, probably to look for more blood.

Thank you, Clorox. I dismissed him and turned back to Scarms and Anastasia. "There was a fight," I lied. "Will called me to get rid of some furniture and some bloodstains. I'm taking it with me, and you've delayed me enough. Molly? Give me a hand?"

I passed the tied-off garbage bag to Molly, gripped my cane, and took a step forward, forcing Miguel to either step aside or plow into an injured girl half his size. Confused, he stepped aside, but Scarms right behind him did not. The werewolf didn't move at all, just stood there and looked at me with a curious, detached expression, like I was a turtle who'd fallen out of its shell.

"A fight between whom?" he said. Anastasia made a quiet crowing noise behind me. I'm sure she was just impressed with the use of "whom."

"We haven't met," I said to him. I kept my voice confident and coldly polite, like the terrifying people who run the DMV. "I'm Scarlett Bernard. You are?"

"Terrence," he said. "Whittaker." I nodded. My name for him was better. "That's Drew," he added, tilting his head toward the house.

"Nice to meet you, Terrence," I replied. Putting my weight on my left foot, I straightened up as tall as I could and met his eyes. "I haven't seen you at one of my crime scenes before, so let me explain how this works. I come and pick up the bloody crap. I take it with me. I get rid of it. I don't get details or names; I'm *just the cleaning lady*," I said, emphasizing each word.

"I want to see inside the bag," he said tersely.

I gritted my teeth and said, "Tough rocks. I do not answer to you, or to Anastasia, or to anyone but Will, Dashiell, and Kirsten. I have another call across town tonight"—total lie— "and I do not have time to fuck around with cutting open garbage bags, cleaning up anything that falls out, and rebagging. So either get out of my way"—I pulled my cell phone out of my jacket pocket—"or I will call Will and you can explain to him why you're interfering with me."

Terrence glanced uneasily at Anastasia. "Don't listen to her," she interjected, her eyes wild. "Let's stick with the plan. We hold her until she gives up the cure."

I could tell Ana hadn't meant to mention "the plan." I fought against a crush of panic, grateful once again that they couldn't smell my fear.

Terrence and Anastasia stared into each other's eyes for a long moment, with Miguel flicking his own gaze from one to the other. There was a palpable intensity between the two, even in human form, and I knew a dominance fight when I saw one. I wasn't going to get anywhere with Ana, so I looked at her opponent and said softly, "Terrence. Will knows Molly is helping me tonight. If you dick around with the treaty, you'll answer to Dashiell."

Miguel made a small noise in the back of his throat. We don't talk about the actual treaty much, because in the Old World, threatening someone with it is more or less the social equivalent of the nuclear option. The treaty is very simple: don't fuck with anyone. People who violate the treaty, or kill another Old World member under any circumstances, go to Dashiell. And everyone was afraid of Dashiell, with damned good reason.

Terrence stared at Anastasia for another long moment, and then stepped out of my way without breaking eye contact with her. Finally his eyes jerked over to me. "Another time," he said roughly. Anastasia folded her arms, anger and frustration written all over her body, but she didn't speak. Molly's presence had ruined her plan, and she knew it.

Molly grunted as she hefted the bag onto her back, showing no sign of its weight. *Go Molly*, I thought. Trying not to lean on the cane too hard, I stumped past the still wolves, careful to keep Molly in my radius.

As she passed Miguel, Molly couldn't resist a last comment. "Nice doggie. Stay." I held my breath, but although the big werewolf's face clouded over with fury, he made no move to touch her.

"Goddammit, Molly," I muttered. I went straight to the van's back doors and opened them for her. Ordinarily, I'd put a body in my van's built-in freezer compartment, but we were passing it off as furniture, so I just pointed to the carpeted back floor and she hefted it in. As she pushed the doors shut I was already rounding the van to the driver's seat, forgetting for a moment that Molly had driven us here. I wanted to get the hell out of there, but she paused at the back doors, leisurely peeling off her surgical gloves and pulling the keys out of her pocket. "Come on, Molls," I whispered.

She slammed the back doors shut finally, but before she could take a single step toward the passenger door the stocky werewolf came tearing out of Will's house. Crap. I had forgotten all about him. "Hey!" he yelled from the doorway. "I know every stick of furniture in this house, and none of it's missing!"

Chapter 6

All four werewolves turned their heads as one to stare at me. Then a slow, devious smile spread across Molly's face, and she gave me a nod. "See you at home," she mouthed. She tossed me the keys, and as they sailed toward me the bubble of tension popped and the werewolves sprang toward the van.

I was already throwing my cane in and hopping up onto the seat. I started the van and instinctively pounded my hurt leg onto the gas pedal, ignoring the responding blaze of pain in my knee. The van shot onto the street (this, folks, is why we always back into the driveway) and I felt Molly leave my radius.

I steered the van back down the little dead-end road, while trying to keep one eye on the rearview mirror. Behind me, the wolves were now right at the end of the driveway, practically in the street. All four of them were silhouetted against Will's house lights, advancing in a semicircle toward Molly, who stood a few feet into the road. Would she be okay? Then again, what could I really do if she wasn't? I needed to call Will.

For a fumbling moment I tried pulling my cell phone out of my pocket with one hand, steering with the other while simultaneously watching the rearview mirror and ignoring the excruciating pain in my knee. It went about like you'd expect—if what you expected is a resounding fail. The van began to list to the side, and I dropped the phone when I had to put my right hand on the wheel to correct my course. Swearing, I mashed the brake with my good left leg, causing the cell to skitter deep into the passenger seat foot well. Awesome.

Abandoning the phone, I stared at the rearview mirror, worried. Molly had always talked like she could take the werewolves easily when they were in human form, but I'd never actually seen *any* vampire go up against werewolves, thanks to the treaty. For a long beat she stood with her arms open in a relaxed, welcoming position—then she abruptly vanished from sight, leaving the angry werewolves standing in the driveway, grouped around nothing. I breathed a sigh of relief. I hadn't been expecting Molly to run away, but she'd be fine. Even in their human form, werewolves are a lot faster than most people, but they'd have to shape-shift to have a chance of catching a vampire. I put my foot back on the gas, gingerly, and began creeping forward again. I needed to go slow until I could get far enough away to put the van in park and rearrange my hurt leg. Not to mention retrieve my phone.

When I checked the mirror again, though, I could see the short figure of Anastasia gesturing wildly at the van, at me. Then she was ripping off her shirt, her pants quickly following, and the others were disrobing too, though not quite so quickly. After a second I realized that she was trying to talk the others into chasing me down in the van. Not good. I didn't have Molly with me anymore, which meant that technically they wouldn't be violating the peace treaty if they hurt me. I pressed down harder on the gas, ignoring the pain. They were going to hunt my van like it was a frickin' buffalo. Werewolves are basically indestructible, and they can run forever. They could just follow me to the nearest red light and—

But as I checked the mirror again, a shadow flew across the street so fast I only had a sense of it, rather than actually seeing it. The werewolf farthest from the house, a man in the process of pulling his shirt over his head, suddenly disappeared in a flying tackle. I grinned stupidly. That had been Miguel, and *that* had been Molly.

I relaxed in my seat. Technically Molly had just violated the treaty by drawing first blood, but I knew she wouldn't kill them. She could still get in trouble, but only if someone told Dashiell or Will, and I didn't see any of these wolves wanting to advertise what had just happened.

I decided not to call Will until I had a chance to talk to her.

A few minutes later, my adrenaline faded, and the pain in my knee crashed into my brain fast enough to make me dizzy. Goddamned vertigo. I pulled over. "Scarlett," I said into the rear-view mirror, "I really don't think you should be driving."

Even after rearranging my leg, it took me almost an hour to finish the job and get back to Molly's. I was too battered to limp up the stairs, so I just stripped and washed off the worst of the night in the downstairs bathroom. Molly had run a load of laundry for me and left the basket of clean clothes sitting on the kitchen table like a gift from the flying spaghetti monster itself. I dressed in baggy running pants and a T-shirt, then sacked out on the couch with a sheet and my downstairs stash of painkillers. I swallowed two pills, enough to knock me out before I had to think too long about the dead body I'd been handling just an hour earlier.

Mostly.

I woke up to an insistent rapping on the front door. "Noooo . . . ," I mumbled, but it didn't help stop the knocking, so I forced my eyelids open. There were stripes of weak morning sunlight on the floor, filtering through the venetian blinds. I squinted to see the clock that Molly has hanging above the television. It was eight o'clock.

"Scarlett and Molly aren't home right now," I yelled at the door. There wasn't even a pause in the knocking, so I finally dragged myself out of the couch nest and grabbed my cane.

My personal physician barely waited for me to pull it open before she walked in. "About time," she snapped.

"Please, come in," I muttered, closing the door behind her.

Dr. Stephanie Noring was an East Indian woman who usually worked at the Mayo Clinic in Rochester, Minnesota. She had one of those short, plump figures that looks sultry on a few lucky women. I wasn't sure how old she was, maybe a well-preserved fifty-five, but she had a lyrical British accent that I might have enjoyed listening to if she weren't perpetually annoyed with me. Today she wore a rose-pink blouse and khaki pants, and her hair, a gorgeous black with elegant streaks of gray, was pulled into a loose bun at her collar. Gold bangles clinked pleasantly on her wrist as she stormed past me into the house.

"Did you bring doughnuts?" I grumbled, closing the door behind her. "Anyone who shows up anywhere before nine should bring doughnuts."

"No, but I brought antipsychotics," she said tartly, her British accent making her sound more crisp than sarcastic. Must be hard, having your accent ruin your demonstrations of attitude. "I heard you were in a werewolf fight and dragged around an eighty-pound bag of trash. I could only assume that you'd lost your *bloody* mind." She followed me back to the couch, where I held up my hand to cover another yawn.

"First of all, you said 'bloody,'" I pointed out cheerfully. "I've never heard anyone actually say 'bloody' in real life. That's adorable. And secondly, the bag wasn't more than seventy pounds, tops. How did you even find out?"

"Carling called me," she said with distaste. The good doctor and Will had some kind of weird hostile relationship I didn't understand, but she'd taken a couple of weeks off to come help me when he'd asked. He probably knew doctors who lived a little closer, but Noring was an oncologist, and she was familiar with the medication that Olivia had forced on me. Noring was also familiar with the Old World—she was a witch.

In lieu of a doctor's bag, she carried the biggest purse I've ever seen in my life, a black faux-crocodile hobo that was massive enough to make Mary Poppins salivate. She pulled out a blood pressure cuff and strapped it around my upper arm, squeezing the little hand pump thingy without mercy.

"How's the vertigo?" she asked accusingly, over the hiss off the cuff.

I winced. "Mostly gone."

"And the edges of your aura?" She meant my radius, the sphere of nothingness that surrounded me. I hated the word "aura," which was Olivia's favorite term for what we could do. I didn't correct Noring, though, because she was a teensy bit scary.

"Still fuzzy," I admitted. When I'd changed Eli, it had been because I'd developed a sudden understanding of my own abilities—I had figured out how to sense the borders of my own power, and how to channel the magic I cancelled out into myself, taking the magic from Eli. But afterward, I hadn't been able to sense the borders of my power like that again. The problem was that I had no idea if losing that ability was due to the concussion, or the coma, or the Domincydactl, or the seizure. And Noring knew even less than I did about nulls.

She nodded as if I'd confirmed her worst fears and resumed checking my vital signs, which were fine. Then she began running me through tests to see if I'd exacerbated the concussion. I nailed the vision, hearing, and memory portion, but failed the balance and coordination section. "That's worse than it was two days ago," Noring said disapprovingly. "Let's see the leg."

I pulled up my pants leg so she could check on my knee. It was so swollen than she had a hard time sliding the brace off, and I held my breath to keep from gasping at the pain. Noring ignored me, either because she has a shitty bedside manner or to punish me for running around on my bad leg.

I'm sorry; that was ungracious. It could also have been both.

When the brace finally surrendered, I had the knee equivalent of cankles. I sucked in air through my teeth as Noring frowned down at it, testing the joint very gently with her fingers. I held my breath so I wouldn't cry out.

"This isn't healing like we hoped," she told me. For the first time since she'd arrived, her tone was mild, and possibly even sympathetic. Let's call it sympathetic-adjacent. "There are physical therapies you can try, but nothing's very effective until the swelling goes down. Meanwhile, I've got some med school friends in the city, so I'll make some calls and get you an appointment with an orthopedic surgeon."

I winced. "Uh . . . I can't really afford that." I make okay money working for the Old World in LA, but I'd had to blow most of my savings to send Jack on a last-minute trip to Europe over Christmas.

"Your insurance should cover most of it," Noring said. When I didn't respond, her lips compressed back into a line. "Let me guess. You don't have insurance."

I shook my head guiltily, and she gave me her biggest, most long-suffering sigh yet. "Of course you don't. What happened the last time you were in hospital?"

"That time I was injured in the line of duty, or whatever, so Dashiell paid my medical bills. This wasn't work-related, though."

Noring gave me a disappointed look and said, "Well, you can try giving it another few days to see if the swelling goes down, but I'm not optimistic. Something is wrong in there, more than a simple torn meniscus, and you need x-rays and an MRI. And you really should be using crutches instead of just the cane now."

"But then I couldn't get around," I protested.

She arched her eyebrows in a way that effectively communicated my idiocy. "Yes, that's kind of the idea."

My right hand was resting on my leg above the knee, and Noring suddenly looked down and took hold of my hand, turning it so she could see my forearm. "That's a burn," she said, puzzled.

I pulled my hand back. "My God, did you go to medical school?" I said sarcastically. It's possible that I'm not a morning person.

Noring wasn't deterred. "How did you get a burn?"

"Making soup. For breakfast," I lied. "Er, I mean a late snack."

After leaving Will's house the night before, I'd still had to get rid of the body, and Molly was busy making sure the werewolves didn't follow me. I'd driven straight to an art studio in the Valley where I have an arrangement with Artie Erickson, the studio's slightly shady proprietor. In exchange for a small fee, he grants me no-questions-asked access to the industrial furnace that came with the building when he bought it. I had my own gate key so I could back the van right up to the door closest to the furnace room. Despite that, it had still taken me nearly twenty minutes to get the body from the van to the furnace. I would take a step with the cane, lift the knot of the garbage bag, and sort of swing the bag two feet forward. Then I'd take another step and repeat. My knee throbbed so much that as soon as I reached the interior doors I started resting against the wall every three steps.

Getting the body to the furnace had been slow and made my knee hurt. Getting the body *into* the furnace was a completely different problem. Usually I toss and run, but I couldn't move quickly now, and even a few seconds exposed to the heat would be dangerous. After some poking around, I had finally discovered a pair of big oven mitts on a hook behind the furnace room door. I put them on, along with a cracked, grimy welder's helmet that I found in a pile of old junk. Then I opened the furnace door, planted my feet, and heaved the body through the opening, like a *boss*. My exposed ears had felt hot for a moment, and I'd gotten a mild burn on my arm where the mitten had gaped, but all in all I considered it a success.

Apparently Dr. Noring didn't agree, though. She frowned at me, but I just shrugged, sticking to my soup story. Noring shook her head and I suddenly felt witch power brush against me, the spell shorting out in my radius like a horsefly on a bug zapper.

I looked at her indignantly. "Uh, can I help you?"

"Sorry," she said, slightly sheepish. "I wasn't trying. Force of habit."

I'd assumed Noring was Old World the moment I'd met her, and I'd felt her power as soon as I concentrated. But we hadn't discussed it until now. "You usually cast spells on your patients?"

"I don't call it that," she said stiffly, "but yes, sort of."

"What kind of witch are you?" The majority of human magic users are trades witches—they can do a little bit of everything, from mild charms to enhance their appearance to (given the time and resources) complex rituals that can protect a building. A few witches have unique skills, though, not unlike how doctors have different specializations. I was guessing that Noring was one of these.

After a moment of hesitation, she sat down on the couch next to me. For the first time since we'd met, her face smoothed into an expression that wasn't a frown or a glare, and she said quietly, "I can sense what's happening in a body and push it toward health."

"Like a healer?" I said, interested. I've heard of witches who can heal, but never met one in person.

But Noring shook her head. "No, no, nothing that dramatic. The body tells me what's happening inside it, and I . . . encourage it. To get better. Sometimes it works, and sometimes the body is just too sick to recover."

"And you were trying to get my body to talk to you just now?"

"Yes," she said briskly. "A reflex." She leaned over to rummage in her enormous bag. "I believe I have something for that burn. But can I give you a piece of advice, Scarlett?"

I doubted that she could be worse at running my life than I was. "Sure," I said with a shrug.

She paused her purse expedition to look at me directly. "You need to stop fighting above your weight class," Noring said simply.

I blinked. "Excuse me?"

"Every day I take care of people who are crippled by a terrible illness, and what you've put your body through . . ." She shook her head. "You're in worse shape than many of them." She had located the burn cream, and she dabbed a generous dollop onto my wrist. Putting the cap back on, she added, "Other than these injuries, you're in good health. That's a gift. Stop squandering it on these"—she waved an arm absently—"these *people*."

Tears stung my eyes. Under ordinary circumstances I probably would have been angry, but I'd been caught off guard, and besides . . . that was exactly what my mother would say.

"It's not that easy," I said helplessly. "There were people counting on me, and I had to help stop—"

"Let someone else help," she interrupted, voice firm. "*You* are getting your ass kicked."

It was such a coarse expression from such a cultured accent that I laughed out loud, a feeble, painful sound.

"You have no idea," I told her.

Chapter 7

Detective First Grade Jesse Cruz was very sick of people.

He'd spent all of the last two days conducting interviews on a hit-and-run homicide just off Fairfax. A dark red—or maybe brown, or maybe purple—minivan had sped off after clipping a nineteen-year-old actress/waitress who had been rushing across the intersection to get to her shift at IHOP. The van had sped off, and the teenager had bled out at Cedars-Sinai after seven hours of surgery. The intersection was within view of three different high-rise apartment buildings, and Jesse and his squadron had been going door to door, asking the same useless questions of useless people. He was tired and defeated, and as he headed back to his department-issued sedan Jesse wanted nothing more than to not speak to anyone for a few hours.

But it didn't work out that way.

A late-model Mercedes S-class was parked illegally at a fire hydrant directly behind Jesse's vehicle. As he neared it, the Mercedes's door opened and an enormous black man began to climb out of the vehicle, his movements purposeful and efficient but not aggressive. Jesse froze on the sidewalk, marginally aware that his right hand now rested on his weapon. The stranger wore a black polo shirt, pressed chinos, and what looked like an empty shoulder holster. He closed the car door gently and held up both hands in the universal gesture for "I mean you no harm." A business card was trapped in the fingers of his left hand. "Detective Cruz?" the man rumbled. A pleasant, professional smile was tacked on his face.

"Yes?" Jesse said cautiously.

"My name is Hayne." The black man extended his arm, holding out the business card. "Mr. Dashiell sent me to get you."

Jesse automatically reached out to accept the white paper rectangle. It was his own card, with the department's official logo and his name, title, and contact info. He flipped it over. On the back was an all-too-familiar address, and the name *Dashiell* in elegant cursive.

Jesse dropped his hand from his gun and looked up at Hayne in disbelief. "He's just . . . *summoning* me? Right now?"

"Yes, sir." Hayne opened the back door and looked expectantly at Jesse, who only gaped.

"I can't come now; I'm working," Jesse protested.

"Your shift ended twenty minutes ago, sir," Hayne said easily.

Anger rippled across Jesse's back, tightening his shoulders. "He's keeping tabs on me? Screw that. I'm not at his beck and call."

He started away, toward his own car, and Hayne's professional smile wavered. "He said you'd say that, sir," Hayne said quietly, forcing Jesse to stop so he could hear the other man. "He said to tell you it's about Miss Bernard."

The manipulation was obvious, but effective. "What about Scarlett?" Jesse asked sharply. "Is she going to be there?"

When Jesse made no move toward the car, Hayne closed the door again and leaned against it, probably trying to look harmless. Instead, the man seemed about to dent the car door. "I don't have that information, sir. But Mr. Dashiell said to tell you that she's in trouble." He stood and reached for the door behind the driver's again, holding it open, and Jesse stared at him for a long moment, trying to read intent in the bigger man's expression. Finally Hayne sighed. "It's not a trick," he said quietly. "Not a trap. Dashiell just genuinely needs to talk to you. Sir."

"I have a phone," Jesse reminded him, trying not to sound sullen. Something about Dashiell always made him feel like an insolent teenager, and it apparently happened whether or not the vampire was actually present.

Hayne broke into a grin, and for the first time his expression seemed real. "And Mr. Dashiell has a way of doing things, sir. You've survived this long, you must have figured that out by now."

Jesse stared at him for a second more, then relented. Ignoring the open door to the backseat, he walked around the Mercedes to the passenger door and climbed in.

Smog hung low over the city's skyline, but the temperature had dropped so low that Jesse could almost pretend it was a nice clean fog instead of man-made airborne poison. The sunlight had faded behind the city by the time they pulled up to Dashiell's Spanish-colonial mansion in the old-money portion of Pasadena. Hayne bypassed the main part of the driveway and pulled the Mercedes into a four-car garage at the back of the property. He hopped out of the Mercedes, but Jesse was faster, getting out of his own side before the man could open his door. Smiling benignly, Hayne guided Jesse toward a service entrance that lead into a Spanish-tile kitchen that he had seen before. They went through the kitchen, and Jesse suddenly found himself back in the same living room area that led out onto the patio.

He blinked. Dashiell was in the living room, having a quiet conversation with Will Carling, the leader of the Los Angeles werewolf pack, and a stunning woman who appeared to be in her late thirties. His wife. Jesse had seen her before.

Dashiell broke off what he was saying as Jesse entered. The vampire was a blandly handsome man who appeared to be in his late thirties, with dark hair and eyes. He wore a perfectly pressed shirt and black slacks. "Thank you for coming, Detective," Dashiell said, turning toward Jesse, who shrugged noncommittally. Like he'd had a choice.

"Detective Cruz," the woman said warmly, rising from her place next to Dashiell on an overstuffed sofa. She stepped toward him, holding out a hand. "I'm Beatrice. It's so nice to finally meet you."

"Right," Jesse said awkwardly. She was a knockout, with long dark hair spilling across a cream-colored sundress that set off her olive skin. Spanish, he figured, which connected to the decor. He automatically took the vampire's hand as it was offered, half expecting it to be icy cold. But no, whatever magic animated vampires kept them room temperature as well. "We've sort of met before." The last time he'd been in this room, he and Scarlett had stopped Jared Hess and a vampire named Ariadne from killing Dashiell and Beatrice.

Beatrice's smile smoothed over into a solemn nod. "Of course. But we weren't exactly introduced then, were we?" she asked, with a little twinkle in her eye.

"No, ma'am."

Jesse realized that Will and Dashiell had gotten up too, fast enough that he hadn't even seen it. Despite the demonstration of speed, Will looked exhausted. After shaking Jesse's hand, the alpha sank immediately back down in an armchair, as though the handshake had been the only thing keeping him on his feet. Dashiell did not hold out a hand to shake, but simply gestured for Jesse to take the last remaining seat in the living room, an ornately carved dark wooden chair. They all sat back down, and Will was the first to speak.

"Have you heard from her?" he asked quietly.

"Scarlett? Yeah." Jesse's hand automatically touched his phone in his pocket, as though it might conjure the girl out of thin air. "She stopped by my apartment about a week ago, to tell me she was gonna join her brother in the UK for a few days to recover from the mess with Olivia." Will's eyes slid over to Dashiell, who smoothed down the front of his spotless shirt. No one said anything for a long moment, and Jesse felt like he had missed something. "What?"

Beatrice finally spoke up, her voice warm and thick like sap running down a tree, smothering everything in its path. "Detective, can I offer you something to drink? Or perhaps a sandwich? We have a well-stocked refrigerator."

Cold realization gripped Jesse, and he jerked his eyes toward the floor. *Stupid*, he cursed himself. Stupid of him to meet their eyes. He'd spent so much time around Scarlett while he was talking to these people that he'd forgotten to be afraid.

And that wasn't the only thing he'd forgotten.

"I've never told Scarlett where I live," he said flatly. "And now that I try, I can't remember what she was wearing or her words. She wasn't really at my apartment, was she?"

"No." Even in that one word Dashiell's calm voice held something, a weight, and despite his resolve, Jesse's gaze flicked hungrily toward the vampire. He suddenly wanted Dashiell to speak again, to ask him for something, a favor maybe that Jesse could—

"Enough," Will's voice was ice-pick sharp, and the spell broke. Jesse's breath rushed into his lungs with a sudden ferocity, and he knocked over the chair as he scrambled away, unconsciously searching for a wall he could put his back against. The glass patio doors were behind him, though, and he had to work on calming the panic.

"You pressed me," he said, hating the tremor in his voice. Terror gripped his body, and Will and Dashiell both turned their heads sharply in his direction, smelling the fear. "You pressed me to think . . ." He shook his head, trying to clear it. One of the vampires had pressed him to believe Scarlett had stopped by his place.

But if that hadn't been real . . . He looked up. "Where is she?" Jesse demanded.

"Will's right, that's enough," Beatrice declared. "Dashiell, please stop. Detective, please put away your weapon." Jesse looked down and realized he was holding his gun. He looked at Beatrice, focusing on the center of her forehead like it had a target on it. "We are not going to hurt you," she said calmly. "We asked you here because we need your help."

She looked at her husband, giving him one of those pointed, nudging expressions Jesse had seen on his own mother's face. That look, more than anything else, helped Jesse quell his panic.

Dashiell took the hint. "My wife is right, of course," he said, the weight gone from his voice. He sounded like an ordinary, tired man. "We do need your help." The vampire gestured to the chair again. "Please, sit."

Reluctantly, Jesse reholstered the gun and squared his shoulders, trying to concentrate on avoiding eye contact. It was harder than he'd imagined. "Somebody just tell me what's going on," Jesse said. "Where is Scarlett? Is she okay?"

"She's injured, but fine," Beatrice assured him, and Jesse nodded his thanks at her.

He was about to ask another question, but Will leaned forward. "Detective Cruz. Remember last fall when Scarlett was in the hospital?"

"Of course."

"Did she tell you why she had to stay for a few days?"

Jesse's brow furrowed. "She said she hit her head during the fight with Ariadne, after I left." He looked at the female vampire. "She was trying to help Beatrice."

"And she did help me," Beatrice confirmed. "She saved me. But she didn't hit her head. She did something that her kind shouldn't be able to do."

She glanced at her husband, who nodded. "She turned Ariadne into a human," Dashiell said gravely. All three of them looked at Jesse, waiting for a reaction. Jesse's eyes moved from face to face, not getting it. "*Permanently,*" Dashiell added emphatically.

Understanding struck Jesse. "That's . . . how is that even possible?"

"It's not supposed to be." Beatrice noted. "But Scarlett is the strongest null any of us have ever encountered. None of us knew . . . well. As it turns out, she's strong enough to turn one of us into a human again."

"But it sort of shorted out her brain," Will added. "I didn't hear about it until much later"—there was the briefest annoyed glance at Dashiell—"but apparently it works on werewolves too, because nine days ago she changed Eli back into a human."

Whoa. Jesse sank back into his chair, trying to process. Scarlett could undo magic, for good? And Eli was human again? What would that even mean? "Why didn't she tell me?" Jesse said out loud.

He had mostly been talking to himself, but Dashiell answered anyway. "I ordered her not to tell anyone," he said firmly. "I was afraid that the wolves and the vampires, in particular, would come after her if they found out. The vampires would either fear her or want her dead. The wolves would all want to become human again—"

"Or want her dead," Will broke in. "There are zealots among the werewolves who believe that we should all be . . . grateful. For what we are." The alpha's voice was weary. "They would consider Scarlett a threat."

"We were also dealing with the Olivia situation," Dashiell continued, "and I wanted time to consider what this development could mean."

And how I could use it, Jesse finished for him. Dashiell was a textbook opportunist, and that kind of ability would be a dangerous addition to his toolbox.

No wonder Scarlett had been so strange during the last few months. Jesse felt a childish sense of betrayal. She could have told him.

And then the rest of the conversation caught up to him. "Wait. You're saying her *brain shorted out* again?"

Will held out a hand to placate him. "No, not that. Her abilities are intact this time, for some reason. But Eli was our beta, and the wolves can feel his absence in the pack. It's causing problems."

"Can't you just . . . pick a new beta?" Jesse asked sensibly.

The werewolf sighed. "It's not quite that simple, I'm afraid. For one thing, we weren't sure that the change was permanent."

Jesse looked from one to the other. Beatrice and Dashiell were still and calm, with a well-mannered detachment that Jesse had noticed the only other times he'd been near vampires without Scarlett. He supposed that when you can live forever, everyday crises don't exactly push you over the edge. In contrast, though, Will looked agitated and restless, one of his legs jiggling up and down at a frenzied pace. "That's why you pressed me," Jesse said at last. "You were hoping it would just go away."

"Yes," said Will with no inflection. "But rumors are spreading in the pack, and we aren't as united as we need to be. And now there's another problem."

Jesse gaped at him. "Another problem? She's hurt, the wolves are panicking, everyone is finding out that she's a *cure*—"

"We don't like that word," Beatrice broke in.

Anger had pushed away Jesse's fear. "Lady, I don't give a shit what word you like. What's the other problem?"

Without speaking, Dashiell picked up a manila folder from the top of a stack of files and papers on the side table. He passed it to Jesse, who flipped it open to find a gruesome eight-by-ten photograph of mangled limbs and torn skin. The woman's face was untouched, but shaded the grayish hue of death, her blue eyes open and filmed over. Jesse flipped past this photo and found another shot of the same woman from a different angle. And another. They were all the same body, and they all had the same date stamp: December 29. Yesterday's date.

They looked almost like crime scene photos, but there were no markers to indicate it was a police-controlled scene. Jesse flipped back to study the top photo. The body was set against a textured green background, like a rug of some kind. He looked up. "Where were these taken?"

Will and Dashiell exchanged another look before Will spoke. "At my house," he said soberly. "Someone left her on my doorstep."

"Why didn't you call the police?" Jesse said automatically.

"Because," Will said heavily, "this woman was killed by a werewolf."

Jesse stared at him for a second, then instinctually looked away. The werewolves couldn't press minds like vampires could, Jesse knew, but Scarlett had once told him that the werewolves communicate with canine body language even in human form. Jesse didn't know much about wolves, but he'd been a uniformed police officer for long enough to know you didn't stare big dogs in the eye unless you wanted a fight.

"How do you know?" Jesse asked.

"I could smell him," Will murmured. He was looking away, almost ashamed. "Even in human form."

"Right," Jesse said distractedly. "Right." He looked at each of them in turn. "So why am I here?" he asked. "You pressed my mind; you must have wanted to keep this hidden from me. Why tell me now?"

Will answered. "Because whoever did this"—he nodded down to the pictures—"wasn't one of mine. I know their scents. And look at the last photo."

Jesse automatically obeyed the alpha, flipping to the last picture in the little stack. It was a close-up of the woman's back. There were marks on it too, and at first he figured it was just another bite wound. As he looked closer, however, he realized that he was looking at a relatively clear patch of skin with only three shallow tears in it. The wounds didn't match the rest of the carnage. They were in a cluster: a little diagonal line, a long vertical one that ran parallel to the woman's arm bone, a short perpendicular line beneath it.

Jesse looked up. "It's a number," he said quietly. "Number one."

Chapter 8

"Obviously we can't be sure," Dashiell broke in, "but it seems likely that whoever did this will try again."

Jesse closed the folder and pushed it toward Will. "Call the police," he said firmly. "Call right now."

"You know we can't do that," Beatrice said genially, as though he'd suggested they all go skinny-dipping.

Jesse turned to her. "Yes, you can. If this woman was human, he's going to go after humans again." Beatrice glanced at her husband, whose face remained unreadable. Jesse continued, "People are at risk here. This is a hell of a lot bigger than me looking the other way while someone from the Old World kills someone else from the Old World." Bitterness had crept into his voice, and Jesse fought to keep it off his face.

"We don't want you to look the other way," Beatrice soothed. "Just the opposite. We want you to find him."

Jesse stared at her, then at Will and Dashiell. Both men—Jesse had to think of them as men, otherwise he'd start to shut down from fear—just gazed at Jesse, waiting for him to put the pieces together.

"Absolutely not!" Jesse exploded. "I'm not getting suckered into doing a half-assed investigation again just so you can keep your fucking secrets. Scarlett almost died last time! *I* almost died last time!"

Dashiell raised his eyebrows at Will, a gesture that very smoothly said, *Told you so.* But Jesse wasn't finished. He took a deep breath, calming his temper, and said tightly, "You need the actual police department, with its resources and experience and tools. Let them deal with this."

Silence. Dashiell, Will, and Beatrice were all looking steadily at Jesse, like parents waiting for a tantrum to blow over. After a second he got it. "You already had Scarlett destroy the body," he said, deflating. He looked at the folder, still in his own hand. "This is all that's left, isn't it?"

"Scarlett wanted us to take those for you," Will said helpfully. "She insisted."

Jesse rubbed his eyes tiredly. "You've known me, what, four months?" he said at last. "What would happen if I wasn't here? What did you do with this kind of thing before you met me?"

Will looked at Dashiell, who shrugged. For the first time his elegant facade faltered, and he looked uneasy. "This has never happened before," he said. "Other than La Brea Park, Los Angeles has never had a situation like this, which has afforded us certain . . . comfort levels." He frowned. "It does seem like there has been an escalation of violence in the last year, but I'm not convinced that it isn't simple coincidence.

"To answer your question, though, we do not bring humans into the Old World. Will would have done what he could to stop the rogue himself, and we would have cleaned up the aftermath as it happened."

Jesse stared. "You'd let him keep killing, and just cover it up."

"Of course not," Beatrice contended. "Will would hunt him. But Will has other responsibilities now, with the pack unstable, and here you are, a trained murder investigator. It seems a shame not to use you."

It was the wrong thing to say. "I am not one of your pets," Jesse said between his teeth. He locked eyes with Dashiell, forgetting his earlier fear. "You and I have had this conversation already. You know what I think needs to be done."

Beatrice and Will were looking at Dashiell now too, and the cardinal vampire nodded. "Detective Cruz feels that a special department should be created within the LAPD," he said to them, his eyes still on Jesse, "one devoted to Old World crime."

"Is that even possible?" Will asked, plain curiosity in his voice.

"Possible? Yes, in theory. I could contact the right people, press a few minds," Dashiell replied in his clipped voice. "But the problem is one of longevity and logistics. A new squadron would require personnel, a budget, annual reviews. It would garner attention. I can press minds to create something, but that kind of long-term maintenance would be too complex and unwieldy to be practical." The volume of his voice never altered, but he was beginning to exert influence as he added, "More importantly, though, *we do not tell humans about the Old World*."

This time Jesse felt the press in time to break eye contact. "Then I'm out," he said stubbornly. He rose and started for the door, shoulders tensed as if expecting a bullet.

Beatrice's quiet voice floated toward him like a breeze. "She still works for us, Detective."

Jesse stopped but didn't turn. He'd forgotten about Scarlett's role in all this, but Beatrice was right: Scarlett would be involved in cleaning up the crime scenes.

"She was attacked last night," Beatrice continued, "by the wolves—"

"Beatrice," Will began to reproach her, but stopped when she held up a hand.

"He cares for her," she insisted. "I do too, in my way. He needs to know."

Jesse sighed and looked back. They were manipulating him with Scarlett again. He had to find a way out of that, but in the meantime, he couldn't help but take the bait. "What do I need to know?"

"She's the only one who can do this job right now," Beatrice said calmly, walking toward him. "The only one who can clean up after this creature if it kills again. It can move in the day, which we cannot, and it can create another . . . scene, which the wolves can't stomach." Being around a lot of blood and meat could force the werewolves into a change, which was a very dangerous prospect in the middle of Los Angeles. "Scarlett is the only one. And she *needs a cane to walk.*"

Jesse caught the emphasis Beatrice put on this last sentence, but it had its effect. His stomach clenched with worry. "Help her," Beatrice pleaded. "Help her keep this hidden, and she can help you find the one who's doing it. Please."

Jesse looked at Dashiell, who was motionless, expressionless. "There is no one else," the vampire confirmed.

"What if I don't?" Jesse challenged. "What if I call my supervisor and report the murder? Or what if I take Scarlett and run?"

The vampires were already very still, but suddenly it seemed like the room around them was frozen. Jesse expected Beatrice to speak next, to jump in with her placating tone, but it was Dashiell who said, in a cool, unaffected voice, "That would never happen. She would never go with you."

Jesse's brow furrowed. The vampire was too confident about what Scarlett would decide. "You have leverage, don't you? What do you have on her?"

He didn't realize he was meeting Dashiell's eyes until the vampire sent a little shiver of pull in Jesse's direction, just enough to remind him who had the power here. "More than enough," Dashiell informed him.

"Then my answer is no," Jesse said firmly.

There was a long, loaded silence. Then Dashiell stood up and strode over to the glass doors, staring out at the darkened patio with his hands clasped behind his back. Jesse could see his reflection in the glass, but the vampire's expression was unreadable. "I could force you, you know," Dashiell mused. He didn't turn around. Jesse said nothing, and after a moment the vampire went on, his voice toneless and detached. "It is what I have done in the past, with other humans. But my wife has persuaded me to try something different in this situation. She believes *you* are different."

Jesse glanced at Beatrice with surprise. As far as he'd known, Beatrice hadn't given him another thought since the last time he'd been in front of her. But now the female vampire gave him a small, reassuring smile and a little nod.

"So I am going to make you an offer," Dashiell said, turning to face Jesse, "and I suggest you take it, because you won't get a better one from me."

His tone clearly implied that Jesse could, however, get a worse offer. "What is it?" Jesse demanded.

"I will arrange for you to have a few days off of work, no questions asked. Make up whatever excuse you like for your coworkers. During that time you will help Scarlett find the perpetrator, with my support and authority behind you. You will report nothing you see or do to any other member of the LAPD. *Nothing*," he added again, pushing power into the word so Jesse flinched. "Beatrice?" he said, turning to look at his wife.

She rifled through the stack of papers on the table and pulled out a single sheet, which she leaned over and handed to Jesse. He glanced at it and looked at Dashiell. "These are LAPD transfer papers," he said incredulously. "And they're already signed." Jesse had known that Dashiell had contacts in the LAPD, and he'd seen the vampire wield power over the police force before. But this wasn't a brief, unofficial word, this was . . . *paperwork*.

Dashiell nodded. "If you can solve this case, and show me that you can protect our way of life despite your misgivings," he stated, "at the end of the week I will arrange for you to be transferred to Homicide Special."

Jesse's mouth gaped. Homicide Special was the LAPD's elite investigative squad, with jurisdiction over the whole city. Homicide Special detectives had fewer cases and were able to spend more time cultivating each investigation. There were only a couple dozen detectives in the unit, and every time a spot opened up there were at least a hundred applicants.

"There's more," Dashiell continued. "If another case should come up involving the Old World, I will have it assigned to Homicide Special. You can work on it from there, in a relatively official capacity. Depending on circumstances, you might not be able to arrest a perpetrator—"

"It's not what you proposed, we know," Beatrice broke in softly. "But it's a good start, Detective."

Will, who had been silent throughout, nodded his agreement, though a troubled expression still stained his features.

Jesse looked away then, trying to pretend for a moment that he was alone. Homicide Special . . . That was the dream for any detective who didn't want to end up spending every day behind a desk. He had hoped to apply himself in maybe a *decade*. And Dashiell was offering a shortcut.

But his instinct was to refuse. It wouldn't be fair to the other detectives, for one thing. There would also be gossip and attention over his swift rise, and Jesse hated both of those things. Not to mention the whole thing reeked of corruption. There was a line, he told himself, and they'd already gotten him to edge over it more than once. Now they were trying to force him over the line again.

And the worst part was that he sort of wanted to go willingly. That was what was really bothering him, Jesse realized. He felt guilty because he wanted to say yes.

For his entire life, Jesse had always been happy to pay his dues, but now there was a part of him that was bored with hit-and-runs.

He knew that there was excitement to be had in the Old World at any given time, and the opportunity to do some real good. For the first time in his career, he was tempted to take the easy way out.

He hated that about himself . . . but he couldn't just turn it off, either. The chance to investigate Old World crimes on the books, with department resources, was appealing as hell. Maybe if he'd been able to investigate Olivia Powell within the LAPD, things could have turned out differently. Scarlett might not have had to shoot Olivia just to save him from doing it.

Besides, if he had Dashiell backing him, Jesse could have a word with the werewolves who'd threatened Scarlett. But taking a deal from Dashiell just felt . . . wrong. Then again, so did letting people kill each other in the Old World and doing nothing.

Jesse's thoughts went back and forth like this for a while, while Beatrice and Dashiell waited patiently and Will began to look restless, his knee jiggling up and down again.

Finally Jesse took a deep breath. *You're overthinking it*, he told himself suddenly. They needed him, and Scarlett needed him, and *someone* had to stop a werewolf who was probably going to kill again. That was what he had signed on for, wasn't it? Stopping killers? He looked back at the three of them, forgetting not to meet their eyes. "I'll work the case," he said at last.

Out of the corner of his eye, Jesse saw Beatrice smiling widely, but in front of him Dashiell just gave a curt nod. "Good. One other thing."

He closed the gap between himself and Jesse in an instant. Jesse tried to wrench his gaze away, but it was too late. Suddenly, a massive force like water from a fire hose slapped into Jesse, knocking his chair neatly backward and pinning Jesse and the chair to the floor. The pressure wasn't crushing him, but Jesse couldn't breathe, as though a thousand gallons of gelatin were flattening him. Panic and instinct screamed alarm bells in his body, but Jesse could only watch as Dashiell stood over him, hands casually in his pockets, and said, "Do not forget your place. You have spent too much time around the girl, and not nearly enough time being afraid." He bent over a little and added conversationally, "I could make you do anything I wanted right now, bestow any humiliation or degradation. And you would *beg me for it.*"

He paused, a cold, inhuman intensity on his face. Even through his panic, the expression shocked Jesse. No one would mistake Dashiell for a regular man, not in this moment.

"Instead, though," Dashiell continued, his voice perfectly conversational, "I am simply flexing a muscle. You will not challenge me again."

He nodded to himself and turned away. As the eye contact broke, so did the magic, and Jesse rolled to one side, gasping for air, legs instinctively curling around his stomach. He used the motion to roll to his hands and knees, and when he looked up, Beatrice and Dashiell were gone and Will was standing next to him.

"What . . . the hell . . . was that," Jesse wheezed.

Will crouched down next to him, elbows resting casually on his knees. "That was getting pressed by a cardinal vampire," he said sympathetically.

"I thought . . . But that was *physical*," Jesse sputtered.

Will tilted his head. "Mmm . . . yes and no. He told your mind to force your body backwards, and then to believe you couldn't breathe or move. He pressed you; he just didn't have to talk to do it."

"That is scary as shit."

"Yup." Will held out a hand, and Jesse took it, allowing himself to be pulled to his feet.

"Suddenly I really miss Scarlett," Jesse noted.

"Well," the werewolf said, with exaggerated patience, "go get her then."

Chapter 9

Dr. Noring insisted I take some more pain pills, and by the time she'd finished fiddling with my knee, I wasn't exactly inclined to argue. The pills made me sleepy, though, so I decided to haul myself upstairs and go to bed for real.

It was the best sleep I'd had since first waking up with the knee injury. I was pretty sure the pills were the only thing keeping me from dreaming about the dead girl I'd destroyed, and I was pathetically grateful for it.

I was awakened hours later by an excessively cheerful vampire bouncing on the foot of my bed. "Ow," I complained sleepily. "You're trampling my bad knee."

"No, I'm no-ot," Molly sang. I opened my eyes. The clock beside me read 5:15, just after sunset. Geez. Apparently I'd been tired.

Molly was grinning like she'd just pulled off a heist. She wore her most pedestrian pajamas: a simple organic T-shirt and light flannel pants that I privately thought had been tailored. "You look happy," I observed. "Kick some werewolf ass, did we?"

"Damn right," Molly said smugly, in a weird foreign accent that I recognized. A couple of days earlier I'd talked her into watching *Bill & Ted's Bogus Journey* with me. "*Man* those guys can heal like nobody's business," she added in her normal voice. "Faster than us, even."

I raised my eyebrows. "You didn't actually hurt them, did you?"

"Me?" Molly fluttered her eyelashes innocently, then grinned again. "Nah, cuts and scrapes only. I just kept knocking them down while they were trying to change. It was *hilarious*." Her face lit up as she recalled. "The bitch got madder and madder, she was stomping her little foot like a three-year-old, and she was stark naked the whole time!" She chortled, mimicking Anastasia's petulant expression.

My spirits sank suddenly. "Go easy on Anastasia," I said quietly. "She's been through a lot."

Molly snorted. "Maybe she has, but that doesn't give her the right to go all cray-cray on my girl." She reached over to tousle my hair, which was hanging loose down my back. And down my front, and sticking up in the air . . . I'd been asleep for a while.

"Stop it!" I protested, jerking my head away. "And nobody says cray-cray."

"It was meant ironically," Molly said loftily. "Besides, she totally was. Scarlett, she thought you had a *cure*! I mean, yeah, being near you is nice and all, but if that's her deal, why not just send her friend to stalk you or whatever?"

"Will has a rule against it."

She arched an eyebrow skeptically. "But kidnapping is cool?"

I sighed. "I don't know, Molls. I don't think Anastasia's really thinking straight anymore."

Molly's face turned serious. "Uh—they don't know where we live, do they?"

"No," I said, thinking it over. "I don't see how they would. Eli and Will both know, I think, but I can't see them telling anyone, especially since Will warned the wolves to stay away from me. Do you know anybody Old World who would tell them if they asked?"

"Nope," Molly replied. "Most of the vampires don't even know where I live, and the ones that do would never tell the dogs. *And*," she added, "the deed isn't in my current name, so I don't think anyone could find us the old-fashioned way."

I always think it's funny when vampires refer to anything as the "old-fashioned way." I yawned. "We should be good then."

"What are you going to do next?" Molly inquired.

I knew she was referring to the complicated situation of my job and the murder, since apparently I was back to work. But I side-stepped her question, saying simply, "I need to shower."

Molly had gone to a drugstore and purchased one of those handles that sticks to the wall of shower stalls, so I could at least shower without anyone having to help me, but keeping one hand on the handle at all times made everything take forever. When I finally hobbled back to my room, I brushed out my damp hair and tied it up, then dressed in a hunter-green pullover and the only jeans I owned that were baggy enough to go over my knee brace. Thank you, boyfriend style. I see your value now.

I made my way downstairs, where Molly insisted that we go to the store for supplies so we could retry the sushi rolls ourselves. I knew she was trying to distract me on purpose, but I gratefully allowed myself to be pulled along by her single-minded enthusiasm. I didn't want to think about the dead woman, or Eli, or the werewolves who had jumped us at Will's house.

After a laborious trip to Trader Joe's, where I essentially turned a cart into a giant scooter, Molly and I made sticky rice in her countertop rice-maker and started spreading supplies all over her small kitchen table. The project escalated, as Molly's projects usually do, until by nine thirty we were eating raw cucumbers and cleaning up a literal explosion of sticky rice.

So when the doorbell rang, I was completely unprepared for it.

Molly and I both froze, staring at each other over the table. She moved first, announcing, "I'll get it!" and trotting off toward the front door before I could respond.

"Dammit, Molly, wait!" I called, exasperated. I grabbed my cane from where it was leaning against the table and hauled myself up to follow her, saying, "At least let me feel if it's something Old World first, okay?"

"Oh, right," Molly said, stopping suddenly. If I'd been moving at a normal speed I would have run right into her. "Good idea." She gestured grandly toward the entryway and intoned, "After you."

I hobbled to the front door, concentrating on my radius until I was satisfied that whoever was out there was definitely human. I went on tiptoes to look in the peephole—and saw Detective Jesse Cruz waiting patiently on the front step.

"Oh," I breathed, rocking back on my heels.

"Who is it?" Molly asked curiously.

"Shh! It's Jesse," I whispered distractedly. "I thought he didn't know I was in town." I stared at the door, uncertain. I hadn't prepared a lie to explain my knee.

Before I could come to a decision, Jesse yelled through the door. "Scarlett, I just came from your boss's house. I know everything."

I opened the door. And whatever I was about to say fell out of my brain as Jesse just looked at me for a moment, a small smile on his face. "Hi," he said softly, the smile widening into a grin.

I always forget how beautiful Jesse is. I don't mean beautiful in an androgynous sense—he's very male, with an athletic, muscular build that looks like he came by it honestly, rather than having his body designed by a personal trainer at a fancy gym, which you see a lot this town. I mean "beautiful" the way you'd call a sculpture or a painting beautiful. Jesse looks like he was deliberately, lovingly crafted by an experienced artist who prefers natural fibers and earth tones. Which is a lot of words, so it's simpler to just think of him as beautiful. I realized I was grinning back at him.

"Hi," I said back. We just stood there for a second.

I could feel Molly looking back and forth between the two of us. "Aren't you guys happy to see each other," she observed, her tone amused. "Say, I think I'll go clean up the kitchen." I heard her walk away, but my eyes seemed to be stuck on Jesse. Then I remembered what I'd been doing and looked down at my clothes. Rice was stuck all over my shirt, and there were a few drops of soy sauce on my jeans. "Sorry, I wasn't really expecting you." I looked back up, puzzled. "Wait, you were at Dashiell's?"

"Yeah, they summoned me after work," he replied.

"They?"

"Dashiell, Beatrice, and Will. We should talk."

"Right." I looked around helplessly. We couldn't talk near Molly—if Dashiell really had told Jesse what was going on, then he knew more than she did. And I'd promised Will I wouldn't tell anyone else about changing Eli. "Um, we better go up to my room."

"Can you make it up there?" Jesse said dubiously. I followed his gaze down to the cane in my hand. I had forgotten about it while I was staring at him like an idiot.

"Oh. Yeah. It just takes a while."

I gestured for Jesse to go up the stairs first. It would have been smarter to go in front of him so he could catch me if I fell, but baggy jeans or not, I vainly didn't want him staring at my swollen leg as I limped up the stairs in front of him. I trailed him into my bedroom, where he doubled back to shut the door behind me. That put our faces about six inches apart and suddenly my small bedroom seemed even smaller than usual. He grinned at me again, white teeth flashing as his eyes crinkled. "I'm going to hug you now," he announced.

I laughed in surprise as he swept me into his arms. I hugged him back enjoying his familiar scent of Armani cologne and oranges. "I was worried," he said simply. "I'm glad you're okay." He leaned back to study my face, and I thought for a second that he might kiss me. And it shamed me, because I wanted him to.

"I'm sorry," I blurted out instead.

"For what?" he asked, puzzled.

"I didn't know that they pressed you. I wasn't a part of that decision."

He sighed and released me, taking a step back. "I know. You were unconscious."

Oh. "They told you about that, huh?" So they had told him about Eli. Awkward.

He nodded. "And, although I don't like it, with everything else that's going on right now I think the fact that vampires pressed me last week is the least of our concerns."

I was starting to list back and forth, so I stumped over to the bed and sat down, shoving pillows under my right knee. Jesse had that look on his face, like he wanted to help me, but he also knew me well enough by now not to ask. I pointed to the folding chair leaning against the wall by the door and said, "You'd better fill me in on what you know."

His smile faded and then disappeared entirely. It was as though he was going from being just Jesse to being a cop by increments. "So you don't accidentally give me more information than I'm supposed to have?"

Ouch. "I guess I deserved that," I said, trying to keep my voice level.

Jesse's jaw stayed clenched for another second, and then he shrugged. "Sorry, that was an overreaction. Being around those guys just makes me suspect every word I hear."

"Welcome to my world," I said without thinking, and for a brief moment we shared a rueful smile. He was definitely in my world now, though I hadn't exactly welcomed him at first.

Then Jesse's face hardened. "Well, I know you changed Eli back to a human, permanently. And Ariadne, last fall." There was a note of professional coolness in his voice and I winced. I had been under orders to keep Ariadne's status to myself. But if I was being honest, I'd also preferred to keep it a secret. It had been easier to just not think about it, especially after Olivia surfaced.

"What was it like?" Jesse asked, softening a little. "Making someone human again?"

"The first time, it was awful," I admitted, remembering the sensation. "It was like . . . I don't know, weight lifting without a spotter. But the second time, with Eli . . ." I closed my eyes, struggling for words. "It was like I held the edges of my radius with one part of me, and with another part, I called his magic." I opened my eyes. "I collected it to me, and then I let the magic go." My knee throbbed suddenly, like it wanted to remind me that nothing came for free, especially magical cures.

"Wow," Jesse said, in a tone that suggested he had no idea how else to respond.

"Yeah."

"Could you do it again?" he asked.

"I have no idea. Not for a while, probably. Will got me a doctor, and she doesn't know if the seizure I had was because of the drug, or the stress, or the coma, or changing Eli. If I try again, I might have another seizure, or . . . you know, die." I shrugged. "Or I could be completely fine."

Jesse had a very thoughtful look on his face, but he didn't say anything else. I couldn't get a handle on his mood and it was starting to make me nervous, so I changed the subject, asking him to fill me in on his evening.

He walked me through his solo visit to Dashiell's house, from when Hayne picked him up to when Hayne drove him back. My mouth dropped open when he got to the part about Dashiell flattening him. The thing is, when someone from the Old World gets in my radius, I get a sense of how much power they have, and Dashiell had always *felt* strong—but for obvious reasons I hadn't ever seen him actually throw his power around. I'd always thought of Dashiell the way cashiers probably picture a really controlling bank president. The fact that he could do that to someone wasn't really surprising, but it was scary as hell.

After I got over that, I realized I'd breezed past the important part of the story. "Wait, so you took Dashiell's deal?"

Jesse flinched. "You sound surprised."

"No, I just . . . I mean, are you okay with that?" I asked, very carefully. Who says I can't learn diplomacy, I ask you. "I mean, helping me with crime scenes?"

"No," he admitted. "It seems like the lesser evil at this point, but it's not really sitting right with me, either." He wasn't meeting my eyes, and his shoulders were stiff, his expression troubled. "Maybe we'll manage to catch the guy before he kills again, and I won't have to . . . you know." He glanced at my face and then looked away again.

"I'm sorry," I said lamely, and Jesse gave me a tight nod in acknowledgment. That explained why he was being so weird—happy to see me one minute, resentful the next. I wanted to lean over and hug him, to tell him that it was going to be okay and he was doing the right thing by helping me. And in theory, I even believed that. The Old World had to stay hidden, period, and what I do is necessary for that. But I also understood that Jesse had just crossed a line he'd never imagined himself even touching, so I just changed the subject. "So . . . where do we start?"

Chapter 10

"We start where we always start," Jesse said, his tone suddenly professional and relaxed at the same time. Back on familiar ground. "With what we know."

"What do we know?" I asked promptly. I know a cue when I hear one.

Jesse pulled out his smartphone and touched the screen in a few places. "I stopped by the station on my way here to make some excuses," he said, eyes intent on the phone. "While I was there, I took a look at the missing persons reports, on the off chance that I could get a hit quickly. We got lucky." He held the phone up to me, showing me a picture of a young woman, blonde and healthy, grinning playfully at the camera as she tried to pull a big orange cat away from her chest. The cat's claws were entangled in the woman's cardigan sweater, and she looked like she'd just finished laughing or talking to the photographer. I recognized the slight hook to her nose and the smattering of freckles. "Would you say this is her?" Jesse asked, though it was obvious that he believed it was.

I nodded. "Who is she?"

"Leah Rhodes, twenty-nine, a marketing associate at a plastic bottling company in Torrance," he recited. "Reported missing yesterday morning by her roommate. She didn't come home Tuesday night."

"Huh. Was she . . . outdoorsy?" Werewolves rarely attack humans, but when it happens it's almost always because a wolf is threatened by a human presence in the wild. I had also heard of humans being infected by werewolf magic on purpose, but it was always a last resort, so I added, "Or terminally ill?"

Jesse shook his head. "Not really, and no. Plus, she called the roommate as she was leaving work, said she would be home in twenty minutes."

"So why her?" I mused. "And why like this?"

"That's what we have to figure out," Jesse said sensibly. "Tell me about the scene."

I paused for a second to order my thoughts. "Well, she was killed by a werewolf, and Will said it wasn't one of his. She died close to Will's house, or maybe in a vehicle. The wolf—I'm sort of thinking it was a he, though I guess it could be a lady wolf too—ate her insides." I wrinkled my nose. "And she had a number one carved into her back. Wait . . . have you found a body with a number two on it?"

Jesse shook his head. "I called my friend in the forensic pathology department; she's going to put out some feelers and get back to me. But the ME's office gossips like a middle school cafeteria, so Glory would probably have heard by now. Anything else?"

I remembered the woman's untouched face and shredded clothes and body. "It was some kind of message," I added.

"What makes you say that?"

"Well, there was that number on the body, like he wants us to know this wasn't the last time. Plus, a werewolf dumps a body on the alpha's doorstep? That sounds like a challenge, doesn't it?"

"Could be," Jesse noted. "But it could be practical too. If you were a werewolf, and you killed someone—either accidentally or on purpose—and you knew that Will Carling had someone on retainer to get rid of evidence . . ." He shrugged. "Maybe it just seemed like the easiest way to dispose of a corpse."

"Maybe," I said dubiously. Jesse's theory was probably as likely as mine, but there was just something about that girl, and the brutal way she'd been killed and dumped that was almost . . . gleeful. Like "look what I'm getting away with!" It was . . . taunty.

"What else do you know about werewolves?" Jesse asked. "I mean, could this be about . . . I don't know, territory or something?"

"I don't know that much. I don't think it'd be territory-related, because a wolf that wants to be the alpha has to fight the alpha for dominance. They wouldn't gain anything from dumping a body at his house." I fiddled with my knee brace, scratching around the edges while I thought. "Other than that . . . I know that they can't change very often, unless they're alpha or beta. The rest of them don't really have the strength."

Jesse's eyebrows lifted. "How often is often?"

"Mmm . . . well, if he doesn't care about staying sane or disobeying an alpha . . . maybe once a week?"

"That's good," Jesse said, nodding. "That means we've at least got a little time to find him. In another day or two, if we haven't stopped him, we should start staking out Will's house, in case he goes there again. What else?"

"Aside from the fact that they get into fights pretty often, I don't know a ton about how they interact with each other," I admitted. "You have to remember, most of my knowledge comes from Olivia, and I don't even really know if anything she said is true." My psychotic ex-mentor had been the one to bring me into the Old World, and she'd gotten off on only doling out snippets of information as she felt I needed them. They were the bread crumbs, and I was the eager, hungry pigeon.

When Olivia had died of cancer, I suppose I could have started asking questions, but for a long time after her death I was just kind of going through the motions of my life. I went running, watched television, hung out with Molly, and waited for a phone call to go clean up blood splatter or animal carcasses. My three co-bosses mostly ignored me, and I mostly ignored anything that didn't come with opening credits and a catchy theme song. I had no interest in trying to be better at what I did.

Or trying to be better, period.

"We need more information," Jesse declared.

"We need a werewolf expert," I said aloud, then immediately wished I'd kept the words to myself.

"Will?" Jesse offered.

"I don't think that's a good idea. He's trying to hold the pack together, and after last night's insurrection it's worse than ever. Besides, he's shorthanded at the bar too." Thanks to me. I sighed. "We need someone who knows werewolves but isn't part of the pack."

Jesse met my eyes, understanding blooming on his face. "You want to go see Eli," he said softly.

I took a deep breath. "I don't want to drag him back into all this, but I don't know who else to ask. Even if the actual killer isn't part of Will's pack, one of the pack members could be involved. Will and Eli are the only pack members that I trust." *Now that Caroline is dead*, I thought. I had missed Caroline's memorial service while I was unconscious, and sometimes I still had the impulse to give my friend a call, just to talk to someone. But Olivia had killed her. She had parents and a couple of sisters in Albuquerque, I knew, but Will would have disposed of her body. They might not even know she was dead. I felt a rush of sorrow at that thought.

"Scarlett?" Jesse said, and I realized he'd been talking to me.

"Sorry, what?"

"I said, it's ten o'clock. Should we go see Eli now, or wait until the morning?"

I bit my lip. "Jesse, listen . . . I know you're the cop, and you have questions. But I need to talk to Eli alone. At least at first." Something unreadable flashed across Jesse's handsome face. I thought it was maybe disappointment, but he didn't say anything. "I haven't talked to him since I changed him back," I explained.

Jesse held my eyes for an interminably long moment, and I swear I could feel a connection vibrate between us like the thrum of a guitar string. "Your thing with Eli," he said quietly. "Where does it leave us?"

And there it was. Before I had changed Eli and gotten hurt, Jesse and I had shared a moment. We had kissed. We had connected. It was a little too late to tell myself that I didn't feel anything for him, or that I wasn't good enough for him. So I opened my mouth to unleash a smart-ass remark—but I had nothing. I blinked a few times, opening and closing my mouth like a fish.

Sometimes I am so smooth it hurts.

Jesse just let me flounder. Finally I said, honestly, "Confused."

He nodded to himself as though that was exactly what he'd been expecting. "Eli seems like a good guy," he stated neutrally. "And he's a human now too."

I could not think of a thing to say. Not one thing. "It'd be easier if he was a giant douchebag," Jesse added, a little ruefully.

"That was how I felt about Runa," I reminded him gently. Jesse had dated a police photographer named Runa Vore for a month or so before he learned that she was a witch who'd been sent to spy on him. Sometimes I wondered if he missed her. Runa was aesthetically perfect, and I had been just the teeniest bit gleeful when she had turned out to be duplicitous—but she'd also helped Jesse save my life. Even with the ulterior motive, I couldn't help but like her a little.

One thing I'll say for Eli: he was a lot less complicated.

There wasn't a whole lot more for Jesse and me to discuss after that. We both knew I had to make a choice. He asked me to call him the next day after I'd spoken to Eli, promised to start researching the victim, and said good-bye. I lay back on my bed, not the least bit tired thanks to my six-hour nap, and thought.

Five short months ago, before I'd even met Jesse, I'd been right in the middle of not allowing myself to fall in love with Eli, despite the fact that we kept falling into bed together. I'd had good reasons, though: for one thing, I'd been convinced that he only wanted to be around me so he could be human again. I'd also been convinced that I wasn't fit to be with anybody after what had happened to me with Olivia and my parents. Okay, fine. I'd thought I didn't *deserve* to be with anybody after what had happened with Olivia and my parents.

But now Olivia was dead, for good, because *I had motherfucking beaten her*. And Eli had proved more than once that he truly cared about me. Moreover, he wasn't even a werewolf anymore. There was nothing standing between us now, except for the fact that I didn't want to pull him back into the Old World when he had the chance to be free. That . . . and Jesse. Who had kissed me. I shivered. It had been a really good kiss.

"Goddammit," I said out loud. I didn't want this. I didn't want to be thinking about *boys*, for cripes' sake. I just wanted to be left alone.

But with that thought, I suddenly *felt* very alone. And I missed my mom. A wave of grief for my parents crashed into me, more powerfully than it had in years. I considered calling my brother, just to hear his voice, but I knew it was a bad idea. If Jack sensed something was wrong and asked me about it, I wouldn't be able to tell him. And if he *didn't* sense something was wrong, I'd feel more alone than ever.

I sighed and got up to change.

Chapter 11

Twenty minutes later, I was driving the White Whale east on the 10. I wasn't going to sleep anyway, so I figured I might as well get the conversation with Eli over with.

I was wearing what passed for work clothes in my life: the same jeans (soy sauce stains be damned!), a clean T-shirt, a thick sherpa-lined hoodie, and my beloved canvas jacket, also known as the "coat o' nine pockets." I had stashed my wallet, phone, and keys into its various pockets, along with my fully charged handheld Taser, which I was delighted to have. I had missed my Taser.

My long dark hair was fixed into a tight bun, and I'd put on my black Chuck Taylors. This was as close to battle dress as I was going to get, since I still needed to replace the leather boots that had been destroyed during the fight with Olivia. I'd briefly considered asking Molly to pick something out for me while I was recovering, but I'd come to my senses. If Molly had her way, I'd end up with five-inch spiked heels and retractable knives coming out of the toe.

Traffic was light by this time of night, and I sailed quickly across the 10 freeway to one of the USC campus parking garages, where I paid a ludicrous amount of money to store the Whale. USC is one of Los Angeles' two biggest schools, but until recently the area around campus was always seedy at best and bleakly dangerous at worst. A few years ago, probably prompted by trust fund parents who worried about the homeless people and drug dealers lurking a block away from their babies' BMWs, the school had made a big push to expand its safe zone of student-oriented businesses, museums, and parking garages. But a few places had resisted the tidal wave of forced urban planning, including a seedy little motel called "The 32nd Street Sleepaway," known locally as the "Dirty 32." I don't know how the Dirty 32's owners survived in the face of all that gentrification—nor do I want to—but I had to kind of respect them for standing their ground.

You can respect a place without ever wanting to visit.

Anyway, seedy or not, the Dirty 32 was where, in the hours and days that I'd been unconscious, Will had stashed Eli. When I heard about the plan, I had to admit it made sense. Very few people hung around this part of town unless they were tied to the university, and none of Will's pack was involved with USC in any way. The students were on winter break, so the motel was deserted, and it was still cheap and dirty enough that the employees wouldn't look twice at a guy who stayed more than a few days with no obvious reason to be there. It was also far inland, which was useful because anyone who knew Eli and was looking for him would probably figure on him staying near the ocean to surf, and close enough that Will could keep an eye on Eli just in case the werewolf magic returned.

It had been just over a week now, however, and it was looking more and more like that wasn't going to happen. Whatever I'd done to Eli had been for good. Or for bad.

You know, one of the two.

I had printed out directions on account of not having a smartphone. Lucky for me, there was a parking garage just around the corner from the motel, so I didn't have far to limp. Gentrification or not, this was not a great neighborhood in which to be injured, alone, or female after dark, much less all three.

The motel was a simple two-story concrete box. Each floor was basically just a long wall of rooms, bookended by twin sets of outdoor stairs with little pebbles embedded into the concrete on each step. To make it classy, I guess. When I'd called Will earlier to get Eli's location, he hadn't known the room number, so I stumped toward the manager's office on the first floor with a $20 bill in my hand. Whoever was working here had to be at least a little hard up for cash. But halfway there, movement caught my eye—Eli himself, walking toward me from the soda machine at the opposite end of the floor. His room must have been one of the ones between us. "Well, that was easy," I said out loud.

Eli heard me and looked up from his drink. He stopped dead for a second, and I saw that he was tired and sweaty-looking. The can made a tinny crackle of protest as Eli clenched it. *"Scarlett?"* he said incredulously.

I found myself blushing. "Uh . . . hey."

He dropped the can and sprinted along the line of doors toward me. I hadn't realized I was braced for his werewolf magic to hit my radius until it didn't happen, but by then he was with me, scooping me up in a breathless hug. I whimpered with pain, and he tried to put me down in a panic. By then I was off balance, though, and started to stumble back the other way. Eli reached out and steadied me, apologizing over and over. The pain flared until I was dizzy with it. My radius seemed to be spinning too.

"Scarlett? Are you okay?" Eli asked from far away. I found his ice-blue eyes and tried to focus as they peered down at me with concern. Eli is tall, a few inches over six feet, with blonde hair and a lean, muscled, surfer build.

"Yep, yep, I'm good," I said through my clenched teeth. "Just give me a second here."

"You're awake," he said wondrously, examining my face like it might have been remade while he'd been away. "When I saw you having the seizure, I was so afraid you . . . but you're okay?"

"More or less," I said, pointing at the ground, where my cane had fallen. Eli bent to retrieve it for me. I thanked him and said, "Wait, Will didn't tell you I was awake?"

Eli's face shifted to something like bitterness. "Will hasn't told me anything. At first he called twice a day to see if anything had changed, but then it's like he gave up and forgot about me. I thought maybe he was punishing me."

"Yeah," I said uneasily. "There's a lot going on there. Can we talk in your room?" I'd kept an eye out and was fairly confident that no one had followed me there, but the open-air motel was beginning to make me deeply nervous anyway.

"Oh, yeah, of course." Eli put an arm around my waist, which almost made it more difficult for me to walk, clumsy as I am, but I let him help me down the hall to one of the plain motel doors, because sometimes guys need you to do that. He had rigged the bolt on the door to keep it open while he'd made his soda run, so he just pushed the door open and we walked inside.

The motel room wasn't the worst one I've seen, but it wasn't far off, either. Everything was shabby and threadbare, from the patchy, faded orange carpeting to the polyester bedspread that looked like it might have been saved from an estate sale in the '80s. Or from a Dumpster. The bubble-front television had actual knobs instead of buttons, which I hadn't seen since I was a kid.

Eli had made his own changes to the room: he'd pushed the bed to one wall, next to a round Formica table, creating a big open space where he'd laid down a clean sheet. He helped me to one of the four chairs next to the little table and took the next one for himself. I nodded at the sheet on the floor. "What's going on there?"

"Oh," he said, embarrassed. "I was trying to exercise."

I nodded. "You must miss getting to surf."

He shrugged. "I go over to the campus every night and run on the track, or do laps around the top of the parking garage. This is more for push-ups and stuff. A little yoga." He ducked his head, embarrassed. "You know . . . man-yoga. For men."

I blinked, finally understanding. I'm used to Eli being human, because he's always been human when he's around me. But werewolves are damn near indestructible, and he'd suddenly lost the ability to survive almost anything. It must feel vulnerable. No wonder he was trying to beef up.

Great job, Scarlett. Had *anything* good come out of what I'd done? "How do you feel?" I said quietly.

He smiled wanly. "I was about to ask you the same thing."

"You go first."

Eli exhaled. "I feel . . ." He thought for a moment, and a slow, building smile spread across his face. It sent a thrill up my skin. "I feel amazing," he confessed. "I know I don't deserve it, after what happened at the bar. But it's like I've been walking around for years with thumbtacks stuck in the top layer of my skin, and suddenly they're all gone. And it's scary in a way, because I'm more . . . easily damaged. But it's incredible," he finished. He reached across the table to take my hand, and for once I didn't pull away. "I was so worried about you," he added. "But now you're awake."

His smile shone across the table, gratitude and happiness and guilt all sewn into it, and God help me, I didn't want to tell him. For a moment, I considered just getting up and leaving. I could wish him luck, make my good-byes, and encourage him to get the hell out of town. I didn't want him to know about the pack, or the murder, and I sure as hell didn't want him to know that the wolves were committing mutiny and coming after me. The nicest thing I could have done for him would be to tell him we were over and walk out of there.

But I needed Eli to tell me more about the pack. And I wasn't ready to say good-bye to him.

I took a deep breath, knowing I was being selfish. "There are some things you need to know," I began.

It didn't take long to fill him in on what had happened since I'd awoken. When I got to the part about Anastasia and her goons jumping me at Will's, Eli's hands tightened on mine, and his lips pressed together like he was swallowing a growl. Old habits.

"I can't believe Ana's terrorizing you for a cure," Eli fumed.

"I don't know," I said tiredly. "I'm starting to think I should just give her what she wants."

He sat up straighter. "You can't do that!" he barked.

I arched an eyebrow, a little annoyed. Scarlett does not respond well to being told what to do. You'd think Eli would have figured that out by now. "Why not? I mean, she wants me to cure Lydia. It's not like she's trying to get me to rob a bank or drown a bag of puppies."

"Because you have no idea if you would survive it, for one thing," he said, holding up a finger to tick off his first point. "Because if it worked and you *did* survive it, every werewolf and vampire in the city—and probably lots of other cities—would come gunning for you. And because if it didn't work this time, Ana would probably just think you were lying and you'd be exactly where you are now." He waggled his three fingers.

"That is a compelling list," I conceded, sighing. "I know, you're right. All I can really do is help Jesse and hope it blows over."

He stood up suddenly, dropping my hands, and went to pace around the big open area on the floor. "This is all my fault," he muttered.

"Don't be stupid."

He paused, turning to face me. "If I hadn't eaten those cookies, you wouldn't have—" he began.

"You can stop right there. *You* didn't change Lydia, Caroline did," I interrupted. I had a weird urge to stand up and pace too, of all things, but it would only make my leg worse, so I settled for playing with my phone, flipping it over and over in my hands. "If you hadn't eaten the wolfberry, Lydia would be just as changed."

He looked away. "Those three people would be alive."

"But they're not," I said frankly. "They're dead. And that's on Olivia, not on you."

He paced again, fingers curling into fists and out again. "I should have kept control."

I threw up my hands. "Stop," I ordered. Looking surprised, he did. I pointed to the chair. "Please, sit. You're giving me vicarious leg pain." He sat. "Sure, if it was possible for you to keep control, that would have been great," I went on. "But you know that it *wasn't*, Eli. You also know that none of this would have happened if Olivia hadn't bumped into me on the street ten years ago. Or if she wasn't thirsty for a kid she couldn't have. Or if she'd never moved to LA." He had dropped his hands and was staring at me. I leaned back in my chair and folded my arms across my chest. "Do you want more? I could do this all day. Or, you know, we could stop trying to figure out where it all went wrong and actually look at *what's happening now*."

We sat there, staring at each other, and I had absolutely no idea what Eli was going to do—cry, scream, throw something at me. But after a moment another smile began to spread very slowly across his face. "You're different," he said, with quiet delight.

I couldn't help it; I grinned back. "Not for nothing, but I think shooting your mortal enemy in the chest will do that to a person," I allowed.

Eli nodded. "That's some serious closure," he said gravely, trying to keep a straight face.

"Closure's my bitch."

He leaned back in his chair, stretching his long legs in front of him. Then without saying anything, he bent forward, gently scooped up my injured left leg, and placed it on his knee. "You should be elevating this," he lectured. A long time ago, Eli had been a paramedic. I smiled. "So," he continued. "What do you need to know about werewolves?"

Oh, right. "Jesse will probably have his own questions," I said hesitantly. I wasn't excited about the two of them getting in a room together. "But for starters, Will keeps saying that the pack is unstable. What exactly does that mean, unstable?"

He tilted his head, gathering his thoughts. "Packs get unstable for a lot of reasons," Eli began, "but most of them have to do with the alpha. He's weak, or he dies suddenly, or he abuses his power. When that happens, the werewolves' magic gets all lopsided all of a sudden. Fights break out, pack hierarchy is challenged, control weakens . . ." He winced. "It's not good."

"Wait, back up. What do you mean the magic gets lopsided?"

"Oh, right." He smiled briefly. "Sorry, it's weird to actually *talk* about this stuff. It's like explaining what it's like to have hair or something. What I mean is, an alpha is the leader of the wolf pack based on a few factors: physical power, magical power—which usually includes control of his wolf form—but also qualities like leadership, authority, kindness. But most important is that the pack agrees that he's alpha. Think of it like . . ." He paused, considering for a moment, and continued, "A magic-based shield, made out of fused patches. Each pack member contributes a patch, and when cobbled together, they make Will stronger and more powerful. He in turn uses the shield to protect the pack."

I looked at him for a long moment, working on the metaphor. "So the patches are like . . . their acknowledgment of him? As their alpha?"

He released my hand and twisted his fingers in the air, looking for words. "Acknowledgment, yes, but also their belief in him. In his ability to do the job. It's all subconscious and almost automatic, but basically every pack member gives up a tiny piece of their magic, their own relationship with their wolf. That power, collected from the pack, builds the alpha's shield."

"So it's like a self-feeding system. They believe he's the alpha so he can be the alpha so they believe he's the alpha." Eli nodded. I frowned. "And when the pack gets unstable?"

"When a pack member stops trusting in the alpha, that magic is returned to him. But it's also taken away from the alpha, creating a little hole in the shield."

"And the more pack members who lose faith in the alpha, the more holes in the shield," I said, understanding.

"I know, it's weird," Eli said, shrugging a little. "Wild wolves have this complex pack structure, and werewolves are emotionally and socially even more complicated than wild wolves. That gap, between wolf and werewolf, is filled in by magic."

Huh. That explained why Will was looking so haggard lately, and why he'd been so busy. He was trying to get the pack's faith back.

"We did it," I said slowly. "I did it. I made the pack unstable when I changed you."

Eli sighed. "How were you supposed to know? Besides," he added, taking my hand again, "I know it looks bad now, but Will is a good alpha. He'll get them back when this stuff with Anastasia and Lydia blows over."

"But how is it going to blow over?" I asked. As long as Eli was around, the pack's integrity was going to be constantly threatened. "Ana seemed more than just irked. She's losing it. You almost have to . . . leave town. And tell everyone you left of your own free will."

Eli considered that for a moment. We both knew that if he left, it would most likely be the end of us. I couldn't go with him unless Dashiell released me from my job arrangement, which was unlikely. And I couldn't run away with him, because Dashiell was keeping my brother under his thumb for the very purpose of preventing that. Eli opened his mouth to answer, his face troubled, but at that moment my phone rang.

We both jumped a little. A tinny version of "Werewolves of London" came burbling out of my pocket. I fished out my phone and answered it without checking the screen.

"Hey, Will."

"Scarlett," Will said, his voice despairing, "there's another one." I met Eli's blue eyes. He raised his eyebrows in question and I just shook my head.

"Another . . . ?"

"Another disaster. At my house."

Chapter 12

After calling Jesse and giving him the address, I drove straight to Will's house, beating Jesse by about twenty-five seconds. I backed the van into the driveway again, opened the van door, and pointed with my cane so Jesse would know to stash his sedan in the empty lot across the street from Will's house.

"There's really another body?" Jesse asked as he joined me. I nodded. Jesse was silent for a long moment, and when I glanced over, he was visibly distressed. So much for trying to catch the guy before he could kill anyone else.

We walked toward the house, with Jesse going extra slow and me working extra hard to keep up. It worked, sort of. It seemed to take forever for me to get out and make my way toward the door, even after Jesse took my duffel bag for me. Will was waiting outside when we made our way to the wooden walkway next to his house. The alpha werewolf paced back and forth, looking cornered and agitated. He had stuffed a towel in the crack underneath the front door, and I realized it was to keep the smell out. Or rather, to keep the smell *in*. That meant that the smell of the body had gotten to *Will*, whose control had always been so total. I shivered in my thick sherpa hoodie, spooked.

Will hurried to meet us on the walkway, possibly so we could talk, or possibly to get in my radius quicker. "I brought her inside, just like last night," he said abruptly. "I figured that would cut down on the amount of flooring I have to replace." Now inside my radius, he took a deep, relieved breath, as though he'd just popped out of the water after a deep dive.

"Was it a werewolf again?" I asked, and Will gave me a tight nod.

"Same one. I could smell him."

I nodded back, glancing at Jesse. His jaw was clenched tight, and he looked as agitated as Will. "I should have been here," he muttered. "I should have been watching the house."

I winced. Will tilted his head quizzically, and I explained, "He thought we should stake out your place, but I told him the guy wouldn't be able to change for a few more days."

Will shook his head. "I would have said the same thing. He shouldn't be able to change this quickly."

"What does that mean?" I asked.

"I don't know," Will admitted. "Come inside. We'll talk there."

The new body was positioned almost exactly like the one from the night before, and I had the strange impression that it had grown through the floor in the same spot, like when a new snack rises to the front of a vending machine to replace the one you took. She was a small Asian woman in her early thirties, with chin-length black hair and the well-defined back and leg muscles of a serious swimmer. She was wearing only a pair of simple satin panties, and like Leah Rhodes, her face was untouched.

But she was different from Leah Rhodes in that no part of her appeared to be . . . missing. Instead, this woman had died the death of a thousand cuts—maybe literally. Wide, messy scratches in clumps of four covered her arms, legs, and torso. Each clump was deep enough to need stitches, but I doubted that any one of them—or hell, any *three* of them—would have killed her. There were so *many*, though. She looked like she was wearing a red-and-white Jackson Pollock painting underneath her underwear. There was a band of untouched skin on each of her wrists and ankles.

Unlike Leah Rhodes, this girl's fingernails were smooth and buffed to a shine. She hadn't fought her attacker. I hoped that meant she'd been drugged and unconscious while he did this to her, but it might have just been because she was tied down.

"Same thing?" I asked Will. "She was on your doorstep?" He nodded.

"Were there any witnesses?" Jesse asked immediately. He dropped my bag inside the door, almost exactly where I had put it the night before, and began walking around me so he could see the body.

"I don't think so," Will said grimly. "My next-door neighbor has been on vacation in Aspen. I got lucky. Again." He shook his head. "But for a lot of reasons, this can't keep happening."

Jesse didn't respond. He had crouched down next to the corpse and was staring intently at her face.

"Jesse?" I asked.

"I know her," he said softly. "I mean, I know her name." He looked up at me. "When I went through missing persons reports at the station today," he went on. "Her picture was attached to one of them. I saw that she was Asian and I clicked past it, but her name is . . . Kathryn. Kathryn Wong."

"You're sure?" I asked, and Jesse nodded.

He looked back at the dead girl, peering at the girl's injuries. "See these?" he said, pointing to the wounds on her shoulders. He moved his hand until he was pointing at her shins. "And these? It's a progression."

"What do you mean, progression?" Will asked, frowning.

"He started at the top and worked his way down," Jesse said absently. "See, the scratches up here stopped bleeding a while ago—they're even starting to scab over. But the ones on her legs are raw."

"Oh my God," Will said, staring. "You're right." Will's eyes unfocused suddenly, calculating.

"What does that mean to you?" Jesse asked, looking at Will's expression. Will didn't answer.

I tried not to imagine how the girl's last moments must have gone, but it was impossible. She must have been in agonizing pain, trying to get away, bleeding. He must have attacked her upper body first, waited a little while, and gone after her torso. Then waited a little longer and come after her legs. It was eerily methodical, like he'd been waiting for something to happen in between each attack.

Playing a hunch, I added, "Will? Is he trying to change them?"

Will's distant eyes flickered back to me. "It's definitely a possibility," he said at last. "I can't tell if she bled out, or if the magic took her."

Werewolf magic is contagious, but only through body fluids, and just a little bit won't usually get the job done. So if somebody gets a single bite or scratch, they'll most often recover and go about their lives. But the more magic-tinged blood or saliva that a person absorbs, the more the magic gets in. And if enough magic gets in, the body will try to make the transformation. Sometimes it works, and the person becomes a werewolf. Sometimes—more and more often in the last couple of decades—it doesn't work, and the magic overwhelms the human body, killing the victim.

Jesse and Will were both staring down at the body, unmoving, so I broke in. "Guys?" I said, snapping my fingers. "Body now? Talk later?"

The men looked up at me, and under different circumstances their identical startled expressions would have been funny. "You're right," Will said heavily. "We've got to get rid of it."

"Her," Jesse corrected. "We've got to get rid of *her*." His voice was loaded with . . . something. Resentment? Anger? I didn't have time to worry about it. It seemed to me like this was a personal, werewolf-to-werewolf kind of thing, but there was still the chance that the guy who'd done this would call a tip in to the police, planning to frame Will for murder. And Jesse definitely couldn't be here

if that happened. Will and I could probably get clear of something like that with Dashiell's help, but Jesse's career would be over.

I stumped over to the duffel bag, which Jesse had dropped inside the door, and pulled out one of my good body bags. Leah Rhodes had seemed like a twisted collection of gore by the time I'd gotten to her, but Kathryn Wong . . . She still seemed like a person. One who had suffered, and one who would now be shoved in a furnace and forgotten. She deserved every bit of respect I could give her.

I instructed Jesse and Will to lay the body bag out next to the body, unzip it, and sort of roll her in. Jesse had seen this done dozens of times on LAPD crime scenes, and Will had covered up more than one murder because of his wolves, so they were both pretty stoic about it—until they flipped her over. The woman's legs and arms looked like her front, but her lower back was smooth and unbloodied. Instead of a hundred gashes, there was just a single knife wound, about five inches long and scabbed over. It was a loop and a quick slash—a number two.

Jesse paused, squatting down to peer closely at the mark. "This one was a knife, I think," he said tightly. "It looks like it happened before the other marks."

When he didn't move, I gave him a little nudge. He looked up at me, startled, and there was anger in his eyes. "We need to move," I reminded him gently. I was getting antsier by the minute.

Jesse nodded, and he and Will zipped the girl into the body bag. Will's face was troubled and thoughtful. "You're going to the Valley, right?" he asked. "I'll ride with you. I might have a theory."

Jesse's eyes widened, but I just shrugged my acquiescence. We had to come back to Will's anyway, so Jesse could get his car. Jesse carefully picked up the body bag and carried it outside, to the back of the van. He didn't wait for me, and by the time I made it back to the Whale, he was closing the built-in refrigerator compartment and hopping down from the vehicle. He gave me a look as I approached, and that one expression was loaded with so many emotions that it seemed to weigh him down, his shoulders slumping forward under the load. I didn't know if he was upset about the girl's murder, or how she'd died, or the fact that we were going to destroy her remains, or the fact that he was helping. Maybe all of them. Now wasn't the time to ask, though.

Jesse went for the driver's door without a word, and I loped silently toward the passenger side, gesturing to Will to climb up in the back. There's no seat belt back there, but if we got pulled over, a ticket would be the least of our problems.

Jesse started the van, driving carefully down the one-way road that led away from Will's. I don't usually like other people driving the Whale, but Jesse was a good driver, and he'd done it enough that the irritation at someone else behind the wheel had worn off for me. Will had climbed in the back of the van and was sitting on the floor in the middle, leaning his back against the rectangular freezer compartment and his feet on the long metal toolbox I have installed on the other side for less mobile cleaning stuff. "Hang on, guys," he said distractedly, and proceeded to spend the next ten minutes on his phone, making arrangements for the bar that night. While he did that, I quietly filled Jesse in on what Eli had told me about werewolf packs.

Finally Will hung up, and Jesse glanced at him in the rearview mirror. "Explain the theory," Jesse said shortly. I bit my lip, but didn't speak. Not how I'd choose to talk to the alpha werewolf of Los Angeles, but I was willing to cut Jesse some slack right now. Hopefully, Will would be too.

"I think it's a nova wolf," Will said promptly. He was squinting at me in the dim light. "Have you heard about novas, Scarlett?" he asked.

I shook my head. "The term sounds a little familiar, but no."

"What the hell is a nova wolf?" Jesse asked impatiently.

Will grimaced. "It comes from the term 'Casanova wolf,' which was a wild wolf in Yellowstone . . . long story." He paused, choosing his words. "The important thing to remember is that werewolves aren't magical creatures. We're magical *wolves*. The magic makes us stronger, faster, and better able to heal—not to mention infectious—but otherwise we're just wolves like any other. And in the wild, wolves need to be a part of a pack. You've probably heard the term 'lone wolf,' but that's not really a thing. It's just a wolf leaving one pack to find another."

"And werewolves need packs too, we get it," Jesse said impatiently. "What are you saying?"

"You have to understand that the pack dynamic calms our inner wolf," he said, sounding like he was working at patience. "It's kind of ironic, but the reassurance of the pack lets us act more human when we're not with each other. The packs are essential to retaining what's left of our humanity."

"So a nova wolf is a wolf that's just been away from a pack for too long?" I ventured.

"No. Wolves never willingly leave a pack, like I said, unless it's to find and join another. A nova werewolf is one who's made and then abandoned." Will's voice darkened. "It happens very rarely, especially now that the success rate for changing a new wolf has dropped so low." Jesse and I didn't interrupt. Nobody knew why transformative magic, which creates werewolves and vampires, seemed to be dying, but it had been happening for a long time now. "Most alphas, like me, can feel the magic shift if one of our pack members creates a new cub," Will went on. "We confront them, get them to find the cub and bring it into the pack."

"Did you feel magic shift?"

"No, but . . . ," Will trailed off, and I turned in my seat so I could squint back at him. His face was troubled. "My connection to pack magic is off," he said finally.

I nodded. If the LA pack was losing faith in Will, one by one, his connection to magic would be fluctuating too. "You think someone in your pack made the nova," I stated.

"Yes. I believe that someone in my pack took advantage of the pack's instability in the last month to change in between moons. But he or she attacked a human and abandoned him." Will shook his head a little. "It's happening faster than I would have thought—usually a wolf has to be alone for a while before he becomes nova—but everything else makes sense."

Jesse sighed, like the wolves were trying to frustrate him on purpose. "If the problem is that the new wolf is alone for too long, can't he or she just join a pack again?" Jesse asked.

I could see Will shaking his head in my peripheral vision. "Nova wolves are almost always male, and no, it doesn't work like that. That's where the name comes in. In the wild, every wolf pack has a male and female alpha who breed. They're usually called the breeding pair, and for whatever reason they're the only ones in the pack who have offspring. That's the norm. But a Casanova wolf is this weird anomaly in nature where a random male wolf sneaks from pack to pack, having sex with the other females."

"Why?" I asked, and then felt myself blush. "I mean, apart from having a bunch of sex."

"Nova wolves are slaves to biology," he said matter-of-factly. "Which includes the natural, evolutionary drive to procreate, and to lead. A nova wolf wants to become a breeding male."

"That's all?" Jesse asked. His eyes were on the road, but a furrow had appeared between his eyebrows. "This is a werewolf that wants to have babies?"

"Werewolves can't procreate the old-fashioned way." Will grimaced again, this time with his teeth showing. "Nova wolves want to create more werewolves. Emphasis on *create*. A nova wolf doesn't want to join a pack or take over a pack. All it can think about, all it can do, is try to make its own pack."

I finally understood. "So you think the person who killed those two women is an indestructible, supernaturally fast and strong apex predator that's specifically targeting humans," I summarized.

Will sighed, and I turned all the way around in my seat to squint at him. He looked tired, and older than I'd ever seen before. "Yes," he said simply.

Jesse and I looked at each other. "If this was Scooby-Doo, one of us would say 'gulp,'" I pointed out.

Jesse made a face at me. "Gulp."

Chapter 13

We hit the canyon road and began winding down toward the freeway. Jesse and Will were both silent, but there was a weight to it, like you could just hear everyone in the van *thinking*.

Will had said that werewolves behave more or less like ordinary wolves with magical enhancements. I'd never really thought of it in those terms before, but it made sense. I'd taken a lot of biology classes in high school, back when I was hoping to become a veterinarian, and I knew a little bit about wolf behavior. Wolves generally don't attack people, not unless they're truly cornered or starving to death. Basically, unless there are no other options. And I knew that werewolves have no particular interest in attacking humans, either. Eli had once mentioned that the one time the LA pack had encountered humans during the full moon, Will had directed his wolves away from the trespassing campers without an incident. That was part of why the Old World was able to stay hidden: werewolves in wolf form just weren't the bloodthirsty, slavering meat fiends bent on eating people that you see in the movies. In their wolf form, they rarely attacked humans, and therefore rarely killed or changed anyone.

So a big, indestructible wolf that specifically hunted humans was a nightmare. And because so few people change when they've been bitten nowadays, it wasn't much better than a serial killer.

"Why women?" I wondered aloud, breaking the silence that

had fallen over the van. "Does he think males will challenge his dominance?"

"No again," Will answered tensely. "Remember, he wants to procreate. He wants to be the male half of the dominant couple, even if they can't reproduce sexually."

"So he's trying to make a mate." I finished, catching on. "Holy crap, it's *Frankenstein*."

"You mean Frankenstein's creature," Jesse corrected me primly. "'Frankenstein' was the name of the doctor who created it."

"No, I mean *Frankenstein,* the work of literature," I retorted. "The title. We're in *Frankenstein,* meaning the title."

"Kids!" Will barked. "Can we get back to the point?"

"Sorry," Jesse muttered.

"What happens if he gets what he wants?" I asked. "If he builds a pack?"

"Wolf packs are territorial," Will reported. "When he's got his own, he'll come after mine. Not to recruit."

"To kill," Jesse stated grimly.

There was another long silence in the van. We'd gotten off the freeway, and Jesse rolled down his window, letting the chilly city air surge into the van. It smelled like Dumpsters and Chinese food and car exhaust.

My city.

It's easy to forget, especially given the last few months, that when it comes to the Old World, LA is supposed to be this oasis of peace. Although certain events or people might intrude on the status quo, compared to most places we have a very unique and somewhat delicate balance. No single supernatural faction runs the city, not even the vampires. But if Will were ousted, if the werewolf pack were obliterated and a new, psychotic alpha stepped in, that balance would be destroyed. Dashiell would have to start interfering with pack business more, just to keep their actions hidden. I doubted the nova would take kindly to vampire interference, and the conflict would escalate. There would be fighting. Soon people who have no business fighting would have to go to war. The peace would fall.

Plus . . . Will was kind of my friend. At the very least, I didn't want him to die.

"I get that he wants to grow his pack," Jesse said suddenly. The sounds of traffic streamed through the open window, and he had to shout a little for us to hear. "But why the two different methods? He ate part of one woman, scratched up the other . . ."

I turned my head and shoulders to look back at Will, who nodded as if he'd been expecting that question. "I think he's experimenting. I've seen attempts to change someone before, successful and unsuccessful, but I've never seen anything this calculating and cold. It's just . . ."

"Nuts?" I volunteered.

"Scientific," he corrected me grimly.

"Hang on," Jesse insisted. "We need to go back to the part where we've got two bodies, two nights in a row, both attacked by werewolves. You said they can't change that often, so is there more than one nova? Could it be something else, like . . . I don't know, a group of random werewolves experimenting with magic, or a werewolf serial killer, something like that?"

"It's possible," Will admitted. Jesse took an on-ramp, and the sudden shift jostled the werewolf, forcing him to tilt sideways and catch himself on the van's carpeted floor. When he recovered, Will added, "But I think perhaps he kidnapped both women at different times, restrained them, and changed. Then he tried the two different methods."

"It just took Kathryn Wong longer to die," I whispered. Goose bumps suddenly broke out on my arms, and it had nothing to do with the air from Jesse's window. "Oh, God," I whispered, so softly that neither man looked at me. I wouldn't have known how to speak if they had.

I'd done it. The LA werewolf pack had been dealt a huge blow when Caroline, the sigma, was killed. And then I'd made everything so much worse by taking away the pack's beta and stirring up rumors and animosity, making everyone doubt Will. I was the one who'd made the pack unstable, creating an opening in the pack's magic for the nova to waltz into town and start killing women. "It's my fault," I said, realizing too late that I was speaking out loud.

Jesse's eyebrows furrowed with confusion, but Will had been looking at me in the dim light, and he had seen the moment when I understood what I had done. He gave me a tired little nod of acknowledgment that said, *I know. You didn't mean to. But now we're screwed.*

Tears stung my eyes, and I swiped at them with the back of my hand. I turned my head to stare out the window, not wanting the two men to see me cry. After Olivia had killed my parents, I'd blamed myself for a long time. But I had been wrong then. It wasn't like I'd made a series of bad decisions or mistakes that had led to Olivia deciding she needed to become my new mommy after dispensing with the old one. I had just *been there*, and she'd decided to take me, and I had no more responsibility in the matter than an apple does when it gets blown off a tree. I finally understood all that now, after I'd seen Olivia again and realized just how batshit crazy she really was.

But this was different from that, and different from Eli feeling responsible for what he'd done after he'd eaten the wolfberry. My actions—my *choices*—had made the pack unstable and crippled Will's magic, leaving it vulnerable to bad behavior and the nova wolf. I had deprived Lydia of the pack's beta and driven Anastasia to a desperate rage that legitimately frightened me. I had carelessly opened a door that I didn't understand and fucked around with a system that was ancient, complex, and delicate. And I had done it on a *whim*, out of pity for a situation I couldn't even comprehend.

When the van stopped a few minutes later, I didn't move. "Scarlett," Jesse said sharply, sounding exasperated, and I realized that this wasn't the first time he'd said my name. I jerked my eyes to him. "This is the place, right?" he asked, in a tone that said, *Get it together*.

"What? Yeah," I said shakily. We were at Artie's studio. I told Jesse to unlock the gate and pull the van around back, and he complied without another word. That was fine with me. I wasn't in a talking mood at that point, anyway.

"Scarlett," Will said quietly, and I turned to look back at him. "Why don't you and I take the remains inside. Detective Cruz can stay here and keep an eye on the van."

I nodded gratefully. I wasn't sure if Will was trying to spare Jesse from having to physically destroy the remains, or if he was just trying to keep the worst of our disposal methods from the police. Either way, I was glad to spare Jesse the sight of Kathryn Wong's body being shoved into the furnace. Jesse didn't comment, which I took as agreement.

Will carried the body bag, I held the doors, and we got the body into the furnace without incident. I thought about saying something as Kathryn Wong's body went into the furnace. If Will hadn't been there with me, I might have.

When we got back to the car, Jesse wouldn't meet my eyes. I didn't blame him. All three of us were subdued and quiet on the way back to Will's.

Finally Will spoke into the terse silence. "I'll call a pack meeting for tomorrow night to try to get things stabilized. What do you two need to hunt the nova?"

I looked at Jesse, who said promptly, "We need a roster of all the pack members."

Will's eyes narrowed. "You can't just go around interrogating the pack," he objected. "That won't exactly help them trust me again."

"Tough shit," Jesse said shortly.

"Jesse!" I hissed.

He looked at me. "I'm past being polite, Scarlett. One of them made a monster. He has to answer for it."

The alpha looked between us for a long moment, and then nodded reluctantly. "All right. Talk to the pack," he said quietly. "But Scarlett can't go."

I understood, but Jesse looked puzzled. "They all hate me right now," I explained. "They think I have a cure and I'm keeping it from them."

"Isn't that . . . sort of true?" Jesse asked, not unkindly.

It stung anyway, and I worked to keep my face straight. "Yes. But Will's right. I can't go rubbing their faces in it."

Jesse looked uneasy, and I realized he was a little afraid to track down the werewolves without me around to negate them. I understood, but there wasn't really anything to be done, and finally he nodded in agreement. "If we're going to split up," he said slowly, "You can at least make yourself useful."

"What do you have in mind?"

"If I'm getting this, there are two ways to stop the nova," he said, glancing at Will. "Either we find out who made him, or we find out how he's choosing his victims."

"You want me to go talk to the victims' families?" I blurted out, my eyes wide.

Jesse nodded. "You can start with Leah Rhodes's roommate and go from there. I'll help you come up with a cover story and give you some questions."

"What if—I don't know if I can—" I sputtered. I had interviewed people without Jesse before, but only Old World people. Talking to civilians had always been Jesse's purview, not mine.

"You'll do fine," Jesse said curtly. "You've done two major police investigations already. You can handle this."

Not wanting to freak out any further in front of Will, I just nodded.

We arrived back at the alpha's house. I had been a touch nervous that there would be flashing police cars waiting for us when we arrived, but the nova wolf hadn't called the police the night before, and he hadn't called them tonight. Whatever was going on, he was keeping it in the Old World for now.

Will went inside to get a pack roster for Jesse, who carried my duffel bag to the van for me and loaded it in the side door. When the door clicked shut, I asked, "While we wait, do you want to talk about those interviews tomorrow?"

"No," he said without hesitating. "I just . . . need some space, Scarlett. I'll go in and get the list from Will, and call you first thing in the morning." He abruptly turned on his heel and marched toward Will's front door, leaving me standing there with my mouth ajar.

I'd seen Jesse mad, distraught, and worried before, often at me, but I'd never seen him be cold. Maybe he was regretting taking the deal with Dashiell. Or maybe he just didn't want to be my partner anymore. *Focus, Scarlett,* I chided myself. Jesse was going to do what he was going to do; there was no use worrying about it.

No matter how many times I told myself that, the nagging fears stayed with me the whole way home.

It was nearly eleven when I parked the White Whale in the structure near Molly's house and limped my way to the back door. My leg felt far away, as if the big lump of pain that had wound itself around my knee like a tentacle was actually separating it from me. I wanted nothing more than to go to bed with several ice packs and some of the good drugs. As I rounded Molly's decorative shrubbery, however, I saw a small figure with shoulder-length blonde hair huddled on the concrete step leading to the doorway, arms hugging her knees, her head turned away so one ear was resting on her legs. I tensed, gripping my cane hard like I might use it for a weapon, but took a few cautious steps forward—and felt her hit my radius. Not a werewolf, not a vampire. It was like my radius had been thrust into a prism.

Another null.

She felt it when I did, and the blonde bob tilted up to meet my eyes. "Corry?" I asked incredulously.

Chapter 14

"Scarlett!" The teenager's face broke into a beautiful grin I'd never seen on her face before, and she jumped up and ran for me, throwing her arms around my shoulders. Her momentum rocked me back a step onto my bad leg, but I ignored it, shifting my weight to my left instead. I was smiling stupidly, and to my great annoyance, I realized I was blinking back tears. "It's so good to see you!" Corry said into my hair.

"Yeah." I released her and leaned back, swiping my eyes as quickly as I could. The pain from my knee, which had been at a low running-refrigerator hum before, now roared into focus, and I fought to keep it off my face. "You too. Come on, let's get inside." I had a dozen questions, but was anxious to get her out of sight first. I didn't think any of Will's pack had found Molly's house, but I didn't want to wait around to find out. If anyone saw Corry here . . .

Corrine "Corry" Tanger was a fifteen-year-old null whom I'd met the previous fall. A teacher at her school had sexually assaulted her, and then blackmailed her by threatening to tell her dad, a Pentecostal minister. Corry had felt like she didn't have any other options, so when a psychotic guy with a yearning to kill vampires offered to get the teacher off her back in exchange for helping him cleanse LA of the supernatural . . . she had gotten all turned around.

I'd done what I could to help her, but then I had told Corry I couldn't see her anymore. Nulls are ridiculously rare, and there are creatures in the Old World who would happily commit murder to get one for their own personal use, especially a young, impressionable teenager with a history of moral flexibility. I'm protected in Los Angeles because of my job, but if anyone else found out about Corry, she'd be fair game. The girl was "in the closet" to the Old World, and I had made it my personal mission to let her stay there.

And here she was, on my doorstep. I wanted to scold her, but I was just so frickin' happy to see her I didn't know what to do.

"Your leg!" Corry cried as we started for the door. "Oh my gosh, what happened? I'm so sorry—I didn't mean to hurt it!"

I waved it off. "It's no big deal; almost healed anyway," I lied. I unlocked the door and led her inside, through the back hallway and into the living room. "Um, sit anywhere you want. I'll take the couch, if you don't mind. Do you want something to drink, or I could make a sandwich . . ." I wasn't used to being a hostess, and I realized that I was babbling.

"Oh, no, here—" Corry ran to the two armchairs, grabbing throw pillows, which she propped under my knee. "I could get you some ice or something," she added hurriedly. There was a pause, and then we both broke into nervous laughter.

"It's weird, isn't it?" Corry said, crossing the living room to perch on the edge of an armchair. "In some ways, I feel like we're family, like I've known you forever. And then I remember that I don't know your favorite color, or band, or if you have brothers or sisters, or . . ." Her voice trailed off, and she gave an embarrassed shrug. "You know. Anything."

"It is weird," I agreed. "And we can talk about all that stuff, but first I need to know how you found me, and why you're here. Are you in trouble?"

Corry frowned, her slightly over-plucked eyebrows furrowing. "Not that I know of. No, I was just, like, worried about you. You sounded so freaked out when I talked to you before Christmas. I called you a bunch of times, but your phone was dead or something." Her eyes lifted to meet mine. "You didn't get my messages?"

I winced. My former cell phone had been lost after I went into the coma—I didn't really know what had happened, but it had something to do with getting everyone's car where it was supposed to be and moving my unconscious body back to Molly's without the police noticing. Nobody had thought to look for or replace the phone until a day or two after I woke up, and if there was a way to get old messages onto the new phone, I had no idea how. I'm not exactly what you'd call "tech savvy." "I'm sorry," I said simply. "I didn't."

She bit her lip, nodding, and I realized how worried she'd been. Corry had been through so much, and she'd been that concerned about *me*. I changed the subject so I wouldn't start misting up. Reputation to maintain and all that. "How did you find out where I live?" I asked

Corry gave a little shrug. "I didn't know how else to find you, so this morning I called Will. He told me where you live." Tentative smile. Will had neglected to mention Corry's call, but I couldn't really blame him for forgetting. "I took, like, three buses. I tried to call first, but my phone's been crappy lately."

I groaned inwardly. "Corry, honey, you're fifteen. You can't take the Metro by yourself at night; it isn't safe."

"I'm fine," she said defensively.

I leaned forward so I could look her in the eye. "Where does your mother think you are right now?" I asked gently.

Corry blushed red, her fingers twisting together in her lap. "She thinks I'm at my dad's place."

That surprised me. "Your mom and dad . . . they split up?"

Corry nodded, suddenly seeming to shrink in on herself. "My mom found out about . . . about my teacher. She told my dad. He kinda freaked out." I winced again. And as if she hadn't been through enough already, now she had to go through all the emotional turmoil of her parents' divorce.

"How did your mom find out?" I asked.

"I told her." Corry swallowed. "My therapist thought I should. My mom took it really well, considering." Tiny smile. "And when my dad flipped, she had my back." I saw her eyes fill, and I wished I could rush over and hug her, but my stupid leg was such a dead weight, it might as well have been part of the couch. "I'm at a different school now, and my dad moved out . . ." Another shrug. "It's a lot of change, but it's better than lying all the time, hiding."

"I'm very proud of you," I said softly. She nodded and looked away with a little smile. I took a deep breath. "But you're right, Corry: no more lies." I leaned to one side, so I could pull my cell phone out of my pocket. I tossed it to her, and she caught it automatically, a questioning look on her face. "Call your mother," I ordered. "Tell her where you are, and that I'll drive you home."

Corry seemed like she was about to protest, but after a long look at my face, she sighed and nodded. I stayed where I was on the couch while Corry stepped into the hallway. I heard snatches of her side of the conversation—her mom was doing most of the talking—and finally she slumped back into the room, holding the phone out. "She wants to talk to you," Corry said unhappily.

Yeeps. I really didn't want to actually talk to an authority figure. I wasn't, like, one of the adults or anything. But in for a penny . . . I took the phone. "Mrs. Tanger?"

"Ellen, please," said a cultured, tired voice on the other end of the phone. I'd met Corry's mom very briefly, but I hadn't even known her first name until that moment. "Anyone who houses my runaway daughter gets to call me Ellen."

"I'm sorry," I said to Ellen Tanger. "I'm glad to see her, but I wish the circumstances were different."

Corry's mother gave a very ladylike little snort. "As do I. Did she tell you that she was grounded?"

I glanced at Corry, who had returned to her seat and folded her arms across her chest defensively. "No, she didn't," I said carefully.

"I didn't think so." There was a long, staticky noise as Ellen Tanger sighed into the phone. "This isn't the first time she's snuck out, Miss Bernard."

"Scarlett," I said automatically. "Anyone who trusts me with their runaway daughter gets to call me Scarlett."

"Scarlett, then," she said, ignoring the lame joke. "I kept thinking that with a new school, a new . . . family arrangement, this behavior would stop." There was a little catch in her voice, and when she spoke again, it was with desperation. "I'm sorry that Corry invited you into our problems, but . . . what am I supposed to do? What did *your* mother do?"

There was no reason for that to sting, but it did. "My mother is dead," I said quietly.

Corry's mother sucked in a breath. "Was it . . . one of *them*?" she asked fearfully.

Oh . . . crapnuggets. I met Corry's eyes. As if she'd heard her mother, she looked away guiltily. Corry had told her mom about the Old World. That was understandable, but very, very bad.

Corry was technically part of the Old World, so she was allowed to know anything I wanted to tell her about how things work. Her mother, however, was purely human, and if Dashiell found out a human knew . . . he'd most likely kill her. We had to make sure Dashiell didn't find out. I added that to my mental list of impossible things to do.

I took a deep breath and processed the question. Had vampires killed my mother? "No, it wasn't one of them," I answered, hoping I sounded at least a little reassuring. *It was one of us*, I added silently. Olivia had been a null when she'd killed my mom and dad. But Ellen Tanger didn't need to know that.

I promised her that I would bring Corry home after we'd talked for a bit, and hung up my phone. When I looked back at Corry, her arms were still crossed over her chest. "You see what I'm dealing with?" she said petulantly.

I put the phone back in my pocket. "You told her about vampires," I said carefully.

Her arms uncrossed as she balled her hands into fists. "I had to!" she said defensively. "She had all these questions, and—"

I held up a hand, "It's done, Corry. I'm not going to yell at you. But do you understand that you may have put her in danger?"

Her eyes widened. "No . . . I mean, I knew I wasn't supposed to say anything, but . . ." she swallowed hard. "Is she . . . what's gonna happen?"

I thought that over for a moment. It was too late to press Ellen's mind—erasing memory only works shortly after the event in question, and she'd obviously known for a while. "I gotta think about it," I said at last. "For now just tell your mom she can't ever talk about knowing, even in front of me. Even in front of you. You never know who's listening."

Subdued, Corry nodded. "And you've got to give her a break, kid," I added. "She just found out that a whole world of magic exists, and everyone in it wants a piece of her little girl. She is balls-out terrified." Corry shrugged noncommittally. Her face was creased down in something resembling a pout. I repressed a sigh. This wasn't exactly what I needed right now.

"She said you've been sneaking out at night," I ventured. The girl reached one hand up to play with a little bead necklace, not meeting my eyes again. "Any particular reason?"

A beat passed, and then Corry looked right at me, pain in her eyes. "I'm not a child," she burst out. "Not anymore. If I want to go out, I should be able to."

"Where do you go?" I asked mildly.

She looked surprised for a moment, her hand going still at her throat. "I just walk," she said hesitantly. "To the movies, or a bookstore. There's a coffee shop that's open late; sometimes I go there. I just . . . don't want to be alone," she confessed. "But I don't want to be with anyone who . . . *knows*."

Well, shit. Once again, I felt woefully inadequate. I wanted to help her, but I was not a frickin' family therapist. There were layers of anguish here, and I had no idea how to peel them back for Corry. I considered telling her to talk to her actual therapist, but that seemed dismissive. "Have you told your mom that?" I said carefully.

The girl's face clouded over again. "She doesn't get it," Corry muttered. "Not like you."

Ah. I saw where this was going. Corry had cast me as the rebellious mother-alternative folk hero. Jesse and I had rescued her once, and now she thought I could save her again. I wished it were true.

She was right about one thing, though—she and I were connected. I knew, in a simple, calm kind of way, that I would die before I let her get hurt again, and that she needed to stay far away from me. "Corry, I wish I could say that things have calmed down for me now, but that's not how it is. My life is dangerous. And after everything you've been through, the last thing in the world I want is for you to get hurt."

Corry took a deep breath, meeting my eyes, and when she spoke again her voice shook, like she was delivering a speech she'd practiced. "About that," she began. "I know what you said, and I get it. But a lot has been going on for me, and I feel like there's this whole other . . . there's this part of my life . . ." She waved one wrist in a frantic circle, searching for the right words. "It's like having your back turned to the ocean, you know? It's just big and vast and I don't understand any of it, and I'm way overwhelmed." Her hands, which had been fidgeting in her lap again, suddenly stilled.

"I need you, Scarlett," she said quietly. "I know you've been trying to protect me by keeping me out of it, but I need to know how to protect myself. I *can't* get blindsided again. I want in."

I stared at her. Well. Goddammit.

Chapter 15

After Jesse had helped destroy Kathryn Wong's body, he'd steered his car away from Will's house only to pull over on Temescal Canyon Road, unsure of where he even wanted to go. He was reluctant to head home when he knew he wouldn't be able to sleep any time soon. His apartment was a tiny bunker that functioned as half sleeping place, half storage compartment; it had zero appeal for him when he was this keyed up.

He turned the engine off, staring out the windshield. The nova may have killed Kathryn Wong, but it was Jesse and Scarlett who'd erased her. She had been a full person, with her own thoughts and parents and probably a hold list at the public library. And they'd just . . . wiped her off the board. And no one would ever know.

Jesse rubbed his eyes with the heel of his hands. "You gotta get your shit together," he said aloud. On top of his agreement with Dashiell and Kathryn Wong's body, he was worried about the fact that he would soon be questioning Old World suspects without Scarlett around as a safe zone. Only a day earlier he wouldn't have found that to be quite so daunting, but after Dashiell had pressed Jesse's mind, he was reluctant to be vulnerable around any Old World creatures.

The problem, he thought, *is that I don't have any weapons I can use against werewolves.*

Unfortunately, the only person he knew who sold silver weapons was a dead serial killer—Jared Hess, who'd made silver handcuffs, silver chains, and presumably other silver weapons as well. But all of Hess's stuff had been seized by the police, and Jesse wasn't about to break into a police evidence locker to steal it.

Then an idea struck him—*Noah is in town.* He checked his phone's calendar to make sure he had the dates right. Yes. A plan began to clink together in Jesse's mind, as he started his sedan and headed for Los Feliz.

Jesse's older brother, Noah, was a stuntman, currently working full-time on a network action-adventure show about an FBI agent who could speak telepathically to his guardian angel. He usually shot on a soundstage in Vancouver, but he'd left Jesse a voicemail a few days earlier saying that he was doing exteriors in LA for the next two weeks. Jesse dialed with his phone's Bluetooth. Noah often filmed his show at night, so he was likely to still be awake, and maybe even up for a minor adventure.

His brother picked up on the second ring. "Hey, Ugly," Noah said cheerfully, by way of hello. Jesse grinned as he drove.

"Hey, Meathead. Whatcha doing?"

"Throwing a tennis ball. Max and I are having an endurance contest." Max was their parents' energetic pit bull mix. Noah had an apartment in Vancouver, but stayed with their parents when he was in LA.

"Getting your ass kicked?" Jesse asked.

"Yes, I am," Noah said airily. "What's up with you?"

"Well, it's after eleven on a weeknight, so I was just wondering if you wanted to go out and do something stupid."

"Come pick me up," Noah said immediately.

Jesse arrived at his parents' home in Los Feliz fifteen minutes later. The cheerfully over-decorated house had been tiny when

Rob Astin and Carmen Cruz had bought it, long before Noah was born. Since then, they had added a new addition every few years until the house had mutated into a stubby maze, with his father's three-room mixing studio fixed to the back of the building, and his mother's kitchen nearly twice its original size. Amidst the clutter, mementos, and family warmth, it was starting to look like a place where hobbits might live, but Jesse was fond of it.

When he pulled up, Noah was sitting outside on the front steps with their parents' dog, Max, who was a strange combination of pit bull and greyhound. Noah let go of Max's collar when Jesse stepped out of his car, and the big dog bolted toward Jesse's knees, jumping up to lick his face. "Whoa, buddy," Jesse said, darting to one side to keep the dog's paws off his chest.

"Max, off," Noah called from the stoop. "Come." The dog immediately abandoned his greeting ritual and trotted back to Noah's side. He sat patiently next to Noah while he and Jesse embraced.

Jesse shook his head in amazement. "He only listens like that to you," he marveled to his brother. "Everybody else has to yell four times just to get his attention."

"That's because he knows I'm the alpha here," Noah said casually. The word set off alarms in Jesse's brain, and it took a moment for him to remember that his brother meant nothing by it.

Noah stretched lazily with a gracefulness that belied his size. Although their faces were different and only Noah could pass for fully Caucasian, the two brothers had almost the exact same frame: same height, same shoulder width, even the same shoe size. But while Jesse had some honest muscle on him, Noah was enormous, the result of spending twelve hours a week at the gym to keep his body up to the same standards as the actor he doubled. For Jesse, looking at his brother was always eerie, like being half of a before-and-after ad for steroids.

"So," Noah drawled, "what are we doing tonight, little brother?"

Jesse plopped down on the stoop next to his brother. "Do you still hang out with that crazy girl?" he replied. "The one who works at the twenty-four-hour pawnshop?"

Noah Cruz had been a stuntman in LA for a decade before he'd gotten the gig in Vancouver, and he had long ago tapped into the industry's network of semi-employed actors, stunt people, prop houses, makeup artists, and so on. Noah called this crowd the Hollywood Peripheral, and he stayed in contact with them even when he was in Canada.

"She *owns* the pawnshop," Noah corrected amiably. "And yes, Tommy and I are still . . . friendly." He grinned. Jesse's brother considered casual hookups to be the best part of his semitransient lifestyle. One of Noah's companions was Tomorrow "Tommy" Vrapman, a former stuntwoman who considered Amy Winehouse to be her personal style maven. Noah's smile faded just a little bit. "At least, I think we are."

"Well," Jesse suggested, "let's go find out."

"What are you pawning, little brother? " Noah asked, eyebrows raised. "Because there are like three pawn shops in between here and there."

"I'm not pawning; I'm buying," Jesse replied. "Come on. What else are you doing?"

Noah shrugged amiably and went to put the dog inside.

Noah directed him toward All That Glitters, the pawnshop that Tommy had purchased with settlement money after an accident on the set of a B-rate action flick. The store was housed in a strip mall in Venice, five blocks from the canals. Against all economic odds, the shop thrived. The building had never been nice, but against the devil-may-care backdrop of Venice Beach, its careworn shabbiness had somehow transformed into grungy chic. A fresh coat of paint on the building would have been ruinous for business, as would fixing the neon sign out front, where the *s* in *Glitters* had long since burned out. Jesse had occasionally wondered if the pawnshop got much business from misguided glitter fanatics.

He had met Tommy only once, at Noah's going-away-to-Vancouver party, and he'd come away glad that the pawnshop was out of his jurisdiction. Tommy flounced around with a devilish "I'm getting away with something, copper" attitude that Jesse figured was intentional—and possibly also accurate. Bad if she lived in your jurisdiction, but potentially good if you needed something only marginally legal. "She still wearing the eye patch?" Jesse asked idly as they searched for parking.

Noah grinned widely. "She goes back and forth between that and the glass eye. There, right there!" He pointed at a space, and Jesse parked in a side alley a stone's throw away from the Venice Canals.

Instead of a bell, a chime played the first two bars of "You Know I'm No Good" as Jesse and Noah went in. Jesse was surprised at how clean and bright the shop was—he'd been expecting something seedy, with a thin layer of grime on each surface, but for a pawnshop the place was surprisingly . . . perky. The main room consisted of smaller goods—china sets, hardcover books, electronics—and a long glass counter against the back wall. There was a wide doorway to Jesse's left that led to a room of what looked like musical instruments. A doorway to the right led to a room of bigger items like suitcases and vacuum cleaners.

Tommy herself stood behind the counter, arguing pleasantly with a man in his fifties who looked just this side of homeless. "Be right with you guys," she called, giving Noah a little wave. The older man glanced at them briefly, then did a slow, cautious double take at Jesse, who gave him a hard stare, just for fun. The guy mumbled something to Tommy, scooped a handful of necklaces off the counter, and jammed them in the pocket of his dirty army jacket. Without meeting anyone's eyes, he skulked past Jesse and Noah and out the door.

"Wow," Noah said, eyeing Jesse with new appreciation. "I had no idea you carried such a stench of bacon."

Jesse held up a middle finger to his brother. "Forget about it," Tommy said, circling the counter to approach them. She was in her mid-thirties, like Noah, with long lean limbs, dark-red lipstick, and what looked like two compacts' worth of blue eye shadow on her lids. She was wearing the glass eye today, and Jesse was impressed at how natural it looked next to her remaining blue eye. Her hair, on the other hand, looked anything but natural: it appeared to have been teased up high with an eggbeater and then shellacked in place with black varnish. She wore skintight jeans and a ribbed tank top that showed off what had to be thousands of dollars' worth of intricate, colorful tattoos. No bra.

"Noah Cruz, as I live and breathe," Tommy drawled, throwing her arms around Jesse's brother. She gave him a long hug, squealing with delight as Noah leaned back to lift her briefly off the ground. "And Jesse 'the Cop' Cruz, I remember you," she added, giving Jesse one of those half handshake, half hugs he mostly expected from other men.

"Hi, Tommy," Jesse said.

"Hey, Toms, did you get new, you know . . ." Noah pointed to his own chest. Jesse backhanded his brother lightly on the arm. "What?" he protested. "I'm asking professionally. As an *actor*."

"It's cool," Tommy said happily. She clutched a breast in each hand, looking down at them fondly. "They were my birthday present last year. To myself. They're good, right?"

"There's only one way to be sure," Noah said glibly, stepping toward her with a hand outstretched.

"Not why we're here, *hermano*," Jesse said, intercepting his brother and steering him away with Noah's own momentum.

"Right," Tommy said, dropping her hands. "You looking for something? Besides a glance at my fabulous new tits?"

"He is," Noah said, pointing a thumb at Jesse. "I'm good with the glance."

Tommy treated him to a flirtatious smile and a wink of the glass eye, and then she turned to Jesse, leaning in a little. "You've got my attention," she said in a low confidential voice.

"I've got a friend," Jesse began, "who's doing a student film. He's really into authenticity—"

Tommy waved a hand. "I don't need the particulars," she said dismissively. "It's LA, baby. This week alone I sold a wax ear and a big-ass box of used dental floss. Nothing surprises me, and I don't need backstory."

Jesse nodded. "Weapons," he said shortly. "I'm looking for a silver blade. And a boot knife." Noah's mouth dropped open a little, but Jesse ignored it.

Tommy's expression grew cagey. She folded her arms across her ample chest and cocked out a hip. "All of our blades are in the glass case on the counter."

"I saw them. They're glorified pocketknives."

"But they're all *legal*," she said solicitously.

Jesse felt his expression harden. His voice too. "Cut the shit, Tommy. I'm not suggesting you're a secret arms dealer. But you must have stuff you keep off the sales floor."

"Jesse, man," Noah said under his breath, "what are you doing?"

Jesse ignored his brother and kept his eyes on Tommy Vrapman, who shook her head, her expression a little smug. "Sorry, officer."

"Detective, now. And you're way out of my jurisdiction," Jesse said coolly. "As long as you're not handing out live grenades with every purchase, I couldn't care less what you do."

Tommy just shrugged, still smiling. Jesse took a step closer. *Fuck it*, he thought. The anger was building again, and he didn't have time for this crap. "I have friends in the West bureau, though," he said softly. "Young cops, like me. Always looking to make an impression with their supervisors, you know? Looking for a bust?"

Tommy's eyes widened a little. "Hey!" Noah said sharply, and it reminded him of Scarlett, the way she'd sounded shocked when he'd talked to Will. He was sick of both of them trying to rein him in when he was doing his job. The job Dashiell had more or less forced on him.

"Stay out of it, *hermano*," Jesse said coolly. "Tommy gets where I'm coming from, don't you, Tommy?"

Her expression was flat. "Oh, I know exactly where you're coming from. You think you're the first cop to come in here?"

"No," Jesse replied, his voice hard. "But I can promise you that I'm the most motivated. And the least charmed by your punk princess bullshit. You're a little girl playing dress up, and I'd bet money that you're doing something stupid just for the thrill of it." Tommy flinched away from him and then squared her shoulders, annoyed that he'd seen her react.

"Jesse!" Noah yelped, but neither Jesse nor Tommy looked at him.

Tommy glared for a long moment, and then her expression softened. "Noah used to say you were the sweet one, you know," she said quietly.

Jesse shrugged. "Things change."

Tommy nodded curtly, her face closed now. She stalked over to the front door and flipped the dead bolt, pulling a chain cord that turned off the neon *Open* sign. Then she looked back at Noah and Jesse and jerked her head. "Noah, wait here. *Detective* Cruz, follow me."

Noah opened his mouth to object again, but Jesse shook his head sharply. He was working now.

Tommy led Jesse toward a door behind the counter and into a long back room that was lined on either wall with cheap metal shelving. She had managed to make the narrow room seem even smaller by adding an additional row of shelves going down the middle. Jesse had to turn slightly sideways to make it through the aisle comfortably, and his brother would have had to crab-walk just to get in the room, but Tommy glided through the narrow space easily. The merchandise piled on these shelves was mostly grimy, broken, or extremely expensive—too nice to keep out front, in case of a robbery. There was a whole stack of video game consoles in perfect-looking condition, and one shelf filled with nothing but small boxes with the Rolex logo on them. "Those fall off a truck?" Jesse asked sarcastically, but Tommy didn't bother to answer. She just stopped in the back left corner of the room. The three-level shelf on this wall was full of weapons.

"Those are all from prop houses," Tommy said immediately, pointing to the bottom shelf, which was piled haphazardly with guns. "The firing pins have been disabled."

Jesse shrugged. "Don't care." There were knives on the middle shelf, at waist height. Some were encased in leather or vinyl sheaths, and some were bare, but they were all spread out on a clean gray cloth, arranged in order of blade length. The shortest blade was fixed to a set of brass knuckles. The longest was a samurai sword that looked authentic to Jesse, though he didn't know anything about them.

He picked up a couple of knives, choosing one in a leather sheath, asking, "Do you have any silver knives?"

She shook her head. "It's not a real practical metal, you know."

"So I've heard," he said wryly. "Do you have *anything* made out of silver?"

Tommy chewed on the inside of her cheek for a second, eyeing the shelf of knives, and then went up on tiptoes to pick up a small, unlabeled box the size of her hand from the top shelf. "You could say that."

Jesse opened the box. "You're kidding." Tommy just shook her head. Not kidding.

The box held homemade silver-plated bullets for a nine-millimeter pistol. "Where did you get these?" he asked Tommy in amazement.

"I've got a dealer in the Valley who makes them. He's a friend, so I always keep one box here. They sell okay, actually, especially in the last few months." She shrugged one tattooed shoulder. "Kitsch value is alive and well in LA."

Jesse almost chortled. Kitsch value. There were probably a couple of customers who liked the novelty of owning actual silver bullets, but he was betting that someone from the Old World had found a place to buy them after Jesse and Scarlett had stopped Jared Hess. Tommy, the girl who liked to flirt with danger, had no idea what she had.

"I'll take them," he told her. Jesse carried a .45-caliber Beretta for work, but like most cops he kept a spare gun at home, and that one was a nine-millimeter. They went back up to the cash register, where Jesse paid cash for the bullets and a knife. Tommy didn't speak during the transaction. Noah didn't say anything either, but he scrutinized both their faces, trying to figure out what had just happened. As Tommy handed Jesse the bag, she spoke to Noah. "Don't call me again."

Noah's eyebrows went up. "Even to apologize for my brother?" he asked, not bothering to keep his voice down.

Tommy started to shake her head, but then shrugged defensively. "I'd give it some time."

Noah didn't speak to him for a long time after they left. After a few miles of freeway, Jesse suddenly found the silence suffocating. "What?" he asked.

"You used me," Noah said wonderingly. Jesse glanced over. Noah was looking at him with a mixture of curiosity and disbelief. "You were . . . a *cop*. With me."

"I'm always a cop," Jesse said flatly.

"You're always my brother," Noah reminded him.

Jesse didn't answer. Minutes ticked by, and finally Noah said cautiously, "Jess, if you're over it—if you want to be done being a cop—nobody would blame you. Hell, *Mamá* would be thrilled to have you off the force. She never understood this urge to serve and protect, anyway."

Jesse's fingers tightened on the steering wheel, and he fought to keep his voice low. "I do not," he said through clenched teeth, "arrange my life to thrill *Mamá*."

"Whatever, man." Noah shook his head. "What do I know? Maybe you're just having a rough day. But that wasn't you back there, man." His voice hardened. "And if I ever hear you talking like that to *Mamá* or Dad, I will put your goddamned forehead through a wall."

Jesse felt a flood of shame. Noah commanded, "Tell me what's going on with you."

Noah waited patiently as Jesse didn't speak for a long moment. Then he said, very quietly, "I agreed to do something I'm not proud of."

His brother answered almost immediately. "So don't do it."

"If I don't, more people could get hurt than if I do."

"What—"

Jesse shook his head. "I can't give you details, Noah. I really can't."

Noah looked like he wanted to argue with that, but after a beat he just nodded. "People have to do things they're not proud of sometimes, Jesse. But that doesn't mean this one decision has to change who you are."

"Doesn't it?"

Noah sighed. "You're such a goddamned perfectionist sometimes. The real world's not always black and white, little brother."

"Do you know how many people I've arrested who said some variation of that same thing?" Jesse asked sourly. "That's a criminal's perspective."

Noah let out a snort. "Now you're just being a drama queen. Nobody forced you to join the LAPD, Ugly. You're the one who signed up to teeter on the moral high ground."

Jesse smacked the steering wheel in frustration. "I did *not* sign up for this," he shot back. That was what was bothering him, wasn't it?

"And yet here you are," his brother said, not unkindly. "So stop feeling sorry for yourself, do what you have to do, and live with the consequences. That's being a grown-up."

"I don't need you to tell me how to live with consequences," Jesse snapped. "You don't know what the last few months have been like for me."

"Maybe not," Noah said quietly. Unlike Jesse, his brother was one of the rare people who got quieter when he got upset. "But I do know that you could have gone to the pawnshop by yourself tonight. Instead, you called me."

The thick bubble of anger in Jesse's chest began to deflate. "Fuck you," Jesse said, but without heat. They rode in silence for a few more minutes, until finally he added, "Thanks."

Chapter 16

I told Corry I needed to think about what she'd said—what else could I do? She was right, but then, so was I. After everything Corry had already gone through because of being a null, she had earned a place in the Old World. But that place was also incredibly dangerous, and if she became part of the supernatural community, it couldn't be undone. How was I supposed to make that kind of decision on her behalf? I couldn't even decide when it was time to water a houseplant. They all died on me.

In true Scarlett fashion, I pushed the problem aside for the moment and went to bed.

When pain from my knee woke me up around eight on Thursday morning, there was a note on my bedside table. *Gotta call biz manager today. Please wake me up during biz hours. M.* I yawned, picked up my cane from the floor, and shuffled off toward Molly's room, my stiff, swollen knee protesting with each movement. I didn't know how long I'd be interviewing victims' families, so I figured I might as well get Molly up now.

She made her call from right outside the bathroom door while I was in the shower. Molly's pretty private about her finances, but I know that she has a business manager who handles all her payments, because I send my comically small rent checks to his office. Like most vampires who've lived long enough to make extremely long-term investments (and press the minds of a lot of bankers),

Molly never seems to worry about money, or even give it much thought. I suppose the whole point of a business manager is to have somebody else worry about it for you.

After I had completed the arduous procedure of getting dressed while Molly waited just outside my door, she came downstairs to have coffee with me at the kitchen counter. We were sitting there with our mugs, talking about the midnight movie Molly had seen the night before, when the doorbell rang. She slowly walked over to open it, with me following just close enough to keep her in my radius. We had a lot of practice moving around the house during the day like this, and had gotten even better at knowing the exact boundaries of my radius since my injury.

I was far enough back in the living room that I couldn't see who was behind the door when Molly opened it, but then she yelled over her shoulder, much louder than necessary, "Scarlett! It's the fuzz!"

"Oh, *man*!" I complained loudly. "She said she was eighteen!"

"You guys are hilarious," Jesse said drily, following Molly into the house and toward the kitchen. He was carrying a small paper gift bag and a to-go cup of coffee. I stumped back to my stool and picked up my mug again, raising my bad leg to rest on the only empty stool. Jesse could stand, as far as I was concerned.

Molly sat back down too and looked at me, silently asking if we needed to be alone. I shrugged noncommittally. If he wanted Molly to leave, he could ask her himself.

But Jesse ignored Molly entirely, coming right over to stand at my elbow. He was wearing jeans that somehow looked both comfortable and very expensive, a simple blue button-down, and a dark-brown leather jacket that made his eyes pop, dammit. "Sorry I was a dick last night," Jesse said contritely. He gave me a look that was so sincere and apologetic that I started to blush. *Damn* his hotness powers.

"But I got you something," he continued. He put the gift bag on the table in front of me. There was red glitter on the paper bag and matching red tissue paper sticking out of it. "Late Christmas present."

"You . . . shouldn't have?" I said uncertainly.

He nudged the bag toward me. "Open it."

I picked up the gift bag, which was a lot heavier than its size suggested, and pulled away the tissue paper. Inside was a long piece of black leather the size of my hand. It had sort of a loop on one end, right next to a handle. "Jesse . . . ," I said uncertainly, and pulled on the handle. A long stainless-steel blade slid silently out of the holster. "It's a knife," I said blankly. "You got me a knife." Jesse knew I disliked violence—when we were hunting Olivia, I had refused to carry a gun even after we learned that, unlike most Old World creatures, she was willing to use to them. I'd taken a pretty firm line on not trying to kill people, and Jesse was now trying to work around it.

"It's a boot knife," Jesse replied. No one should ever be that cheerful before 10:00 a.m. "To go in your leather boots. I already sharpened it. If you won't carry a gun, at least you'll have something to protect yourself with if the werewolves come after you again . . . what?"

Happily, I had a great excuse for rejecting his newest attempt at arming me. "It's a really nice knife, Jesse," I said, putting it back in the holster. "But my boots were destroyed the night of the solstice." It's pretty hard to shred leather boots, which is why I wear them whenever the weather's cool enough. But I'd had to crawl around in a great big mess of broken glass and blood when Eli had lost control of his wolf, and even if the boots had survived the glass, there was way too much DNA embedded in them. They'd gone into Artie's furnace.

"Oh." Jesse's face fell.

But just then, Molly jumped up and grabbed my hand. "Come to the bottom of the stairs a sec?" she coaxed, tugging.

"Uh, okay." I grabbed my cane and hobbled to the bottom of the staircase. Molly zipped up to her bedroom and back down, just barely managing to stay in my radius the whole time. When she trotted down the stairs, she was carrying a huge cardboard box with *FRYE* printed on the side.

"Back to the kitchen," Molly sang. I let her lead me back to my chair at the counter. She placed the box in front of me ceremoniously. "I was saving this for your birthday," she explained happily, "but I think you should open it now."

I lifted the lid obediently. "Oh," I breathed. Inside the box lay a pair of black calf-high boots, with a sturdy two-inch rubber heel and small silver buckles at the ankle and calf. They smelled of leather and polish, and were simultaneously simple, functional, and gorgeous. And my size. "They're *beautiful*, Molly," I whispered.

"Nice," Jesse said smugly. "Those are totally you."

Damn if he wasn't right. I had figured that if I gave Molly money and asked her to buy new boots for me, she would come back with the kind of boots she'd wear—something thigh-high and bad-girl sexy with a five-inch heel. But she'd surprised me. These were exactly the boots I'd choose for myself . . . if I had four or five hundred dollars to spare.

"They're too much, though," I said sadly. "Way too much." Molly and I do exchange gifts on special occasions, but I think the Sandra Bullock Blu-ray I'd gotten her for Christmas cost, like, twenty bucks. I pushed the big cardboard box toward her. "I can't accept them."

"Oh, don't worry." Her smile was predatory. "I got *quite* the sale price."

Jesse shot her his Suspicious Cop eyes. "You didn't steal them, did you?"

Molly regarded him disdainfully. *"Please,"* she sniffed. "I pressed a personal shopper at Nordstrom *years* ago. She gave me her discount. And a sale price." She pursed her lips in thought, then added, "And a coupon."

"Oh. Uh . . . good," Jesse said uncertainly. He turned back to me. "Anyway, now you can carry the knife."

"I still don't think it's necessary," I protested, but more feebly. "I have a Taser, Jesse." A really, really good one that I thought was still illegal for civilians, but I wasn't going to mention that part. "It has all the stopping power I need."

He reached over and pulled out the left boot, picking up the knife holster and hooking it on the leather so the handle would be just visible on the inside of my leg. "It's not about stopping power," he said patiently. "If you tase one of the werewolves and run, he'll heal as soon as you're a few feet away and come after you again. And again. Which gives him time to get more werewolves together." I bit my lip. He was right, but I didn't want to admit it.

Jesse reached across the counter to touch my hand. "I know you're not comfortable, Scarlett, but you need to be able to kill one of them if you absolutely have to. I'm not saying don't use the Taser; I just think you should have a backup plan. Just in case."

He looked at me, waiting for a response, and after a moment I nodded reluctantly. I didn't have to use it, right?

He circled the counter to stand over the stool that I was still using as a footrest and held out the boot. I slid my left foot into it. Perfect fit. "I put it inside left so you can draw the knife with either hand. Do you know anything about knives?"

"No," I said absently. I was drunk on the scent of boot leather and barely listening. I carefully pulled the right boot on too. It came to just below the swollen area of my knee, so the calf was a bit tight, but wearable. With both my legs propped on the extra stool, I pointed my toes slightly to admire the boots. So pretty. I felt like the underworld Cinderella.

"I'll show you a couple of things when your knee gets better," Jesse was saying. "For now, though, you just need to know how to angle for the heart. Be careful—I sharpened it." He drew the knife easily and put it in my hands, holding it there with both of his.

I finally tore my eyes away from the boots so I could study the wickedly sharp blade that I was now holding. "Jesse . . ."

"It's okay," he reassured me, gently guiding the blade toward himself. "The heart is here, as you probably know," he said, tapping the blade *very* lightly against his chest, just right of his breastbone as I was facing him. "But to stab someone in the heart, it's best to go between the ribs, from here, at an angle." He took my right hand off the knife and pressed it to his chest under the knife, guiding my fingers down to touch his rib cage. I smelled coffee on his breath. "You feel that?" he asked, his eyes searching mine.

"Honey, *I* feel that," Molly murmured, and I shot her a glare.

"Don't look at her, look at me," Jesse said calmly. I met his eyes again. "This is important. Do you feel the space between the ribs?" I nodded. He moved my left hand down and tilted it so the knife blade would travel up through his ribs if I added any pressure. "Like that. Okay?"

His hands were warm, and I could feel his chest rising and falling under my hand. He trusted me with a knife to his heart. "Okay," I said finally.

"Good." Jesse dropped his hands and backed up a few steps.

"Thank you for the knife," I said to him. "And for the boots," I added to Molly. "I will wear them with pride and lethality."

Molly put one hand over her heart and pretended to wipe tears from her eyes with the other. "That's all I ever wanted," she said dramatically.

"You're welcome," Jesse added, his voice turning sober. "Molly, could you excuse us for a bit?"

I got Molly back to her room, where she would "sleep" for the day. To anyone but me, she would actually appear to be dead—minus the decay—but we liked to pretend she was simply nocturnal. It was just easier to deal with, emotionally. I got dressed while I was upstairs too, and by the time I made it back down, Jesse had taken Molly's seat and refilled his coffee.

When I was settled back on my stool, he passed me a small stack of index cards. "The bottom card has the name and address for Leah's roommate, and Kathryn's boyfriend and her parents. The other cards are questions you should definitely ask," he explained.

Right. I had forgotten for a moment that I was supposed to go play detective today. "Don't take the cards with you when you go in, though," Jesse added. "It doesn't look natural."

I glanced through the cards. "Who do I say I am?"

He reached into a jacket pocket and dug out a laminated card on one of those little claw clips. "This is totally unofficial, so if someone pushes you, get out of there. I made it on my mother's laminator." I took the ID card, which had my driver's license picture, the LAPD shield, and a title: Civilian Consultant. "Laverne Halliday?" I asked, wrinkling my nose. "Do I look like a Laverne to you?"

"There really *is* a Laverne Halliday, and she really *does* consult for the department," he countered. "That way if someone calls to just verify that you exist, it'll pass through."

"Oh." I looked down at my outfit. I had changed into a pair of wide-legged, dressy khakis over the new boots, a lightweight cowl-neck sweater that matched my green eyes, and a black blazer that belonged to Molly and probably cost almost as much as the boots. After a moment of consideration, I clipped the badge onto the hem of my sweater, so it wouldn't leave any marks on Molly's expensive blazer.

Jesse eyed me up and down, but in a professionally appreciative manner, if that's a thing. "You look perfect," he concluded.

"But what am I supposed to be consulting on?" I asked dubiously. My areas of expertise, after all, were stain removal, body part disposal, and the primetime television schedules of the greater LA area.

"You're part of a new missing persons support program," Jesse said promptly. "Checking to see if they need anything, finding out more about the victim—the missing person, I mean. That way you don't have to try to sound like a cop; you can just talk to them. The most important thing is to look for connections between Leah and Kathryn. I looked around this morning, but I couldn't find anything on the Internet."

It was weird to me, how he kept referring to the victims by name. I hadn't dealt with many dead bodies, but when I had to, I always thought of them as "the body" or "the victim." I wondered if Jesse was trying to humanize them on purpose, to remind me. Or maybe that was just really how he thought of them.

Either way, I couldn't really blame him.

"You seem nervous," Jesse observed. "Don't worry, you're going to be great."

I blew out a breath. "I just wish you were going with me."

"I wish I was too, but we don't have that much time before this guy can change again. Splitting up makes the most sense."

He was right, I knew. "Okay," I said finally. "I'm ready."

More or less.

Chapter 17

Leah Rhodes and her roommate had shared a two-bedroom apartment in a big concrete box of a building just off the 405 freeway, near the border of West LA and Culver City. I had the van's window down as I parked, and the sound of traffic from both the 405 and Sepulveda was loud enough that conversation would have been difficult. It was a still, cool January day, with no breeze to speak of, and when I stepped out of the White Whale at Leah Rhodes's apartment, a thick haze hung over the city like a canopy of poison. The chemical scent of car exhaust stung my nose. The building's architect hadn't bothered adding balconies to the apartments, and I understood his reasoning.

Cane in hand, I limped up to the apartment directory and was extremely grateful to see that the *Rhodes and Lewis* apartment was on the first floor. I pressed the button, expecting to have to go into a long detailed explanation, but to my surprise Leah's roommate bought the consultant story with absolutely no fuss and buzzed me in.

Inside the building, I made my way down the hall and found Amanda Lewis waiting for me in her apartment's doorway, leaning against the frame with her arms crossed over her chest. She was a short, plump Caucasian woman in her late twenties with strategic clothing that probably made her look slimmer than she really was. She had long, white-blonde hair tied in a careful, high ponytail, almost at the very top of her head, and bubblegum-pink lip gloss that practically showed my reflection in its shine. "*You're* Laverne?" she asked, a little doubtfully. "You don't look like a Laverne."

"That's just what I keep saying," I said lightly as I approached.

Amanda Lewis led me into a small, cluttered living room. All of the furnishings, down to the threadbare rug, had obviously outlived their expiration date from IKEA. She pointed me to a lumpy sofa, and lowered herself into an adjoining armchair that had been dressed up with a pale-blue cover. I sat down in one of the two obvious ass-dents and pulled a little reporter's notebook and pen out of the blazer pocket. Jesse had instructed me to download an app that would let me record the conversation on my phone, and had been comically dumbfounded when I informed him I didn't have a smartphone.

"I'm not sure what I can tell you," Amanda began, a little frown creasing her features. She wasn't really pretty but had access to high-quality makeup that enhanced her pleasant-enough features until she was almost there. "I mean, Leah and I have been roommates for . . . oh, five or six years. But we aren't exactly close."

"You've been roommates for that long, and you're *not* close?" This felt so weird, learning about someone after I'd already covered up her murder. I had to work not to use the past tense as we talked.

She bobbed her head. "We roomed together at UC Riverside; randomly assigned, you know, by the school. We got along okay, stayed out of each other's way real well, but we didn't, like, socialize. When we both got jobs in West LA—she's an industrial designer at this place on Overland; I manage a restaurant at the Bev Center—it just made sense to get an apartment up here together." Amanda gave me a tiny smile. "Leah always says that there's friend chemistry and romantic chemistry and roommate chemistry, and we have the last one like nobody's business." For the first time, a look of genuine emotion came over her face. "I hope she's okay," Amanda added softly.

I clenched my jaw so I wouldn't wince. Sorry, Amanda. I threw her into a furnace twelve hours ago; she's probably not okay. "Is there someone she may have decided to go visit? A friend or boyfriend?"

"The cops at the station asked me that too," Amanda sniffed. "I don't know of anywhere she'd go and not be back by now. She has a boyfriend, but it's pretty casual, I think, and he's out of town a lot for his work."

"Does she have family nearby?" I asked.

"Her family is all in San Diego; they haven't heard from her, either," Amanda replied. "Diane—that's her mom—she's planning to come up late tonight to file another report or whatever. She's really freaking out."

I wrote *Diane Rhodes* in my notebook. "Do you know her boyfriend's name?" I asked.

Amanda shrugged again. "She just introduced him as Henry. I don't think I ever heard his last name. He was older, maybe in his forties."

I wrote *Henry—40s.* Amanda was looking at me, a little impatient. "You said you guys weren't—aren't," I corrected hastily, "really friendly, but you must know how she spends her time. She's here, she's at work. What else does she do?"

Amanda leaned back in the armchair, her eyes going distant as she considered the question. "Well, she likes to knit. She has a knitting group at the library on Thursday nights. She goes to San Diego once a month or so to visit her family—her sister just had a baby." Her hands unconsciously clasped and unclasped in her lap. "She volunteers at the Humane Society, walking dogs, and she was active in a couple of animal rights groups, although I'm not sure she's still doing that."

Walking shelter dogs to werewolves was kind of a big stretch, but my ears perked up anyway. "Which groups?"

"Uh, let's see. It's P-A-W . . ." Amanda stared at the ceiling, squinting to remember. Then she met my eyes in sudden triumph. "Protect America's Wolves, that was it."

This time I did wince. Leah Rhodes had been mauled to death by a werewolf. Irony-wise, that was pretty brutal. But it couldn't be a coincidence, could it? I wrote down the name.

I talked to Amanda for a bit longer, but all I really learned was that Leah had liked *The Bachelor* and had recently developed a case of baby fever, after the birth of her new nephew. "She's been talking about kids lately," Amanda added, shaking her head in amazement, like having kids was some weird thing they only did in Japan. "I mean, Henry just doesn't seem like the dad type to me"—she wrinkled her nose a little—"and I can't picture Leah as the 'hear me roar' do-it-yourself type."

I felt another stab of sadness as I pocketed my notebook and thanked Amanda for her time. Leah Rhodes was never going to have a baby. She was never going to have a conversation with her nephew, either.

You didn't kill her, I reminded myself. *Go find the fucker who did.*

Back in the van, I called Jesse and left him a voicemail describing my interview with Amanda Lewis. Then I headed toward the South Bay to talk to Kathryn Wong's boyfriend. I was getting the hang of driving with just my left foot, but my injured knee ached even when thrown over the passenger seat, a powerful, insistent wave of pain that was always cresting. It only seemed to recede when I downed one of the Vicodin that Dr. Noring had given me. I was doing my damnedest not to take them, though. Not because I was trying to be a hero, but because the pills made me feel sluggish, like I'd just had an intense workout and two glasses of wine.

If Leah and Amanda's apartment had come across as the typical LA early professional habitat, then Kathryn Wong's place screamed "South Bay Money." It was a condo one block away from Manhattan Beach, with a spacious emerald lawn that pretty much guaranteed the grass was never greener anywhere else. The air smelled of saltwater and sunshine, and there was careful, minimalist landscaping lining the sidewalks and side of the building. The lobby had been decorated just as carefully, with ornate pots of fresh flowers on glass-tipped end tables in each hallway. However the nova wolf was choosing his victims, it definitely wasn't for their socioeconomic similarities.

I hadn't wanted to make the trip south unless I knew that Kathryn Wong's boyfriend would be there, so I'd called ahead with my victim support story and David Mailt had agreed to see me. After he'd buzzed me through the entryway, I limped toward a bronze-door elevator and rode up to the fifth floor, careful not to get fingerprint smears on the pretty interior paneling.

Mailt opened the door of 5E a heartbeat after my knock.

"Did you find her?" Mailt demanded immediately, before the door had swung all the way open. I felt an instant twinge of disappointment when I felt him in my radius—he was human. It would have been so much easier if he'd just been the nova wolf. I tried to adopt Jesse's professional cop voice. "I'm sorry, sir. We have no new information on Kathryn." *Liar.*

Mailt sagged against the door frame. He was a skinny white guy in his mid twenties, with narrow square-framed glasses and a look that could be best described as "student filmmaker." "You'd better come in anyway, I guess," he said, defeated, and turned around without another word, trudging back into the condo. I followed.

The interior would have been gorgeous under other circumstances. It was airy and filled with light, all cream-colored walls and light wood-paneled floors. Decorative accents of bright fuchsia, deep violet blue, and emerald green popped out against beige or wood furniture. There were two distinctive work stations in the large living room, each covered with electronic equipment. Mailt pointed me toward a nearby Pottery Barn sofa that would never deign to be dented by a human ass. I perched on its edge just in case I was inadvertently dirty.

"What can you tell me?" Mailt asked wearily, tugging at his tousled black hair. "Or do you need something from me? Pictures of Kate, or you need to get her fingerprints or whatever?"

"No, no," I said, retrieving the pad and smoothing down the blazer. "I'm not in charge of evidence collection. Mostly, I'd just like to check in on how you're doing, and see if you can tell me a little bit more about who Kate"—*don't say was, don't say was*—"is."

Mailt stared at me, and now I could see the bleariness in his eyes from lack of sleep. "How will that help you find her?" he asked bluntly.

What would Jesse say? "Please, Mr. Mailt. Just humor me. I want to do everything I can to help you find your girlfriend," I said, feeling like a worm.

I felt even worse when he apologized. "You're right, I'm sorry," he said, holding his hands up deferentially. "I've just been frantic. Kate's never done anything like this. She doesn't just . . . disappear." He leaned over to rest his elbows on his knees. "What can I tell you? Ask me anything."

"Well, why don't you start by telling me what Kate does for a living," I said gently.

"Right, right." He bobbed his head. "Let's see . . . we both graduated from the film program at UCLA a few years ago. Kate went right into a job at Sony, and I worked for an indie producer. After a couple of years, she decided she didn't want to deal with the politics, and she started working on some short films. Kate, ah . . ." He hesitated, trying to read my face. "Well, Kate has money. But I don't get any of it if something happens to her," he added hurriedly.

He didn't have to worry. I'd known he wasn't a real suspect the second he'd hit my radius. "Where does the money come from?" I asked anyway, because it seemed like I should.

"Her grandfather left Kate and her sister trust funds when he died, uhh"—he looked at the ceiling a second, doing some mental math—"six or seven years ago now."

Okay. That didn't seem likely to be connected to her death, so I switched tacks, mentally shuffling the index cards Jesse had provided. "Does Kate have a lot of friends? Does she go out a lot?"

He leaned back in his chair, thinking it over. "We hang out with people from college, but nobody really close. Kate's sister is her best friend, but she's in San Diego with the rest of the family."

I remembered Leah Rhodes's interest in wolves and asked if Kate liked animals. Mailt shook his head. "She's funny about animals—she's a vegan, and I think she even used to be in PETA, and now she's in HPA. But she's super allergic herself. The family across the hall asked us to feed their guinea pigs once, and Kate couldn't even go into the condo without sneezing. I had to do it."

I'd at least heard of Humans for the Protection of Animals, which was one of the big three animal rights groups, along with PETA and the Humane Society. I wondered if there was a connection between Kate being in HPA and Leah being in PAW—but then again, this was LA, where your "activism" could be as much of a status indicator as your haircut or job. I wrote Mailt's info down just in case.

David Mailt was looking at me with desperate eagerness, just hoping I would ask him a question so he could answer it. Meanwhile, I had helped destroy his dead girlfriend only a few hours earlier. I asked him some more questions about Kate's activities, and found out that Leah and Kate had gone to different schools, lived in different parts of town, and worked at jobs that didn't seem like they'd intersect. They weren't from the same area, or even the same tax bracket. Other than being about the same age, same size, and not all that social, they seemed as different as could be. I was flailing. So much for Jesse's assurances that I had enough investigative experience to do these interviews.

Finally I ran out of ideas and thanked Mailt for his time. I also promised to call if I got any new information. Which I wouldn't. As I limped out to the car, leaning on the cane, I started to wonder if Jesse had given me this assignment just to punish me. I wasn't finding any connections, but I *was* learning an awful lot about the two victims. Was he trying to make me feel guilty on purpose?

And if so, was it working?

Chapter 18

By mid afternoon, Jesse was beginning to have doubts about his own plan.

With Scarlett working the victim end of the case, Jesse had to try to find the nova by figuring out who'd created him. Jesse also just wanted to talk to the werewolves who had clashed with Scarlett and her roommate. It annoyed him that Scarlett and Molly seemed to be taking the attack as just another part of life. No one should have to live with that kind of threat over their head, much less find it mundane.

Luckily he could do both things at once. Will had given him a list of the nineteen other werewolves in the pack, in rough order of their place in the pack hierarchy. He'd suggested that the nova had been created by either someone very high on the list, or someone very low on the list. The stronger and more dominant a werewolf was, the more likely he'd be to ignore the alpha's wishes that they not change in between full moons unless they were with other pack members. The pack members who were the lowest on the list, on the other hand, were more likely to have trouble controlling themselves in between moons.

Jesse had figured he'd start with the top three wolves and the bottom three wolves on the list, a group which included Drew Riddell and Terrence Whittaker, two of the wolves who'd ambushed Scarlett. The plan, he'd decided, would be to simply interview the werewolves and try to get a sense of their truthfulness. Jesse wanted to ask the kind of questions that would give him a sense of how each person felt about Will, the pack, and being a werewolf in general, and hope someone gave himself away.

Will had also pointed out that whoever turned the nova wolf had successfully kept it from the rest of the pack without stinking of deceit. He (or she) had to be a world-class liar, but Jesse had had plenty of experience figuring out when suspects were lying. At any rate, it'd be good to get a better sense of wolf pack behavior from the point of view of someone who *wasn't* the alpha. So he plotted all six addresses on his phone's GPS and loaded his backup gun with the silver bullets he'd bought from Tommy Vrapman.

It was a tenuous plan to begin with, and he just kept striking out. Two of the wolves on his list—Lydia, the lowest werewolf in the pack, and Astrid, the fourth highest—weren't home when Jesse called on them. Ryker, number eighteen on the list, turned out to be a broody, obnoxiously well-groomed aspiring actor who answered his door shirtless and stayed that way for the whole interview. He came off to Jesse as too vain and one-dimensional to deceive the rest of the pack, and when Jesse pushed him, Ryker immediately cowered into his chair. He was all bluster.

The next closest werewolf, number seventeen, was a meek Hispanic woman named Rosarita Hernandez who was so grateful that Jesse could speak to her in Spanish that for a moment he thought she might cry. She pushed tamales and iced tea at him and showed him pictures of the cats she used to have before she'd become a werewolf. She was not going to be the one who'd lied about the nova, either.

An accident on the 10 freeway forced him to slog through forty-five minutes of traffic, and by two thirty, Jesse was tired, frustrated, and really needed to use the bathroom after all the iced tea. The whole endeavor was starting to feel like a waste of time he didn't have.

After a pit stop to use the bathroom, though, Jesse found his first real possibility. Drew Riddell, number three on the list, was a short, thick Caucasian man with short, curly hair and a restless energy that practically came off him in gusts. After a few calls to Riddell's home and office, Jesse tracked him down at a construction site off Fairfax. Riddell was a contractor, and when Jesse walked up, he was deep into a heated argument with an older man in a hard hat with an electrical company logo on the side. Jesse hung back and watched the two men for a few minutes. If you knew to look for it, Riddell's body language had "dominance" written all over it.

After the electrician had slunk away, Jesse approached Riddell and identified himself. The shorter man jerked his head toward an RV parked nearby. "Let's talk in there," Riddell grunted. He had a hint of an accent, maybe midwestern.

After a few minutes, conversation with the werewolf, however, Jesse wasn't convinced that Riddell was the guy who'd turned the nova. He was aggressive, but no more so than most of the LA residents Jesse had pulled over back when he was on traffic duty. Riddell denied changing in between moons and attacking a human. And he didn't seem to have any particular animosity toward Will.

"Then why are you trying to . . . I don't know what the term is . . . overthrow him?" Jesse asked.

Riddell shrugged his beefy shoulders. "I don't know that *any* of us want to overthrow Will, so much as help Ana." He paused, and then added, "Okay, there are some who want to overthrow Will. Not me, though. I don't want to be alpha, so I don't really care who is. But I do want Ana to get her answers."

"Even if it meant kidnapping and torturing someone?" Jesse asked, unable to keep the anger out of his voice.

If Riddell was distressed about being accused of a felony by a police detective, he didn't show it. "You're talking about the girl, right? Bernard?" Riddell shrugged. "I'm a werewolf," he said seriously, his voice low and unapologetic. "And a contractor. If there's one thing I know for sure, it's that sometimes you have to get your hands dirty to get what you want."

"All the same," Jesse retorted, his voice hard. "If you go near her again, I'll arrest you for kidnapping, assault, and conspiracy to commit murder, just for starters."

Riddell looked at him speculatively for a long moment, his nostrils flaring slightly, and Jesse realized the other man was searching him for signs of a lie. "I believe you would," he said at last. "You'd catch hell from Will and Dashiell, but you don't care about that, do you?"

Jesse shook his head. There was another long silence, interrupted by the buzz of a table saw just outside the trailer and the traffic noise from Fairfax. "All right," Riddell said finally. "I'll leave her alone. Not because I'm afraid of you, but because if I got arrested, Dashiell would make sure I died in jail before the full moon."

As he drove toward the next name on the list, Jesse thought back over the interview. The werewolf could have been lying about not attacking any humans, but there was really no reason for it. Why lie about that if he was willing to be up front about conspiring to kidnap Scarlett? And he had believed Riddell when he said he didn't want to be alpha. The man might be aggressive, but he didn't seem like a leader.

Half an hour later, Jesse was knocking on the door of the second name on Will's pack roster: Terrence Whittaker, another one of the guys that had gone after Scarlett outside of Will's house. Whittaker lived in one side of a ramshackle old duplex in central LA, on a street with rusted cars parked on every lawn and pockets of loud music blasting out of half the driveways. Whittaker's lawn, like all the others, was strewn with pieces of litter in varying stages of decomposition. A big, muscled Harley was parked alone on a strip of blacktop next to the paint-thirsty building. Jesse parked behind the Harley and circled the motorcycle to get to the peeling front door. No doorbell, so he raised a fist to knock.

The door popped open before his knuckles made contact. A thin, shirtless black man in his late thirties opened the door and looked Jesse over, leaning casually into the door frame. Long, thin scars were scattered over his arms, including one on his shoulder that strayed most of the way across his chest. A forty-ounce can of beer dangled from the fingers of one hand.

"Terrence Whittaker?" Jesse asked briskly.

"What can I do for you, officer?" Whittaker drawled. He took a long pull from the beer, his eyes never leaving Jesse's. He was about the same height as Jesse, but he somehow managed to loom over the detective, challenging him. *Showing off his dominance*, Jesse thought.

"Detective Cruz," Jesse corrected. "Will Carling sent me. Is there somewhere we can talk?"

Whittaker's eyes sparked just a little at the mention of Will's name. Slowly, he looked over his own shoulder at the dingy living room. Jesse saw a bong and some lighters amidst the trash on the crappy old coffee table. Whittaker turned back to Jesse with a smirk. "Let's go around back. The house isn't real *presentable*."

Jesse stepped back to let him pass, then followed Whittaker through the overgrown lawn to the back of the house, where an obviously stolen wooden picnic table stood next to a massive barbecue. Whittaker hopped effortlessly onto the picnic table, sitting on top with his feet on the bench. He took another long drink. "What brings you here, Detective? Noise complaint again? That Spanish mama down the street mad about me revving my bike?" His speech seemed to get more and more choppy, like a gang thug in a bad movie.

Jesse frowned. He was already sick of this guy. "Cut the ghetto bullshit, Whittaker," Jesse said brusquely. "I looked you up. You have a PhD in astrophysics from Berkeley. Until recently you were a full professor at UC Santa Cruz. I don't know what happened to you"—he glanced around the tattered backyard, the broken blacktop—"but you're not fooling anyone with the act."

Whittaker's grin disappeared, and for a second something flashed across his face—real anger. His teeth bared, but then he got control back and glared at Jesse. "I took my three best grad students and a telescope to the desert. That's what happened," he hissed, the choppy speech pattern vanishing. He spread his arms wide. "And now this is my kingdom."

Jesse contemplated the litter-strewn yard, the blistered house paint. "The kids survive?" he asked quietly. For the first time, Whittaker looked away from Jesse's face. He took that as a *no*. "That where you got the scars?" Jesse said, nodding at the man's arms.

Terrence shook his head. "Misspent youth." He looked down at his naked biceps with a wry smile. "I studied in London for a year, took fencing. We thought it was more fun with real blades."

Jesse shook his head a little. He may not have always been a werewolf, but Whittaker had been wild for a long time. "Why come here?" he asked, gesturing around the dingy yard. "They fire you?"

Whittaker jerked his head up in defiance. "Naw, man. But I couldn't be around students anymore. Wasn't safe for them. My grandma left me this place." His fingers twitched emptily, and he dug into the back pocket of his blue jeans, pulling out a pack of cigarettes. After a second of hesitation, he held it out to Jesse, grudgingly. When Jesse shook his head, Whittaker shrugged and pulled out a lighter, tilting his head toward the duplex at the same time. "I own the whole building. Collect rent on the other half." His fingers shook as he flicked the lighter open. Jesse had seen that kind of tremor many times.

"Scarlett thought you were pretty together at Will's place the other night," Jesse observed. "But I bet you've been drinking since you got up this morning. Smoking too."

Whittaker smiled bitterly around the cigarette in his mouth. He didn't speak until it was lit and he'd taken a long, desperate drag. "We're two days closer to the full moon now. Only five out. For me it's tied hard to the moon." He held up the cigarette and looked at it speculatively. "Every little bit helps."

"That why you change between full moons?' Jesse asked offhandedly. "Does it help keep the magic under control?"

This time when Whittaker looked at him, his eyes were calculating. "Is that why you here, Detective Jesse Cruz? You Will's new hall monitor?"

Jesse hadn't mentioned his first name.

He must have reacted, because the werewolf laughed. "Oh, yeah, we know who you are. You've been running around town with that, that"—Whittaker's eyes burned—"that pretty little atrocity. We keep tabs on her."

"Will know you do that?"

Whittaker's upper lip curled. It was nothing like a smile. "Will may be our alpha, but he doesn't speak for all of us."

"So you do change between moons," Jesse stated, getting back on topic. Whittaker's nostrils flared but he remained silent, not denying it. "You ever bite anybody," Jesse asked casually. "Maybe leave 'em for dead?"

It happened so fast that Jesse thought for a moment that he'd been sucked into the ground. The werewolf's speed was disorienting, and before he knew it Jesse had been tackled and Whittaker was on top of him, hands on Jesse's throat, snarling.

"I would *never*," he screamed, straight into Jesse's face. Spittle flew. "I would *die* before I did this to anyone, you piece of shit, coming here like you know the *first thing*—"

His rant broke off suddenly as he felt the cold barrel of Jesse's Glock press into his temple. Jesse hadn't been able to get it out of the holster before he'd hit the ground, but he had it out now. "I can survive that," he growled at Jesse.

The werewolf was pressing down on Jesse's throat, but not quite hard enough to cut off all his air. "Silver . . . bullets . . ." Jesse wheezed.

Surprised, Whittaker sprang back, twisting a little in midair to land in a graceful crouch on the bench of the picnic table. Then he remembered where he was and glanced around. Jesse did too.

No one was watching. Nobody looked out of their windows in this neighborhood.

Jesse stood up warily, not bothering to brush the dead grass off his clothes. He kept his gun out, but pointed at the ground. "Someone . . . someone was attacked?" Whittaker said. His brow was furrowed, as if he were trying to add large numbers in his head. "She said . . ." He trailed off and shook his head. "It wasn't me."

"Who's she?" Jesse asked.

Whittaker waved a hand. "I meant your girl, Bernard," he said offhandedly. "She didn't say anything about attacks when we met the other night."

Jesse studied the other man. "You're high up in the pack," Jesse reminded him. "If you know something . . ."

"Yeah, I'm high in the pack," Whittaker interrupted, his voice sour. "Because I'm powerful. Too powerful, which is exactly why I'm so fucking dangerous. Nobody tells me anything."

The werewolf seemed calmer, like his burst of rage had helped him somehow, relieved a little pressure. "Ironically," he added, "I have much better control as a wolf. But then it becomes worse, afterward. To come back."

Jesse could see Whittaker giving in and changing between moons, even going against his alpha . . . but his reaction to Jesse's question hadn't been faked. He hadn't turned someone between moons. However, there was still the problem of Terrence Whittaker's interest in Scarlett.

"I believe you," Jesse said finally. "And honestly, I don't give a shit what goes on within the pack." He stepped closer. "But you need to stay away from Scarlett Bernard."

Whittaker's eyes went hollow. "She has a cure," he said feverishly. "She can make it all go away. She could give me my life back."

"No," Jesse said carefully, "she can't." It was the truth. Scarlett might be able to change people, but it also might kill her to try. And she could never give this man back what he had lost.

Whittaker looked at him just as Riddell had, searching for signs of a lie. Jesse stared him down. Finally, without breaking eye contact, Whittaker muttered, "We'll see. You're just a cop. You can't keep us away from her."

Jesse took a deep breath, letting his senses focus on the noise of the neighborhood. He made the calculation, and decided to take the risk. "Maybe I can't," he said. Then Jesse raised his gun and shot Whittaker through the meatiest part of the thigh. The werewolf howled and flew to the ground like he'd been knocked down with a wrecking ball. "But I can slow you down," Jesse added.

If Whittaker heard this, he didn't respond, because he was busy screaming as the silver bullet burned its way through his leg. As Jesse understood it, the wound would heal slowly, at a normal human rate, at least until Whittaker changed again. And it would hurt like hell.

Jesse got back in his car to head west, back toward the 10 freeway and Scarlett. A half mile away from Terrence Whittaker's house, though, he had to wrench the wheel to the right, pulling the car across two lanes of angry traffic. As soon as he was off the main lanes he threw open the car door and vomited all over the pavement.

So much for calculated risk.

Chapter 19

"You *shot* a guy?"

My voice had been too loud, and Jesse made a shushing motion with his hand. Luckily it was four thirty in the afternoon, and nobody else was seated at the little outdoor taco stand on La Cienega. I hadn't gotten lunch yet, so this was supposed to be a working meal to compare notes on the case. At least, I had *thought* we were working on the case. Apparently Jesse had decided to appoint himself my own personal assassin instead.

"Just in the leg," Jesse muttered. "It was a perfect through-and-through. Just to slow him down, buy us a little time."

"This is not a Johnny Cash song, Jesse. You can't just . . . *shoot* people who come after me," I hissed at him. "You're a cop."

"I know," Jesse said, his voice miserable. He was hunched over his untouched basket of chips and guacamole, his shoulders slumped in guilt or defeat or both.

"I didn't ask you to step in," I went on. I couldn't seem to get my mouth to stop moving. "I didn't need your help. Molly and I had it covered."

Now Jesse looked up, his gorgeous eyes skeptical. "For how long, Scarlett? They were just going to come after you again while you weren't with Molly. For all we know, Anastasia is waiting outside your house right now."

"They don't know where I live," I retorted, trying to keep the uncertainty out of my voice. "But that's not my point," I added. "My point is: don't shoot people." I took a bite of my burrito and shook it at him for emphasis. "Use your powers for good," I said, around a big mouthful of chicken and rice.

"It was a bad decision, okay?" he said tiredly. He poked lifelessly at the chips. "For a second there I thought I could play in their league, go on the offensive. But I didn't become a cop so I could punish people for things they *might* do."

We sat there for a few minutes in silence. I didn't know whether to hug him or hit him. Whatever Jesse might say about the shooting, he'd done it to protect me. For obvious reasons, Terrence Whittaker was never going to press charges, but Jesse had still risked his entire career as a cop for me. And that felt . . . big. Too big.

Jesse continued to stare gloomily at his food. I was eating ferociously, though, because . . . well, I was hungry. And I've never been the type to lose my appetite easily. My basic philosophy regarding eating during an emergency breaks down along the lines of "Moral crisis: bad. Spicy chicken burrito: good."

Jesse was looking at me with a complicated expression that I couldn't interpret. Guilt? Resentment? "You were going to tell me what you learned from Leah and Kathryn's people," he stated.

"Yeah, but I got a little sidetracked by 'I shot a guy.'" Jesse gave me a look that I could definitely interpret as annoyance, and I added in a softer voice, "Kate. She went by Kate."

He nodded. "What did you learn about Leah and Kate?"

I passed him my shoddy notes and filled him in on everything I remembered. "So I have a list of names of people that were connected to them—Leah's boyfriend, Kate's sister, and so on. And I know of a few activities each one liked. But I couldn't find any obvious connection between them. The only thing that even comes close to a match are the animal rights groups, but Leah was in this

PAW group and Kate's a member of Humans for the Protection of Animals."

Jesse sighed. "Because that would have been just too easy, wouldn't it." It wasn't really a question, but I nodded anyway. "Well," he said thoughtfully, "we'll widen the circle. You should talk to the parents, if you can find them, and friends, and so on. I'll try to get some membership rosters for the animal rights groups, too—it's possible that Leah was in PETA or Kate was in PAW and their roommates just didn't know about it."

"True," I said, brightening a little.

"And I'll keep talking to the werewolves," Jesse added. I began to protest, but he overrode me. "I know you want me to stay out of your business. But we need to stay on top of the threat against you, and we need to find out if there are any more connections between the nova wolf and the rest of the pack, aside from one of the pack members accidentally attacking someone." He finally picked up a chip, dunked it liberally in the guacamole, and chewed. "I just *know* that there's another connection here. I know it."

I sighed. "So who are you going to talk to next?"

Jesse's eyes gleamed. "Anastasia."

Oh shit. I didn't like it, but I didn't bother to protest. I doubted that Anastasia was involved in the nova wolf debacle, but she had certainly proven herself willing to go against the alpha's orders before. I texted Will to get Ana's address.

When my phone chimed I used my hand to shield the screen from the afternoon sun and squinted at it. "Huh."

"What?" Jesse asked. Traffic was picking up on La Cienega, and we had to nearly shout to hear each other.

"Anastasia's working at the bar tonight."

I glanced across the table at him. His eyes were practically bugging out of his head with surprise. "Will's letting her work, after all the shit she's stirred up?" he said indignantly.

I shrugged. "I guess he's just too short-handed." Since both Caroline and Eli were . . . off the payroll.

"Oh, yeah," Jesse said, remembering. Then he added, "And I suppose the bar gets busy on New Year's Eve."

"That's today?" I said stupidly. I had completely forgotten.

Jesse snorted with laughter. "You forgot?"

"Hey," I protested. "I lost track of the days because I was *in a coma.*" I reached across the table and stole one of his chips. Just out of spite.

"To be fair," he admitted, "it may have slipped my mind for a minute there too." His eyes drifted away into what I think of as his "Pensive Cop Face."

"There's not much point in trying to interview more people today," he concluded. "Everybody's going to be getting ready for New Year's Eve stuff."

"What do you want to do, then?" I asked. He was still staring off into space, so I picked up another chip and threw it at his nose.

"What? Hey," he sputtered.

"Just getting your attention, Detective," I said sweetly. "What's the plan? Go home and ice our extremities?"

"No," he said slowly. "I have another idea."

Of course he did. "What's that?"

"Let's go stake out Will Carling's house."

Chapter 20

We knew the nova wolf had changed two days ago, Jesse explained, because Leah Rhodes had died not long after he had attacked her. The nova should need twice as much time before he could change again, but according to Will, he was already more powerful than he should be. "You people are always telling me magic is unpredictable," Jesse finished. "So it seems possible that the nova wolf can change faster than we expect."

"Even if he can," I argued, "and even if he attacks someone else, there's no guarantee she'll . . ." I winced. "You know. Die right away. *And* there's no guarantee that he'll dump the body at Will's again."

"I think he's going to keep leaving the women at Will's," Jesse contended. "It's too good of a 'fuck you' to the werewolf pack. And you—I mean, *we*," he amended, "keep helpfully disposing of the dead bodies for him."

"Still," I said, unconvinced.

"Do you have something better to do?" Jesse asked, innocently raising his eyebrows. I glared at him, not speaking. We both knew I have essentially no life. "I'll buy you a great big bag of ice," he wheedled.

"You can get ice free at any fast food place."

Jesse held up two fingers. "Then I'll buy you two bags of ice," he said playfully.

I rolled my eyes and reached for another chip to throw, but he pulled the little paper carton out of my reach. "Is that a yes?" he persisted.

"No, that's a 'fine, I give up.' Totally different thing."

We split up for a couple of hours. Jesse wanted to stop at his place to shower and change, and I wanted to restock my cleaning supplies from my big stash at Molly's, just in case. At six, we met up on Temescal Canyon Road, which was completely deserted. I left my van on a side street and rode with Jesse in his sedan the rest of the way. On Will's street we parked as far away from Will's house as we could while still keeping it in view. I wanted to keep the White Whale close by so we could get to it easily if the nova showed up, but we also wanted it to look like there was nobody around, so the nova would feel like he could get away with dumping another body. And if he'd done any research about the LA Old World, he might know my van.

We were settled into our stakeout by six thirty. I was sitting in the passenger seat with the promised ice packs above and below my bad knee. They were wrapped in place with an old flannel scarf I'd brought from my van. Jesse had stopped for snacks at a 7-Eleven on his way over, and he was subjecting me to a lesson in the art of the stakeout food.

"It has to be able to stay in the car for hours," he explained very seriously, "but not go bad. And it can't make you have to . . . you know, go to the bathroom right away. So salt is good, because it helps you retain water." He handed me a small package of pretzels.

"I thought for sure there would be doughnuts," I complained. I could not get a friggin' doughnut on this case.

"Doughnuts are bad for you," Jesse said around a mouthful of pretzel shards. "These are naturally fat free." He swallowed and dug through the plastic grocery bag between us. "But I've also got apples, granola bars, let's see . . . peanuts, Naked Juice, and Diet Coke." He looked up at me expectantly.

"*Naked Juice*? Do the other cops know you're a closet health nut?" I grumbled.

"Plenty of cops eat like this," Jesse said, with great dignity. "You're just prejudiced. Against the fuzz."

I couldn't help but laugh at that.

Time passed slowly. We got on the topic of car games—as it turned out, both of our families had taken us on road trips as kids—and for a while we played Twenty Questions and My Mother Owns a Grocery Store, which turned out to be basically the same game. After a couple of hours, though, I started to fidget, flipping the compartment between our seats open and closed. I peeked inside—nothing there but CDs. "Do you have any gum?" I asked, and without waiting for an answer I opened the glove compartment. When the little interior light turned on, I saw a glossy black pistol resting in a specially contoured piece of foam. "Whoa. How many guns do you need?"

"That should have been locked," Jesse grumbled. He reached over my lap to close the glove compartment, locking it with the ignition key. "And no, no gum. But I'll put it on your stakeout wish list for next time." He put the keys back in the ignition, eyeing my face. "You look cold," Jesse commented.

I nodded. It was chilly in the car, and though rotating the ice packs on and off my knee felt great, the ice wasn't doing me any favors when it came to body heat. I put the ice packs on the floor of the car, and Jesse twisted around to dig in the backseat. He handed me a fleece pullover that smelled like oranges and Armani cologne. I thanked him and spread it over my lap.

"So *did* you have any plans for New Year's Eve?" he asked.

"Nah," I admitted. "I was just going to stay up and watch TV or something."

"With Molly?"

"No, she usually . . . goes out." Party holidays like New Year's and St. Patrick's Day are big feeding opportunities for the vampires, especially the ones like Molly who can pass for young people.

It's not that I don't know anyone else in Los Angeles. I know a few people from my hometown who've ended up here too, and one of Jack's ex-girlfriends—not to mention Jack himself, who lives in the city and works at a blood lab owned by Dashiell. But, even aside from the fact that knowing me can be hazardous for one's health, for the most part I don't trust myself around humans anymore. It's too easy to start talking about my day and accidentally let something slip about the . . . people . . . I spend my time with. Then I'd have to go begging Dashiell or Molly to press someone's mind for me, which would put that person on the Old World's radar. So I just keep to myself, mostly. It's not that hard, in a city this big.

"What about you?" I asked Jesse. "Are you missing any big New Year's plans right now?"

"My parents usually throw a big party," he said. "My brother Noah's usually in town for it, and we team up and assault the food table."

"Noah's the stunt double, right?"

Jesse smiled. "Yes."

"Is it weird for you, that they all work in Hollywood and you don't?" I asked.

"Sometimes," he admitted. "Mostly because they don't understand why I wanted to be a cop. My mom, especially, was sort of hurt by it. She doesn't understand why someone wouldn't want to work in the movies."

"So why *did* you become a cop?" I'd brought up the topic idly, but I realized it was a pretty good question.

Jesse looked away for a moment, thinking. "There was this detective," he said slowly. "When I was a kid."

"Did he, like, solve the murder of your best friend or something?" I asked lightly.

"It was my cousin," Jesse said gravely.

I must have looked horrified, because he laughed out loud, his face brightening. "I'm kidding, I'm kidding." I smacked his arm, and he picked up the story. "No, I used to go to movie sets with my folks once in a while, you know, and once on a teacher in-service day, my dad had to take me to this preproduction meeting with him.

"I was waiting in the reception area, with my Spider-Man comics, you know, and this guy walked in. You could just tell right away that he was somebody important. He had this . . . mmm . . ."

"Presence?" I offered.

Jesse snapped his fingers. "Yes, exactly. I just figured he was a movie star at first, but there was something different about him. A vibe, I guess. Anyway, he came and sat down with me, asked me about my comic books, and chatted with me a little bit. He was a homicide detective."

"What was he doing at the movie studio?"

"Oh, he was there as a consultant. The movie Dad was working on was this cop drama, and this guy had come to advise them on the real-life procedures and things. They do it all the time."

There was a loose strand of black hair on his forehead, and for a second I could picture exactly what he'd looked like as a little boy, waiting for his dad with a big stack of comic books. "What did this guy say to you?"

"He . . . ," Jesse trailed off, caught in the memory, and started again. "It was something he said, exactly. The thing was, I had already seen so many cool things on movie sets: fake car accidents and space aliens and exploding buildings. And I figured out pretty early that there wasn't anything you could do or imagine that couldn't be faked by good filmmakers. And if anything could be faked, how did you know if something was real?" He looked at me for a moment.

"And that detective wasn't fake," I prompted gently.

Jesse took a breath. "No. He was real. And I wanted to do something real too." Even in the streetlight, I could see his face color a little. "Of course, now I know that *magic* is part of the world, so I guess I don't know what's real anymore." He looked forlorn for a moment.

I leaned back in the seat. "Sounds like the guy made quite an impression on you," I said gently.

Jesse smiled wistfully. "He was . . . he was absolute. He just gave off this confidence and certainty, like there wasn't anything that he couldn't handle. He was really nice to me, friendly. But at the same time his eyes were just . . . scary."

"Would you say," I began, straight-faced, "that he had lifeless eyes, black eyes, like a doll's eyes?"

Jesse laughed out loud, and I felt the thrilling click of connection that you get when someone understands your movie reference. "You know, I might. Which I thought was cool." He shrugged. "It's just how cops look sometimes, I think. When you've seen enough of the things people do to each other, it just kind of takes over your face."

I studied him for a long moment. "You don't look like that," I mused. "Not yet, anyway."

"You do," he said softly, and then looked surprised, like he hadn't known he was about to say it. "Except sometimes, when there's nobody from the Old World around, and you don't think anybody is trying to get something from you, and you forget who you are."

My mouth dropped open, and tingles of surprise prickled through my nervous system as a long silence passed between us. Jesse was staring at me with just a hint of defiance, like he was daring me to say something real, certain that I couldn't do it. But this time he was wrong.

"I'm not a lost soul, Jesse," I said quietly. "And I'm not an innocent. Nobody has done anything to me that I didn't invite."

He looked indignant, which was sort of adorable if you thought about it. "Dashiell—" he began, but I held up a hand.

"Dashiell is a vampire and he plays vampire games. Olivia was a psycho who made it her mission to fuck with my life. But it's the scorpion and the frog story, Jesse."

"The scorpion kills the frog," Jesse pointed out. "It isn't the frog's fault."

I sighed. "The dumbass frog should've just run like hell. Well, hopped like hell. Swam like hell? Whatever frogs do to get away, but really quickly," I amended. "Instead he agrees to give a scorpion a ride across the river. He definitely deserves some of the blame."

"He didn't choose to be a frog. And you didn't choose to be a null," Jesse reminded me.

"True." I fidgeted in my seat, unable to find a position that felt comfortable for my knee. I pretty much needed to give up on the idea that a comfortable position was even possible.

Jesse was still looking at me expectantly. I sighed. "Look, when I was eighteen, something happened to me that wasn't fair. But I *chose* to fuck around with the wolf pack. I invited all this." I waved a hand.

A shadow passed over his face, and I was about to ask him about it when my phone began vibrating in my pocket. I pulled it out and squinted at the screen, which seemed extra bright in the dimness of the car. It was Jack. I pushed the button to ignore the call. He was probably just calling to wish me a happy New Year's, but he'd want to know what I was doing, and I couldn't tell him.

I turned my head and saw Jesse regarding me with a frown.

"What?" I said.

"Do you ever get sick of hiding things from him?" Jesse asked.

"Yes," I said wearily. "Do you ever get sick of poking me about how I live my life?"

"No," Jesse answered promptly.

There was silence in the car for a long time after that.

Chapter 21

Around ten, Scarlett dozed off, and Jesse let her. He was used to the long hours of staring at nothing, and she wasn't. Besides, she seemed like she needed the rest. The last few months were taking a toll on her. He saw it in the hollows under her eyes, the pallor of her face, not to mention the knee that was visibly swollen under her yoga pants. He suspected that her knee was worse than she was letting on, or maybe worse than she was admitting to herself. Maybe it had been selfish of him to bring her along. He could have watched Will's house without her.

He considered driving her back to her van, but Jesse was afraid that if he did leave, even briefly, that would be the moment the nova wolf chose to dump the next body. Jesse didn't want to miss the chance to stop him from hurting anyone else. And if the nova wolf was really so powerful, he would want Scarlett along to turn it human again.

Besides, she looked like she was finally resting now. After a while, he reached over and pulled the fleece pullover up to cover her lap better. His hand brushed Scarlett's as he was pulling his arm back, and Jesse was startled at how cold her fingers were. He twisted the key to run the car's heater for a while before leaning over to put his arm around her, pulling her close to him. She mumbled a sleepy thanks, tucking her hands under her arms for warmth, and he felt a rush of tenderness for her. Since first finding out about the Old World, Jesse's experiences there had been so connected to his relationship with Scarlett that he forgot sometimes that she was technically human. She'd gone up against things that were more powerful than she was, and her very best weapon only leveled the playing field for a short time. It wasn't fair. He pressed his lips to her hair for a moment. Then Jesse settled back to watch the entrance to Will's house, leaving his arm still tucked around Scarlett.

Hours passed. The alpha had left his porch light on, but the little street was quiet, even on New Year's Eve, and Jesse wondered idly if the whole street took vacations at the same time. He turned the car's heater on whenever it got too chilly and sipped Diet Coke to keep himself awake.

By two in the morning he desperately needed to urinate and decided it was time to give up for the night. He wasn't really surprised that they hadn't managed to catch the nova, but he was disappointed anyway. It would have been nice to get a break in an Old World case. For once.

Jesse had already retracted his arm from Scarlett's shoulders and was about to start the sedan when he decided he wasn't going to make it all the way home without peeing. "Scarlett," he said, and she made a sleepy annoyed noise at him. "Scarlett!" Jesse said again, shaking her shoulder a little.

"What?" she mumbled.

"I'm going to go . . . uh . . . well, I'm gonna go pee in the woods real quick," Jesse said sheepishly. "Then we should go. He's not coming tonight."

"'Kay," Scarlett replied drowsily. She hadn't even opened her eyes.

Jesse got out of the car, leaving the keys in the ignition in case she needed to run the heater again. He circled Will's house, heading for the trees. *It's too quiet up here*, Jesse thought, as he relieved himself. And damned cold, for Southern California. He zipped up and stretched out his neck, feeling stiff from the long stakeout.

Because of the silence, Jesse had no trouble catching the sound of movement far off in the woods. He froze, his head still bent at an angle, and listened. It had just been a rustling, but fast, like someone had thrown a rock through the trees. Jesse had spent his whole life in the city and had no idea if this was a normal sound for the forest or not. Maybe a big bird?

But no, the sound was coming again, from somewhere lower. He thought of the nova, and his hand went to the gun on his right hip. He was carrying the nine-millimeter Glock, loaded with the silver ammunition.

Now the sound was even closer, and it seemed . . . spread apart. More than one animal? Jesse peered into the woods, unnerved by the total darkness. He took a few steps backward on the lawn, back toward the lights of the house. Then he heard rustling again, much closer now. Jesse lifted his gun and took aim at the woods. Whatever it was, it was coming *fast*.

A huge wolf exploded into the clearing, and Jesse almost shot it dead on pure reflex. It was charcoal-colored from nose to tail, an efficient running machine that didn't even slow down as it took in Jesse's presence. He had seen wolves at the zoo, but those topped out at maybe eighty pounds. This one looked to be nearly *twice* that, and his finger instinctively tightened on the trigger. But Jesse understood immediately that if he took a shot, it would miss. The wolf was just too fast. Besides, it was moving *away* from Jesse. He wasn't in danger, and he couldn't be sure this was the nova.

Jesse forced himself to take a breath in and out, relaxing his hand on the gun when the second wolf burst out of the woods, and he almost fell down from the shock. This wolf had more traditional coloring: it was a dusky tan that faded down its legs into white paws. Impossibly, it was even bigger than the first, two hundred pounds or more. Jesse had a sense of immense power, of gorgeous, kinetic grace. Then he realized the new wolf was favoring one leg, and that there was a series of long rusty stripes down its body that didn't seem natural—blood. It was bleeding.

The tan wolf paused in its chase to look at Jesse. Jesse's stomach twisted with cold fear as the tan wolf gazed calmly at him. It wasn't growling or anything, but it was so goddamned big that Jesse felt a rush of stupidity. What was he doing out here with this creature? He raised his gun automatically, and now the animal's lip curled up, a growl starting in the back of its throat. Its canine teeth were enormous, almost as long as Jesse's thumb. It moved laterally to put itself between Jesse and the charcoal wolf, which had stopped too, a few hundred feet away. With its enemy distracted, the charcoal wolf began to creep back in the direction of its pursuer.

Shit. Jesse didn't know how intelligent the werewolves were in their other form, but it seemed like the tan wolf understood the gun. Very slowly, he put the gun back in the holster, hoping to pacify the big tan wolf, who must surely be . . . Will? Jesse cursed himself for not thinking to get pictures of the wolves in the LA pack. As his gun went down, the tan wolf's growling softened, though it kept its eyes fixed on Jesse. The charcoal wolf saw an opportunity and leapt at its pursuer with the total, determined commitment of hunters. The enormous tan wolf sensed the leap and instantly turned to meet the charcoal wolf as it crashed into him with unnatural speed and power.

The two werewolves were a blur of dark and light movement, like animal fights in those old Looney Tunes cartoons, where there was just a cloud of gray smoke and the occasional paw or tail sticking out. Jesse jumped back to avoid being trampled, trying to make out what was happening in the weak light from Will's porch. The tan wolf was trying to protect itself, but not really attacking its smaller opponent with any seriousness. The charcoal wolf, on the other hand, was enraged, launching forward to snap at the other wolf's legs and hindquarters. The tussle took both animals a few yards away from Jesse, and he began to edge back toward the car.

But before he'd gone very far, the wolves separated and the charcoal one let out a hacking bark of frustration. Then it froze, blinking, and Jesse was struck by how eerily human the gesture was. The werewolf had an idea. It wheeled around, snarling, and made a sudden beeline for Jesse.

"Shit!" Jesse yelled, scrabbling for his gun again. He got it out but couldn't get the safety off before the charcoal wolf had two paws on his chest.

Jesse went down hard, instinctively dropping the gun as he brought his arms up to protect his head. He felt the werewolf's jaws clamp down on his raised forearm in the same moment, and cried out with pain. The charcoal wolf just bit deeper.

The tan wolf hit the charcoal wolf with a rolling tackle, but the smaller wolf had a perfect lock on Jesse's arm, and it dragged Jesse with it as it rolled, wrenching his forearm in its jaws. He screamed with the pain as he was flipped sideways, nearly landing on his attacker. The charcoal wolf slipped nimbly out from under him and stepped right onto his goddamned chest, the unexpected weight making him gasp. It never let go of his arm.

Suddenly, the sharp pop of a gunshot exploded in the night. Jesse felt the charcoal wolf's jaw loosen its grip with surprise, and both of them looked toward the source of the sound. Scarlett was on the lawn in front of them, silhouetted against the house lights, her hand extended in the air. She had his service Beretta raised toward the sky, and was grimacing with pain. Jesse didn't see her cane anywhere.

"What the *fuck*," she said, her voice ragged but calm, "is going on here?"

Chapter 22

Jesse grinned with relief. Scarlett lowered the gun to her side and began limping toward them, taking little hopping steps and dragging her bad leg behind her. The charcoal wolf snarled with frustration and launched itself off Jesse, forcing a little *oof* of pain out of him as it pushed off his chest. Then it raced back toward the woods, leaving Jesse and the tan wolf alone in the yard.

Jesse staggered to his feet to go help Scarlett, but there was a sudden movement to his right, and by the time he turned his head Jesse could see a very human Will, stark naked, rolling to his feet. Without even looking at Scarlett, Will squared off opposite Jesse and demanded in a panting voice, "Did it break the skin?"

"Huh?" Jesse looked down and realized he was clutching his forearm. It throbbed with hot pain, but he didn't see any blood. He held it up, angling himself so he could inspect the arm in the dim light. The thick leather of his jacket had caught the werewolf's teeth—one or two had gone all the way through, leaving perfect little holes in the leather, but the shirt underneath it was okay. "No, my jacket stopped it," he said, and Will's shoulders sagged with relief.

It was only then that Jesse understood the alpha's anxiety. "Wait, could I . . . could he have turned me into a werewolf just now?"

"She," Will said wearily. He'd dropped down onto the lawn, sitting with his elbows propped on his knees. The shadows hid most of his body, but his nudity didn't seem to concern him anyway. "That was Anastasia. And it's unlikely that one bite would have changed you . . . but yeah. It was possible."

"Oh," Jesse said. He didn't really know what else to say.

Scarlett took one last hopping step to Jesse and held out the gun without a word. He accepted it. A glance passed between them, and then Scarlett looked away. Jesse realized how much it must have cost her to get the gun out of the glove compartment, knowing she might have to use it against someone. "Thanks," he said quietly. Meaning it.

Without meeting Jesse's eyes, Scarlett looked down at the alpha. "Will, you okay?" she asked. The concern in her voice made Jesse squint at Will again. The alpha was still breathing heavily, and he had a long, shallow tear down his side that was oozing blood.

"I thought you healed when you changed form," Jesse said stupidly.

Will smiled briefly, obviously in pain. "A normal change boosts my magic, which boosts the healing." He tilted his head at Scarlett. "But this time she forced the change—thank you, by the way." Scarlett nodded. "So I didn't get the extra healing."

"Oh," Jesse said again, feeling like an idiot.

Will rose unsteadily to his feet. "Detective, if you would please take Scarlett inside," he said. "The back door's unlocked. I'll grab some clothes and join you shortly. We can talk then."

"Do you need help, or . . . ," Jesse began, but he noticed Scarlett trying to suppress a smile. "What?"

"He wants us to go ahead so he can heal, dummy." Scarlett held out her arm. "Be my cane," she commanded.

Jesse holstered his Glock, keeping his service gun in his injured right hand after making sure Scarlett had put the safety back on. His fingers could barely close tight enough to hold it. He slid his left arm around Scarlett's waist, bending awkwardly to compensate for their height difference, and guided her through the unlocked back door, which opened right into a kitchen. It was tidy but well used, and surprisingly homey: shining hardwood floors and rustic cabin-type accents made the room feel like the kind of place where you could have a cup of coffee and share secrets. Jesse helped Scarlett to the solid oak table, which was clearly used hard, often and lovingly. When she was settled in a chair, he went back out to put the Beretta away in his car's glove compartment, retrieving Scarlett's cane from where she'd dropped it just outside the sedan.

"How's your arm?" Scarlett asked him when he returned. She looked shaky and a little pale.

"It'll be sore as hell tomorrow, but I don't think she broke it." He took the chair next to hers and held open his good left hand. She took it without a word, wrapping both of her hands around his.

They sat in silence for another moment, and then Will entered the kitchen, dressed in jeans and a simple blue pullover. Scarlett drew her hands back into her lap. If Will saw it, he didn't comment.

"Did you guys want anything to drink?" he said tiredly. "Coffee, beer, water?" They both accepted a glass of water, and Jesse took a long gulping drink from his, feeling dehydrated after all the soda.

"What happened tonight?" Scarlett said to Will. "Why did Anastasia attack you?"

Will sighed heavily. He showed no signs of injury now, but he still had the strung-out weariness that Jesse had noticed earlier. He sat down in an empty seat next to Scarlett.

"It wasn't our most constructive pack meeting," he muttered.

"You met with them *tonight*?" Scarlett asked, raising her eyebrows quizzically. "On New Year's Eve?"

Will shrugged, wincing at the movement. "You saw how things have been; it couldn't wait. The bar started clearing out a little after midnight, so I just put out the *Closed* sign and told the pack to meet in the woods." He tilted his head in the direction of the national park that met his backyard. "There's a clearing about a mile in, which we consider the beginning of the pack's territory in the park. That's where we start to run on full moon nights."

"Why not just meet here at the house?" Scarlett asked.

Will hesitated, searching for words. "We don't . . . we try not to have too much conflict here, partly because the house is a place of peace, and partly so if someone loses their shit, they'll be far away from humans. If it seems like there's going to be some kind of big argument, we go out in the woods."

"What happened at the meeting?" Jesse asked.

"There was a lot of tension," Will admitted. "I tried to explain that Eli was unavailable without going into too much detail. Some of them believed me, I think, or just didn't care either way. Eli's made calls to them, but Ana's got them all stirred up that he's being forced to lie or something. She's got half of them convinced about this cure, and we kept arguing, getting nowhere. Finally she challenged me to a fight for alpha."

Jesse's jaw dropped, and he saw Scarlett looking just as incredulous. "But . . . ," Scarlett began. "I mean, Ana's not a delicate flower or anything, but did she actually think she could *win*?"

"No," Will said flatly. "Ana's not stupid. Even if I wasn't the alpha, I could take her. This wasn't about winning, though. She knew I wouldn't kill her, so she put me in a position to look bad. If I refused the challenge, I was weak. If I fought her, I was beating up on a weakling."

"That's kind of brilliant," Jesse observed.

"Yes, it is," Will said matter-of-factly. "So I told her I would fight, but the rest of the pack had to stay human, so they couldn't interfere. And as soon as we changed I moved the fight away from them." He shrugged. "I was going to just let her tire herself out, and then change back and try to have a serious conversation with her. But she went after you."

"Why?" Scarlett asked. "I thought you guys didn't usually attack humans. I mean, Jesse hadn't, like, cornered her."

"No," Will agreed. "I suspect it was a calculation. She figured she'd either distract me enough for her to really hurt me, or she'd kill Jesse, which would hurt you."

"Oh," Scarlett said in a small voice. Without looking at him she reached over and grabbed his good hand again. Jesse wasn't sure she even knew she'd done it. He squeezed her hand briefly and didn't let go.

"Things are getting worse," Jesse said quietly.

"Yes," the alpha agreed. "And it's only going to *get* worse the closer we are to the full moon."

"What happens then?" Jesse asked, alarmed. His stomach was already churning from the adrenaline and soda, and the anxiety wasn't helping.

"The nova will *have* to change again," Will explained. "We all will."

And he'll attack more women, Jesse realized.

Will was looking back and forth between the two of them. "I take it the stakeout was unsuccessful."

"Yeah," Jesse acknowledged. "It was a long shot anyway."

"What else have you come up with?" Will asked tiredly. "I noticed Terrence Whittaker was limping badly tonight. Do you know anything about that?"

"Uh . . . yeah . . . ," Jesse said uneasily. "About that."

Chapter 23

Will wasn't thrilled with Jesse's decision to shoot Terrence Whittaker. Jesse couldn't really blame him. When the werewolf finally calmed down and they had filled him in on the rest of the investigation, Jesse noticed Scarlett's eyes drooping and proclaimed that they needed to go get some sleep. He dropped Scarlett off at her van and headed back to his apartment.

It was after three in the morning, but when Jesse climbed into his bed he found himself staring at the ceiling, his brain churning as fast as his stomach. He was still jittery from all the caffeine and adrenaline, not to mention the pain in his wrenched arm. Jesse got out of bed and went over to the kitchenette, where he swallowed three Advil and a liter of water, before making himself a couple of sandwiches. Then he sat down at the little card table that served as his dining area to think about the case.

They needed to make progress before things got any worse for the werewolves—not to mention before the nova wolf had time to change again and kill anyone else. There had to be some sort of logic to the nova's choice in victims, Jesse reasoned. There *had* to be. Will had said that the nova would try to create a mate first. And you wouldn't just go to the Grove, point at a woman, and say, there's my mate for life, right?

But how *would* you pick a mate? Or more importantly, how would a man who'd just been turned into a werewolf pick a mate?

That line of thinking got Jesse exactly nowhere, so he went back to trying to figure out how the two victims might be connected. He spent the next hour on his laptop, trying to match both Kate and Leah to the same school, gym, church, anything. It was endlessly frustrating. There was plenty of information on the Internet, but there were also plenty of potential connections that he *couldn't* look into. They might have just used the same dry cleaner as the nova werewolf or something.

Jesse paged through Scarlett's notes again. Both women had been involved in an animal rights groups: Leah had been in PAW, which—judging by the amateur website—was a fairly small, local thing. The PAW members had a web page and a Facebook group, and they got together in person once a quarter to discuss the wolf situation in America. Jesse got the sense from their site that it was mostly about getting together to drink coffee and bitch about legislature.

Kate, on the other hand, had been part of Humans for the Protection of Animals, which was enormous. Jesse spent some time investigating whether the two groups had worked together on anything—a fund-raiser, volunteer opportunity, charity work. There was nothing online to suggest the two groups had so much as encountered each other.

He sent both PAW and HPA a message identifying himself and requesting that a senior member of the group contact him immediately. Then, bleary-eyed and still sore, he pushed the laptop away and finally fell into bed around four thirty.

Just two hours later, however, his phone began to vibrate insistently on the nightstand. Jesse was only dimly aware of its buzzing, and he felt a sleepy surge of gratitude when it finally danced its way off the table and fell to the cheap carpet with a dull thump. But seconds later it began to buzz from the floor, and with a groan

Jesse reached down and fished around for it. He cracked his eyelids open and squinted at the screen, seeing a small picture of Glory. That was unusual enough to get his eyelids all the way up. Gloria "Glory" Sherman was the lead forensic pathology technician at Jesse's LAPD station. She was also the only other human Jesse knew of who was aware of the Old World.

He answered the phone with more of a grunt than an actual greeting.

"Jesse," Glory said in a low voice. "I've got one that you need to see."

"One what?" he mumbled.

"One murder?" Glory answered, her voice slightly annoyed. "It's weird. And our mutual acquaintance told me that I was to report anything really weird to you."

"He did?" Jesse said, digging the heel of his hand into his eye socket, trying to wake up. It was a stupid question. Of course Dashiell was using Glory as a scout for Old World trouble. Most of the time, Jesse had been told, humans who learned about the Old World had their minds pressed to forget, and then went about their lives. If time or trauma didn't allow for that, though, they were given a choice: join the Old World or be killed by it. Since the odds of successfully turning into a vampire or werewolf had gotten so low, this was often a death sentence, regardless of what they chose. Dashiell was willing to allow Glory to remain alive and human, however, in exchange for the occasional forensic favor. But he also kept leverage—he'd made it clear to Glory that he knew everything about her two children, including where to find them. If Dashiell had told Glory to keep Jesse informed of weird homicides, that's exactly what she would do.

"Yeah. After that car accident case last month, remember?"

Sitting up now, Jesse gritted his teeth. The car accident in question had been part of the Olivia Powell investigation, nearly two weeks earlier, but he'd agreed to help Scarlett destroy crime scenes only a few days ago. The cardinal vampire was playing the long game. Typical. "How could I forget," Jesse said wryly. "But I can't come in right now, Glory. I'm on leave."

"Just trust me, okay?"

A thought pinged in his tired brain. "Was it a woman? Mauled, or scratched, or something like that?"

"No," her voice had lowered, and he could just picture her cupping one hand around the receiver. "Not a woman."

Probably not the nova, then. "Glory . . . ," he complained. "I've had about two hours of sleep, and I'm on leave anyway—"

"Hang on," she interrupted, a new tone in her voice. "There's someone here who wants to talk to you."

There was a muffling on the phone, and then another familiar voice said, "Hey, Jess."

All trace of sleepiness vanished when Jesse heard his ex-girlfriend on the phone. "Runa?" he said stupidly, like they were playing *This is Your Life*.

"Yeah. Listen, you gotta get down here."

"I'm supposed to be off," he said, hesitation in his voice now. Runa Vore was a witch who had taken a job as a crime scene photographer, partly in order to get closer to Jesse. Things had been deeply awkward between the two of them since he'd learned who she really was and broken up with her, so if she was willing to talk to him now . . . Jesse kicked off the covers and started for his dresser.

"Who's in charge of the scene?" he asked, wedging the phone between his ear and shoulder so he could dig for clothes.

"DIs McHugh and Bine," she replied, and Jesse almost whistled. He'd heard of McHugh, a veteran Homicide Special detective who was a couple of pay grades above Jesse. Bine must be his partner. Homicide Special usually took the really weird cases, so it was possible that their presence was just a coincidence. It was also possible, though, that Dashiell had gotten Homicide Special assigned to the case to prove to Jesse that he could. "Bine's a friend; I'll get you in," she went on, urgency in her voice. "I'm texting the location. Hurry up."

She hung up the phone, and Jesse went to get his gun.

Chapter 24

For a moment Jesse thought Runa's text was a prank. Leaving a dead body—or in this case, two—at a graveyard seemed too much like the beginning of a joke. Something about cutting out the middleman. But she wouldn't do that, and so ten minutes after the phone call had ended Jesse found himself driving toward Evergreen Cemetery.

Jesse had been there once as a kid, for the funeral of one of his mother's cousins. It was enormous, nearly seventy acres, but, although it was the oldest graveyard in LA, it lacked the star power that drove tourists to Hollywood Forever or Forest Lawn. There were some historical heavyweights among the three hundred thousand graves, but what was local history compared to global celebrity, especially in Los Angeles?

He followed his phone's GPS instructions to the ornate concrete pillars that marked the entrance to Evergreen, showing his badge to one of the two uniformed officers guarding the gates. Passing through, he headed toward the island of bright lights and activity he saw in the south end of the graveyard, winding past row after row of silent graves.

At last, Jesse arrived at the end of a long trail of department vehicles parked on the right side of the road. All of the police activity was on his left, marked by crime scene tape circling enormous metal spotlights on tripods. The bulk of the cemetery that

Jesse had just driven through lay beyond the bodies. He pulled the sedan over as far as he could behind a patrol car that was still flashing its red and blues, probably to discourage curious onlookers who might otherwise wonder if the bright spotlights indicated a film shoot.

As he approached the closest uniformed officer, Jesse registered the unusual size of the cordoned-off area. It was enormous, more than twice as big as what Jesse was accustomed to. He could hardly see the bodies themselves, fifty yards away behind a throng of technicians in overalls and booties. But there were definitely two of them, which was all Runa had mentioned. Why cordon off so much area if the bodies were way over there?

He reached the first cop outside the caution tape, a pear-shaped African American woman with *Waters* stenciled across her right breast. "Sir—" she began, but he showed her his badge. She didn't move to lift the tape, shaking her head slightly.

"Detective Cruz from Southwest robbery-homicide," he said, in case she was having trouble making out the words. The spotlights weren't doing much at this distance. "You from Hollenbeck?" he asked, naming the nearest division station.

"Yes, sir. But they want as few people within the tape as possible," she explained, with professional pity in her voice. Jesse had used the same tone many times. *It's not my rule, sir, the boss just makes me enforce it.* Lowering her voice, Waters added, "There's blood all over the place."

That explained why the technicians had cordoned off so much of the cemetery. They would want to collect samples of all the blood. Jesse nodded, hoping Runa had done whatever she needed to do to get him in. "I'm looking for Runa Vore, the photographer. She asked me to come."

Waters nodded, no expression on her face, and automatically turned her head away to speak into her microphone in a low inaudible voice. Jesse had done that plenty of times too and wasn't offended. She listened for a moment and said to Jesse, "She's coming to get you."

Jesse nodded and took a few steps back and to the side, giving Waters room to see her assigned area. While he waited, he studied the area behind the tape. The whole scene almost looked like a blast radius, like a bomb had gone off in the cemetery. He'd never seen anything like it. Blood pebbled on the gravestones, saturated the grass in wide swaths, dripped down the sides of shrubbery. The blood splatter experts were going to be here for days.

"Who found the bodies?" he asked Waters.

Her eyes flicked back toward him with benign interest, like she'd forgotten all about him. "Neighbors, sir. They reported strange noises two hours ago."

Jesse nodded and went back to surveying the crime scene. He realized that it wasn't actually a blast site, but almost an optical illusion: the center of the taped-off area hadn't been leveled by an explosion; it was just a wide, flat clearing created by four rows of in-ground placard markers, the kind that everyone said were easier for the cemetery groundskeepers. It had just been hard to see them at first because of all the blood.

The boundary dividing the rows of placards and the skewed rows of gravestones was an enormous monument, a great rectangle that would have reached Jesse's chest, topped with a stone tiger the size of a beagle. When he looked closely Jesse saw the red blood streaking down the side of the monument, splattering the tiger's back like so many stripes. His eyes moved down to the bodies just in front of the tiger's perch, and beyond them to scan the in-ground grave markers more carefully.

Many of them had been cracked in half. Most of them were splattered with blood. There were little numbered evidence cards scattered over the markers and the ground around them. Marking more blood.

What the hell could crack in-ground grave markers?

One of the technicians in coveralls and paper booties hurried over, and Jesse saw that it was Runa, a black camera strap around her neck, her corn silk pigtails backlit by the spotlights. Jesse's heart ached for a moment. She was so beautiful, even in the stupid coveralls: lithe and poised, stepping with her feet turned out slightly like a dancer. "Jesse, hi," she said, speaking fast. Tension saturated the air between them for a moment, and Jesse struggled to push through it. Runa solved the problem by reaching across the caution tape to hand him a pair of booties. "Put these on and come with me." To Waters, she added, "Bine wants him to look at the bodies close up."

Waters shrugged and nodded, the responsibility of minding Jesse officially handed off to someone else. Jesse had to stand on one foot at a time to put on the booties, wobbling a little but managing to not fall over. Then Runa lifted the tape for him and he ducked under.

"Watch your step," she ordered. "They put markers near the blood splatters they could find, but they keep finding more. Try not to step on any." Jesse nodded and concentrated on stepping around the little yellow evidence markers.

"I'm just about done here," Runa said over her shoulder. "But the ME is already getting his stuff out to take the body. You've only got a minute."

Jesse followed her into the spotlights. There was a small crowd of crime scene technicians still moving around the scene, Glory among them, and the medical examiner's people were waiting with a stretcher. Jesse nodded to a couple of techs he'd worked with before, feeling his cheeks redden self-consciously. It made no sense for him to be in the middle of such a complicated crime scene. He looked around for the Homicide Special detectives. "Runa, where's . . ."

His voice trailed off as he noticed a woman in her late thirties approaching them. She was exactly as tall as Jesse's six feet, a skinny woman with a splatter of freckles across her face and slightly frizzy red hair that she'd grown too long and tied back in a lifeless ponytail that hung down her back like a kicked dog. Despite her gangly limbs, she had no trouble negotiating the evidence markers. She made a beeline straight for Jesse with her right hand extended.

Runa started to introduce them. "Jesse, this is—"

"Sarabeth Bine," said the red-haired woman. Up close she was a little older than he'd first thought, with plain weathered features. She shook Jesse's hand vigorously. "And you're Cruz. I'd introduce my partner, but he went to inform the next of kin. Runa tells me you have an eye for the weird ones. I appreciate you taking a look at this."

"Not a problem," Jesse said, trying to sound confident.

Bine looked thoughtfully at Jesse for a second, then pointed a finger at his chest. "You're the one who wrapped up that La Brea Park thing a few months back, right? The golden pretty boy?"

"I'm not—I wasn't really," Jesse stammered, blushing fiercely.

Sarabeth Bine continued as though he hadn't spoken. "That *was* weird. Okay, well, sign the register, take a quick look, and update me before you go. I gotta talk to the evidence guys about the search."

"Search?"

She glanced at Runa. "You didn't tell him? Good." Bine smirked. "More fun if it's a surprise." To Runa, she added, "You should start packing up, but be ready to step in if they find anything."

"Yes, ma'am," Runa promised. Bine rushed off again like a questing bumblebee, and Jesse let out a breath he'd somehow been holding. "I gotta get back to work," Runa murmured. "You good?"

"Yeah. Thanks," Jesse said, off balance. He automatically reached out a hand to touch Runa's shoulder, but stopped the gesture halfway there, awkwardly turning it into a professional clap on the back. Runa rolled her eyes and went off to finish her job.

Jesse put both women out of his mind and stepped up to the bodies. Both were nude, with male genitalia. The unforgiving spotlights washed out their skin tones, but Jesse could tell the man on the left had been white and had been shorter than the man on the right, who had been slim and black. They both looked like they'd been chewed and torn and sliced into ribbons of tissue. Jesse had seen a couple serious maulings back when he'd first joined the department, and this looked sort of like a super-powered version of that. The skin on all of the extremities had been *shredded.* Both bodies also had enormous, gaping torso wounds that must have flooded the ground with blood. The biggest single injury, though, appeared to be facial. Jesse inched even closer, trying to stay out of the worst of the blood splatter, and peered at the bodies for a long moment before his eyes were able to translate what he was seeing.

Both men were missing their lower jaws. It looked like they'd been *torn off.*

"That's fucked up," Jesse said aloud. He glanced around and saw Glory frowning over at him. She had been painstakingly tweezing bloody plant matter into little evidence baggies.

"Did you guys find the jawbones?" he asked her.

"No. But Bine has a team looking," she said, her voice hushed. "I've never seen anything like this, Jesse."

"I've never *heard of* anything like this," Jesse replied absently. His first thought was *werewolf*, just based on the savagery. But this didn't feel like the nova wolf's kills, which had been methodical, calculated. Cold, but with purpose. This was messier than that. And why would any werewolf, nova or not, take the victims' jaws?

But if it wasn't a werewolf, what else could it be? Jesse thought suddenly of the La Brea Park murders, which had been committed by a human nutcase who liked playing with body parts. Those killings had been farther down the spectrum of gruesomeness, much more scattered and frantic than the nova's previous kills. But these killings just didn't have the same chaotic, sadistic glee as the La Brea Park murderer. His brow furrowed. Was it possible that this had nothing to do with Old World at all?

Jesse adjusted his weight, preparing to stand, but the movement caused the light to shift on the victim as well, and something shiny caught his eye. He shifted back, then again. There. Amidst the gore, he spotted the shiny surface of deep scar tissue. He played his flashlight over the body's chest, and then moved the light up so he could stare at the top half of the face.

"What is it?" Glory asked anxiously. The bustle around them was picking up; Jesse was officially in the way of the ME's people. But he wasn't paying any attention, because he recognized the corpse.

"Hello, Terrence," Jesse said aloud.

Chapter 25

Werewolves. Someone had torn up two werewolves.

Once he'd realized that the taller man was Terrence Whittaker, it didn't take long for Jesse to recognize the shorter, stockier guy as Terrence's sidekick, Drew Riddell. He'd talked to both of these men just the day before. And now he knew why there was so much blood and gore at the scene. Scarlett had told him that unless you were with a null, werewolves were nearly impossible to kill; they healed too quickly. He knew that Scarlett hadn't been anywhere near this scene, so whoever had done this had needed to essentially wound these guys faster than they could heal, until they finally bled out.

Could the nova do that? What about Will? After all, Will had openly admitted to there being conflict between him and the other wolves. If Terrence had pushed him far enough, could *he* have done something like this?

No, Jesse reasoned, if this had been Will, he'd have gotten rid of the bodies himself, or at least called Scarlett, who would have called Jesse to help. Whoever this was didn't have access to Scarlett's "services." But even the nova didn't leave bodies out in the open, in public. And he still didn't understand the thing with the jaws.

Jesse got to his feet, getting out of the ME guys' way, and leaned a bit to put his mouth close to Glory's ear. "Call Dashiell, tell him it's Old World," Jesse told her. "These guys were werewolves."

"You know them?" Glory said hopefully. "Are you gonna give their names to Bine?"

Shit. Jesse paused, considering. If he told Bine the victim's ID, she would immediately ask how he knew them. Then again, if he *didn't* tell Bine, and in the course of the investigation she found out that he'd talked to both of those guys earlier that day, his career would be over. Worse than that—he might even be a suspect, especially if anyone found out that he'd shot Whittaker in the leg. Jesse cursed under his breath in Spanish, and said, "No. I'm not gonna say anything about the IDs for now. Let's give Dashiell a little time to work."

"Jesse, the sun's coming up," Glory pointed out.

Jesse glanced up. It was hard to see past the lights of the city, but sure enough, warm pink light was beginning to break over the LA skyline. Dashiell would be dead for the next twelve hours or so. "Oh, come *on*," Jesse complained. He stepped away from the body, pulled out his own phone, and called Will, who picked up right away.

"We have a problem," Jesse said into the phone. He tried to keep his words vague, like Scarlett always did, on the off chance that anyone was listening. Scarlett's paranoia was really rubbing off on him. "I just got a call from a work friend. Two of your . . . erm . . . family members were killed tonight. The top two on your list."

Silence. Then Will said, "You're sure it's them?"

Jesse considered that for a second, and said, "With the taller one, I'm sure. With the shorter one, I'm ninety-five percent."

"How did they die?" Will inquired. There was a note of hope in his voice, and for a moment Jesse thought the alpha was asking for details over the phone, which seemed out of character. But then he understood: Will was hoping that Drew and Terrence had been hit by a bus, or drowned accidentally, something like that.

"Well," Jesse said, glancing back toward the crime scene behind him, "it wasn't a nice quiet stroke in their sleep."

"Okay," Will said, disappointed. "I gotta think about this. Thanks for the call."

"Wait!" Jesse protested. "You're not getting it. Two dead, and it's after sunrise."

There was another long silence, and Jesse checked his phone's screen to make sure the call hadn't dropped. "Will?" he said.

"*Dammit,*" Will said with feeling. "We're not set up for this. LA is not supposed to be a place where this kind of thing happens."

"What do they do in other places?" Jesse asked, trying to keep his voice reasonable. "You guys have stayed hidden for an awfully long time. How does it work?"

"Different things, in different places," Will said tiredly. "Corruption, more murder, tighter control on everyone. That's not going to help us right now. But I don't have Dashiell's contacts. He's kept them from me in case—well. You're just going to have to stall until sundown, and let Dashiell throw his weight and money around."

Stall. Right. That was just what Jesse wanted to do right now. He'd agreed to this whole deal so he could *stop* deceiving his fellow cops, but saying so wouldn't help right now. "Fine," he said, working to keep the snap out of his voice. After a moment's thought, he added, "Hey, Will? Have you ever heard of . . . your kind of people . . . being killed, looks kind of like a mauling, but their lower jaws are ripped off?"

There was a sudden crash on Will's end of the line. Jesse had heard the sound before, and knew Will had dropped the phone. He waited, mystified, for the alpha to return to the line. "Pick up Scarlett," Will growled. His voice had changed, becoming deeper and more terrifying. "Meet me at Dashiell's in an hour."

"I have to tell them *something* here," Jesse protested. "Besides, it's after sunrise—"

Will cut him off. *"One hour!"* he roared, his voice barely human. And the line went dead.

Chapter 26

Jesse left the crime scene without a word to anyone, even Glory and Runa. He hated looking like a flake in front of Bine, who was expecting a report, but it seemed like a better option than lying to her face.

He drove straight to Scarlett's. She didn't answer her phone on the way over, so he was prepared to wait on her doorstep for quite a while, knocking and ringing the bell. To his surprise, though, she answered the door a few seconds after the first knock. She looked tired, but she was dressed in a clean thermal shirt and clean yoga pants, her hair damp from the shower, a piece of peanut-buttered toast in the hand that wasn't steering her cane. "Couldn't sleep," she explained around a mouthful of toast. There were dark smudges under her eyes, which stood out against the paleness of her skin. *She's pushing too hard*, Jesse thought guiltily. Swallowing, she added, "I saw the missed call. I was gonna call you back after breakfast. What's up?"

"You . . . don't look so good," Jesse said tentatively. "Have you seen your doctor lately?"

Scarlett rolled her eyes. "I'm fine, Cruz. Well, I'll be fine as soon as we find this asshole and I can spend a whole week icing my knee. Now, what's going on?"

Ten minutes later they were heading toward the freeway on-ramp in Scarlett's van. She had insisted on taking it because, as she pointed out, Will hadn't actually said whether or not there would be a crime scene to clean up. Jesse hadn't argued with her because he suspected it was easier for her to get in and out of the van with her swollen knee. And because she had let him drive.

Murders or not, the morning was lovely. The smog that had hung heavy over the city the day before had lightened just enough to let sunlight filter through, and the last bits of gorgeous sunrise colors were still fading as Jesse drove east toward Pasadena. It was early in the morning on New Year's Day, so traffic was blissfully light. For a moment Jesse felt tension lift from him as he cruised down the empty freeway, crossing the lines of shadow created by the palm trees that grew along the side of the road. Damn, he loved this stupid city. He hated it too, once in a while, but he'd never live anywhere else.

He told Scarlett about the two dead bodies in the cemetery, and Will's weird reaction. When he'd finished, Jesse asked, "The thing with the jaws, does that mean anything to you?"

Scarlett frowned in the seat beside him. "I think . . ." She shook her head. "You know when you can almost remember something, but it's just not quite there? I feel like Olivia said something about jawbones once, but I just can't remember the context."

"Maybe it'll come to you if you stop trying to remember," Jesse suggested. "Do you know why we're meeting at Dashiell's instead of Will's or the bar?"

He glanced at Scarlett as he said it, and Jesse thought he saw a flash of something on her face—fear. But she just shook her head.

Hayne answered Dashiell's door wearing the same polo shirt and chinos he'd worn on Jesse's last visit, this time with a Desert Eagle strapped in the holster on his shoulder. Jesse had always considered that particular handgun too ostentatious to take seriously, but Hayne was large enough to make it seem completely rational. When he greeted Scarlett and Jesse he had the same neutral expression Jesse had seen before, but there was something about his tone and posture that seemed . . . troubled.

"What the hell's going on?" Scarlett said bluntly, and Jesse felt a rush of appreciation. Will and Dashiell might be frequently cryptic, but at least his partner didn't play games.

"I don't know, exactly. But I do know that Mr. Carling wants you to go wake Dashiell and Beatrice," Hayne said simply.

Jesse was surprised, but Scarlett's expression merely tightened, and he realized she'd been expecting this. "You know I can't do that," Scarlett said levelly. Her eyes were locked on Hayne. "He'll kill me."

"Why?" Jesse asked, focusing on her. "Is it really that big of a deal?"

"Why don't you two come inside," Hayne said smoothly. "We can talk in the living room. Will should be here any second."

Slowly, so Scarlett could keep up on her bad leg, Hayne led them into the same room from earlier, the one with the glass doors that led out onto the patio. Jesse was really starting to hate this room.

Nobody sat down. When the door closed behind them, Hayne began, "To answer your question, Detective, it is a very big deal. Dashiell is very . . . private."

Scarlett snorted, turning to face Jesse. "It's a power thing," she said simply. "A cardinal vampire couldn't allow a simple human like me to choose when he lives and dies. At least, not without some kind of fatal gesture to swat me back down to my place." She turned her head to glare at Hayne. "I'm not going to do it."

"Yes, you will." The new voice came from just outside the door. Will twitched as he stepped into the room, and Jesse realized he'd hit Scarlett's radius. The werewolf was dressed in khaki pants and a simple button-down that hid the hard muscle Jesse had seen the night before. His eyes were wild, searching the room like he expected ninjas to jump out and attack.

Jesse took an instinctive step closer to Scarlett.

She crossed her arms again. "No, I won't," she said stubbornly. "Why do you need to talk to him so badly? What can't wait until sunset?"

"The jaws," Jesse guessed, watching Will closely. "It's got something to do with the werewolf's jaws."

Will pulled at his hair, which was already sticking up. Usually he was blandly handsome in a forgettable, Disney Channel dad kind of way, but even this close to Scarlett, he looked practically feral. "They have to know," he muttered. "She met them before, she said, and he has to know they're here."

Scarlett gave the alpha a worried look, her brow furrowed with distress. She glanced at Jesse. He hated the expression on her face, like she was right on the brink of panic. "Will's gone bye-bye, Scarlett," he said solemnly. "What have you got?"

She flashed him a grin that pierced his heart. Before she could speak, though, the doorbell rang, a long series of notes that echoed through the house. Will said, "That'll be Kirsten."

Hayne looked surprised, and a little uncomfortable, and Jesse remembered that Hayne and Kirsten had been married once. What did Kirsten have to do with any of this? Scarlett looked as confused as he felt, like they were watching a disc that had skipped.

If the bigger man was upset about his ex-wife's arrival, though, he kept it to himself, leaving the room to answer the door without a word.

Will wheeled on Scarlett. "You need to do it," he said firmly. "You have to wake him up."

Scarlett shook her head. "You know I can't do that. He's forbidden it."

Jesse had never heard Scarlett use the word "forbidden" before, but it sure sounded like something Dashiell would say.

"Hold on," Jesse jumped in, stepping between the two of them. "Scarlett has worked for you guys for years. This has to have come up before, right? That you might get in a jam and need to bend the rules?"

"You were with me on the two worst situations I've ever seen," Scarlett said, with a little more control in her voice. "And I don't think we even discussed it."

"Things were never this time-sensitive," Will objected. He bared his teeth, adding, "I'm your employer too, you know. Anything Dashiell can do to you, I can do just as easily."

"Hey!" Jesse began, stepping forward, but just then Kirsten walked through the doorway with Hayne at her heels. The semi-official leader of the city's witch population was a blonde woman in her mid-thirties, wearing a tiered wool skirt, tall boots, and a white sweater with sleeves long enough to cover the second knuckles on each hand. The sweater made Kirsten look feminine and angelic, but Jesse knew better than to underestimate her. He'd seen some of the things she could do with magic.

Kirsten took one glance around the room and made a beeline for Will. "What on earth is going on?" she demanded.

His eyes latched on to her with sudden desperation. "They're here, Kirsten," he said, anguished. "The Luparii came to town."

Jesse glanced at Scarlett, who appeared to be as confused as he was. Kirsten looked suddenly unsteady on her feet, her alabaster skin paling further. Hayne stepped up beside her with concern on his face, placing a hand gently on her arm. She seized it and hung on, tilting her head way up to see Hayne's face.

"Bring them up, Teddy," she said quietly. "Bring them up here and Scarlett can wake them. I swear on my craft that you won't be blamed."

There was a moment of silence in the living room, punctuated only by the sound of Will pacing back and forth in front of the patio door. Finally Hayne nodded. He turned on his heel and left the room.

They left a long, terrible silence in their wake, and then Scarlett let out a choking sound. "Scar?" Jesse asked, concerned. She made the sound again, and Jesse realized she was laughing. "What?"

She chortled. "His first name is *Teddy*?"

Chapter 27

It took me a little while to stop laughing, but only because of the law of inertia—once I started, it just seemed easier to keep going. Teddy. What a stupid name for such an enormous man.

Eventually I calmed down and remembered that Jesse and I still had no idea what was going on. The Luparii . . . that name jangled in my brain, and I closed my eyes, trying to remember. Olivia had been telling me stories about the European Old World. I opened my eyes and looked at Kirsten. "They're the boogeymen for werewolves, right?" I asked Kirsten. My voice came out thin and sober.

"Something like that." Kirsten looked suddenly tired. "I'll tell you all about it, but it'll be easiest if we wait for them," she said firmly. I shrugged and went to sit down in one of Dashiell's nice padded chairs.

Minutes ticked by. Part of me was ready to take a handful of Advil and go to sleep right there, but at the same time my stomach was thrashing around like a shark on a boat deck. Hayne may have been the one actually moving him, but I knew Dashiell was going to blame me for resurrecting him during the day. Besides, completely apart from the fact that I wasn't supposed to wake him without permission, Dashiell hates being near me. I don't blame him, really. If you spend a couple of centuries becoming the most powerful creature in a hundred square miles, the last thing you want to do is be near someone who can immediately relegate you to the bottom of the food chain, which is what humans are. He gets in my radius every once in a while just to prove he isn't afraid, but he always looks twitchy when I've foisted humanity on him. And now I was going to do it without his permission or foreknowledge? It just seemed like the pickle on the crap sandwich of my week.

Hayne brought Beatrice and then Dashiell to the hallway outside the living room, and then called for Will to help. The werewolf went out and collected Beatrice's limp form, and the two of them carried the vampires into the room, a sober procession that was only somewhat tempered by how ridiculous Dashiell looked in a fireman's carry on Hayne's shoulders.

When Hayne took the last step into my radius, Dashiell exploded with sudden life, taking in an enormous breath and struggling to disentangle himself from Hayne. Beatrice, right behind him, got her feet under her without much trouble, but Dashiell looked undignified and silly for a second, flailing around to get himself oriented without his usual vampire grace. And thanks to the world's most reliably terrible luck, when he finally got his feet under him, the vampire was about six inches away from me with murder in his eye.

Before anyone could speak, Dashiell raised his palm to slap me—but Will had anticipated this and darted forward, grabbing his hand. "*Stop,*" he roared at the vampire, and Dashiell froze in surprise. I had never heard Will—or anyone, really—talk to Dashiell like that. "It's not her fault; I made her," Will said in a quieter tone. You know things are bad when the unhinged werewolf is the most reasonable person in the room.

Then Will added, very simply, "The Luparii are in town."

The word hit Dashiell like a blow. He seemed to suddenly forget all about me as he turned around as fast as a human can, managing to arrive at Beatrice's side just in time to catch his wife as she fainted dead away. No pun intended. Jesse looked at me with his mouth open.

So. That happened.

It took a few minutes, but Hayne got everyone seated and more or less calm. I stayed in my armchair, mostly because it was so overstuffed that I wasn't sure I could get up by myself. Dashiell and Beatrice were on the adjoining sofa, which was still in my radius. Bea looked pale and shaky, and I suspected that she was only sitting upright because she was leaning on her husband. Will took the hard-backed chair on the other side of the sofa from me, and a wary Jesse had simply sunk down on the floor to my right. I knew he didn't want to be too far from me in case everything went to hell again, but I didn't exactly mind. Hayne brought in a chair for Kirsten, who set it between Will and Jesse so we formed a loose oval around the coffee table. Hayne stood guard at the door.

Between the Luparii and Beatrice fainting, Dashiell seemed to have forgotten he was furious with me—although every once in a while he shot me a suspicious look that I didn't at all like.

When it seemed like we were more or less settled, I jumped in. "Olivia talked about the Luparii once," I ventured. "I don't remember her exact phrasing, but I had the impression that they were magical imaginary villains, something older werewolves used to scare new wolves into silence. Like the Loch Ness Monster or something."

Will frowned at me from across the coffee table. "Oh, they're very real, unfortunately. And technically they're witches. A family of witches."

I looked at Kirsten, whose frown matched Will's. That explained why the witch queen of LA was here. "What do you mean, 'technically'?" Jesse asked.

"The Luparii are witches the way Hitler was German," Kirsten said stiffly. She held a hand up to Will to indicate that she'd take over, and he nodded. "They are a family, a very old French family. There are stories about them going back as far as the Middle Ages."

I blinked in surprise. Unlike vampires or werewolves, witches pass their magic on hereditarily, not through infection. I knew that there were old witch families, but I'd only heard of, like, *Mayflower*-old, not medieval. "Back then, they were called the Gagnons," Kirsten continued. She did the full French pronunciation of the name in a careless, natural way that I envied. "As you know, different witches are skilled differently."

"Like how Runa finds things," Jesse said quietly, and Kirsten nodded.

"Different families sometimes pass down the same . . . specialties." She bit her lip. "Our history suggests that the Gagnons had a gift for . . . twisting things. Changing the purpose of things, usually to something dark and cruel."

"Example?" I asked. I was feeling very attentive. If it meant I got to sit down and no one was trying to smack me, Kirsten could lecture all day, as far I was concerned.

She swiveled her hand idly in the air, her eyes searching the air above my head for an example. "Like . . . farmers who competed with the Gagnons would suddenly discover all of their crops were poisonous. I don't mean that the crops were poisoned, I mean they became toxic. Or a young woman who rejected one of the Gagnon men would have miscarriage after miscarriage, and the babies would be born . . . disfigured." Kirsten shuddered. "Anyway, the Gagnons caused a lot of deaths. Eventually even Charlemagne noticed. Do you . . ." She raised her eyebrows at me, and I rolled my eyes back.

"Yes, I know who Charlemagne is. My father taught history."

Kirsten nodded and continued. "Well, in the ninth century Charlemagne figured there was no point in arresting the Gagnons. There was never any proof, and anyway every kind of law enforcement that went after them simply disappeared. So instead, he gave them a job."

"Come again?" I asked, confused.

Kirsten sighed. "It was a tactic. If your two-year-old is about to throw a tantrum, you ask him to help you water the flowers or bake some cookies."

"I'm guessing the Gagnons aren't known for their amazing snickerdoodles," Jesse guessed. I flashed him a grin.

"No," Kirsten answered, her expression soured. "Charlemagne gave them the office of the Luparii, the official wolf hunters for the crown."

Will's lips curled back with rage. "He paid them a reward for each dead wolf."

"The jaws," I said softly, putting it together. "They used the jaws to prove the kill."

"Yes," Kirsten confirmed. "It was easier to drag around a bag of jaws"—she wrinkled her nose distastefully—"than the complete carcasses."

"Did it work?" Jesse asked.

"Oh, yes," Will said darkly, "it worked. The Luparii grew rich slaughtering wolves for the crown. They *excelled* at it." He stood up and began to pace the length of the room restlessly again. The pacing took him in and out of my radius with each loop, which was harmlessly distracting, like when a fly keeps dive-bombing your head. I wasn't about to ask him to stop, though.

"And this is regular wolves?" I asked hesitantly. "I mean, not werewolves?"

"Right." Kirsten nodded. She glanced furtively at Will. "They used their magic occasionally, but . . . mmm . . . well, they mostly used 'regular' methods to hunt wolves: poisoned meat, packs of hunting dogs, that kind of thing. It was a point of pride for them that they could do it without magic. In all fairness," she added, with an apologetic glance at Will, "wolves were a genuine threat to human settlements at the time, and the Gagnons felt that they were performing a public service. A lucrative one."

Will turned to face us, and I saw the bones in his jaw flex with anger. "Wolves were hated then," he snapped. "They were the rabid baby-eating monsters of fairy tales."

"Many of which were based on werewolves," Dashiell pointed out conversationally, an unfathomable expression on his face. Apparently the vampire was still feeling hostile.

Will snarled back, a human sound in his currently human throat, but Dashiell didn't rise to the bait. I almost opened my mouth to intervene, but decided I'd rather they were mad at each other than at me.

"Anyway," Kirsten said hurriedly, "this went on for centuries. The last name changed from Gagnon to something else, and changed again, but the family line continued killing wolves. In the eighteenth century, though, the crown could no longer afford to finance the office of the Luparii."

"So they had to find something else to kill," Will growled.

"They started hunting werewolves?" I guessed, and Will nodded grimly. "Just for fun, or what?"

"By then they were true believers," Kirsten said softly. "They thought it was their family's calling, the same way some families turn out many generations of teachers or policemen. They began to travel. And werewolves began to die."

"People must have noticed," Jesse protested. "I mean, the werewolves were people most of the time. *People* were disappearing."

"Oh, they noticed," Dashiell spoke up. He and Beatrice had been suspiciously quiet through all of this. "The French monarchy realized that people were disappearing around the Luparii again, so they reinstated the office ten years later, hoping to get them back on track. The position exists to this day, I believe, although now it's called the Wolfcatcher Royal."

"But it was too late—the Luparii didn't want to go back to hunting regular wolves," Kirsten added. "I don't condone or agree with what they do, but to them, werewolves are a plague. And generation after generation of Gagnons have spent their lifetimes training to destroy that plague."

Jesse met my eyes, and I thought we both thought of the same thing: a conversation we'd had with Jared Hess, back in the fall. He had been crazy, and he had loathed everything about the Old World . . . but he'd also hinted that he wasn't the only one. *Don't you think there are a few humans who know what's going on, who want to put the animals down?* "How many werewolves did they kill?" I asked.

"All of them," Will said flatly. "To this day, there are no werewolves in mainland Europe or the United Kingdom. The Luparii killed most of them, and the few who survived ran for their lives."

There was a moment of silence. I was awed by the scale of what Will was saying: *all* of the werewolves in mainland Europe and the United Kingdom? All those different countries, different cultures . . . I couldn't imagine a clan of witches claiming that big a territory.

"Excuse me," Jesse said finally, mindful of Will's anger. "But aren't you all supposed to be really hard to kill? And aren't werewolves smart enough to evade those guys?"

"We're not always as smart in our other form," Will answered. "But yes, we could avoid the Luparii at first. Then they adapted to us."

"They began to incorporate their magic," I guessed. Will and Kirsten both nodded. "How?" I was genuinely curious, apart from our current troubles. Magic doesn't work very well against itself, which means witches can't put spells on other Old World creatures. So how would you use magic to kill werewolves?

"That's the thing," Kirsten said softly. "I don't really know."

Jesse met my eyes, and without discussing it we both turned our heads to look at Beatrice and Dashiell. The cardinal vampire's arm tightened protectively around his wife, but she sat up straighter, her shoulders back. "Do you know something about them, Bea?" I said softly.

"They . . . my . . ." Beatrice cleared her throat and looked helplessly at Dashiell. I'd never seen her look so unsure of herself.

Dashiell pressed his lips to her head, then looked back up and said with stormy eyes, "The Luparii killed her younger brother."

Chapter 28

Dashiell looked like he was ready to slaughter the first one of us to ask a question, but luckily Beatrice patted her husband's arm gently and said, "I will tell them." Her voice was small and fearful, but strong.

"You don't have to," I rushed to say, ignoring the look that Jesse shot me. We needed whatever information we could get. I knew it, but I just didn't want to make Beatrice relive whatever was causing that expression on her face.

"It's all right," Beatrice said, letting out a long breath. "It was a long time ago."

Back in Spain, she explained, she'd had a little brother she was close to. Esteban had been twelve years younger than her, and their mother had died giving birth to him. Beatrice had more or less raised the boy, and he'd followed his big sister around with worshipful eyes. In 1911, Dashiell had passed through Barcelona and spotted the twenty-five-year-old beauty. He was enchanted, and began to court Beatrice—always at night, of course. They fell in love.

For years, Dashiell pressed her mind to keep her from asking too many question about his strange habits, but eventually he loved her so much, he didn't want to lie anymore.

"So I told her what I was," Dashiell broke in. He was human in my presence, and I wondered if he would still have that look of guilt and grief if he weren't. "As soon as I did, the local cardinal vampire made sure I turned her."

Beatrice took his hand. "It's what I wanted too, love." She looked back at me with tears pooled in her eyes. "We planned to leave town, as is the custom when one is turned. You leave everything behind. Esteban was sixteen, though, and he didn't want me to go. He followed Dashiell one night, to talk to him, and he . . . realized what we were." Her voice broke. I winced. The poor kid had probably seen his big sister drinking someone's blood. And by finding out about the Old World, he'd have to join or be killed.

Dashiell picked up the story so Beatrice wouldn't have to. "Because of the boy's age, we decided he should join the werewolf pack, rather than the vampires. Even back then, sixteen was too young to . . ." He cleared his throat. "Anyway. Becoming a werewolf would keep him alive, and let him and Beatrice have many long years together . . ." His voice trailed off for a moment. "We contacted a local alpha. The change was successful—"

"And the Luparii came to Barcelona three months later," Beatrice finished. She took a deep breath. "They killed the whole pack, including Esteban. They took their jaws."

"You didn't . . . try to get revenge?" Will asked, as tactfully as possible.

Dashiell's expression darkened. "The cardinal vampire of the city forbade it. He had no love for werewolves, and the Luparii were not interested in vampires. He wanted to keep it that way." Then Dashiell looked away, and I realized that he was ashamed. "I wasn't as strong back then," he said formally.

"We left, and never went back to Spain," Beatrice said in a clearer voice. She smiled sadly at her husband, who squeezed her hand. I hadn't really registered it before, but both of them were dressed in simple, comfortable clothes: T-shirts, yoga pants, gym trunks. Beatrice's long dark hair was mussed, and Dashiell was squinting a little, like he might need glasses as a human. I had never seen either one of them in anything less than business casual. It was so strange to see them like this. Like . . . people.

"Why don't more people know about them?" Jesse wondered. "If they've killed every werewolf in Europe, why hasn't the entire Old World . . . I don't know, gone to war against them?"

Kirsten bit her lip. "For us, the Luparii are a disgrace—and yet none of us want to cross them. Think of it like . . . having an uncle who's a convicted murderer. You'd be ashamed, but you'd also want to stay far away from him."

"And the wolves," Will growled, "are afraid of them."

I didn't bother asking Dashiell why the vampires hadn't stopped the Luparii. "So . . . what? We think the Luparii finally got around to expanding into America?" Jesse said doubtfully. "And they decided to start in LA exactly when there's a nova running around killing people?"

"No," Will said morosely. "They've never hunted in America, so far as I know . . ." He looked at Dashiell, who nodded his head in agreement. ". . . and I doubt they would send someone for an ordinary werewolf."

"But a nova wolf," I continued, catching on. "That might be rare enough to be worth the trip."

Kirsten nodded slightly. "Europe is enormous, and there's a lot of territory to cover," she said softly. "And I doubt that the Luparii have had much of a hunt for years. Werewolves are that frightened of them." Her eyes dropped with shame.

"So they're all sitting around sharpening their wolf-killing silver, or whatever," Jesse said skeptically, "and they just randomly hear about a nova wolf running around LA?"

"No." Will had stopped pacing and was leaning against the glass patio door, resting his head on the glass. When we looked at him he straightened up, looking more tense than ever. "Someone called them."

That left me speechless, and Jesse looked like he was in the same boat. Dashiell's face was grim: he'd obviously come to the same conclusion. But Beatrice jerked her head toward Will in shock. "Who would do that?" she cried. "Who would bring them here?"

"Someone who put the missing women together," I surmised. "They came to the same conclusion you did—that it was a nova—and told the Luparii."

"Or," Will said tersely, "whoever changed the nova to begin with summoned the Luparii to come clean up his or her mess."

Every eye in the room turned to Will, and I was suddenly certain that he was right. "We need more information," Jesse said pragmatically. "How many of the Luparii would they send here?"

Will shrugged. "We don't know."

"They send one first," Beatrice said softly. We all turned to look at her. "That's how it was in Barcelona. First a scout. One wolf dies, a few days before the full moon. It puts the rest of the pack in a frenzy, makes them careless. Then suddenly there are a dozen Luparii in the city, to kill the others."

"But how do they *do* it?" Jesse asked, his voice strained. "How do the Luparii kill them?"

Beatrice shook her head, and Dashiell shot Jesse a glare. "We don't know," he said flatly. "They picked them off one or two at a time, over several days. The wounds themselves looked like maiming, but each corpse was missing the jaw."

"So we have to find the scout," Kirsten surmised. "If we stop him, maybe that will be the end of it."

"I don't think so," Will contended. "If we kill the scout, they're just going to send more. Lots more."

Jesse blinked at the frank discussion of killing someone, but didn't speak. Everyone sat in silence for a moment. We were stuck between a psycho werewolf and a terrifying hunter who was auditioning LA for the role of his family's new stomping ground. And we had no idea where to find either one of them.

Finally Jesse made a noise of frustration. "We need to know more about the Luparii," he concluded grimly. "We've got to get them out of the city." *My city*, was the unspoken claim.

"And we still have to find the nova," I pointed out. That one was on me, and I was determined not to get too sidetracked.

There was silence around the room. Dashiell usually had the world's greatest poker face, but right then he looked sort of politely murderous, like he was gearing up to go kill the hell out of someone. Which was fine with me, as long as it wasn't anyone I cared about. Beatrice's expression was lost in the past. Kirsten's was thoughtful, and a little ashamed, although I couldn't see how the Luparii could be her fault. Will was staring out the window with his hair sticking up again. He must have been pulling at it when I wasn't looking.

"I can put out feelers among my people," Kirsten volunteered finally. "As far as I know, none of them have crossed paths with the Luparii, but it's worth asking."

"Beatrice, Dashiell, is there anyone else you can ask for more information?" Jesse asked.

Dashiell gave him a hard look. "No one who is awake during the daytime," he said frostily.

Jesse winced and shot me an apologetic look. I gave him a tiny shrug. The news about the Luparii seemed to have downgraded Dashiell's reaction from homicidal to grouchy. I could live with grouchy.

"But after the sun sets, I will begin contacting people in France," Dashiell relented. "I will see if the Luparii will speak to me."

"Why?" I asked, before I could stop myself.

Dashiell's regal face soured, and Beatrice answered for him. "To ask them to retract the scout," she said softly.

I made a little *bleep* of surprise, but managed to stifle any further comment. I had sort of expected Dashiell to declare war on the Luparii scout for coming into his city, but I realized that that wouldn't really be his style. Beatrice and Dashiell wanted to be smart and look after LA more than they wanted revenge on the Luparii. Will flashed her a grateful look, but Beatrice's eyes were on Dashiell. She took his hand.

"Will, what about your wolves?" Jesse said quickly, obviously trying to change the subject before Dashiell remembered he was furious with us. "Do any of them know anyone—"

"Wait," Will said suddenly, turning to face us. His face flushed with sudden excitement. "I know who you can ask. We have someone who's run into the Luparii before."

"One of your wolves?" Kirsten asked, looking puzzled.

"No," Will answered. He met my eyes. "Scarlett's doctor."

The plan came together quickly after that. Hayne would take Dashiell and Beatrice down to their . . . well, if ever there was a good time for the word *lair*, this would be it. Dashiell would call me for an update after the sun set. Kirsten and Will were both extremely motivated to stop the Luparii, for different reasons, so they would go home and start calling their people on the off chance that someone had more information. Will also wanted to warn all of his wolves not to change—they weren't really supposed to anyway, but with the Luparii scout in town, it could be fatal.

And Jesse and I would go talk to the good doctor, who was more likely to talk to me than Will, who had an adversarial relationship with her, or Kirsten, who she didn't know. "After you talk to her, get back to finding the nova," Dashiell said firmly, looking at Jesse and me as though one of us might actually protest. Jesse had helped me climb out of the overstuffed chair, and we were standing in the doorway as the "meeting" was breaking up, waiting for Beatrice to finish having a quiet word with Kirsten. "Let *us* work on the Luparii," Dashiell finished.

"There's something else," Jesse said as he shrugged into his jacket. Dashiell arched an eyebrow at him. "You said if I took this case I would have your support and authority."

"I did," Dashiell said coolly.

"But that was when the only official crimes were two missing women." Jesse shook his head. "The case has expanded into the normal world, and now it's intersecting with an official LAPD homicide investigation. Working on this during my time off isn't going to cut it anymore. I need to be able to do this as a cop, not just as an investigator."

"What exactly are you suggesting?" Dashiell asked.

Jesse jutted out his chin, and I winced. *Don't say anything stupid*, I begged him silently. He wasn't looking at me, though. "I'm suggesting you use some of that pull with the department you're always bragging about and get me assigned to the murders, officially," he said levelly. "Maybe Homicide Special puts in a request for a little extra manpower, or maybe my station decides to loan me out as a floater to Hollenbeck. I don't care how you do it. But I need jurisdiction over the whole city, and I need to be able to use my badge when I ask questions."

He met Dashiell's eyes boldly, and we both looked at the vampire, waiting for him to react. Behind Dashiell, Beatrice heard the silence and broke off whatever she was saying. The concern on her face made me nervous. If I had to, I could just throw myself backward, get out of Dashiell's radius maybe, except my stupid knee would slow me down . . .

But after a moment a tiny smirk appeared on Dashiell's face. "Well done, Detective," he said approvingly. "You're beginning to understand how to work in and outside of the system at the same time." My shoulders slumped in relief, although Jesse kept a straight face. "Give me a moment," Dashiell continued. He took a couple of steps back toward the couch, pulling a cell phone from his shorts pocket.

While he was on the phone, Will came up to us, already holding his car keys. "Let me know if you two need anything else from me," he said tightly. "I need to go make calls."

He started to move past us, but I reached out and snagged his sleeve. "Will," I said softly, to show that there were no hard feelings about our argument, "be careful, okay? If the Luparii found Drew and Terrence, they may know who you are too."

The alpha werewolf went still. "I'll take that into account," he said quietly. I nodded, and he left.

A few minutes later Dashiell returned, looking a little smug. "It's done," he said to Jesse. "You're a—what was the word you used? A floater. You're being loaned to Homicide Special to do some footwork on some missing persons cases that may or may not be related to the homicides. Now go find the good doctor."

Chapter 29

Will had put up Dr. Noring in a mid sized chain hotel just off PCH, not far from Molly's house. I wondered why she wasn't staying in one of Will's guest rooms—I thought he had at least two—but decided not to ask. I fully intended to get to the bottom of their weird frenemy thing, but it could wait until the nova was caught and the Luparii scout's ass had been kicked back to France. Meanwhile, Noring had agreed to meet us in the coffee shop at her hotel in twenty minutes, which was about the amount of time it took to get there.

The coffee shop was the most blandly generic room I'd ever been in. Simple wooden tables surrounded by four cookie-cutter wooden chairs with maroon pleather stretched over half an inch of padding. Plain, industrial carpeting. No signs or decorations of any kind. There was a haggard-looking African American barista with short, tight dreadlocks and suspiciously red eyes behind the counter. He gave us a bleary nod when we walked in and went back to leaning his head on his arms. At least someone had had a fun New Year's Eve.

Jesse ordered us some coffee and we got settled at one of the tables. It had been varnished to a high gloss, and I suddenly longed to gouge out a chunk of the wood, just to add some character. Jesse gave me a suspicious glance like he knew exactly what I was thinking, and I just smiled sweetly.

Noring bustled in a moment later, wearing loose, comfortable-looking jersey pants and a red T-shirt with lace detailing around the collar. Her long black hair with its artful streaks of silver spilled down over her shoulders and chest. She looked irritable, which might have meant that she'd still been sleeping when I called. Then again, every time I'd seen her she'd looked irritable.

"Morning, Doctor N. Love your hair," I said cheerfully.

Noring ignored the remark and sat down primly in the only chair at the table that wasn't occupied by Jesse, me, or my leg. The barista slumped toward our table to deposit our coffees in front of Jesse and me, and Noring swiftly scooped my mug toward her own chest, claiming it for her own. Jesse raised his eyebrows at me but I decided to let the theft slide, mostly because I found her a teensy bit scary. "Dr. Stephanie Noring, this is Detective Jesse Cruz," I said formally. "Jesse, this is Dr. Noring."

Jesse held out his hand, but Noring ignored it. She eyed me up and down as she took a long sip of the coffee formerly known as mine. Then she snapped, "How is it that you look worse than before? What have they tangled you up in now?"

"Oh . . . the Luparii are in town," I said offhandedly. And Noring choked on her coffee, which was shamefully satisfying. Apparently invoking the Luparii was the equivalent of announcing a Beatles reunion tour—with all the original Beatles.

She coughed for a few moments, and Jesse shot me a glare that said, *You did that on purpose*. I shrugged at him. You have to take fun where you can get it, even if your idea of fun is getting middle-aged women to gag on hot drinks.

Eyes watering, Noring finally sputtered, "That's impossible; this is America." Fear was threaded into her voice, as if she were asking me to make it not true. Suddenly, I wasn't having fun.

"They're here," Jesse said quietly. "And we need to know what you know about them."

Noring looked from his face to mine and back. Then she abruptly stood, pushing her chair back with her knees. "No," she said, shaking her head. "We do not talk about them." She looked around furtively, like talking about the Luparii might make them manifest in front of her.

I was too lazy to haul myself back to the counter for a replacement coffee, so I reached over and grabbed Jesse's, taking a sip. He gave me a look. "We're sharing now," I informed him. Looking back at Noring, I asked, "Is it like a Beetlejuice-Freddy Krueger thing? You think if we talk about them they'll appear?"

"No. We believe talking about them will give them more power," Noring corrected stiffly. Tension had pervaded her entire body. "Names, stories, legends—these things have a degree of magic attached to them, especially when told with feeling and memory."

"I didn't know you were superstitious," I said mildly. I don't spend a lot of time worrying about how magic works, since it doesn't work at all near me. I've picked up a little bit of knowledge from working at witch-related crime scenes, and one thing I know is that witches don't create magic—it already exists in the world, all around and part of us. Witches simply channel it into doing things. And at least some part of the reason that witches can access magic is because they believe that they can, which is why there are people with the innate ability to manipulate magic who live their whole lives without even knowing it. If Noring believed that talking about the Luparii would give them more power, and her belief was tied to her magic in any way . . . it was theoretically possible.

"There's just one problem with that," I said out loud. I set down my coffee and pointed my thumbs at myself. "Null."

Noring's eyes widened. "I keep forgetting," she said slowly. I felt the subtle buzz of her magic flare up suddenly as she sort of . . . flexed it.

Jesse looked between us. "What's going on?" he demanded.

I answered him without looking away from the other woman. "I'm not sure she's even aware of it, but Dr. Noring is trying some kind of spell right now." The magic fizzled out against my radius. "See?" I asked her.

She nodded. "But that was a direct use of magic, you know . . . against you," she admitted, her cheeks coloring slightly. "A conversation about the wolf-killers would just be putting magic out in the universe."

"It doesn't work like that," I told her. "My radius extends in a sphere around me, not in a direct line between me and the nearest witch."

"How do you know?"

I was sipping my coffee, but Jesse understood and answered for me. "Because," he said, "the wolves can't smell her when they're in wolf form. We talked to a werewolf last fall who said she was a space in the smell."

I nodded my head. "Their enhanced sense of smell comes from magic, and magic can't interact when I'm around. As long as you keep your voice down, nothing you say can . . . go out into the universe," I said, feeling silly about invoking the universe in a conversation. Witches, man.

Noring held my eyes, and I knew she believed me. But she still leaned back in her chair, folding her arms across her chest. "I'm still not going to say a word," Noring said firmly. "Unless Scarlett promises to meet with an orthopedic surgeon."

I snorted. "I didn't know you cared, Doc."

She gave me a piercing look. "You don't get it, do you?" she snapped. "You've no idea what you even have here. Los Angeles isn't *like* other cities. Haven't you noticed the new members of Will's pack? The new vampires who've made the city their home in the last few years? The Los Angeles Old World has gained a reputation for peace, for balance, and it's growing." She pointed a perfectly manicured finger at my chest. "You are part of that,

Scarlett. Like it or not, you're important to this town. You have to take better care of yourself."

I stared at her. I didn't want to admit that I'd had no idea that the supernatural population had been getting bigger. Was that why I'd had more crime scenes lately? I suddenly felt very stupid. And very young.

Luckily Jesse jumped in for me. Unluckily he said, "I'll take her to the doctor. I promise."

She eyed him up and down. "Swear by your honor," she said finally. The word should have sounded silly—who talks about honor at a hotel coffee shop? —but she used it with such gravitas that it would be hard *not* to take her seriously.

Jesse flinched, and I knew he was thinking that his honor was tainted. Without thinking I reached out and covered his hand with mine. He gave me a startled, grateful look, and said to Noring, "I swear by my honor. I'll take Scarlett to a surgeon as soon as she can get an appointment."

"Excellent," Noring said with a smirk. She reached into her wallet and pulled out a business card from a doctor's office, the kind with the lines on the back for appointment times. "I've already scheduled you to see Dr. Shapiro next Tuesday. He's the best orthopedic surgeon on the West Coast. You're welcome."

I withdrew my hand. "Wait," I protested. "Jesse, I can't just—"

"We'll be there," Jesse said firmly, shooting me a glare. "Please, tell us about the Luparii."

Noring looked down at her empty coffee cup. "What do you want to know?" she asked, careful to keep her voice down.

"Let's start with how they manage to kill werewolves on a regular basis," I said promptly.

For the first time since I'd met her, Noring looked genuinely shaken. "They use a spell."

"I thought you couldn't use magic against itself," Jesse pointed out.

Noring shook her head. "Not a spell against the werewolves. They use a spell to create a creature that can fight werewolves."

Jesse and I exchanged a look. "What creature?" Jesse asked, his patience obviously thinning.

Noring drew in a breath and blew it out slowly through pursed lips. "It has a few names," she said hesitantly. "I've heard hell-hound, or demon dog." She turned her mug around and around in her hands. "But witches usually call it a bargest."

Chapter 30

"Isn't that like a fairy-tale thing?" Jesse said, somewhat less politely than before.

Noring waved a hand dismissively. "There are many stories about the bargest. *The Hound of the Baskervilles*, for example. But the bargest is real, although it's not at all natural." She asked, "Do you know how modern hunters kill wild wolves?"

I knew about as much about hunting as I did about water polo—nothing—so I shook my head, but Jesse answered grimly, "They use dogs."

Noring nodded. She glanced at the barista, who appeared to have nodded off on his stool with one hand propping up his face. She continued, "The Luparii used packs of dogs to hunt wolves for centuries. But when they tried to adopt the same plan to hunt werewolves, the wolves simply killed the dogs. They were too strong, too fast—even a single werewolf versus a whole pack of dogs. They tried crossbreeding different kinds of dogs next, even breeding the most vicious of them with wild wolves." She shuddered. "There are stories about some of their creations, which I try not to think about."

I winced. My mother had been a veterinary assistant, and she had spent more than one family dinner venting about recklessly negligent dog breeders. She'd firmly believed that anyone who breeds dogs should be required to spend a week in their dogs' conditions.

Noring drained the rest of her coffee. Jesse looked impatient, but Noring didn't seem in any hurry to continue the story. I prompted gently, "They crossbred dogs with wolves . . ."

The doctor hardened her face to keep any expression inside. "But none of it worked, so they incorporated their magic. The Luparii make things . . . twisted," she said distastefully. "Corrupt. They still breed the dogs with wolves, as big as possible, and they channel a tremendous amount of magical energy into one dog, usually a male. As a side effect, the spell turns him coal black, which is where the stories about the black demon dog originate. But the main purpose of the spell was to design a creature, something they could control, that was able to keep up with a werewolf physically."

"Genetic experimentation by way of magic," Jesse said thoughtfully. "It's interesting, in a diabolical super-villain kind of way."

Noring snorted. "The Luparii are not super-villains, I can promise you that. They're more like a cult of magically gifted thugs."

"Even so," I said helplessly. "We're up against evil dogs from hell."

"That's not entirely fair," Noring said, frowning. "Magic itself isn't good or evil. The bargest spell simply creates physical abilities that are then twisted into killing. The bargest is as fast and tireless as a werewolf, with tough skin that the wolves can't bite through, and they can heal as fast as werewolves. They live for a long time too, because the Luparii didn't want to put all that work into the creature for a ten-year life span. But its brain is still the brain of a dog. The Luparii are the ones who train it to kill."

I glanced at Jesse, who looked disgusted. "Like bully breeds," he said to me. To Noring he said, "We have degenerates here who breed pit bulls and rottweilers, and then pour pain and hate into them until they're basically a weapon. I've seen those dogs. The people who do that to them . . . they're monsters."

Noring nodded. "That was the Luparii's plan too," she said crisply. "They see werewolves as monsters and vermin. So they created their own monster to fight them. Killers who can hunt and smell magic. And it worked: a bargest can handle a werewolf without much difficulty. Two, even."

I thought I picked up a note of bitterness in her voice. "Will said you ran into them before," I said neutrally. "But you're obviously not a werewolf."

"I'm an oncologist," she retorted. Her chair pushed back suddenly as she stood up. Noring stalked a few feet away, out of my radius and toward the doorway where the coffee shop opened into the hotel lobby. She surveyed the lobby with her back to us. Jesse started to speak, but I touched his arm again, shaking my head. I glanced at the barista, but he was still half-asleep on his arm.

Finally Noring paced back to our table, sitting down with stiff limbs. "The Luparii work with death magic. Sacrifices," she hissed, her voice brittle with tension. "And the bargest spell requires a human."

I blinked. I've encountered witches who used sacrifices, but I'd only seen small birds—chickens and doves, mostly. Images from movies filled my mind. As if she could see them, Noring shook her head. "It's not as melodramatic as it sounds. Money has never been a problem for them, so they go into a hospital, find a terminal patient with lots of medical debt and a family to support, and they *buy* him."

"And you're an oncologist," I said, finally understanding. "They bought one of your patients?"

She nodded. "They tried to. That's when I asked around and found out about the Luparii. I was young and idealistic; I tried to intervene. This was twenty-five years ago, in Suffolk."

"Why?" Jesse asked. "I mean, you clearly have no love for the werewolves, and your patient would get lots of money."

She stared at him coldly. "You know nothing about my relationship with werewolves. And I believe in the soul. Death magic is like using the soul as *fuel*," she spat out. "It's sick."

"What happened?" I asked. "Did your patient go through with it?"

She turned away, as much as the wooden chair would allow. "I don't know. The Luparii weren't pleased with my interference. I came to the States to get away from them."

My fingers clenched into fists. Who *were* these clowns? Who had the power to scare Dashiell, Beatrice, and Dr. Noring out of Europe altogether?

"How do we kill it?" Jesse asked, trying to get us back on track. "The bargest, I mean."

"You don't," Noring said simply. "Their hides are too thick for bullets, and bigger weapons are too conspicuous for the Old World. Spells don't work on them, because they're already made from magic." She nodded at me. "Even you wouldn't be able to undo the spell, I believe. Bargests are permanently changed."

"Dammit," I complained. "How do bad guys keep finding these frickin' loopholes?"

Jesse ignored me. "Could you undo the spell?" he asked Noring. "I mean, if we captured it, could it be . . . I don't know, dissolved?"

She shook her head. "It doesn't work like that, not when there's a sacrifice involved. A trade has already been made: a human life in exchange for the magic to be placed in the creature. To undo it, you'd need a second human sacrifice and a full coven of witches, or a very powerful boundary witch—not to mention an ancient strain of mandrake root." Noring realized her voice had gotten louder and leaned forward to continue quietly, "Even then, I doubt anyone outside of the Luparii could pull it off. They haven't exactly shared the secrets of the bargest spell."

"Boundary witch?" Jesse asked, eyebrows raised.

"Witches whose particular skills are in death magics," Noring said shortly. "They are anathema even among other witches. I've never even met one, or at least a witch who would admit to being one."

I winced. The first dead body I'd ever destroyed, back when I was working with Olivia, had been that of a witch who had died playing with death magics. We wouldn't be undoing the bargest spell anytime soon.

We asked a few more questions after that, but we'd reached the limits of Noring's knowledge on the subject. Jesse asked if we could call her if we thought of something else, and Noring shrugged her assent. "I won't be here much longer, though," she warned. "My deal with Will was to stay until Scarlett was healed or she could be handed off to another doctor. And now you have an appointment."

"Ha!" I cried. "I knew it. You don't actually care about getting me better; you just want to go home."

Noring gave me a hard look, then fixed a glare on Jesse. "You. Take her home *right now*, make her rest for at least two hours, with ice for the knee and anti-inflammatories."

Whoops. I had maybe been a little too mouthy just then. Jesse gave me a sidelong glance, clearly uncomfortable. "We're in the middle of an investigation—"

The doctor snorted. "With the wolves, I know. The full moon's still two days away. A couple of hours aren't going to hurt. Look at her. She's going to fall over."

"Hey!" I protested, but Jesse was already assessing me like I was a used car he might buy. And it was true, I felt like shit. But in a way, focusing on the investigation kind of helped—at least it meant I wasn't sitting around dwelling on the pain. I made a face at him, and he gave me a tiny smile.

"She's right, a few hours won't hurt. We could both use the rest," he told me.

Noring added stiffly, "I probably won't see you again, Scarlett."

"But . . ." Dammit, I kind of liked having a physician on hand for when I inevitably fucked up and hurt myself. But it made sense—she'd been here almost two weeks, and she had to get back to her own life. I swallowed and started again. "I understand. Thank you for everything."

Noring sniffed. "Tell Carling to find someone else next time. This was my last favor." She stood to leave.

Before she could walk away, I said quickly, "What is it between you and Will, anyway? You act like you hate the guy, but you flew halfway across the continent to do his bidding."

Whoops. Noring glared death rays at me, and I realized I could probably have phrased that more tactfully. She said icily, "Ask Will."

"I did. Right before we came here," I replied. "He looked pointedly at his watch and suggested we should shake a leg."

"Or four," Jesse muttered under his breath. We high-fived.

Noring ignored us. "Maybe he thought it was none of your business."

"He trusted you enough to give you full access to my body while I was unconscious," I pointed out, more serious now. "Doesn't that kind of make it my business?"

Noring dug her key card out of her pocket and straightened her top, and I figured she wasn't going to answer. But she relented. "Will," she said severely, "trusts me because I was his doctor too." She spun on her heel and marched out of the coffee shop.

Jesse and I looked at each other with matching "what just happened" faces. "Did she just . . . say that Will used to have terminal cancer?" he asked incredulously.

I nodded and mused, "I guess I've never asked Will how he was changed. He probably decided to become a werewolf when

Noring couldn't cure him medically. Or maybe it was the other way around—Noring's a witch, so she could have arranged it for him."

"Why would that make her hate him, though?" Jesse said quizzically. "I mean, if she helped him become a werewolf, why would she be pissed at him?"

I shrugged. "Maybe it's a God complex thing, like she's mad that magic succeeded where she failed. Or maybe she wanted him to stay in Minnesota or something, and he left."

"Maybe . . . ," Jesse said dubiously. "Anyway, we need to figure out what to do about the Luparii and the nova wolf."

"Oh. I know exactly what to do," I announced. "I'm thinking maybe we should find them and stop them." I wiggled my eyebrows up and down. "You know. In their tracks."

He rolled his eyes. "If you say 'The hunter will become the hunted,' I'm gonna throw your cane out of the car window."

Jesse drove me back to Molly's, where he fetched an ice pack and a glass of water, helped me up to my room, and handed me the bottle of Vicodin. After I'd swallowed two of them, there was a moment of awkwardness while he arranged pillows under my knee, the two of us in close proximity. He smelled the way he always did, like Armani cologne and oranges. The oranges had always been a pleasant mystery, since I'd never seen him eat one. "Do you need anything else?" he asked softly, and maybe I was imagining things, but I felt like there was another question beneath it: *do you want me to stay?*

"I'm good," I said with cheer that fell flat. Sleeping together now would be a bad idea for a lot of reasons, even if it was just sleeping. I was sure of my romantic interest in Jesse, but not sure about pretty much everything else. And my knee hurt. It just wasn't the time or the place—especially considering the pills I had just taken.

"But maybe you could just crash on the couch for a couple of hours?" I added. *Didn't make sense for him to go all the way home, either*, I told myself.

He nodded. "If you need anything, just yell," he told me, but my eyes were starting to droop already. I mumbled something that even I didn't really understand, and fell asleep with the impression of him smiling on the way out of my room.

The next thing I knew, someone was gently but insistently squeezing my hand, over and over again. "Scarlett," Jesse said quietly, "Wake up. We need to go."

"Time's it?" I muttered, but Jesse understood.

"It's five o'clock. I just got a call back from the woman who's in charge of Humans for the Protection of Animals, Cassey Maximus."

I yawned, squinting at him. "Sounds like a fake name to me."

"Scarlett," he said patiently, "three members of her group went missing last night. Three women."

Chapter 31

Jesse used his phone to read up on the HPA while he waited for the e-mail that Cassey Maximus had promised to send. Humans for the Protection of Animals was the third-largest animal rights organization in the country, with chapters in most major cities. They weren't quite as militant as PETA, or as do-goody as the Humane Society, but what they lacked in positive media coverage, they made up for with political influence. HPA focused their time and funding on lobbying politicians directly, one animal-related cause at a time.

The leader of the LA branch, Cassey Maximus, was a former socialite who now spent her time designing purses and running her part of the HPA. To his surprise, though, Jesse had liked her when they spoke on the phone. She had seemed genuine, and also genuinely worried, promising to send him the roster of all the LA HPA members, as well as photos of the missing women.

The e-mail arrived while Scarlett was freshening up, so Jesse borrowed her computer to read it on a bigger screen. Cassey had created a simple Word document and pasted in information on each of the three missing women: Ruanna Martinez, Samantha Wheaton, and Lizzy Thompkins. She'd even included a separate photo of each one, likely cropped from photos taken during some sort of group event since none of the women were looking at the camera. Beneath each photo, Cassey had added each woman's contact information and a little description of the woman depicted.

Rue has three kids and loves horses. Sam has a new baby and can't stand the sight of blood. The last page in the document was the roster of the LA branch's members.

In a stroke of luck, the leader of PAW had e-mailed him back as well, and by the time Scarlett returned from the bathroom, he had printed off the rosters for both organizations.

"You wanna go talk to their families now?" Scarlett asked as they headed out of the house. "The missing women's?"

He considered it for a moment, then shook his head. "Not yet. If the nova wolf took those three women early last night, he may have already tried to change them. Which means he may be dumping bodies tonight."

"You wanna go back to *Will's*?" Scarlett said dubiously.

Jesse held up the printouts. "I want to kill two birds with one stone. We go back to Will's and go through the two rosters in the car. If we can find a name that's on both lists . . ."

"That might be the nova," she finished for him, newly excited.

An hour later, they were back in their spot across the street from Will's house, and Jesse's hopes were quickly deserting him. He squinted down at the list of PAW members. "The next name is Orlando Rajes, age twenty-two."

Scarlett rustled through the HPA roster, looking at the names in the dim glow from the van's reading light. She sighed heavily. "Yup, he's on here too."

Jesse swore, not for the first time. There were twenty-nine names on the PAW roster, each listed along with their DOB, but so far almost all of them had *also* been on the HPA roster. He'd been hoping to find just one or two matches, but instead there were almost twenty. There was no way they could chase down twenty names quickly, especially not before the nova attacked the three women he'd taken.

This stakeout was becoming more and more like a vigil.

"Jesse," Scarlett said patiently. "You with me?"

"What? Oh, yeah."

"Next?" She was actually trying to stay positive, which was definitely a sign that everything had gone to hell.

"Henry Remus," Jesse said in a monotone. "Age forty-four."

"Hang on," Scarlett said suddenly, staring straight ahead. Jesse peered out the windshield, both hoping and not hoping to see the nova. He wanted to catch the fucker, but he didn't want to see any more dead bodies. But there was nothing out there.

"What?" he asked Scarlett.

"Henry in his forties . . . Henry in his forties . . . I've heard that before," she said, snapping her fingers idly. "Do you have those notes I took from the interviews?"

Jesse reached into his jacket pocket and dug out the little notebook, passing it over to her. Scarlett flipped to the right page and stabbed it with a forefinger. "Here," she said. "When I was talking to Amanda Lewis. She said that Leah was dating a guy in his forties named Henry."

"It could be the same guy," Jesse said. "Is the guy in HPA too?"

Scarlett lifted the printout again, trying to get the right section of the paper into the light. "He's here!" she crowed, before looking over at him. "What now?"

"Now we find the guy."

First things first: Jesse took out his phone and googled Remus. The only things that popped up were a couple of PDFs, and when he downloaded the appropriate files he found Remus's name mentioned in a couple of newsletters from local public schools. Huh.

At his request, Scarlett called Leah Rhodes's roommate, Amanda Lewis, and asked for any further details on Leah's boyfriend. Jesse waited impatiently as Scarlett went "Uh-huh" a few times. Finally she hung up and turned to him. "She doesn't remember much else," Scarlett reported. "Except that he drives an old blue pickup truck, pretty small, and she thinks he still lives with his parents, because Leah almost never spent the night at his place."

Jesse checked the white pages on his phone and called a friend at the LAPD, ending up with an address and phone number for Ezekiel and Sharon Remus.

"You're smiling," Scarlett observed from the passenger seat. "Did we get him?"

"Maybe," Jesse said. "Don't get too excited, though. Let's see if the guy's even home. Then we can go over there and you can feel him out, so to speak."

He called the Remus house, where the phone was picked up by a nervous-sounding woman, maybe around his own mother's age. Without identifying himself, Jesse asked for Henry.

"Oh, he's not home, dear. Are you calling about his classroom presentations?" she asked.

"Yes, ma'am," Jesse responded. "My daughter goes to"—what was the name of that school?—"Roosevelt Elementary, and she's been raving about Henry's performance. I just wanted to thank him."

"Why, that is so nice!" the woman exclaimed, sounding relieved. "Unfortunately, Henry is camping right now. But he checks in with me every week, and I'll be sure and let him know you called."

"When are you expecting him back?" Jesse inquired, trying to sound polite.

The woman's voice changed again, picking up a stronger note of nervous energy. "Oh, we never quite know about Henry's comings and goings," she said, trying to sound cheerful. "But—"

"Jesse!" Scarlett yelped, and he looked up. She was pointing frantically at the windshield. "Look!"

He hung up the phone and peered into the darkness of Will's yard. There was a beat of stillness, and then he saw it: past Will's house, at the edge of the woods, some of the bushes were moving. Then a man emerged, staggering, with a weight on each of his shoulders. Whatever they were kept getting caught on tree branches, and as Jesse watched, the man had to repeatedly pause to tug them free.

Bodies. They were bodies.

"Shit," Jesse breathed. "That's why nobody ever saw him. He came through the woods." He reached for the door handle, but Scarlett grabbed his arm. "Hold on," she hissed. "You'll never catch him if he runs now. Let him get closer, and be ready. I'm gonna try something."

Jesse clenched his teeth, but he nodded, trusting her. Scarlett closed her eyes, brow furrowing. After a moment her expression smoothed out, and a look of calm replaced it. Jesse glanced back toward the trees. The nova was moving easily across the lawn now, free of the branches. They didn't have much time. Whatever Scarlett was going to do needed to happen *now*.

When the nova was halfway to the house, though, he suddenly collapsed under the weight of the bundles, and Jesse realized that Scarlett had expanded her radius. "Go now," she whispered without opening her eyes. Jesse threw open his door and bolted.

He was running as silently as he could, but the man clearly knew something was wrong. He frantically tried to get out from under the bodies he'd been carrying, which were pinning him to the lawn. The nova managed to push one of them off and was wiggling away from the second. Jesse was going to lose him. Hoping to distract the guy, he shouted, "Stop! LAPD!"

For a second the nova looked like every criminal Jesse had ever encountered—he jerked upright, a look of fear and horror plastered across his face. The guy wasn't much to look at, really—just a skinny, narrow-shouldered punk with bulging eyes, buzzed hair, and horizontal Slavic cheekbones. Then, with a burst of energy he finally wriggled free of the second body, stumbled toward his feet, and darted for the woods.

Jesse raced after him. He ran three times a week, and boxed and lifted weights on alternate days. As a human, this guy didn't look like he'd ever heard of exercise, and Jesse was gaining fast. The guy was almost to the trees, but Jesse was just twenty feet away—and then Scarlett's radius ran out.

The guy stumbled as he left it but regained his footing with unnatural grace, and Jesse knew he was about to lose him. Trying to throw him off, he screamed, "*Henry Remus!*"

The guy paused, just like Jesse had hoped, but only for a moment. He shot Jesse a toothy smirk, looking feral. Then he turned back toward the woods and vanished.

Jesse kept running, hit the trees, and immediately snagged on a branch that carved a long scratch across his left cheek. Realizing the branch could have hit his eye, he cursed in Spanish and froze, listening. He could hear movement ahead and to the left of him. Why hadn't he grabbed a flashlight?

Furious, Jesse knew he had to give up. He turned in a slow circle until he saw the lights from the house. Panting, he trudged back toward the bodies. A car door slammed, and he saw Scarlett hobbling toward him with her cane, a heavy-duty flashlight in her free hand.

"Why didn't you tell me you could extend it?" he yelled to her.

That brought her up short for a moment. Then she started moving forward again, and Jesse waited for her, still catching his breath from the sprint.

"It was . . . fuzzy, after the thing with Olivia," she said, when they were close enough to hear each other without shouting. "I wasn't sure if I could do it."

"You should have gotten out and walked toward us. I almost had him!" Jesse snarled, unable to stop himself.

"I couldn't concentrate on my radius and walk at the same time," she explained. "I'm sorry, Jesse."

"Give me the flashlight," he snapped. He knew it wasn't her fault, but he was shaking with adrenaline and rage. They had been so *close*. The guy had been right there.

Scarlett's eyes widened, but she obliged, handing over the light. Jesse pointed it at the bodies in front of him. Both women were obviously dead.

"Only two," she said quietly.

"Maybe he didn't have time to go back for the third," Jesse muttered.

The woman on his left was Hispanic, with a long tangle of hair, about twenty extra pounds around her hips, her big open eyes staring at nothing. He recognized her from the picture in the van: Ruanna Martinez. The woman on his right was Caucasian and slim, with a short brunette pixie haircut: Samantha Wheaton. Both of them were wearing tattered underclothing that was soaked in blood.

The nova had duct-taped both women's arms and legs—not as restraints, Jesse realized, but to keep the limbs from flopping around as he carried them. Jesse crouched with the flashlight, trying to see past the blood that stained and crusted both bodies. Ruanna Martinez had long scratches all over her body, but they weren't shallow, like Kathryn Wong's injuries. These were horrible, deep scores, each one more than a foot long, and they'd sliced her skin into long, thin flaps. Jesse's stomach turned, and he looked over to Samantha Wheaton's body. He squinted against the light, reluctant to touch her. "Oh, God," he whispered.

There were chunks missing from her. The nova had taken bites out of Samantha Wheaton, presumably while she was still alive.

"He's still experimenting," Scarlett said softly.

"You think?" Jesse snapped. He couldn't meet her eyes. His gaze was glued to the women he had failed not once, but twice.

First by not stopping the nova in time to save them, and second by not being able to catch the son of a bitch when he'd turned up to dump their bodies. Gritting his teeth, Jesse reached out and gently took Ruanna by the arm, shifting his weight so he could roll her over. There was a big number three scored into her back.

Scarlett started to bend down toward Samantha, but he waved her aside. "I got it." Samantha was light, and with her limbs taped together she flipped over easily. Jesse pointed the flashlight beam at her back, expecting to see a four.

It was a five.

Scarlett saw it too. "What does that mean?" she whispered.

Jesse shined the light back and forth between the two of them for a moment, then reached down to lift up the taped bundle of first one woman's legs, then the other, checking the degree of rigor mortis. Then he stood up. "I'm not an expert, but it looks like they were killed at the same time," Jesse said shortly.

"So?"

"So, the nova's getting impatient. He got sick of the one at a time thing and took three women at once, hoping one or more of them would change. And one of them did."

Scarlett nodded, understanding. "Number four."

"Lizzy Thompkins," he corrected. "She's a werewolf now. Or will be in two days, I guess." He looked at her over the bodies. "How ironclad is the timeline? Any chance she won't change for this moon?" They were closing in on Henry Remus, but he wasn't sure they could find the guy by the following night. If they had even a few more days . . .

But Scarlett shook her head. "The shift takes two days to complete, but it's different if there's a full moon in those two days. Easier for them, actually." She looked down at the women, and for a moment Jesse thought he saw sorrow on her face. But all she said was, "We have to clean this up."

Jesse looked at her, the just-cooled rage building pressure in his chest again. "That's what you have to say?" he demanded, not bothering to keep the fury out of his voice. "We have to *clean this up*? These were people!"

"Do you get this upset about every murder you work?" Scarlett said, ice in her voice. "I'm amazed you have enough energy left to get up in the morning."

"This is different. You *know* this is different," he spat.

"Don't snap at me, Jesse," she said, eyes narrowing. "I'm not the bad guy here."

"That's right, I forgot," Jesse said angrily. "You're the bad guy's cleaning lady."

Tears spilled down Scarlett's cheeks, but when she spoke her voice was steady. "I can't do my job if I let it—"

"Your *job*?" Jesse yelled. "Do you think I give a fuck about your job right now? Or my job, for that matter? Do you think I'm still in this for a *promotion*?"

Scarlett flinched. "You know why we do this. You know why people can't find out."

Jesse clenched his fists. He was working so hard to keep his voice below a scream. "Bullshit. We were so *close*. If we'd had the resources, we could have been faster, we could have warned these women. We could have prevented this."

Scarlett looked skeptical, and he felt a wave of irritation with her. She was keeping her eyes on him, and he suddenly wanted to grab her head and force her eyes downward, like a puppy that's had an accident. Instead he pointed at Samantha Wheaton. "She couldn't stand the sight of blood, Scarlett. How do you think the last day has gone for her?" Scarlett trembled, but still kept his gaze, so he pointed down at Ruanna Martinez. "And *she* has three kids at home, and no husband. Two boys and a girl who get to spend the rest of their lives without parents now." Scarlett stubbornly kept her eyes on his. He could hardly make out the green through her tears, but he kept going. "How's that working for *you*, Scarlett?"

Her whole body went rigid. "Get away from me," she whispered.

"Happy to," he said nastily. He stomped back toward the main road, leaving Scarlett standing over the bodies, alone.

Chapter 32

I kept it together for a while, I really did.

I called Will, told him he needed to get there right away. I was calm as I lied and said Jesse had run off in pursuit of the nova, while Will helped me dispose of the bodies, and while I faked a phone call from Jesse saying he'd lost the guy in the woods. If Will had had his werewolf hearing and scent, I would have been screwed, but if he suspected me of lying, he didn't say anything.

Then again, maybe he was too preoccupied by the fact that the nova had made a mate. As bad as it had already been, things were going to get worse for the pack. I asked if the nova was going to come after them the next night, but he said, no, Remus would want to build up his own pack first. Which was a nice way of saying that Remus was going to try to infect as many people as possible during the full moon. Unless we found him first.

I dropped Will back at his house, promised to call him in the morning with an update, and cried most of the way back to Molly's house.

By the time I got there, I felt like one of those ceramic figurines my mother had collected: fragile on the outside, hollow on the inside. I had run out of tears, thoughts, and ideas. I had nothing left but pain in my leg and ashes in my hair from Artie's furnace.

Molly's car wasn't in the driveway when I got home, which was okay by me. I wasn't in the mood for quality time. I shucked my dirty jacket and left it near the door so I'd remember to get it washed. I wanted nothing more than to collapse in my bed, but I was filthy and sore and needed a shower. Sitting on my butt, I dragged myself up the stairs, letting my cane bump along the stairs next to me. Since I was on my butt anyway, I just kept going on it, scooting my way into the bathroom. I pulled off my boots, slid my knee brace off very carefully, and wriggled out of my clothes, leaving all of it in a messy heap on the bathroom floor.

I showered, shampooing my hair several times, wrapped a towel around myself, and snagged my knee brace on the way out, leaving my clothes where they were and hobbling back to my bedroom. After putting on underwear, an enormous Chicago Bulls jersey from my father, and the knee brace, I stretched out across my bed. The pain in my knee roared even louder by then, so I carefully rolled sideways to the bottle of Vicodin on my bedside table. I swallowed two dry and flopped back onto my pillow, closing my eyes as I waited for them to kick in.

Just as I started to drift, though, I heard a small crash from downstairs.

I opened my eyes. "Molly?" I called, but there was no answer from below. "Molls?"

Silence. Then a soft creak, somewhere in the house.

Panic raced to life along my body, fighting the stupefying medication and urging me to take action. I tried to focus, to sit up and swing my legs over the side of the bed, but the pills were kicking in and that was suddenly too complicated. I realized with sickening fear that the vertigo had returned. I settled for rolling onto my stomach and sliding into a heap on the floor, on the opposite side of the bed from the door. The skin on my bare legs goose-pimpled where it touched the cool carpet. I peered over the side of the bed, staring at my open doorway. The hallway was dim, lit only by the light trickling up from the stairs to the right of my door. I could see Molly's bedroom door and a light switch, nothing else. I squinted my eyes, focusing hard. A dark shadow passed through the light, and I ducked my head below the top of my bed. There was a long, heavy moment of silence. I shivered with fear and cold, my head clearing despite the drugs.

I was being stalked. And my Taser was still in my coat pocket, downstairs.

When I couldn't stand it any longer, I slowly raised my head again. As soon as my eyes rose above the mattress, a wolf sprang at me from the hallway.

At least, that's what was supposed to happen. Before she made it through my door, however, the werewolf hit my radius and changed instantly into a snarling, tumbling naked woman. Momentum carried her through the doorway and a few steps into the room, where only the bed stood between me and her. Anastasia stood up and squared her shoulders, unaffected by her own nudity. Her short afro was matted to her head in places, and her black eyes were reddened and furious.

"You," she spat at me. "You worthless *cow*."

I felt silly all of a sudden, hiding behind a bed while a crazy naked lady calls me a cow. I mean, who talks like that? But then she took a step closer to me, and I saw her eyes. There was more than just fury in them now. They were mad with rage. Emphasis on the *mad*.

Ana wasn't home anymore.

My own eyes widened, and I was glad she couldn't smell my fear. "Hang on," I said very gently, holding my hands up. "Ana, look, about Lydia . . ."

She howled with rage, a wolf reaction but a human sound. *"Don't say her name!"* she screamed at me. And she lunged.

Social norms are funny. Anastasia was willing to break into my house, attack, and probably even kill me, but there's something about someone's unmade bed that you just instinctively avoid, because it's not polite. So instead of the shortest route to me, over the bed, she launched herself around it. By memory and instinct I threw myself over the bed, scrambling for the hallway.

I'd forgotten about my knee. I blamed the drugs.

Pills or no pills, searing pain drove through my leg as I landed on it, and I screamed. The pain helped me focus, though, and I managed to scoot backward on my butt. Ana had recovered quickly and was on my heels, diving at me as I made it to the doorway. She expected me to turn right, toward the stairs, so I dodged left instead, and her grasping arms hit the wall with a loud crack that could have been either her finger bones or the plaster of the old house. She bellowed with rage and pain, and in the dim light I could just see her clutching at her right hand. I continued my useless backward escape, keeping my eyes on the werewolf. The stairs were behind Anastasia, and there was nothing down at this end of the hall but the bathroom and the little laundry area.

With no other options, I dragged myself backward toward the bathroom, hoping I could lock myself in and scream for help. If I stayed right on the other side of the door, Ana wouldn't be able to change into a werewolf; she'd have to break it down as a human, and if her fingers were broken—

The half-assed plan turned out to be futile anyway, because the damned hallway was too long. I felt, rather than saw, when I scooted too far and Anastasia left my radius. Her howls of pain cut off abruptly, and I could see her backlit figure straighten up, flexing fingers as they healed, bones knitting together almost instantaneously. I froze with indecision: move forward toward Ana and keep her wounded, try to extend my radius again, or race for the bathroom door as best I could?

I went for the bathroom. There were still at least five feet between me and the doorway, and I felt like the tendons and ligaments holding the parts of my body together were dissolving. I scrambled hopelessly for the door, dragging my leg behind me, even as Anastasia's silhouette took a long, deliberate step in my direction. Stalking.

She tackled me just as I reached the threshold of the bathroom. There was no time to even drag myself in before she was on top of me, her fingers clawing for my throat, her legs smashing down on my bad knee. I cried out with pain, but she cut off my air, hands around my throat. The tackle had pivoted me onto my back in the doorway, and my right arm flailed out, as I tried to punch her in the eye, the nose. But her reach was longer than mine and she dodged easily. I was panicking, every cell in my body screaming at me as I reached out, fingers scrabbling on the bathroom floor for *anything* that could help me—and they brushed against soft leather. A boot.

Terrible hope erupted in my brain. *Please be the right one*, I begged silently. A fifty-fifty chance. Ana pressed down harder, trying to crush my throat as she strangled me. Haze started to darken my vision as I laboriously worked my fingers around to the opening of the boot . . .

I pulled out the knife and thrust it between her ribs in one smooth movement, like I'd practiced it every day of my life.

I gasped as her fingers finally loosened and sweet, glorious air rushed into my lungs. And then I let out a pathetic, wheezing scream, because blood was *everywhere*. On television, people never really bleed until you pull the knife out. But I had stabbed Anastasia in the heart, and her blood spurted immediately, pouring down onto my stomach, drenching my arms, my clothes, and finally soaking into the hallway carpet beneath us. It was so hot that it seemed like its own living thing, like her life was deserting her for me, and for the first time I understood what the word *lifeblood* truly meant. I managed to tilt my body enough to get her mostly off me, but after that the last remnants of my strength disappeared, and my head slapped down against the linoleum of the bathroom like it had been pushed there. For the first time since my fingers had touched boot leather, I looked at her face.

It was slack and staring, no traces of surprise or hurt or pain left. She was dead.

I closed my eyes and welcomed the darkness.

Chapter 33

When I was nine, there was a whole week in the summer where my mother just stayed in bed.

My father, a history teacher who taught driver's ed during the summer, was the one who called my mom's boss at the veterinary clinic and said that she was sick. She didn't sound sick when I heard the two of them talking in their room, so I kept trying to get to her, to show her my crayon drawings or beg her to play Crazy Eights. My father was usually the pushover of the two, but he kept intercepting me at the bedroom door. First he tried to calmly redirect me toward the backyard or my room, but I was stubborn and prone to running headfirst toward anything I was supposed to leave alone. Finally he came right out and ordered me not to bother Mom unless there was a fire. I momentarily considered starting a small controlled fire, but even I wasn't willing to go that far. Plus they'd hidden the matches.

By the third day I was sick of all of it: being alone, not understanding. After Dad had left for work, I stomped up the stairs and to my mom's door, opening it just a bit before bumping it all the way open with my hip. "Momma," I announced, with as much righteousness as my nine-year-old self could muster, "you have to get up now."

She didn't move, so I sighed dramatically, like she did when I didn't want to get out of bed to go to school. There was still no response, so I marched across the room and circled around the bed. There, I saw that she looked . . . like a ghost. Her face was pale and wrinkly, and her eyes were rimmed in red like she'd opened them underwater in the city pool. When she saw me, the line of her mouth trembled and she flipped back the corner of the sheet as an invitation. Temporarily shocked into compliance, I climbed into the bed and snuggled my back against her belly as she wrapped her arms around me. "I don't get it," I complained after a moment.

"Scarbo," she sighed into my hair, creating a circle of warmth on the back of my head. "I hope you never ever do."

Years later, I would learn that our long-estranged grandmother had died that week, and my mother had been torn up with grief and guilt and regret. And it was years after that, when I lay on the floor in Molly's hallway, staring at Anastasia's corpse, that I could finally understand why she had stayed in bed. Unmoving.

I'd seen so much death. More in the last week alone than anyone should see in a lifetime. Ana wasn't even the first person I'd killed, but while I hadn't *enjoyed* killing Olivia, I hadn't felt one moment of remorse about pulling the trigger. Olivia had been truly evil.

Ana, though . . . Ana was never evil. She was just lost. And I'd killed her for it.

The first thing I heard was the sound of footsteps on the stairs. My eyes opened, but a murky haze had settled over me like a lead apron, pressing me into the floor. I was curled on my side, still drenched in blood, and now staring at Ana's forehead. Her eyes were still open, but I had stopped looking at them. The haze encouraged me to keep my eyes higher, to just focus on the smooth brown oval of her forehead and keep it in my sight line. And I listened. Because the haze was my friend.

There was some more noise, but I was untouched. I ignored it with easy detachment, letting the haze keep me pinned and deaf. Then there was nothing else for a long time, and I ignored that too.

Then there were more footsteps, and more noise. To my irritation, some of it was filtering through the haze.

"Holy *shit*. Is she . . ."

"Dead? No. I thought so too, but she's breathing, and I don't think any of that blood is hers. She's in shock, I think, but then there's the body. You're her assistant, right? You can take care of the body?"

"I . . . I mean, yeah, but I'd like to stay with Scarlett."

"I'll stay with her."

"But *in the room*, right?"

"Yeah. I have to . . . eat. Tonight. But I can wait until you get back from wherever."

"Okay."

Ana's forehead disappeared suddenly, dragged out of my view. I could feel a vampire in my radius, but now it was quiet again, so I didn't care. I preferred the quiet. I unfocused my brain, staying curled under the haze. Some more time passed, and then I grew annoyed because there were more fucking footsteps.

"Scarlett? Scarlett!"

"Oh, yeah, saying her name. Why didn't I think of that?"

"Not helping, Molly."

A pause. Then—"You're right. Sorry."

Suddenly, there was warm breath on the back of my neck, and I felt hands underneath me, a little awkward, but so careful. Eli picked me up very gently, cuddling me into his chest like you'd hold a small child or a broken doll. His T-shirt was soft and smelled like ocean air and hamburger grease. The blood had dried tackily on my father's jersey, and crusts of it broke apart in protest as we moved. I didn't care, personally. It made no difference to me where I *was*.

Then warm liquid exploded against my face, and for just a moment I thought it was more blood, and I almost screamed. But no, he had carried me into the big shower/tub stall in Molly's bathroom. The shock began to wash away, down the drain with the tacky blood. Eli put my legs down and helped me stand, balancing me against his chest so I could keep most of my weight off my bad leg. I sputtered in the water, gasping for air with panicked breaths, my fingers knotting into his shirt. He made comforting shushing sounds. "You're okay," he murmured over the sound of the spray. "You're going to be okay."

My haze had washed away too, and I screamed, a raw howl that may have started out as a word but I couldn't tell you which one. "I can't, I can't," I sobbed into Eli's chest, smearing tears into his shirt. "It's all over me, I *can't*."

"I've gotta . . . I'm going to go get something to eat," said Molly, from the doorway. Her voice was shaking, but I didn't think it was from the blood. It was from the sight of me.

Eli didn't bother even looking at her as she left. He shushed me again, a sound of comfort, and gently pulled my bloody shirt over my head, then bent to pull my underwear down. The blood had soaked through everything, and I yelped when I saw how it had stained my skin underneath. Eli picked up a bar of soap, my plain everyday Dove bar, and helped me wash it off. Naked, crying, I went up on tiptoes to wrap my arms around his neck so I could bury my face in his neck. "I can't, I can't . . ."

"Scarlett," he whispered in my ear, smoothing my hair. "Come back, come back to me."

We stood like that for a long time, with him murmuring my name. Eventually, he planted gentle kisses on the rim of my ear, distracting me. When he reached my earlobe he kissed his way down my neck, my skin calling for my attention wherever he touched it. Slowly, giving me every chance to pull away, he slid his hands under my butt so my legs could wrap around his waist, which they did before I'd had a chance to even consider doing it. He kept one warm hand cupped gently under my swollen knee, making sure it didn't dangle. My hands began pulling up his shirt.

This was how it always was with Eli, natural and explosive at the same time. There was such comfort in my body's reaction to his, something so familiar, so safe. His mouth found mine, and I was home.

Chapter 34

I opened my eyes and registered *pain*. The pills had worn off, and my leg ached terribly. My back hurt where it had hit the floor when Ana tackled me, and my neck hurt where she had tried to strangle me. It all hurt, and reminded me that I was getting my ass kicked, just like Noring had said.

But that wasn't what had woken me. There had been a sound. What had it been?

Knocking.

Someone pounded on the door again, and I sat up. I was naked, and in a tangle of slightly damp sheets on my bed. There was enough light filtering through the window for me to make out a Post-it note on the pillow next to me. It said simply, *You have no breakfast foods. Back soon with Coffee Bean. -E.*

Eli.

Anastasia.

I remembered all of it. And as someone knocked on the door for a third time, I pushed it all away.

Numbly, I grabbed a robe off the floor and my cane. Tying the robe, I limped to the bedroom doorway and yelled down the stairs. "Who is it?"

"It's Lydia."

She didn't give a last name, but I didn't need one. The only Lydia I knew of was Anastasia's girlfriend, the woman who Caroline had changed. We hadn't officially met, although I'd seen her after the attack while she'd been unconscious.

When I didn't respond right away, she knocked sharply on the door again. "Open up, Miss Bernard. We need to talk."

I let my head fall forward with a *thunk* against the door frame, which was unhelpful on so many levels. Lydia was *here*? Was she looking for Anastasia? Oh, God—I glanced down the hall, expecting to see the red pool of Anastasia's blood, but instead I saw that the floor on either side of the bathroom floor had been ripped up. Eli must have gotten the carpet knife from my duffel and cut out a big piece of carpet and a smaller piece of linoleum. I stepped closer. There was still a pinkish stain on the floor underneath, but it looked damp. I sniffed the air.

Bleach. I'd trained him well.

"Miss Bernard!" Lydia yelled again, through the door. "I know you're in there. If you don't open this door, I'm going to come through it." There was no anger in her voice, just determination.

"One second," I called down. "I need to get dressed, and I'm injured. I'll be right there."

There was a brief silence, and then another shout from the other side of the front door. "Three minutes."

I had to get her away from the house before Eli returned. On autopilot, I yanked open the drawer where I kept my running clothes and pulled out baggy sweatpants, a T-shirt, and a running jacket with a collar. I dressed as quickly as my knee brace would allow, zipping the running jacket all the way up. I checked the mirror. The jacket hid the bruises that Anastasia had left on my neck. I rushed out to bump down the steps on my butt, the fastest way to get down.

How much did Lydia know? What would happen if she found out that I'd killed Ana? Did she already know? How could she already know? *Stop, Scarlett,* I told myself. The important thing was to get Lydia away from the house before Eli got back. If she found out that he wasn't a werewolf anymore, my whole life would implode.

Before I opened the door I grabbed my dirty coat o' nine pockets off the floor so I could transfer my wallet and keys to the pockets of my sweatpants. After a moment of hesitation, I put the Taser in my jacket pocket too. Just in case. I felt terrible about Ana, but not enough to let Lydia kill me, if it came down to it.

I swung the front door open. Lydia, who had been surveying the street, turned her head to eyeball me. She was a petite Asian woman with the kind of enviably glossy hair that women are always flipping around in shampoo ads. I knew from when I'd seen her before that she had a climbing vine tattooed on one arm, but today it was hidden by a leather bomber jacket that she wore over tight jeans and a ribbed tank. You could see her lacy black bra pretty clearly through her shirt. Lydia's eyes were outlined in thick rings of black kohl, which would have looked trashy on me. On her, they perfectly complimented the whole "exotic badass" look.

I had an instant to take all of that in before Lydia's eyes widened, and although she was motionless, she seemed to lose her balance suddenly, putting a hand out to the door frame to steady herself as she bent almost double. "Oh my God," she breathed. "Oh . . . you . . . wow."

"Sorry . . . ," I said uncertainly. I had been expecting her to . . . I don't know, slap me across the face the second I opened the door. But I'd forgotten that Lydia was a *new* werewolf. "It has kind of a strong effect the first time. Are you okay?" I saw something clear dripping onto the porch underneath her, and for a stupid moment I thought the overcast gray skies had yielded some rain. But when Lydia lifted her head, I saw her wet eyes. Her lips trembled like she was struggling to speak.

"There's a diner a couple of doors down," I offered, desperate to get away from Molly's house. "We could talk there." She nodded, and I stumped down the porch steps to the sidewalk, taking off at as brisk a pace as I could manage. Which wasn't very brisk at all.

I was discovering that you could learn a lot about people by how they walked when you couldn't walk very well. Lydia was fairly patient about it, taking small, slow steps to accommodate my speed. Or maybe she was still off balance because of my radius.

"This is the place?" she asked, as we rounded a small apartment building and the diner came into view. It was the first time she'd spoken since we'd left Molly's house. I nodded. It was just a greasy spoon, with lots of emphasis on the "greasy." I generally only stopped in when I was hungover or hiding from Molly, who would never frequent a place that allowed homeless people to sit at the counter for the cost of a cup of coffee.

A little bell chimed as Lydia opened the front door. We didn't talk to each other as we passed the *Seat Yourself* sign and headed to one of the booths against the far wall, nor as a depressingly indifferent waitress took our orders for coffee. I don't know about Lydia, but as I looked around, I found the atmosphere comforting. It was so steeped in the tiny rituals of humanity: fixing your coffee, checking your teeth in a compact, signing credit card receipts. If we had to have this very uncivilized conversation, I was grateful we could have it somewhere so civilized. Well, relatively speaking.

"Ana didn't come home last night," she began abruptly. I didn't speak, but Lydia didn't seem to be expecting me to. She paused for a moment, expressions flickering across her face like changing TV channels. "We heard about Terry and Drew yesterday. They were our friends. Last night, I . . ." Lydia broke off, shaking her head. She tried to speak again, but choked on the words.

I studied her. I don't know how I knew, but somehow I did. "You tried to end your life," I whispered.

Lydia cringed, a werewolf gesture, and I knew I was right. We sat there for a few minutes without speaking. I didn't want to push her to talk about it—and every minute we were away from Molly's house gave Eli more time to get away too.

Finally she cleared her throat and met my eyes again. "I don't have any illusions about Ana. I know she can be too intense. And, you know"—she gave me a tiny smile—"dogged."

"I think she's mostly just been trying to help you," I said carefully. Here I was again, in a conversation where I couldn't use the past tense for a dead person. Only this one was one that I'd killed personally.

Lydia flinched. "She's been so worried. She's been doing things . . ." She shook her head. "Things I never would have thought she'd do."

"Like changing in between moons?" I said gently, on a hunch.

Before Lydia could respond, the waitress came back with a pot of coffee and filled our mugs.

Lydia took a long sip of hers before meeting my eyes defiantly. "I figured you knew about that. She thought it would help me if we went up to Kings Canyon, away from the pack." She shook her head and continued, voice quiet, "Something changed, though, and she's been scheming with Terry ever since, giving me these looks like I might suddenly sprout fur at any moment . . . But that's not the point. Last night, she said she was going to follow you. Get you to give her the cure."

She paused, as if waiting for my reaction, but I stayed silent. My dad used to say that it was a lot harder to get in trouble if you kept quiet. "Ana and I have been together seven years, did you know that?" Lydia added abruptly, her expression shifting around again. I shook my head. "The whole time, I had no idea what she was. Seven fucking years." She set her coffee cup down hard and leaned forward. "But now I know. And I know what you do for them now, your job. And my thinking is that Ana came after you last night and you killed her."

"I . . ." I swallowed, at a complete loss for words.

Lydia watched me steadily for a moment, and then leaned back with disappointed satisfaction on her face. "That's what I thought," she said, in the same quiet, eerily calm voice. "I'm not going to ask you where she is, or whether or not she's coming home. But there's something I do want to ask you."

I nodded, trying to keep myself together. I kept seeing Anastasia's blood pouring down, the way it had felt splashing hot on my stomach.

"Where is Eli?" Lydia asked me.

That wasn't what I'd been expecting. I didn't answer. Couldn't. Instead, I took a long sip of my coffee, which is the lamest way to stall, but I had no idea what to say. A big part of me wanted to just come clean, consequences be damned. This woman deserved to know what had happened to her girlfriend. She deserved the truth. But if I gave it to her, would I be making things better, or worse? I had thought changing Eli would make things better, and I'd been so wrong . . .

Sensing I wasn't going to respond, Lydia added, "Because here's the thing. If Eli wasn't cured, if Ana really was just losing her mind this whole time, then that's really sad, but I kind of get it. A crazy werewolf, running around stirring up trouble . . . I hate it, and I miss her, but I understand too. Now more than ever."

She leaned forward, eyes piercing me. "*But if Anastasia was right*, and you-all killed her just to keep things convenient for some goddamned asset, then may God have mercy on your souls."

I blinked, and a chill went through me as I realized that I was the asset. I sat frozen in my seat, Lydia staring at me, as waitresses and busboys and customers bustled around us, laughing and yelling and complaining to each other. The sun had drifted out from behind the clouds at some point, and a beam of sunshine had traveled through the blinds on the big picture window next to us, striping the skin on my wrist. I suppressed a weird urge to recoil from it.

Finally I said the only honest thing I could think of. "I don't know where Eli is."

Lydia nodded again, the same weird twitchy expressions moving across her face. She dug in her pocket for a moment, and by the time it occurred to me to be afraid of a weapon she had produced a $5 bill. "Then I'll make it really easy for you. The pack is gathering tomorrow night for the full moon. If Eli's there before the moon sets, we'll make plans for a memorial for Anastasia." She stood up, keeping her voice low. "But if he's not there, or not one of us, then I'll get whoever will join me and I will bring fucking war down on all of you." Her eyes closed and she swayed as if in pain. "And we'll lose," she whispered. "But I'll take you with me."

Lydia opened her eyes and tossed the bill on the table, while I sat there with my mouth open. "Coffee's on me," she added, and walked out the door.

Chapter 35

When I got back to Molly's, I checked out the front window to make sure Lydia had really driven away. Then I took a few steps toward the stairs and yelled, "Eli? Are you here?" Listened. Nothing. I hadn't seen his truck out front, but he could have parked on a side street, or in the garage where I kept my van. I sighed. I was going to have to stump all the way up the stairs to make sure, wasn't I? Great.

Then there was a sudden knock on the door right behind me, and I jumped, heart suddenly ping-ponging around my rib cage. I hobbled back to the window and peeked through the curtain before opening the front door.

"Hey," Jesse said. His face was expressionless. "We need to go talk to Henry Remus's parents."

I blinked at him. A lot had happened in the few hours since we'd spoken, but not enough for me to forget how hard he'd come down on me. "That's it?" I said, my voice hard. "No 'I'm sorry, Scarlett?' 'I shouldn't have yelled at you, Scarlett?' 'My sincerest apologies for being a dickweed, Scarlett?'"

Jesse shifted his weight from one foot to the other. "Last night wasn't your fault," he began. "I was angry about the nova getting away, and it was wrong to take it out on you."

There was a telltale little catch in his voice. "But?"

"But . . ." He paused, choosing his words. "I'm not sorry that I got upset. That seeing those women affected me. I'm not sorry that it bothers me when it *doesn't* bother you."

Images bombarded my thoughts: Leah. Kate. Ruanna and Sam. Anastasia.

I sagged against the door. Sometimes I think pushing those thoughts away is my one real superpower. "You really think that seeing those dead women didn't affect me?" I whispered.

Jesse stared at me, unrelenting. "Did it?"

I gritted my teeth. What did he want me to do, put on a play for him? I was too tired and too strung out to continue this fight. I glanced down at my sweats. "If we're gonna interview the parents, I should change," I said tightly. "You can wait out here."

I swung the door closed.

It was a very tense ride to the Remuses' apartment. I had decided to take the "if you can't say anything nice" approach, and Jesse probably had too, because neither of us spoke the whole way there. The only non traffic sound was the voice in Jesse's phone's GPS, telling him when to change directions. I sat and played with the dark green scarf that I was wearing to hide the bruises on my neck.

The Remuses lived in Temple City, one of a small cluster of towns just outside the border of the city of Los Angeles. I forget sometimes how big Los Angeles County really is. I had lived there for more than five years, and it seemed like I was always running into huge swaths of the area that I'd never seen before. Temple City was fairly nondescript in a Southern California kind of way: palm trees, decent houses on tiny lots, signs everywhere in a multitude of languages. I saw a lot of Asian women chattering in clusters outside store windows, often with a small child tugging at one of their hands.

The Remuses lived right on the border of the North San Gabriel area, in a big stucco hive of a building with cactuses (cacti?) instead of flowers planted along the walkways. We went into the lobby only to discover that the Remus apartment was garden-level, so Jesse decided we should find the exterior door rather than warn them that we were coming. I may have done some grumbling as I hobbled after him around the side of the building, but then I'd never promised anyone I would be gracious about it.

After a couple of false starts, and one of us threatening to smack the other with her cane if there was any more walking, Jesse and I found the right door. He held up his fist to knock, and I reached out without thinking and grabbed his wrist. He gave me a questioning look.

"Let me feel first," I whispered, and closed my eyes. When a null spends as much time as I do around the Old World, the supernatural can start to feel like background noise in the way regular Los Angeles residents can stop noticing traffic, or creepy people on the public transportation. I would feel really stupid if I got distracted and didn't notice that we were walking right into the nova. But I didn't feel anything. I focused on the edges of my radius and pushed them outward again, but still didn't pick up anything nonhuman. I opened my eyes and nodded at Jesse, who drummed his knuckles on the door. Nothing happened for a moment, but we could hear the sound of the television blaring through the door, so Jesse knocked again, harder.

The door was jerked open by an annoyed-looking man in his sixties. He was very tall, with deep vertical creases in each cheek that gave the impression of gauntness, although he had a pretty average build. "Ezekiel Remus?" Jesse asked, authority hardening his voice. He held up his badge. "I'm Detective Jesse Cruz. This is a civilian consultant, Scarlett Bernard." Now that Jesse was investigating for the department semi-officially, I could no longer pretend to be Laverne Halliday. Which was fine with me. "May we have a few minutes of your time? It's about your son," Jesse continued.

The tinny cheers of a football game jumped in to fill the silence Jesse's words left behind. Ezekiel Remus's face didn't change as he absorbed who we were, but his rigid shoulders slumped a little bit. For a second, I thought he was going to slam the door in our faces, but instead he abruptly swung it open. "Well, come in, then," he muttered, like a pouting kid. "I guess I'll turn that down."

The door opened straight into a small living room decorated in Martha Stewart for Kmart. There was an afghan-covered yellow couch along one wall and a blue velvet easy chair sitting adjacent to it, both facing a modest flat-screen television mounted on the wall. The chair was still rocking a little from when Ezekiel Remus had stood up to answer the door. There were three beer bottles on an IKEA-style side table between the couch and chair, one still mostly full.

"Sharon!" he yelled. He picked up a black remote from the arm of his chair and switched the TV off, cutting off the announcer's voice. "You call me Zeke or Mr. Remus." he said gruffly. He pointed toward the couch. "Sit."

I glanced at Jesse, who stayed on his feet. I was beginning to pick up on the psychology of Jesse's interviews, and I was guessing that he didn't want Remus to feel like he was in charge. I played along, although I *really* wanted to sit down. I tried not to look longingly at the couch.

A woman who was also in her sixties came through the open doorway. Sharon Remus, presumably, was a thickset, unadorned woman with sensible short hair the color of cement blocks. She wore plain, unflattering jeans and an equally plain and unflattering blue button-down that did nothing for her sallow complexion. Her eyes, unlike the rest of her, were stunning: big and Elizabeth Taylor-violet, with a thick fringe of black eyelashes that couldn't have been anything but natural. On a pretty or even pleasant face, the eyes would have made Sharon Remus a knockout. Instead, they seemed jarringly out of place.

She blinked those big eyes at us in combined terror and relief, like she'd been expecting the police to knock on her door for a long time now. "This is my wife, Sharon," Zeke said, nodding at her. "I already forgot your names."

"Detective Jesse Cruz," Jesse said again, reaching out to shake hands with both of them. "And this is Scarlett Bernard; she's a civilian consultant." I shook their hands too. Sharon's was plump and a little damp, like she'd just dried her hands on a towel that wasn't dry to begin with. Zeke Remus's hand was big and rough, and he squeezed just a little too hard. He eyed my leg and cane as though he was dying to ask me what had happened, but had thought better of it.

"Please, sit down," Sharon said nervously, and this time Jesse moved toward the couch. I followed gratefully. "Let me just grab a chair from the kitchen. Do you all want coffee or some lemonade . . ." she trailed off, unsure of the social protocol of a police visit.

"They're fine, Sharon," Zeke said dismissively. He reminded me of an old-fashioned country preacher, although I had no idea if the family had any connection to religion. There was just something about the commanding, self-possessed way he stood, and the way Sharon Remus kept glancing at him with nervous deference. She scurried toward the kitchen, coming back with a plain straight-backed wooden chair.

"What do you consult on?" Sharon asked me as she took her seat.

I opened my mouth, though I'm not sure what I would have said, but Jesse jumped in and saved me. "Missing persons cases," he said immediately. "Ms. Bernard is a coordinator with that department."

Sharon nodded, looking confused. Zeke grunted. "Let's get this over with," he said stiffly. He looked at me, then at Jesse. "I have three sons. But I'm guessing you're here about Hank."

"Henry," Sharon added, in case we were confused.

"Yes, sir," I answered Zeke. Unlike Jesse, I'm allowed to call members of the public anything I want—but he was just the kind of guy you called "sir."

"He's not missing," Sharon said hurriedly. "He lives here with us . . . but he camps a lot."

"That's not why we want to speak with him," Jesse said to her. "We think he may know something about some other disappearances."

"Who disappeared?" Zeke broke in.

"Five women in LA have gone missing in the last two weeks," Jesse said evenly. "They were all involved in environmental causes, just like Henry."

He didn't come out and say that he suspected Henry of murdering them, but the implication lay thick and obvious on the table between us. I expected Zeke, at least, to raise his voice and demand that Jesse apologize. He looked like the kind of guy who demanded a lot of apologies. But instead, Zeke and Sharon Remus exchanged a complicated look.

"Hank—Henry, I mean, he prefers Henry—wouldn't hurt a fly," she said slowly, as if she *really* wanted it to be true.

"I understand, but it's important that we ask him some questions," Jesse responded. "When was the last time he was here?"

Zeke looked pointedly at his wife, and she scanned the ceiling, considering the question. "Maybe three weeks ago? He was going up to the Sequoias," she added. "He has a little pickup truck that he took up there."

The Sequoias. Why was that chiming in my brain?

"Raided the fridge first," Zeke grumbled. He'd picked up the black remote control and was fidgeting with it.

"Have you heard from him since then?" Jesse asked.

Sharon Remus nodded eagerly. "Oh, sure. We have a system, you know. Henry calls or texts every Sunday to let me know he's okay, when he's traveling. He texted me this past Sunday, said everything was fine." Understanding dawned on her face, and she said to Jesse, "Hey! You were the one who called me last night!"

"Yes, ma'am," Jesse said. Unapologetic.

Sharon looked disappointed. "I thought—I thought some parent really did like his show. He goes around to schools in the area, you know, and gives little presentations to the kids about preserving their world and all that." Without looking down she began worrying at a cuticle. "He does it on a volunteer basis."

Zeke snorted. "They would never pay him for it, is what she means. The schools tolerate the boy because he's free and he brings his own photos." Jesse and I exchanged a quick look. "The boy" was forty-four. "The other two're straightened out," Zeke continued, "but there's something off about Hank. Always was." Sharon shot him a despairing look. To his wife, Zeke added irritably, "You know I'm right, Sharon."

"We tried everything," Sharon said to us, desperation in her voice. "Private school, tutors. I even took him to a therapist in Van Nuys. He means well, and he'd never hurt anyone, honest. He just . . . prefers the company of wildlife to the company of people." One of her cuticles ripped a small line of blood, and she frowned and stuck it in her mouth.

Jesse glanced at me. "Mrs. Remus," I said gently. "Do you have a family photo?"

Her face lit up. "Oh, yes." She jumped up and grabbed a framed photograph off an end table. It was the only picture in the room. "These are my boys," she said proudly.

The photo was a few years old, judging by the depth of the wrinkles on Zeke Remus's cheeks. Zeke and Sharon were posed in the center, sitting on wooden stools, while three younger men stood in a line behind them. "That's Phillip, he's the oldest," Sharon said, pointing at the one on the far right, a weary-looking man with graying temples. "He's an accountant in Bakersfield now. And that's Mikey, he's my baby," she added, touching the man on the left, who looked about thirty in the photo. "He just got married last winter to the nicest girl, from San Luis Obispo. I'm hoping they give me some grandbabies soon." She smiled fondly at the photo.

"And that must be Henry in the middle," I finished for her. All three "boys" had similar features: their father's long face, dull sandy hair that had probably come from Sharon before hers grayed. Phillip and Mike both had empty, obligation-filled smiles, the kind that said "look how nice I'm being, to do this for my mother." But Henry's grin was different: a little too wide, a hair too crazy. Maybe I was just seeing what I expected to see, but he seemed . . . well, off. Neither of us had gotten a great look at the guy the night before, but this certainly could be him.

I showed the photo to Jesse, then handed it back to Sharon. "They're very handsome, ma'am."

Sharon Remus beamed at me. "Thank you." She placed the picture carefully back on its end table and returned to her kitchen chair.

"How much time does Henry actually spend here?" Jesse asked.

"Oh, he'll stay a stretch of about a month, at the most," Zeke drawled. "Then he's back out in the woods. Usually he stays at the public campgrounds. Police've brought him home twice, though, when he was camped out somewhere he wasn't supposed to be."

"I put a card in his wallet," Sharon added helpfully, "so they'll call if they find him. He's not actually . . . you know . . . *retarded*. But sometimes he gets agitated."

"Stubborn is what he gets," Zeke grunted. "I don't get it. You thinkin' Henry killed those women?"

Sharon gasped and her hands flew up to clasp at her breastbone. Zeke ignored her. He seemed absurdly satisfied with the direction of the conversation, as though he'd been just waiting for someone besides his wife to show up so he could bad-mouth his son.

"There's no evidence of that," Jesse said. "But we're talking to people who know the missing women, and that includes members of their environmentalist clubs." He looked at Sharon, clearly the gatekeeper to current information on Henry. "So you don't know where he is right now?" Jesse asked. "Where does he go when he camps?"

Sharon and Zeke looked at each other. Zeke gave a little shrug. "Heard him say he'd been to Lake Casitas, once," he said doubtfully. "And I know he goes over to Mammoth once in a while."

"You said he went to the Sequoias," I said hesitantly. "Would that be Kings Canyon National Park?"

Sharon beamed at me again. "Why, yes."

Jesse gave me a questioning look, but I shook my head slightly. A little piece had fallen into place, but now wasn't the time to talk about it.

"When the police brought him home," Jesse said, "where did they find him?" I knew he was thinking of the werewolves running in the LA parks at night.

"At Griffith Park," Sharon said immediately. Her voice was soft and a little sad. "I used to take the boys for picnics there, when they were little. He loved it."

"Where in the park?" Jesse asked sharply. "The big picnic area to the south, by the playground?"

Sharon blinked at the intensity of his voice, and Jesse flushed. "Sorry," he said. "I just know that park pretty well. I take my parents' dog for walks there."

"No," she said hesitantly. "Northwest of the observatory, by where the tunnel comes out."

Jesse's face clouded over for a moment, then he nodded in recognition. "Ma'am," he said to Sharon, "would you try calling Henry now, and ask where he is?"

She hesitated, her loyalties torn. Zeke Remus made an exasperated noise. He really did have quite the versatile range of grunts. "For Pete's sake, Sharon," he barked. "If he hasn't done anything wrong, they'll figure it out when they talk to him. And if he has, well, he's gotta answer for it."

Biting her lip, she acquiesced. "I'll call but I can promise you he won't answer. He only turns the phone on to call me on Sundays. He said it saves the battery that way."

She was right. After retrieving her phone from the kitchen, Sharon Remus put it on speaker before Jesse could ask her to and placed the call. It went straight to voicemail. "You've reached the voicemail of Henry E. Remus," said an overly cheery male voice. He sounded odd, like that moment right *after* you suck in balloon helium and talk in a Munchkin voice, just before it goes back to normal. I felt an unexpected stab of sympathy for Zeke Remus. That voice would annoy the shit out of me too. "If you're calling about my classroom services, please leave a message, and I'll get back to you just the second I can. Have a *wiiiiild* day!"

"Henry, it's your mother," Sharon said hesitantly. She looked at Jesse, who just pointed a finger at her. Nodding, she continued, "Please call me back when you get a chance. I—" Her voice faltered, and for a moment I thought she was going to warn him about us. But she just swallowed and added, "I love you, honey."

Once the excitement of the phone call was over, Zeke Remus seemed to lose interest in the conversation. "If that's all you-all need, we'd like to get back to our day," he said impatiently. I glanced at the beer and the remote. Yeah, that looked more important than his son killing people.

Jesse ignored the comment. "What about his brothers?" he asked. "Would he go to either of them?"

"Nah," Zeke said, unwilling to be ignored. "Neither of them have much to do with Hank."

"Can we get their contact information anyway?" Jesse asked, looking at Sharon.

She nodded, looking terrified as she clumsily scrolled through her phone's contacts and held it out so Jesse could copy her sons' numbers. "When you find him, please don't hurt him, all right?" she begged, her eyes flicking back and forth between Jesse and me. "He's a good boy, he's just . . . a little different, is all." She focused in on Jesse. "You won't let him get hurt, right? You're police, you have to protect him even if he does . . . know something about those girls." Her beautiful eyes flicked away uncomfortably and then came back to fix on Jesse again. This time he squirmed. Detective or not, he wasn't used to making promises he couldn't keep.

That was my department.

I stepped forward and took Sharon's hand. "No, ma'am," I said solemnly. "We won't hurt him."

Chapter 36

Back in the car, Jesse asked, "What was that about the Sequoias?"

I hesitated for a second, unsure how much to tell him. I didn't want him to know that I'd killed Ana, or that I'd slept with Eli. But didn't he deserve to know both of those things? Was I protecting him from having that weight on his conscience, or was I just protecting his opinion of me? Was there even any point in that anyway?

"Lydia came to see me this morning," I said finally. "She mentioned that she and Ana drove up to Kings Canyon a couple of weeks ago and changed."

"Why didn't you tell me?" Jesse exclaimed. I didn't answer, and after a moment's thought he added, "So one of them changed the nova."

"Yes, that's what I think. My guess would be Ana, because Lydia didn't seem to know anything about an attack on a human. But I suppose it doesn't really matter."

"But was she also the one who called the Luparii?" Jesse asked, talking mostly to himself.

The Luparii. Shoot. I'd been so focused on the nova, I'd almost forgotten that there was another player in the game. "It's possible," I said. "But it's also possible that Ana told someone about the nova, and *they* called the Luparii."

"Terrence," Jesse concluded. "Terrence and Drew were the one who met with the scout at the cemetery."

Lydia *had* said that Terrence and Ana were scheming. "Okay, but how did he know to do that?" I wondered. "I kind of doubt the Luparii have a number in the Paris phone book."

"When I went to see Terrence before," Jesse said slowly, "he had these scars on his arms."

"I remember those."

"He said he studied in England for a year, practiced fencing with real swords." Jesse shook his head in amazement. "I wasn't sure I believed him, but if he really was in Europe for a whole year, he may have made some connections."

"Who may have known about the Luparii," I concluded.

"Maybe. I don't think it matters, at this point," Jesse said, shrugging. "That link is broken. Terrence is dead."

"We need to call Will," I said firmly. It was time for an update. Jesse nodded, and I pulled out my phone. While I was finding Will's number, he gave me a sidelong glance. "Are you going to tell me why Lydia came to see you?" he asked quietly.

I put the phone to my ear. "No. It's personal."

Will picked up on the third ring, and I filled him in on what we'd learned at the Remus house. "So you're pretty sure this is the guy?" he asked anxiously.

"We're pretty sure Remus is the guy, right?" I said to Jesse, holding the phone away from my chin.

"You know, if we were in my car, we could put him on Bluetooth," he reminded me.

I blew him a raspberry. Then: "Oh, wait, I think I've got speakerphone."

Jesse rolled his eyes as I figured out the button that would let us all talk to each other. Once I had everything set up, he and Will greeted each other, and then Will repeated his question.

"Yeah, we're sure," Jesse said loudly. I told Will about Remus's weird camping habits, and his interest in the outdoors.

"That makes sense," Will said thoughtfully. "I couldn't figure out how someone could turn into a werewolf, keep it a secret, and just . . . go about his life."

"But this guy was off anyway," I finished for him. "I wonder if that's why he ended up becoming a nova. Maybe all novas are created when a crazy person becomes a werewolf and then gets ditched?"

There was a long pause, during which I squinted at my phone's screen to make sure the call was still connected. "Maybe," Will said at last. "As far as I know, no one really understands the relationship between a nova and his pack. Or if they do, word hasn't gotten out about it."

"So we have to figure out how to find him," I said aloud. "Hey, Will? Can I ask you a hypothetical?"

Will knew me well enough to be wary. "I guess."

"Let's say you're the nova wolf. All you want in the world is create a massive werewolf pack and murder the shit out of the current one. You've finally found a mate. What do you do now?"

He sighed. "It's hard to say. We're getting into a magical gray area here. The female—"

"Lizzy Thompkins," Jesse said, looking irritated.

"Lizzy Thompkins can't be feeling very favorable to him right now. He kidnapped her and killed her friends, maybe in front of her, and now she's going through physical hell. And he intends to keep her as his mate. I don't know if that's even *possible* against her will."

"So he's gotta have a place where he can contain her," Jesse reasoned.

"Yes. He can't order her around as her alpha until she's completed her change," Will finished.

I said, "The guy's a planner. He fancies himself a scientist; that's why he gives the school presentations, why he marked all their backs like it was a controlled experiment. He must have come up with a hidey-hole where he can restrain her." I thought back to the silver-barred cage I'd seen back in September, the one in Jared Hess's basement. I shuddered.

"If he's got her in some big wild area he could just dig a really big hole and put her inside until the change is over," Jesse pointed out.

Will said, "My guess is that he'll park her somewhere for the full moon so she can finish her change, then he'll go attack as many people as possible, hoping to build a pack. He'll kill a lot more people, but his chances of changing them increases during the full moon."

"It's a numbers game," I said thoughtfully. Jesse gave me a glare, but I just shrugged defensively. It was.

"Where will he go to find his victims?" Jesse asked the phone. "He's got his mate, so I assume he'll be less discerning."

"Good question," Will said slowly. "Probably an outdoor area somewhere because he'd be too conspicuous as a wolf running around a movie theater or something. A place that he knows well, that's public enough for people to be around but private enough that he can pick them off one or two at a time. No huge crowds."

"Okay, thanks, Will," Jesse said suddenly. "Any luck with the Luparii?"

"Not yet," Will answered heavily. "But Kirsten and I are both still working on it."

There wasn't much Jesse and I could do about the Luparii, especially if we were gonna find Henry Remus before the full moon. But . . .

"Will, what happens if the scout is still in town when the moon goes up tomorrow night?" I asked.

There was a pause. When he finally spoke, his voice was miserable. "I don't know. It's possible that he'll be so busy tracking the nova that he'll ignore us . . ."

His voice drifted off, letting Jesse and me fill in the blanks. If the scout was still in town and he couldn't get to the nova, he would probably come after the LA pack.

"Can you guys get out of town?" I asked hopefully.

Another long sigh. "I've urged those of us who have another safe place to go during the full moon to do so. The problem is that there just aren't many of us with a second secure location."

"I could come sit with you guys," I offered hesitantly. In theory, I could hang out with the pack on the full moon, and as long as they stayed in my radius they wouldn't have to change at all. But we'd never done that before. Will had told me once, a long time ago, that the pack needs the release of changing during the moon. They already spend so much time tamping down their instincts, and if they don't get a chance to change, it makes everything worse. In these desperate times, though, it seemed like a viable one-time option.

But Will said, "No. I thought about that, but you're our best chance of stopping the nova before he attacks or kills more people. I can handle the pack." His voice betrayed his uncertainty, but he just continued, "For now, you just worry about finding the nova."

I had been planning to tell Will and Jesse about Lydia's ultimatum—really. But in that moment, when Will sounded so broken, I resolved to keep it from them. It was my mess. I needed to figure out a way to clean it up. Again, I wondered what had happened to Eli. I needed to call him as soon as I got a moment alone.

"Okay. Let me know what you find out," Jesse said shortly, in a telltale "I have an idea" tone. He nodded at me, and I shrugged and hung up the phone.

"What is it?" I asked.

Jesse looked at me. "Griffith Park."

I frowned. "I thought the LA parks close at sunset. If the guy wants people around . . ."

"Not Griffith. It stays open until ten thirty, because of the Observatory."

Oh. I thought that over. "A few people around, lots of dark, an area he knows well," I said slowly.

Jesse nodded. "It's our best guess. But that's plan B."

"What's plan A?"

He glanced at the dashboard clock. "We've still got thirty-some hours until the full moon rises. Let's see if we can find the bastard before he tries to attack the public."

"How?"

Jesse gave me a pleased little smile that said, *You're gonna hate this.* "Old-fashioned police work," he proclaimed.

Yep. I was probably going to hate it.

Jesse explained that we needed to start calling everyone involved with the animal rights organizations to see if they knew where to find Henry. There was a good chance that one of them was hiding him, or knew of a place he would go. Calling almost one hundred and fifty people sounded horrible, but I didn't have any better ideas.

Since Jesse's phone battery was low, he suggested we head for the nearest residence that had a landline and where we would be more or less welcome: his parents' house in Los Feliz. Which would have been fine, except I really didn't want to meet Jesse's parents.

"What's the big deal?" Jesse asked when I demurred. "My dad will probably be in his studio anyway. And my mom's really nice. *And*," he added, "I know you want to see Max."

Well, he had me there. I had a serious pet-crush on Jesse's parents' pit bull mix. But I was also still a little raw from Jesse's comment the night before about living without my parents, and I didn't want to see him—or anyone else—being part of a happy family just then. It would hurt too much.

But I couldn't actually say that out loud, of course. Not my style. "Didn't you say your brother was in town too?" I objected. "They'll be distracting. Besides, though I love him, Max will probably knock me down and hurt my leg," I added piteously.

We were at a red light, so Jesse took his eyes off the road long enough to search mine. I don't know what he saw there, but his expression softened almost imperceptibly and he nodded. "So we'll go to Molly's."

Oops. We'd been so busy talking to the Remuses that I'd forgotten for a moment that I'd murdered someone at Molly's the night before. And that Lydia had put Eli and me on a ticking clock. And I still didn't know where Eli was.

"Scarlett?" Jesse asked impatiently.

I snapped back to the present. "Fine," I said. "Let's go to Molly's. We'll need to stay downstairs, though, so we don't . . . you know. Wake her up."

Which is exactly what we did. It was after lunchtime, so we picked up sandwiches—well, Jesse ran into the place to buy sandwiches, so I didn't have to hobble around more than absolutely necessary—and ate in the van on the way. Traffic was still light, so thirty-five minutes after we'd left the Remus apartment, Jesse and I were sitting at Molly's card table–sized kitchen table with the rosters from PAW and HPA. Jesse gave me the PAW list, keeping the much longer HPA roster for himself. Still, I looked down at the thirty names on the paper in front of me with dismay. "Are you sure we need to do this?" I complained. "I really don't like . . . people."

"Too bad," he said cheerfully.

"What do I even ask?"

"Do they know Henry Remus? If so, do they have any idea where he might hide out? Try to get a sense of who might be lying or holding something back, and we can visit those people in person. Oh, and ask everyone who Henry hung out with at meetings. Hopefully we can get a sense of who his friends were, and then we can go after them hard."

Ugh. "Who do I say *I* am?"

He considered that for a moment. "Do the missing persons consultant story. You're specifically looking into Leah Rhodes's disappearance. Talking to people about her boyfriend would be a logical move for the police to make."

"Got it."

Jesse took the cordless handset into the living room so we wouldn't be heard in the background of each other's calls. When I was sure he couldn't hear me, I dialed Eli's number. It rang five times and then went to voicemail. Crap. I hung up without leaving a message. There was nothing to do but get to work.

Chapter 37

I've never actually wanted to be a cop. Any kind of cop. Up until this point, helping Jesse with Old World investigations had been alternately terrifying, frustrating, and exhilarating, but because of my unique circumstances, it had never really been dull until I started calling the PAW members. Because as it turns out, *real* police work is boring as hell.

At least, that was my conclusion by our second hour of calling strangers and trying to keep them from hanging up in the first two seconds. Most of the people on the PAW list were women, and those who were able to answer the phone in the middle of the day were not really interested in anything a stranger had to say. A bunch of them snapped at me for calling in the middle of their small children's nap times. Because I was supposed to just know when that was, apparently.

I did find one interesting new fact, though. When we'd worked on the PAW list the night before, I hadn't gotten all the way to the bottom—we'd found Remus and gotten distracted. But now I saw that two of the names near the very bottom of the roster looked familiar. I went and borrowed Jesse's list of the LA werewolves. Sure enough, two of the wolves were on the PAW list: Esmé Welch and Corbin Hurd.

It actually made sense, I realized. Why *wouldn't* the werewolves want wild wolves to be protected? If no one was allowed to kill wolves, that made it all the safer for the pack to run around the woods during the full moon. When I looked at it in that light, I was actually surprised that there weren't more of the pack members on the list. And it wasn't like either Esmé or Corbin could be the nova—they'd both been werewolves in the pack for years. I shrugged and resolved to call Esmé and Corbin just like they were anyone else on the list. Well, maybe I'd have Jesse call them instead.

I went back to work. Two hours later, I had made actual contact with a total of twenty people. I thought that was a pretty high percentage of the list, all things considered, but the holidays were probably working to our advantage. At any rate, of the twenty people I'd talked to, almost all of them remembered Henry Remus as the "guy with the crazy eyes and the do-it-yourself haircut," as one chatty lady put it. Her name was Heaven Centuri (for real), and she told me that at their last meeting in October, our boy Henry had given a speech about some alleged wolf sightings in Northern California, suggesting that PAW should send a group up there to stake out "these magnificent creatures."

"He said 'magnificent creatures', like, six times," Heaven snorted. "I mean, we were at a noodle place in Brentwood, and this guy's talking about building tree stands out in the woods so we can what? Take pictures? Get a head count? More likely we'd end up getting stuck out there waiting for the wolves to go away again so we could come down. If we even *saw* them."

"I take it he wasn't getting a lot of support," I said neutrally.

"Ha. No. Everybody thought he was crazy." After a moment of hesitation, she added, "I mean, the guy's heart was in the right place, you know. But it was like the more he talked, the more people's chairs just scooted sloooowly away from him. By the end he was just *shouting*, and someone from the restaurant came and escorted him out." There was a bit of awe in her voice, like she couldn't imagine being so invested in something.

"What about Leah, his girlfriend? Was she there too?"

"I think so," Heaven said dismissively. "There was a girl with him, anyway. I didn't get much of a read on her; she was real quiet. Kind of mousy. When Henry got thrown out she just followed behind him silently, like she knew when she got up that morning that she'd be getting thrown out of a restaurant."

"Did it seem like either of them had any other friends there?"

There was a brief pause while she considered the question. "You know, I think there was another woman who got up and left when they did," Heaven said finally. "But she may have just been leaving at the same time."

"What did she look like?" I said eagerly.

"Short, brunette, pretty in a bland soccer mom kind of way. Maybe thirty, but not, like, a well-maintained thirty. I only remember because she looked really edgy, like she was strapped to a bomb or something."

That was kind of a general description, but it did match Esmé Welch, one of the werewolves on the PAW roster. I thanked Heaven and hung up.

Most of the calls were like that one. Everyone who had attended that meeting remembered Henry getting thrown out and Leah following him, but no one besides Heaven remembered the brunette woman who'd left at the same time. I made a note of it and kept going.

I was done with my list—minus the people who hadn't answered—by four, so after checking to make sure Jesse was still talking in the living room, I tried calling Eli again. I'd checked upstairs when changing clothes that morning, but there had been no further note or message. It wasn't like him to just disappear. Had I done something wrong?

You mean besides slaughtering one of his fellow pack members? I thought sourly.

The phone rang five times, and then his voicemail picked up. "Eli, where are you?" I said quietly. I struggled for a way to tell him that I was worried, that it scared me that he hadn't called. Instead what came out was, "And where the hell's my breakfast?"

As I hung up, Jesse came yawning into the kitchen. "Need a coffee break," he mumbled. "You find anything?"

I told him about the October PAW meeting, and the two werewolves I had skipped. "I'll give them a call," he said, nodding. "Are you thinking that they told Remus about being werewolves?"

I paused. "You know, that hadn't even occurred to me. I'm so used to the Old World being so insular . . ." I considered it for a second, then shook my head. "I just can't see it. But they might have insight into Henry, like anyone else. How did you do?"

Jesse went past me to circle the counter, heading for the coffeemaker. "Well, first I called the two Remus brothers. Supposedly neither of them knows a thing about Henry's activities. They only see him at holidays."

I leaned back in my chair, flexing my knee just a little, half expecting a creaking sound. The swelling had gone down some, but the pain was still there. Shouldn't have sat so long without moving or elevating it. "That's not very helpful," I said absently.

His face darkened. "Yeah. I'm not finding out much from the HPA, either. I can't ask about *all* the girls without giving them the chance to connect the dots, and we don't want that. When the LAPD figures out the five missing women are connected, it won't take them long to find Henry Remus's name. Then again . . . maybe we want them to." He shrugged. "Maybe we want to set up Henry as the fall guy now. And by 'fall guy,' I mean 'guy who actually did it.'" He pulled a bag of coffee grounds out of the fridge and held them up. "You mind if I make some coffee?"

"No, go ahead," I said cautiously. Things had been tense between the two of us all day. And now I had to make it worse. "Look, Jesse, we can't tell anyone about Henry Remus until after we've . . . found him." If the cops arrested Henry the night before the full moon, Dashiell would have to get involved. I didn't know much about how he pulled strings in the police department or the city government, but I was betting it wasn't easy to have someone killed or released from prison on twelve hours' notice. "Which brings me to the subject of what we're going to do when we catch up with the guy."

"Go stop him," Jesse said promptly. He switched the pot and turned the coffee machine on, then turned around to lean onto the counter island so he was bent at a near-ninety-degree angle. "But that wasn't what you meant, was it?"

"No." I watched him carefully for signs of tension. We'd been down this road before, when we were going after Olivia. Jesse believed in the justice system; it was as much a part of his identity as his face or family. He'd wanted to arrest Olivia, despite orders from Dashiell that she was to be killed. We had managed to avoid the problem when I shot Olivia so Jesse wouldn't have to be responsible for her death. But now we were up against a similar situation, and while I didn't have a problem with killing an insane werewolf who'd murdered four women, there was no guarantee that I would be the one to confront him.

"I know I can't keep riding the fine lines on this," Jesse said quietly, echoing my thoughts. "But if we do what I think you're suggesting, if we just put him down like a rabid dog . . ." His voice trailed off.

"You're scared you can't be a cop anymore," I finished for him. Looking a little surprised, he nodded. "Even though you more or less agree that the Old World has to stay hidden." Another nod.

The coffee was done, so Jesse straightened up and started looking for cups. *Maybe there was an alternative*, I thought. The Luparii wanted the nova too, and they certainly had no qualms about killing. What if we just let *them* kill Henry? I turned that idea over for a moment while Jesse rummaged for milk and sugar.

I doubted Will or Dashiell would go for it. Aside from their personal hatreds, they wouldn't want the Luparii to gain any footing in America. Besides, Jesse probably wouldn't feel like handing Henry Remus over to be killed did much to solve the problem of him not wanting to kill anyone.

Jesse circled back around the counter and plopped himself in a chair across from me. I envied his easy movements. My leg was feeling more and more ungainly, like I was dragging around one of those old-fashioned ball-and-chain things. "Could you change Remus into a human again?" he asked me, unable to hide the hope in his voice.

That shocked me. I had been so busy trying to hide the fact that I could change someone permanently that I hadn't realized it could be a viable option to save Henry Remus from death. As I looked at Jesse, I remembered the moment in my bedroom when he'd asked me if I could do it again. This was what he'd meant all along: he wanted to use what I could do to get justice in the Old World, without having to just kill. Of course he did. I felt like an idiot.

If it had been Dashiell or Will asking, I would have felt used, but I couldn't even blame Jesse. He wanted so badly to keep his integrity, and what I could do might actually make that possible. I opened my mouth to say I would try—but I closed it again. I thought about my knee, and the vertigo that had returned the night before. Then I remembered what Noring had said about taking care of myself.

"Not yet," I whispered. Clearing my throat, I added in a clearer voice, "I have to get better first, Jesse. I have to finish healing before I can try something like that again. I'm so sorry."

He nodded, unsurprised. "If it's a choice between you and Remus, there's no choice at all," he said earnestly. "But if we could figure out a way to contain Remus until you got better . . . would you be willing to try?"

I found myself nodding. "And listen, Jesse," I continued, "about last night . . ." Crap. Why on earth had I brought that up? Stupid mouth.

He raised his eyebrows over the rim of the coffee cup. "What about it?"

I struggled for words and finally ended up with, "Just because you don't see something that doesn't mean it isn't there."

His gaze softened and he put his cup down. "What are you saying, Scarlett?"

My eyes unfocused as I felt something stir on the edge of my radius. "Molly's coming downstairs."

"Huh?" He blanched, and then the stairs behind him creaked as Molly came into the room.

"Is this all you guys do, sit and drink coffee?" she asked cheerfully.

Jesse and I exchanged a glance. "Pretty much," I said, shrugging.

The smile faded from her face. "Scarlett, can I talk to you for a minute?"

My eyebrows lifted. "Uh, sure . . ."

Jesse rose. "I'll go back to the living room and make some more calls," he said. Nodding a farewell, he vanished through the doorway, taking his coffee with him. Molly sat down in his chair.

"What's up?" I said nervously. It's rare for Molly to actually be serious about something. No good ever comes of it, in my experience.

She held up a finger, leaning back to check on Jesse in the other room. I heard his voice start up on a phone call, and she leaned forward again. "I take it you haven't told him about last night?"

For a moment, I wasn't sure if she meant sleeping with Eli or killing Anastasia. Then I realized the answer was the same either way. "No, I didn't . . ." I trailed off and then repeated, "No."

Molly nodded. "Listen—"

"I'm really sorry about your carpet," I interrupted. "I'll pay to have it fixed, of course."

She gave me a thin smile. "I don't care about the *money*, Scarlett. Money I have. But last night was the second time in two weeks that someone broke into my house looking for you." Molly paused and took a deep breath. "Whenever vampires put down roots, there's a time limit on how long it lasts. I want to enjoy the time I have in this house before I need to move on. Meanwhile, your whole situation keeps escalating, and . . . I don't think I can continue on this journey with you."

I tried to swallow, but the inside of my mouth was suddenly dry enough to be a fire hazard. "You—you want me to move out," I managed to say.

She nodded reluctantly. "Not, like, today or anything. But as soon as you catch this guy, I'd like you to start looking for another place to live."

I nodded, unable to stop the rush of tears that spilled down onto my cheeks. I couldn't even blame her. I *had* put her life in danger; kicking me out was completely fair. If anything, it was surprising that she hadn't done it the first time, when Olivia had broken in.

But in that moment I realized that as much as I had *tried* to hold myself back, to keep a distance, I thought of Molly as my friend. Vampire or not, spy or not, justified or not . . . it hurts when your friend doesn't want you around.

Molly, unaccustomed to genuine emotion, looked distressed by my tears. She stood up and patted me awkwardly on the shoulder. "Uh . . . I'm gonna go out for a while. We can talk more later."

She speed-walked out the back door. A moment later, Jesse finished his call and came into the room.

“What was that about—” he began, then saw my face. I was trying to get my tears under control but not having a whole bunch of success. “Oh, hey . . . what happened?”

“Can you—” I pointed at the roll of paper towels on the counter, and he went to retrieve it for me.

“She wants me to move out,” I said shakily, blowing my nose on a paper towel. I have never pretended to be a pretty crier.

“*What*? Why?”

Oops. I still didn’t want to tell him about Anastasia. Things were delicate enough between us. So I just said, “Too dangerous.”

Jesse ripped another paper towel off the roll and handed it to me. I nodded in thanks. “Well, I can’t really blame her,” he said frankly. I looked up from the paper towel to gape at him. “Come on, Scarlett. You know as well as I do that all this wasn’t what she signed on for.”

I flinched. With an effort, I met his eyes, my voice hardening. “Are we still talking about Molly?”

He looked away. A minute of awkward silence ticked by, and then Jesse stood up. “I can finish these calls by myself,” he announced.

Something had shifted between us. I could actually *see* his body language changing to professional detachment. “Why don’t you take the rest of the night off, get some rest,” he added. “We’ll start early tomorrow.”

“Good idea,” I said flatly.

Chapter 38

After Jesse left, I got my cane, swung my leg down carefully, and made my way toward the living room, collecting my cell phone as I passed the counter.

I got myself settled on the couch. Screw going back up those stairs, I was too tired. I held up my phone and realized that I'd missed a text from Dashiell. He had found the Luparii in France, but they weren't responding to his requests for negotiation, and there wasn't time for him to push it any farther. It was a dead end. And Will and Kirsten hadn't contacted me, so I was assuming they were coming up dry too. There was no way to call off the scout.

Not knowing what else to do, I tried calling Eli again. This time the phone went straight to voicemail, so either his battery had died or he'd switched his phone off. Frustrated, I ended the call and dialed Hair of the Dog. The bartender transferred me to Will.

"Have you heard from Eli?" I said loudly. The back room was a lot quieter than the main bar area, but it still wasn't actually *quiet*.

"Huh?" Will said distractedly. "Sorry, what?"

I repeated the question. "Oh." Now Will sounded . . . reluctant. "Um, I'm sorry, Scarlett, but he checked out of the motel, and I don't think he's been back to his place. I think he left town."

Oh.

I fought back tears. I did not want to cry again, goddammit. I had already cried too much this week. This year. And it wasn't like

Eli and I had been going steady. I'd saved him after he killed someone; he'd saved me after *I* killed someone. Maybe he just figured we were even now. And the night we'd spent together . . . that must have been good-bye.

Could I really blame him?

I leaned back on the couch, staring at the ceiling. Sometimes you are just so completely screwed that you almost have to admire it. Eli had left town right after sleeping with me which, aside from being humiliating and sad, also meant that Lydia was demanding something I couldn't produce. The nova was going to attack a bunch of people tomorrow night, and the Luparii scout was going to go after the werewolf pack if he couldn't find the nova, which *we* hadn't been able to do even with knowledge of the city and a week's lead time. Jesse and I were . . . complicated. Molly was evicting me on justifiable grounds.

The steady thrum of pain from my leg suddenly intensified, as if to remind me it existed. "Yes, thank you," I told my leg. I had almost forgotten to catalogue my messed-up knee. Fantastic. I honestly didn't know what to be most upset about. I leaned back on the couch pillow, feeling trapped and frustrated.

I wish I could say I tapped into reserves of inner strength and struck upon a plan to fix everything, but that's not really my style. Instead, I laid there for a good long while, alternately pouting and feeling sorry for myself. I wasn't even twenty-four, dammit! Most of the people I knew from high school were currently being supported by their parents while they figured out what to do with their useless but enjoyably obtained liberal arts degrees. I shouldn't have to deal with all of this! It wasn't *fair*.

I might have lain there sulking until Jesse arrived the next morning, except that it was still pretty early when he left, and by nine o'clock I was starving. I tried to ignore the hunger cramps in my stomach, but after a while my head began to ache too, and I realized that, unless I got some food, it was only going to get worse.

So I took a deep, slow breath, and did what anyone would do in my dire situation: I called for pizza.

While I waited for the food, I ran through my options. I needed to do something. Will and Kirsten were both trying to find out more about the Luparii scout. Jesse was making phone calls. Everyone was busy, hard at work fixing my mess while I laid around waiting for pizza delivery. I felt a rush of shame. This had all started with my mistake, after all.

What I really wanted was someone I could talk to about all this, who could help me work out a plan—but my options were limited. I couldn't exactly hash it out with humans. I considered calling Corry, but even if I had been certain that bringing her all the way into the Old World was the right play, she was fifteen and probably couldn't help much. I knew that if I called Molly right then, she wouldn't answer. She would have already begun to distance herself from me. And everyone else I knew in the Old World were people who were dumb enough to need help cleaning up a crime scene.

I tried Molly anyway, just in case, but her phone went straight to voicemail. I sighed, tapping the phone against my forehead. There was one other person I could try, but I really, really didn't want to. "Suck it up, Scarlett," I said, my voice suddenly seeming loud in the empty house. "Nobody cares about your stupid weird feelings."

I dialed the phone.

A few minutes later, the pizza guy rang the doorbell. I limped to the door to sign the receipt and collect my delicious cheesy goodies. I had barely gotten the door closed when the doorbell rang again, and I opened it, expecting the pizza guy had forgotten to give me a receipt or something—but even before I saw her, I recognized the familiar sensation of a witch in my radius.

"Um . . . hi," Runa Vore said hesitantly.

"You have a really nice place," Runa said politely, looking around Molly's kitchen. I set the pizza box in the middle of the table, pulling out a chair for myself.

"It's not mine," I said, a little shortly. I pointed to another chair, and as Runa was sitting down I said, "Do you want some pizza?"

"No, I ate. And I'm a vegan," she added.

Of course she was. I looked down at my greasy, cheesy, sausage pizza. What with the dead animal on it and everything. "Will it bother you to have it here?" I asked reluctantly. I really, really didn't want her to say yes.

But she waved a hand. "Oh, no. I don't expect people around me to live the same way I do, that's just silly." I relaxed an inch and swooped up a slice, taking a huge first bite. I was *so* hungry. "But . . . I guess I don't really know why I'm here," she continued, looking almost apologetic.

"Then why'd you come?" I asked, my mouth still full.

Runa gestured helplessly, not sure what to say. I swallowed and said with effort, "I'm sorry, that was rude. What I meant to say was, 'Thanks for coming.'"

She nodded, her short blonde pigtails bobbing along with her head. I was really having to work hard not to hate her on sight. It wasn't just that she'd dated Jesse—she was also annoyingly put-together, artistic, and graceful. She gave off a sense of inner peace that I envied much more than her beauty. Lots of people are beautiful, and you don't live in Los Angeles very long before you notice that, hey, a whole bunch of them congregate here. But Runa also seemed so comfortable in her skin. I, on the other hand, couldn't even feel comfortable in my sweatpants and ratty T-shirt. I felt a pang of grief for my dad's Chicago Bears jersey, which Eli had taken away, presumably to destroy.

Focus, Scarlett. "I asked you here," I began, "because I need to talk to someone about a really big Old World mess, and frankly my options are limited. Very limited." She smiled a little ruefully, and I liked her for it. "Sorry again," I added.

"What about Jesse?" she said carefully, keeping her face still. "Can't he help?"

"Jesse and I are not okay right now," I answered. No sense tiptoeing around it. "But I'd rather not talk about him."

Runa nodded again. "I can respect that."

"Thank you. Please hang on a second while I inhale a little more pizza." This time she grinned at me, and I finished off the slice and reached for another. "I think my body's still hungry from being unconscious for a couple of days," I mumbled.

Runa blinked. "When was this?"

I stilled. "You don't . . . Kirsten didn't tell you?"

Her eyes flinched away. "Kirsten and I are not okay right now," she said softly.

Kirsten was the one who'd sent Runa to get close to Jesse, in hopes of finding out if he was telling Old World secrets to anyone, especially other cops. He'd dumped Runa when he'd found out. I was guessing that this had been what created the rift between Runa and Kirsten, which was interesting, but not really my business. "Fair enough," I said, shrugging.

"But I don't mind being a sounding board, if that's what you need." She fidgeted for a moment, pushing loose strands of blonde hair behind her ears.

"I guess I'll start at the beginning then. Stop me if you've heard this one."

So I walked her through the whole thing: the confrontation with Olivia, waking up to Will, getting called back to work, the nova, the investigation with Jesse. She told me about being assigned to the Evergreen crime scene and calling Jesse, after which I picked up the story again. By the time I got to the Luparii, we had moved into the living room, drinking coffee that she'd made. Apparently the coffee Molly bought was already vegan.

I told her everything, except for the parts having to do with changing Eli back into a human. Will had told me to keep that a secret, and it was the least I could do for him. And besides, it wasn't really connected to the mess with the nova, not anymore.

"So Jesse's still making calls, but I don't know how we're going to find the nova," I summed up. "And the full moon is tomorrow night."

Runa sat back in her chair, looking thoughtful. "And you don't know where the nova is," she said slowly. "But you think you know where he's going to be."

"Right. But even if Jesse's right, Griffith is too big, and the Luparii scout is still out there too."

"Hmm." Runa stared off into space for a moment, considering. "And I suppose it wouldn't do any good for you and Jesse to split up and go after the nova and the scout separately."

I shook my head. "Jesse's a good cop, but he can't go up against a witch with a lethal dog-monster, or a werewolf in a big natural area." Griffith wasn't a clear field where you could see anything coming; it was a dense tangle of brushes, trees, and rocky outcroppings. A werewolf would have no trouble getting the jump on a human, with or without silver bullets.

Sighing, I pushed hair away from my face. I'd taken out my ponytail so I could rest my head comfortably on the couch. "It'd be different if we could track the nova somehow, or know exactly where he's going to park his car and change. Then we could get him in my radius, let Jesse subdue him, and problem solved."

A slow smile was spreading over Runa's gorgeous face. "What?" I asked, confused. "What'd I say?"

Runa leaned forward. "You think you need to find the nova, but technically that's not true. You just need something that can find him."

"Isn't that splitting hairs?" I asked doubtfully.

Then I got it.

I grinned at the gorgeous witch, suddenly fully appreciating what Jesse had seen in her. "Runa Vore, you clever minx."

Chapter 39

Jesse was having a long night.

He'd finished all the phone calls, including doubling back on the people who hadn't answered the first time, by just after ten. It was mostly a fruitless effort. The more he pressed, the less anyone seemed to know about Henry Remus. The guy was a ghost, one very lost soul in a whole city of them.

The last two on his list were Esmé Welch and Corbin Hurd, the werewolves. Hurd wasn't home, and a quick text to Will revealed that he had a business meeting in Santa Barbara and wouldn't be back until the following afternoon. Esmé wasn't home either, but Scarlett had said she was picking up a few shifts at Will's bar, and Jesse managed to get a hold of her there. When she answered he could tell she'd picked up the office extension, just based on the lack of bar sounds in the background.

He explained who he was and why he needed to ask her about Remus, and there was a long, pregnant pause. "Esmé?" he said cautiously. "Are you still there?"

"It was totally an accident!" she burst out.

"What was an accident?"

"Corbin and I were chatting a few months back, while we were waiting for the PAW meeting to start," Esmé said, and now Jesse could hear tears in her voice. "And we were just talking about our weekend plans, you know, and some of the latest pack drama, and there was this guy, he'd overheard the whole thing, and we said . . ." She took a gulping breath.

"Let me guess," Jesse interrupted. "You talked about being werewolves, and changing in between moons."

"I didn't see him," Esmé wailed. "Then he was running away, and I was gonna call the vampires, you know, like you're supposed to, but nobody remembered his name and nothing bad happened and I just kind of . . . forgot about it. I mean, who would believe a story about *werewolves*?"

Said the werewolf. Jesse managed to refrain from banging his head on the door frame. "What *exactly* were you guys talking about?"

There was another long silence. "Esmé, I can come down there, pitch a big fit, and demand some answers, right in front of Will. Or you can just tell me what I need to know right now and save us both the trouble."

"There—there's this place," she whispered into the phone. "Up by the Sequoias. It's like a three-hour drive, no chance of running into Will or any of the other pack members. Every month, on the new moon, some of the pack goes up there."

"What about you, Esmé?"

"I went once," she mumbled. "But I was too scared of disobeying Will. It wasn't even any fun."

Jesse sighed. Well, at least they knew how Remus had found out about the werewolves. Only a guy who desperately wanted to believe in wolves would overhear that conversation and think it was actually true.

"Why did you run out of the October meeting?" Jesse asked.

"How did you—"

"Esmé," he said tiredly, "maybe you should just assume I know everything, and tell me the truth."

"I—I realized that he was nuts," she admitted. "That was the day the guy overheard us. I went to find Corbin, to tell him the guy might be nuts, because Corbin had missed his speech. By the time I got Corbin out of the bathroom and we came back, they were long gone."

"Did you tell anyone else about this?" Jesse demanded.

"Just my friend Ana," she insisted.

Jackpot.

Jesse asked Esmé a few more questions, but she didn't seem to know anything else about Remus, especially not where he might hide. By the time he was finished talking to her, Jesse was exhausted, having fueled the last few days on too much coffee and not enough sleep. He texted Scarlett to let her know about Esmé, then went and laid down on the bed in his little studio apartment. Jesse's thoughts were just spinning, stuck on finding the nova wolf. They knew how the nova had been made, but that didn't actually *get* them anywhere.

Despite his churning mind, Jesse's exhaustion tugged at him. After a few minutes, he gave up and set his alarm for seven, before giving in to it.

He awoke feeling just as stuck, but at least a little more capable of rational thought. He showered and dressed quickly before leaving for Scarlett's. The LA morning was cool and overcast, with a heavy gray sky that seemed to be drifting slowly downward to cover the ground in haze. Jesse had to shake a sudden impulse to stomp on the gas, to see if he could outrun the weather. It was the weekend, and this early in the morning the streets were practically empty. He made it to Scarlett's in record time.

To Jesse's surprise, Scarlett answered her door quickly, with a phone to her ear and her cane tucked under the same arm. She was half hunched over to keep the phone from falling. "I'm on hold," Scarlett said briefly, and gestured with a shoulder for him to come inside. "Come on in."

Without another word she took hold of her cane and hobbled back to the couch. She looked better than she had in days, dressed in jeans and an oversized cowl-necked sweater that went to her fingertips. Her hair was damp and sweet-smelling from the shower. She'd wrapped it up in a bun, and when she turned back toward the room Jesse saw what looked like a blue pen stuck through it. He followed her, perplexed. "Who are—" he began, but she half turned to him and held up a hand.

"Yes. Yes, I'm still here," she said into the phone. "Nobody? All right, I must have the wrong information. Thank you." Ending the call, she collapsed onto the couch, careful to keep her knee free. Scarlett picked up a yellow pad of paper that was tucked into the couch between the arm and the cushion. She pulled the pen out of her bun. "There's coffee in the kitchen if you want it," she said through a yawn.

"I had some on the way. What's going on?" he asked, still mystified. He perched in the armchair, more so he wouldn't be looming over her than because he needed to sit.

She scribbled something on the pad before looking up. "You're not going to believe this, but I came up with a plan. Well, Runa and I did."

For a second he thought he must have misheard her. "*My* Runa?" Jesse said incredulously.

Scarlett stuck out her tongue and crossed her eyes for a moment. "No, the *other* bearer of that globally popular name."

"Shut up. What . . . why were you talking to Runa?"

"I figured it was time we had a long talk about your expertise in the bedroom," Scarlett said gravely. When Jesse's eyes more or less fell out of his head, she laughed. "Sorry, I've had, like, a *lot* of coffee. Like a lot."

Jesse shook his head slightly to clear it. "Okay, let me start all over. Good morning, Scarlett. How was your night?"

"Good morning, Jesse," Scarlett said gamely. "My night got a lot better when I invited your ex-girlfriend over for a chat. I needed to talk through this whole thing, and I couldn't really think of anyone else." Off Jesse's look, she rolled her eyes and said, "No, we didn't talk about you."

He must have looked relieved, because she added, "I mean, just your penis size, but that was it."

"*Scarlett . . .*"

"Okay, okay." She flapped a hand. "I told Runa most of what's been happening, and she pointed out that, since we know where the nova is going to be, all we have to do is show up and hunt him down."

"Well, yeah, but that park is enormous . . . ," Jesse began, but she waved him into silence.

"I know; just listen. We need a way to find a renegade werewolf, and we just happen to have a trained werewolf-finder in town."

Jesse stared at her. "You're not suggesting—" he started to say, but stopped when Scarlett bounced a little in her chair.

"Yes, I am," she said gleefully. "I'm suggesting we steal the bargest."

He eyed her suspiciously. "Wait," Jesse said. "*How* much coffee have you had?"

She pulled a face. "Think about it. If we take the bargest away on the morning of the full moon, the Luparii scout won't have time to get a replacement or get his pals here to help him. It'll cut his legs out from under him, and that's one problem solved. Then we take the bargest to Griffith and use it to find the nova."

"That's . . . huh." Jesse stood up and began pacing the length of the living room, thinking it over. "There are so many unknowns," he said, mostly to himself. "For one thing, even if we could pull off finding and stealing the bargest, we have no idea if it will listen to us."

"But remember, the thing started out as a dog," Scarlett contended. "And you and I know dogs. We have as much chance as anyone outside of the Luparii at controlling the thing. What else?"

He turned to face her, considering the problem. "Well," he said, "we don't know the bargest's range. If Remus isn't right where we expect, there's no guarantee that it'll be able to scent him from one end of the park to the other."

"True," Scarlett allowed, "but the Luparii have spent, like, three hundred years perfecting this creature to hunt wolves. The friggin' *werewolves* are afraid of it. I think we should trust that the Luparii wouldn't be as successful as they are if the bargest wasn't a complete werewolf-hunting badass."

She must have seen the doubt on his face, because her enthusiasm waned suddenly and she said in a more desperate tone, "Look, Jesse, I know it's kind of crazy, but it's our best shot."

Jesse thought it over once more, and had to admit that she was right. The bargest was their best option. "Even so," he said slowly, "we have no idea where the scout *is*. Will and Kirsten haven't been able to find him, and they know way more than we do about the Luparii."

Scarlett clapped her hands together, enthusiasm back. "Ah, yes. But you and I have been so busy working on finding the nova, *we* haven't tried finding the scout until now." She leaned forward and held out the pad of paper she'd been writing on.

Jesse crossed the space between them to take it from her. "Beverly Hills Hotel, the Four Seasons . . . what is this?"

"A list of places where the scout might be staying. The Luparii are rich, and a lot of the really swanky LA places let rich people bring their pets into the hotel . . ." She shrugged. "It's a work in progress."

"It's a good idea," Jesse mused, "but the problem is that they could also be in a rental house, or an unoccupied private home, or somewhere out of town." He put the list down. "This is a good plan B, but there's gotta be another way to find the Luparii."

"Yeah?" Scarlett said. She grinned at him, a look full of such excitement and hope that it pierced his chest, hollowing out the spot where doubts about her had begun to collect. "What do you got?"

Jesse sat down and leaned back and thought it over for a moment. The Old World leaders had been trying to find the guy using their own channels. But Scarlett was right; no one had tried coming at the problem the way the police would. If he was at work on a regular investigation, what would he have done?

"Start at the beginning," Jesse said. He stood up and paced the living room again. "Henry Remus goes to the place where the wolves run between moons. Ana was there, and she knew Remus might show up. She changed him and then abandoned him. Then she told her good buddy Terrence, who had connections in Europe, possibly from his time in London. He called the Luparii and told them about the nova wolf. The Luparii got interested and sent someone to LA to hunt him down."

Scarlett shrugged. "That's the working theory, yes."

"But then the scout killed Terrence and his sidekick, Riddell. Why?"

Scarlett's brow furrowed. "Maybe he found out that Terrence and Ana don't really know who or where the nova is."

"But then why bring the Luparii to LA to begin with?" Jesse ground out, frustrated. He looked at Scarlett. "Ana is the last link in the chain. We need to talk to her right away."

To his surprise, Scarlett paled, unmoving. "What?" Jesse asked.

Her lower lip trembled for a second, but then she lifted her chin and met his eyes. "Ana's dead," she told him. "She came after me two nights ago, upstairs in my room, and I killed her with the boot knife you gave me."

Jesse sank down in the nearest chair, flummoxed. "Scarlett . . ."

"That's why Molly is evicting me. And I didn't tell you, because I didn't want you to know that I murdered someone," she rushed on. "And I didn't want you to look at me the way you are right now."

He stared at her. "Anastasia's really dead?"

"Yes," she said in a small voice.

Sighing, he leaned back in the chair, taking that in. "You're not a murderer," he said, toward the ceiling. Deciding that was unfair, he sat up and looked at Scarlett. "I know I've been hard on you," he said quietly. "And I know we haven't been on the same page on this case. I should never have taken Dashiell's deal; it's knocked everything out of whack. But I also know you well enough to know that you wouldn't have killed Anastasia if you'd had any other choice."

Scarlett visibly relaxed in her seat on the couch. "Thank you," she whispered.

"You're welcome." He absently rubbed his arm, which still hurt where Anastasia had wrenched it. "I just don't know where that leaves us, as far as the investigation goes."

Scarlett looked at him thoughtfully, her fingers fidgeting in her lap. "You said Ana was the last link in the chain. Ana and Terrence made the nova and brought the Luparii."

"Yeah . . ."

"But we've been assuming that they brought the Luparii here to go after the nova," she pointed out. "What if they made the nova in order to bring the Luparii here?"

He stared at her. "Why?"

"What do the Luparii do?"

"Kill werewolves," Jesse said promptly.

She sat up, swinging her legs to the floor and leaning forward. Despite wincing a tiny bit at the movement, Scarlett plowed on. "Ana's upset about Lydia. So she comes after me, for the cure. And maybe she goes after Will, for not protecting her girlfriend from

Eli in the first place. She's not strong enough to kill him herself, and her pal Terrence is too crazy to do it. So she gets the Luparii to send a scout here who can take care of Will. But the scout doesn't appreciate being used as someone else's tool, so he kills Terrence and his henchman."

Jesse considered Scarlett's explanation. It made sense. It would have been much easier for Anastasia to just shoot Will with a silver bullet, but even that might not necessarily kill him unless the circumstances were perfect. And then Ana would have had to face the rest of the pack for killing their alpha.

Instead, Ana had managed to arrange for someone else to do all her dirty work, without even paying them. It wasn't a bad plan, except for the part where the Luparii aren't anybody's puppet. "Why go after Will, though?" he asked Scarlett. "Why not go after Eli?"

"For one thing, she couldn't find him," she pointed out. "But more importantly, everything that happens in a wolf pack is the alpha's fault, good or bad. To Ana, part of Will's job was to keep Eli and Caroline from attacking humans. He failed at that."

"So she and Terrence found a bigger, badder asshole to go after Will," Jesse said slowly, shaking his head a little in amazement. "If it's true, I don't think Terrence even knew the whole plan. I could see him calling the Luparii, but when I suggested he made the nova, he flipped out on me. I don't think it was faked."

"Ana used him," Scarlett said simply. "I don't know how much of it was always the plan, or how much of it was her taking advantage of a moment, but Lydia's change was ripping her apart. It was destroying their relationship. Add that kind of stress to the regular tension and discomfort that the werewolves have to deal with every day . . ." She shrugged helplessly, looking a little sad. "It's kind of tragic. Ana and Terrence were both miserable, but they were too weak to get what they wanted. They found someone stronger to do it for them, but then they were too weak to survive the help."

"And now we have to clean up their mess," Jesse grumbled. "Okay. I think we're right about what's happening—"

"Jesse," Scarlett broke in, fear in her voice. "If we're right, then the Luparii scout knows who Will is. And tonight's the full moon. There's no guarantee that he'll go after the nova when he could go after the pack."

That chilled him. "Remember, if we can take away the barg-est, the Luparii isn't going after anybody, not today," he said to Scarlett. She nodded resolutely, and he went on, "But how do we find the scout?"

"You're asking *me*?" Scarlett asked, wide-eyed.

"Shh. I'm thinking aloud."

"Oh."

Jesse snapped his fingers. "Phone records." He pulled his phone out of his pocket again and began scrolling numbers.

"Who are you calling?" Scarlett asked.

Listening to the phone ring, Jesse said quickly, "If Terrence called the Luparii in France, maybe he and the scout talked once the scout was here."

"Unless they set up their meeting before the guy left France," Scarlett pointed out.

"Shh. Be hopeful," Jesse told her. She gave him a tiny smile, and motioned that she was going to the downstairs bathroom. He nodded and she hobbled away.

After five rings, Glory finally answered her phone. "Sherman."

"Glory, it's me. Has Bine identified the two bodies yet?" he asked. No point in tiptoeing around it.

"Well, hello to you too. Yes, they got the IDs in this morn-ing. Terrence Whittaker and Drew Riddell. But you already knew that," Glory said angrily.

Jesse blinked. "You know why I couldn't tell her," he said, and then winced at his own voice. He sounded just like Scarlett when she talked to him.

"Yeah, but you left Runa and me holding the bag. Bine really tore into us."

"What'd you say?"

Glory sighed into the phone, a heavy static sound. "I don't know; Runa made something up."

"Good, good," Jesse said distractedly. "Listen, I need to get Terrence Whittaker's phone records. Just for the last week."

There was a long, pregnant silence. "I can't just drop everything to chase some hunch for you, Jesse," Glory said. "I have my own work to do."

Jesse pressed on. "I know, Glory, but it's important. I need to know if he called a number in France, and any calls he made here in the city."

There was a pause. "Is this coming from you or Dashiell?" she asked icily.

He swallowed. Dashiell was using Glory's kids as leverage. Jesse would never do that . . . but at the same time, there was too much at stake to dick around with a distinction that didn't really matter. He was working for Dashiell now, after all. "Both, I guess."

"Then I'll see what I can do," Glory said shortly, and hung up the phone. Jesse stared at it, feeling about two inches tall. He already regretted lumping himself in with Dashiell. He hoped she wasn't thinking that he was on Dashiell's side now instead of hers.

With an acidic burn in his stomach, Jesse tried to ignore the thought that if she was, she might be right.

Chapter 40

While we waited for Jesse's friend to call back, I sat back down on the couch, stretching both legs out on the carpet in front of me. After a few minutes of uncomfortable silence, Jesse said uneasily, "How are you doing over there?'

I had been half dozing, but I jerked awake at his voice. "I'm okay," I said automatically.

Jesse came over and sat down next to me, our elbows touching. His legs were stretched out next to mine. "Listen, while we're waiting . . . I think maybe we should talk." He turned his head to look at me, direct and frank. "About us."

"Is this really the best time?" I said tentatively. Because I am a coward.

He gave me wry smile. "I don't think you and I are going to get a best time."

That was fair. When I didn't say anything more, Jesse began, "Scarlett, listen." I was expecting the "let's just be friends" talk, considering the way things had been between us for the last couple of days. But to my surprise, he said firmly, "I want us to be together."

My astonishment must have shown on my face because he added, "I know things have been weird lately. I agreed to take this position because you were hurt and you needed help. But we've been arguing a lot, and I know I haven't been much use."

"You *left* me," I reminded him, the hurt like an itch in my chest. "You left me with two bodies to move by myself."

He nodded. "And I'm sorry I left you after I promised to help. But this whole thing . . . it's just really made me see how toxic your life is right now."

I blinked, taken aback. "*What?*"

He leaned forward. "Hear me out, Scar," he continued. "Everything you do—hiding bodies, erasing all the violence and bloodshed—it all has ripples. It affects people, and eventually that's gonna catch up with you. I know Dashiell and those guys want to keep things quiet, and I don't necessarily disagree. But it doesn't have to be *you*."

Blanching, I said quietly, "Someone has to do it. And I have a unique skill set. Because it's me, there's a lot less risk, less violence."

Jesse waved a hand. "That doesn't mean it's not corrupting. I worry that every time you do this stuff, you're giving up a piece of yourself. This isn't good for your soul, Scarlett."

I winced. "You might be right, Jesse," I said, keeping my voice very calm, "but then again, it's *my* soul. What makes you think you can tell me what to do with it?"

"Grow up, Scarlett," he said, not unkindly. "You know this isn't some misogynistic dominance thing. That's not who I am, or who we are. I love you, and I don't want to watch you giving up yourself."

I shook my head. "I can't just quit," I said weakly. "Even if I wanted to, there are other factors . . ."

"I know Dashiell is holding your brother over your head," he interrupted. "To keep you in line."

That surprised me. "How did you . . ."

Jesse rolled his eyes. "I'm a trained detective, remember?"

I smiled. "Right, sorry."

"Anyway. I know you can't just quit without Jack getting blowback from Dashiell. But maybe we could work something out with him, or get Jack out of town. Or we could just leave—you could make a deal with the Old World somewhere else; offer your null services in exchange for getting Dashiell to back down. You said that LA wasn't very notable in the supernatural world. There have to be a lot bigger fish than Dashiell."

I thought about that. I do make a little money from freelance jobs doing the kind of stuff Jesse was talking about—escorting vampires to daytime meetings, guiding werewolves through stressful occasions, that kind of thing. Certainly nothing that involved throwing murdered women into furnaces. But it had never occurred to me to try to start over with that stuff somewhere else. I felt dread sloshing in the bottom of my stomach. True, I had always kind of viewed my job as a temporary thing, something I'd do out of necessity for a few years and then get out. But when I did, it wouldn't be to jump right back into bed with the supernatural. "I don't want to work for the Old World somewhere else," I said quietly. "I just want a normal life, like I used to have."

Jesse snorted, which took me by surprise again. He was just full of surprises today. "No, you don't."

"There you go again," I said irritably, "telling me about my feelings."

"You *think* you want normalcy," Jesse retorted. "But you've been special for too long. What you *want* is control over your life." He spread out his hands. "I'm saying, let's find a way to make that happen, together."

I stared at him. Was he expecting an answer right this second? Did I have one?

"You don't have to answer right now," Jesse said, grinning. He'd read my mind. "I know you have to sort some stuff out. But after we catch this guy, I *am* going to ask you again."

His phone buzzed loudly, but he didn't so much as look at it. Instead, he held my eyes, quirking one eyebrow up, waiting for my response. "Okay?" he said, still smiling devilishly.

"Okay, okay!" I answered hurriedly, smiling back despite myself. That face was impossible to resist. "Answer the phone!"

Jesse answered the phone without looking. "This is Cruz," he said, eyes never leaving mine. "Yeah . . . okay . . . sure." He glanced around the room and crossed quickly to my abandoned pen and notepad, scribbling something in a margin. "Go ahead . . . okay, got it. Thanks, Glo—" He stopped and held the phone away from his ear, peering at the screen. "She hung up," he said to himself.

"What'd you find out?" I asked impatiently.

He grinned. "We got an address."

Chapter 41

The Luparii scout, Jesse told me, was staying at a rental condo in Huntington Park, not far from Evergreen Cemetery. According to Jesse's friend Glory, Terrence Whittaker hadn't made many phone calls. Shortly after the run-in with Molly and me at Will's house, however, he had called a handful of numbers in Europe. The last had an area code for Versailles, France, when he must have gotten in touch with the Luparii. After that conversation, all of Terrence's subsequent calls were to one of three phone numbers. Since there were so few, and she figured Jesse would ask, Glory had tracked down addresses for all three numbers. One was Anastasia's cell phone, one was Drew Riddell's cell phone, and the last was a rental property in Huntington Park.

Now that the LAPD had the number it wouldn't be long before they pursued the lead too, so Jesse spent a few minutes on the phone with someone named Bine, explaining that he was going to check out Terrence Whittaker's cell phone info himself. The conversation went on for a while, and when he hung up Jesse was shaking his head a little. "She said I've got twenty-four hours before she puts someone else on it," he told me. "I got the sense that she wants to kick me off the case, but whatever Dashiell did to make me a floater is apparently working."

Next Jesse tried calling the property's owner to find out who was renting the condo, but the guy didn't answer his phone. We still had the address, though. I was ready to pretty much get my jacket and go kick in the guy's door—well, okay, supervise Jesse as he kicked in the door—but Jesse pointed out that we needed, you know, a *plan*. He went upstairs to retrieve my laptop from my bedroom and sat down next to me on the couch. I entered my password, and he opened a browser and typed in the address for something called Google Maps.

"You've never heard of this?" Jesse said disbelievingly, fingers flying on my computer's keyboard. "What do you even use this thing for?"

"Oh, you know. E-mail. Wikipedia. Looking up movie times."

Jesse snorted and pulled up a satellite image of the address in question. The rental condo was one of four rectangular buildings clustered around a few green blotches. "Coooooool," I breathed. "What's with the giant spears of broccoli?"

"Those are trees, dummy," Jesse said good-naturedly. Then he frowned. "They're blocking the satellite from really seeing what the space looks like, but I'm guessing it's a yard. Or a really big garden."

I nodded. It made sense that the Luparii scout wanted more space and privacy, especially if the bargest was so big or terrifying that it actually couldn't pass for a dog. It also kept both of them from being seen by a bunch of hotel employees who might gossip.

"You can't really see all the entrances and exits, which is a problem," Jesse observed. "We'll be going in blind."

"So what do we do?" I said, sitting back on the sofa.

Jesse looked disconcerted. "I have no idea," he answered. "I'm not usually on the criminal end of this kind of thing. How does one go about dognapping?"

I thought about it for a moment. We could stake out the guy's place and hope he'd go out for food or something so we could steal the dog. But if I had a magical creature that my family had perfected after centuries of trial and error, not to mention made using a human sacrifice, I probably wouldn't let it out of my sight on the day of the full moon, not even for In-N-Out Burger.

Then I grinned. "Jesse," I said sweetly, "would you be a lamb and run upstairs for my Taser?"

There were still a few more things to take care of. First we went by Jesse's place so he could get his police uniform. Then we stopped at a pet supply store for an extra large muzzle, a leash and collar, and some dog food. I had no idea what bargests ate—it could be exclusively squirrel livers, for all we knew—but Noring *had* said the thing was at least part dog. We got the expensive canned stuff that promised to be the most meatlike.

I thought we were done by then, but Jesse insisted on stopping at Home Depot.

"Why Home Depot?" I asked dubiously.

Jesse gave me a mysterious smile. "You'll see." Then he said, "Hey, if I keep receipts, will Dashiell reimburse me?"

I waited in the car while he went into the store, mostly because Home Depot is the size of a football field and I wasn't up for the exercise. When Jesse came out, he wasn't carrying anything—but he was pulling a big utility wagon, the kind serious gardeners use to pull potted plants around. I could see a roll of duct tape rattling around the back. "Oh," I said. "Well. Good thing we have the van." I held up my hand for a high five.

Up until then, we had been pretty cheerful about the whole ridiculous plan, but for the last few miles the mood in the van grew subdued. I was having . . . well, not second thoughts, exactly, but certainly some new reservations, now that some of my initial excitement (and caffeine high) had waned. I didn't know about Jesse, but I was painfully aware of how tenuous our plan was.

But then again, we were taking a gamble no matter which way we turned. And there was one thing I *was* sure of: if the bad guy has a weapon, you have to take it away. Even if we couldn't use the bargest, at least keeping it away from the Luparii scout meant that he couldn't go after Will's people tonight.

"This is it," Jesse said finally. We had arrived at the condo building, a three-story, white and pale blue affair with archways everywhere. Like, *everywhere*. I don't know anything about architecture, but I do know when a building looks like someone drew wavy lines on it with crayon. Its ornateness wasn't feminine, exactly, but it was too elegant for the neighborhood by half.

"It looks like it belongs on top of a cake," Jesse observed, leaning over the steering wheel so he could stare at it better.

"It looks like it *is* the top of the cake," I countered.

He drove past the building to the next block and pulled over to the curb. "Okay. I'm gonna change," Jesse said. He wasn't using his "official police business" voice, but he did sound like a cop: in control, serious, trustworthy. The effect was kind of ruined when he added, "No peeking while I'm naked."

I snorted as he crawled into the back of the van, grabbing the hanger with his old uniform. "I'm a professional," I said loftily. "Professionals do not *peek*." He hadn't wanted to drive around the city in LAPD garb, for some reason. I debated turning my head just a little to peek despite my words, but I figured that would be taken for flirting, and I wasn't ready for that, exactly.

He ducked back between the two front seats. "Okay," Jesse said, tension thickening his voice. "Are you ready?"

"Not really," I admitted. "But let's do it anyway." I pulled on my old USC baseball cap. We'd loaded the dog supplies and Jesse's street clothes into an old backpack, and I put that on as well.

To my surprise, he leaned just a little farther and planted a swift, gentle kiss on my lips, tweaking the brim of my hat as he pulled back. "Good luck," he told me.

"Uh . . . right. Yes. And you as well," I sputtered, and opened the door.

I began walking back toward the condo. There was no security team or anything, and I didn't spot any obvious cameras, although it was hard to really look and keep my head down at the same time. It would make sense for the Luparii scout to want to stay somewhere that valued privacy over ostentatious security, though.

The building was shaped like a long rectangle, split lengthwise by a pretty open-air courtyard that ran the whole length of the building. There was a tasteful fountain burbling dead center in the courtyard, between a modest swimming pool on one side and several sets of café tables and chairs on the other. No one was using either area, and I breathed a sigh a relief—we wouldn't have to try to do this with witnesses.

A narrow cobblestone path framed the courtyard and provided little walkways to each of the ten or twelve doors that framed the long sides of the rectangle. I started down the path, figuring number 144 was probably on the ground level. Each condo had picture windows on either side of an ornate, Spanish-style wood-and-iron door, but almost every single window had closed blinds. It was a shame—all that fancy landscaping for the courtyard, and nobody was willing to sacrifice their privacy to look at it.

The landscaping suited my purposes, though. There was a waist-high hedge that ran between the cobblestone pathways for each condo, underneath the windows. That would make it a lot easier to sneak up on the Luparii scout. I didn't want to give him time to see me coming. If he got skittish and tried a spell, he might figure out what I was. And although he couldn't hex me, he could still send the bargest to eat me. And I had no idea how the Taser would work against a magical dog-monster.

I spotted the iron placard for number 144 and kept right on going. The barking began when I was still a good twenty feet away, a low sound that seemed to come from a *very* deep chest. Damn. The thing really did have strong senses. A female voice shouted inside the building, a guttural blur of a word that had to be French, and the barking ceased abruptly. It was well trained, if nothing else. I saw the white blinds shift in one of the condo's windows as fingers with red nails made a vertical hole between them. I made a special effort to look purposeful and confident, feeling the comforting bump of the Taser in my pocket. I never so much as glanced at the window for 144, and after a few seconds I saw the blinds snap closed again out of the corner of my eye. I kept going, making my slow way to the next footpath.

My thoughts spun. A woman. The Luparii scout was a woman. I felt like an idiot. Of course she was a woman; the vast majority of witches were. Why had we assumed that she'd be male? Because she was evil?

Stupid Scarlett. Ladies can be bad guys too.

I walked right up to the door of number 112, listening closely. If there were people at home, they were being quiet about it. I glanced around—still no people—and dropped down to all fours. The space between the building and the hedge was just wide enough for me to crawl through without brushing against the shrubbery, and almost tall enough to hide me completely. I lifted my cane and set it very gently a few feet in front of me, without making noise. Then I crawled after it on my hands and one knee and repeated the process, making my way under the condo's picture window and toward number 144. I was agonizingly slow, which I hoped would work in my favor. Who would expect an injured burglar with a cane, who attacked in broad daylight? Hopefully no one, although if any city was going to have a handicapped, crawling daytime burglar, it'd probably be LA.

Focus, Scarlett. As I reached the bottom of the picture window by 144, I felt the scout in my radius on the other side of the wall. Up close, I could see that the condo's windows had a latticework of sturdy bars, painted white so as to be almost invisible against the blinds. Huh. Between the security sticker in the window, the bars, and that heavy wood-and-iron door, we'd better hope this plan worked. We weren't getting into the condo otherwise.

I was under the center of the window when I heard a loud creak right on the other side of the wall, stunningly close to where I was. I froze. A female voice murmured something in French again, and I felt a stab of fear. What if she wasn't alone? I closed my eyes, concentrated, and extended my radius. No other witches, but there was a muted yelp, and I felt something new in my radius. Emphasis on the *new*.

A witch in my radius felt like a faint buzz of white noise, and this new thing was similar, but the . . . *shape* of it, for lack of a better term, was different. Subtler. There was another spark to it too: something *wild*. I might not even have noticed that spark if I wasn't concentrating so hard, tuned in to Radio Scarlett.

I heard footsteps. Leaning forward, I peered beyond the hedge and into the pathway for 144. Jesse was just rounding the fountain, marching in my general direction, looking handsome and professional in his police uniform. He spotted me—or maybe the condo number—and abruptly altered course to head straight for 144, not trying to hide it. Our eyes met, and I thought I saw him give a little nod.

Still on my hands and knees, I flicked my index finger at the door and mouthed, "woman." Since we'd been expecting a man all along, I didn't want him to let his guard down when a woman opened the door. Confusion flickered across his face, and he faltered a step. "Woooman," I mouthed again, eyebrows up emphatically. "Lady," I tried. But he wasn't getting it. He was getting very close now, so I rolled my eyes, leaned back on my heel, and mimed giant breasts in front of my own very average-sized ones. "Woman," I mouthed again, pointing at the door. He nodded, comprehension flooding his face. Finally. I ducked back down below the hedge just in time—I heard the metallic rustle of the blinds right above my head as the Luparii peeked out again.

Jesse arrived at the door, only inches away from me, and rapped three times, causing the dog to bark again. Maybe not *that* well trained.

The door did not open, but she shouted through it. "Who ees zhere?" she asked in heavily accented French.

"LAPD, ma'am," Jesse said sternly. He held his ID up to the peephole. "We've had a complaint from one of your neighbors about a barking dog."

"I do not . . . my Eenglish ees . . ." She faltered. I frowned. We had not anticipated her being unable to understand us.

But to my very extreme surprise, Jesse jumped in with, "*Je suis avec la police, madame. Ouvrez la porte, s'il vous plaît.*"

My eyes bugged out of my head, but I could feel Jesse very pointedly not looking down at me. He didn't want to give me away, but it was still kind of funny.

I caught the words "*police*" and "*porte*," which I assumed was "door," but I totally lost the thread when the woman yelled, "*Le chien ne sera pas aboyer plus. Je te le promets.*"

"*J'ai besoin de vous parler, madame. Attachez le chien. Ouvrez la porte.*" He held up the ID again.

I stared at Jesse, trying to pick up from his expression what the hell was going on. But he remained very firm and professional. I waited. After a long moment of silence, I heard at least three bolts thrown open, and a crack appeared in the door.

My Taser is very special. It's a police-issued, drive stun model, meaning I hold it directly against a target and it hurts like a bitch. Unlike most drive stun models, however, mine has been modified to affect the central nervous system the same way a Taser gun does. It's the best nonlethal weapon for a null because it means I don't have to dick around with trying to shoot a weapon at supernatural creatures who are probably moving really fast. By the time you're close enough to me to be a physical threat, you're close enough to tase.

It's basically a pocket-sized cattle prod.

I could have given it to Jesse to use, but since I had to be right there anyway to make sure she couldn't use her magic, we had decided it was best for me to do the tasing while Jesse distracted her. It works through clothes, but when the Luparii scout finally opened the door all the way, I opted not to take chances. As Jesse began to speak in rapid French, I slid up the cuff of her sleek black pants, pressed the Taser against her skin, and pulled the trigger. The whole thing was over faster than she could say, "Ooh la la! A Taser!"

Or whatever French people say.

Chapter 42

I held the Taser on her skin until the woman crumpled forward. Jesse was ready to catch her though, dragging her quickly into the condo and dumping her just inside the door. I hauled myself to my feet and followed as fast as I could. I slammed the door closed behind me, and we exchanged a relieved grin while I caught my breath. From deeper in the condo, the bargest began to bark again.

I looked at the woman at my feet. She was very tall, maybe six feet; blonde and beautiful in a harsh, imperialist kind of way. In a movie she'd be cast as a German Nazi ice queen, French heritage or not. She glared at me with her lips moving, but I knew from experience that she lacked the fine motor skills for talking.

The condo's front door opened directly onto a living room/dining room combination, with the kitchen off to our left. She must have had the bargest restrained in a back bedroom. "You told her to put the dog away?" I asked Jesse. He nodded.

"So," I said to Jesse, "You speak French."

"A little," he admitted. "I already spoke Spanish, so in high school my mom made me take French. Haven't used it in years, though." Jesse wrinkled his nose. "Smell that?"

I glanced around the condo. It wasn't even furnished, not really, but what little furniture was there probably cost more than my van. "Money?"

"Piss," Jesse corrected. "I think she pissed herself."

"Oh. Yeah, that happens."

He nudged the Luparii scout's body with a toe. She glared up at us, conscious but unable to access the ability for speech. Jesse glanced down at my Taser. "Is that thing street legal?" he asked doubtfully.

"Let's call it legal-adjacent," I suggested.

"Will she be okay?"

The barking from the back room had gotten so loud that he had to repeat himself twice before I understood. "She'll be fine," I yelled back. "We should get her tied up before she recovers though."

Jesse produced the roll of duct tape from behind his back, where he must have tucked it into his belt, and we got to work taping the woman's ankles, wrists, and mouth. We used more than half the roll before Jesse declared her officially subdued. As he tore off the tape, I spotted a very expensive handbag sitting on the countertop. "Hey," I called, crossing the empty kitchen to the bag. I almost didn't want to put my grubby hands inside it, it looked so expensive. I solved the problem by flipping the damn thing over. A small mound of purse paraphernalia scattered across the counter.

Jesse picked up a French passport. "Her name is Petra Corbett," he called over the sound of barking.

"Doesn't sound very French," I yelled back. He just shrugged.

"We gotta get it to be quiet, or someone's gonna call the LAPD for real," Jesse pointed out. I nodded, and he started for the back bedroom. I hobbled after him.

Jesse opened the bedroom door very slowly, but the barg-est didn't dart out and trample him. It must have been in a crate or something. But when the door began to move, the thing went suddenly quiet, and Jesse and I exchanged a nervous glance. He pushed the door the rest of the way open.

I swung the backpack around so I could dig the dog stuff out of it, but I looked up when I heard Jesse's gasp. He was planted in the doorway, frozen, mouth wide open. "Holy shit," he breathed.

"What?" I said, making my way toward the doorway.

"That," Jesse said, eyes huge and round, "is the ugliest fucking dog I have ever seen."

I came up behind Jesse's shoulder and got my first look at the bargest.

The back bedroom was fairly large and had no furniture, but a lot of space was taken up by an enormous wire crate that didn't look sturdy enough for what was inside. The bargest stood tense and growling within it, paws planted in all four corners of the crate. I had been expecting big, and it was very big. Almost three feet at the shoulder, and I was guessing about a hundred and eighty pounds. Big, yes, but not the biggest dog I'd ever seen.

But Jesse was right; it was hideous. Except for the ears, the bargest looked like someone had taken a Scottish deerhound, shaved off huge swathes of its fur, and dipped it in the blackest of black ink—except that its face was lumpy and not quite symmetrical, giving the overall impression that it had recently lost a prizefight. Tufts of short, coarse fur covered part of the back and one ear, while the rest of its skin was hairless, with a pebbly reptile-like texture that looked a little like . . . armor. The hairless ear had been torn at some point and had healed not quite right. The good ear flicked forward, and I realized that it was a perfect wolf's ear.

If Frankenstein made a dog . . .

It snarled, drawing black lips up over terrible white teeth. Jesse took an involuntary step back, stretching out his arm protectively. "This isn't gonna work, Scar," he warned. "That thing is dangerous." Jesse held out his hand. "Give me the Taser. We'll tape it up and take it to Dashiell or Kirsten. They'll find a humane way to put it down."

I stared at the bargest. Once you got past the ugliness and the size, it looked . . . like a dog. A terrified, confused dog. "Let me talk to it," I suggested.

"And say what?" Jesse said disbelievingly. "That thing only knows French commands."

"Well, try one. Tell it to sit."

Jesse shook his head at me, but said, "Uh—*asseyez-vous*." He looked at me. "I don't know the command tense."

I pushed gently past his arm and approached the kennel. When I took a few steps into the room, though, the bargest hit my radius, and suddenly it's growling stopped and it whined uncertainly. It shook itself. Jesse began to say something, and the bargest snarled again, the tufts of fur on its back rising with tension.

With some effort, I lowered myself to the floor a few feet in front of the kennel, stretching out my bad knee and pulling my opposite foot in to touch my thigh. "Jesse," I said softly, not meeting the bargest's eyes, "I saw a wad of paper in the purse. Would you see if any of it is for the dog? Vet papers or whatever?"

I wasn't looking at him, but I could practically feel a suspicious look coming from Jesse. "First promise me you won't go any closer," he commanded.

"I won't go any closer."

I heard soft footfalls on the carpet, and the bargest looked at me, slightly calmer. It tilted its head, puzzled. Maybe having multiple people in one room had been a little overwhelming

"Hi, puppy," I said soothingly, keeping my eyes on the floor. "I'm Scarlett. What's your name?"

I glanced up to see the bargest yawning, displaying enormous jaws that could possibly be described as "slavering." "Hoo boy," I breathed. Despite the shadows in the crate, I thought I saw it wag its tail once, tentatively. Encouraged, I crooned some more nonsense at it.

Jesse chose that moment to reenter the room. The bargest went on alert again, feet planted, tufts of hair standing on end. Jesse didn't notice; he was focused on the unfolded wad of papers. "You were right, they had to register it with the airline. Paid a *fortune* to fly it too."

"Jesse," I murmured, "you're too big. Be smaller."

"Oh. Right." He sat down on the carpeted floor, and the bargest stopped growling and shifted its feet nervously, totally confused by the situation.

"What's her name?" I asked softly.

"Her?" He looked at the crate again, but the dog was black and there were shadows. It was impossible to see between its legs.

"Call it a hunch," I said.

Jesse flipped a page while the bargest eyed both of us. "You're right, it's a female," he noted, scanning the paper. "They claim she's a Peruvian Hairless mix, which strikes me as total bullshit. Her name is . . . heh. Belle."

"As in Beauty?" I said incredulously. I don't know much French, but my childhood had been infiltrated by Disney, just like everybody else's.

"Yep. The Luparii might be a bunch of assholes, but at least one of them has a sense of humor."

"Guess so."

Jesse looked at his watch. "We need to move. We've already been here too long. If any of the neighbors saw us . . ." The bargest, hearing our friendly voices, began to tentatively wag her tail again. "Well, look at that," Jesse said softly.

I nodded. "I don't think she's actually that aggressive. I think she's scared and confused."

"Scarlett," Jesse said patiently, like he was talking to some bleeding-heart moron. "She's evil."

"Hush. She's no such thing, are you girl?" Hearing the question in my voice, the bargest's tail started wagging double-time.

"She slaughtered those two werewolves, Scarlett," Jesse said gently. "Just because you *want* something to be true . . ."

For the bargest's sake, I kept my voice low and calm, even as I said, "I'm not an idiot, Jesse. Look at her: before it started wagging, that tail was tucked between her legs. She's not cowering—they probably trained her not to run from scary stuff—but she's leaning sideways so she'll be ready to recoil. She doesn't understand if she's supposed to listen to us or attack us, and we haven't given her the right cues for either."

There was a long pause behind me, and then Jesse said defensively, "She was snarling."

"We scared her, and she's trapped in a little box. You'd snarl too."

"She's dangerous, Scarlett."

I turned my head slightly so I could look back at him. "So is your gun, but I trust you with it. Now trust me."

My partner locked eyes with me for a second, and then nodded warily. "Okay. So what do you want to do?"

I told Jesse to go move the scout into the bathroom so she wouldn't distract the bargest. I also gave him his jeans and T-shirt out of the backpack so he could change. When Jesse closed the door to the bedroom we were in, I approached the bargest's crate by crawling in a curve toward it, never facing her head-on or making eye contact. I crawled on my hands and good knee until I was at the side of her kennel that had the latches. Making sure I wasn't blocking her escape route from the crate, I took a deep breath and undid them. The door sprang open.

The bargest exploded out of the crate, suddenly seeming to fill the room with her presence. It was overwhelming, terrifying, but I forced myself not to cower. She could probably smell my fear, but there wasn't much I could do about that, so I just sat there as calmly as possible while she raced around the room—which had seemed fairly big only a moment ago—in tight controlled circles. Now that I could see all of her . . . well, she was just as ugly as before, with a strange club-like tail that just naturally looked like someone had docked it at ten inches. But there was something else going on with her too: a graceful power and intelligence that had nothing to do with magic and everything to do with how she was built. I could see why the Luparii had chosen this particular puppy for the bargest spell.

After a few minutes, when I didn't seem to be going anywhere, she calmed down and came over to sniff me. I held very still. After she'd snuffled her muzzle around my hair and clothes, I very slowly lifted my hand from the floor, my fingers curled in a loose fist, and held it out to her. She sniffed it for a long moment, and then gave me a single approving lick. Her club tail wagged again.

"I'm not sure that Belle suits you," I said, lowering my forehead to touch hers. "It seems a little pretentious and cruel." She was wearing a collar, a formidable spiked leather thing. I scratched her neck under the collar, and she panted appreciatively.

I pulled the new canvas collar out of my backpack and let her sniff it. When she didn't object, I fastened it around her neck and then undid the buckle on the leather collar, letting it fall on the floor. The bargest was a huge investment of time, money, and magic, and if I were the Luparii, I wouldn't have been above putting some kind of GPS chip in the collar to protect my investment.

She sniffed the discarded collar once, and looked back up at me. She had a quizzical expression that said, *What now?* "We got this," I told her. I repeated the procedure with the new leash, letting her sniff it before fastening it. She gazed at me evenly, her tail still wagging rather hesitantly.

Even though I trusted her in that moment, alone together in a room with no stimuli, it was better safe than sorry. I took the soft canvas muzzle out of the bag and let her smell that too. "Okay?" I said. She gave me a resigned look. "You've done this before, I take it." At my voice, her tail wagged once.

I fastened the muzzle behind her head and let out a breath I'd been holding.

We left the Luparii scout tied up in the bathroom. I was tempted to hand her over to Dashiell, to be killed or used as leverage. But, aside from the fact that I didn't know how Jesse would react to that idea, we weren't up for getting her into the van in broad daylight, especially with my injury.

The bargest seemed to accept Jesse more now that she wasn't stuck in a little box while he loomed over her, so I gave him the leash to hold on the way to my van. I was a little nervous that the bargest might take off as soon as she hit fresh air—which prompted a funny mental image of her racing flat-out down the center of the street, with Jesse dragging behind her like a prisoner in a Western—but I needn't have worried. The bargest heeled perfectly, staying exactly in step with Jesse's left foot as we walked.

"All that work, and you didn't get to use your big wagon," I said sadly, as Jesse stowed it sideways in the back of the van to make room for the bargest. He patted the bottom of the van and the bargest hopped up effortlessly. Despite the graceful movement, the whole van shuddered as she climbed aboard.

"The night is young," Jesse said, his voice still a little tight. He was doing a good job of appearing calm, but I knew that committing daylight crimes was bothering him. Or maybe he was just a little nervous about the bargest. "We may get a chance yet."

We climbed in the van, both of us craning our heads around to check the back. The bargest had curled into a tight knot on the floor, laying with her head facing forward so she could keep an eye on us. "I've never seen a dog do that in a car," Jesse said, amazed.

"She's a lady," I intoned.

As he pulled away from the curb, Jesse jerked his head back in the direction of the building we'd just left. "You think she can hex herself out of there?" he asked.

I shook my head. "I've never met a witch yet who could do a spell with their thoughts only. And if she could, I'm guessing she would have done it by now. We're waltzing off with her prize."

He nodded, accepting that, but looked a little regretful. "She'll be fine, Jesse," I added. "That bitch forces animals to kill people. A day or two locked in a bathroom is the least we can do to her."

"That's true," he said thoughtfully. Looking a little more cheerful, he headed toward the freeway.

We rode in companionable silence for a few minutes, and then he glanced over at me. "How did you know?" he asked.

"Know what?"

"That she wasn't going attack us."

I considered the question for a moment. "The body language, for one thing. My mom was really interested in dog body language; she talked a lot about their cues."

"Yeah, but we didn't know if it would follow dog rules," Jesse pointed out.

"That's true," I allowed. "But, look, the Luparii have to *use* her. That means they have to direct her to specific purposes. The Luparii haven't lasted this long or prospered this much without being smart. And which is smarter, to have a psychotic cave troll that you can only let loose at your enemies, or to have something so well trained that you can point to five people out of a crowd of a hundred and say 'kill *them*'?"

Jesse adjusted the rearview mirror so he could check on the bargest. "So you're suggesting she's more effective as a weapon than as a monster."

"Yeah. And the Luparii built her that way." I shook my head. "The bargest spell is probably the most complex I've ever heard of. It makes sense that they'd start with raw material they could control. If it were me, I'd keep a whole bunch of these dog-wolf hybrids trained and ready at all times, and just do the bargest spell when I knew of a werewolf threat somewhere."

"That would save on resources." Jesse thought it over for a few minutes. "So she may not even have had these powers for that long. If they did the spell just a few days ago, she might be as new to killing werewolves as we are to the Luparii."

I nodded. Jesse turned his head and smiled at me briefly. "Sorry for doubting you," he added.

I sniffed imperiously. "Don't let it happen again."

Chapter 43

We got away from the Huntington Park area as quickly as we could, pulling over at a fast food restaurant so I could call and update Will while Jesse ran in for caffeine replenishment. With the Luparii scout taken off the board, the whole situation got a lot less complicated, but we still had almost six hours until moonrise. Jesse thought we shouldn't arrive at Griffith Park too early, for fear of the nova wolf spotting us as he arrived and taking off for another location. That left us with a lot of time to kill—and not a lot of places where we could take a 180-pound dog-monster.

Molly's was out, as was Jesse's tiny apartment. "What about taking her to Will's house?" Jesse asked, taking a sip from his Diet Coke. "It's secluded, and there's parking."

I shook my head. "That whole place stinks of werewolf. I don't know how she'd react to that, especially if she wandered out of my radius."

"Good point. Dog park?" Jesse suggested.

"No way. We have no idea how she'll react to other dogs. She might eat them."

"I guess that rules out taking her to my parents' place," Jesse mused. "I don't want Max to be eaten."

I thought it over for a moment. "Actually . . . maybe it's worth a try? At least then we could see if she can pass for a dog in mixed company." With her color and intelligence, I couldn't imagine thinking the bargest was anything but a magical creature, but I was hoping that was only because I knew for a fact that magical creatures existed.

Jesse shot me a dubious look, but called his parents' house anyway. They were both out, but his brother Noah was home, and willing to participate in a doggy friendship experiment. Or rather, a dog-bargest friendship experiment. Possibly the first of its kind. Jesse brightened a little. "If we're stopping at my folks', I have another idea too."

When we pulled into the driveway at Jesse's parents' house, there was a man already standing on the front steps with Max on a leash beside him. My eyes bugged out a little at the sight of him. It was like Jesse had taken another Jesse and swallowed him. "Whoa," I said in awe. "It's Jesse version 2.0."

"Can it, Bernard," Jesse said good-naturedly. "That's Noah."

I took a closer look as he put the van in park and we got out. Noah stayed on the steps, standing calmly as Max started jumping straight up and down in the air, thrilled beyond measure by our presence. Noah had lighter skin, for sure, and wasn't as handsome as Jesse. He had the exact same smile though, which I noticed as we walked toward the house and he stepped down from the steps, holding out his hand. I shook it while Max cheerfully head-butted my legs, delighted to have me within love-attack range. It hurt, and I winced. "Max," Jesse reproached. Max turned to him with a wounded look and did his best to love my femur by wagging his whip tail against me instead. Not a big improvement. I patted him on the head anyway.

"It's nice to finally meet you, Scarlett," Noah said playfully. "Jesse never, ever talks about you, so we know you must be special."

"Noah," Jesse warned, in the exact same tone he'd used on Max. His brother took him about as seriously as Max had.

"All right, where's this monstrous dog?" Noah asked.

Jesse and I exchanged a look. "In the van," I said simply. I looked down at my knee. "Jesse, can you . . ."

"Yep, I'll get her. Hang on to Max's leash," he warned Noah. "She's . . . big."

Jesse went to the back doors of the van and cracked one door open a little. "What's he got in there, King Kong?" Noah said under his breath. I smiled.

The bargest stepped daintily down from the van, hardly needing to hop at all with her long legs. Max went stock-still, his hackles rising. "Holy shit," Noah whispered. I glanced at him. He was staring at the bargest with a mixture of wonder and respect, but no fear. "That," he said with awe, "is the ugliest fucking dog I have ever seen."

I laughed. Definitely Jesse's brother.

Jesse took it slow, but she walked toward us with perfect calm, head up, eyes alert. I'd never seen such a self-possessed dog before; she seemed to be *controlling herself*, not because we'd told her to, but because it was her nature. As someone who has spent a lot of time around dogs, I found it almost spooky. Then she paused and rubbed her face against Jesse's leg, trying to push the muzzle off, and I had to laugh a little.

"What kind of dog *is* she?" Noah asked me quietly.

"Technically, she's a lurcher," I replied. More or less honestly. Anytime you breed a sighthound, like a deerhound or an Irish wolfhound, with any non-sighthound breed, that's called a lurcher. Don't ask me why.

Max whined as Jesse and the bargest drew closer, shuffling his feet the same way she had in the crate. He didn't know what to do. Jesse stopped when the bargest was just close enough for the two dogs to smell each other's heads, and we let them do so. Then Max did something I never dreamed I'd see him do: he plopped on the ground and rolled over, belly in the air.

And that was that.

Fifteen minutes later, we were sitting on the kitchen table, watching the dogs chase each other around the house. I could have sold tickets to this view. Max, who was already a fast, intelligent, strong dog, was tearing around the house, playing with a creature that was twice his size, speed, and intelligence. Noah had wisely put all the breakables up high before we arrived, so while they thundered around, the cupboards rattled a little, but nothing actually broke.

After a few minutes, Noah vanished upstairs to take a phone call. Jesse and I had started out sitting on the couch, but had elected to move to higher ground for our own safety.

"Let's change her name," I said to Jesse, watching the two of them play. Max was panting heavily, but although I'd removed the bargest's muzzle, she still seemed unfazed. "She's not responding to how I pronounce Belle, and anyway, she should get to be called something a little less annoyingly ironic."

"What are you gonna call her instead?" Jesse asked with a tiny smile. "Frenchie? Blackie? Inky?"

"Those are terrible bargest names," I informed him. "Everybody knows that."

A grin broke out on his face. "What, then?"

"Well, it should really be Hunter, but that's a boy's name, and I'd like to think she can escape the trappings of her upbringing." I pursed my lips, watching the bargest lope after Max as he made joyous circles around the house. Where he was lively, excited, and rambunctious, she was more serious, grave. It was like all the natural liveliness of a big high-energy dog had been taken away from her through her training. What was left was restrained grace and dogged pursuit. Max was probably the fastest dog I'd ever seen, but the bargest looked like she could have run right over him whenever she felt like it. But she stayed glued to his heels instead.

"Shadow," I said aloud.

When I turned to look at him, Jesse was watching me closely. "You're not getting attached, are you?" he asked, not unkindly.

I shook my head. "I know she'll have to be put down," I told him quietly. "She's too dangerous in the wrong hands."

Jesse looked like he wanted to say something, but fell silent instead. After a moment, he said, "Shadow, huh? Well, I guess we have to call her something."

I took a sip of my tea. "We should probably work on our plan for tonight."

Jesse smiled. "Hang on, I gotta go get something." He jumped up and left the room, and a second later I heard his footsteps on the staircase in the other room. Max and Shadow changed course to go investigate what he was doing, and I smiled as Shadow easily overtook Max, leaving him looking after her with a confused expression.

A few minutes later, Jesse and the canines came back down the stairs with a decoupage cardboard box, the kind my mother used to have for storing photos. "Take a look at this," he said, climbing back onto the table and discarding the lid. "I think I might have some pictures of the spot Sharon Remus was talking about." He began sifting through the photos.

"Why?" I asked. "Magical premonition?"

"That, or because my mom got a new camera a couple of years ago and I wanted to mess around with it." After sorting through the box for a few minutes, he finally pulled a little wad of photos out of the box. "My mom is a chronic photo developer." He leaned forward and began laying them out on the table in front of us. "Max is in most of these, but you can get a sense of the background."

I leaned forward too, scanning the photos while he spoke. "See, this is the road that leads up to the Observatory—the tunnel's right over there—and then just down the hill there's this long clear path that goes to a circular picnic area," Jesse said. He pointed to the relevant photo, which showed a seated Max panting happily in the middle of a clear-cut, sand-colored trail. The trail was like the landing on a staircase: on the left side, the hill rose steeply enough to create a natural wall, and the right side of the path, the hill dropped off completely. In the distance behind Max, the path seemed to dead-end at a big flat area with blurs scattered around. I squinted. Picnic tables.

"What's behind the picnic area?" I asked. "Does the trail go off in another direction?"

"No, see, that's why I think this is the spot," Jesse said excitedly. "That picnic area is a big flat circle, and behind it there's nothing—the ground drops off to form a cliff. There's this short winding path that goes for a little ways below it, kind of like a narrow bridle path, but with rocks and brush everywhere. You'd basically have to be a mountain goat to navigate it in the dark."

"Or a werewolf," I concluded.

"Right. But it's a fantastic overlook; you can see the whole city from there." He raised his eyebrows significantly.

"So you think Remus will hide on the bridle path, for lack of a better term, waiting for someone to come see the pretty view, and then pick them off?" I said skeptically. "How can he be sure anyone will show?"

Jesse shrugged. "I've never been up there at night, but it makes sense. The Observatory's right there. If the parking lot is full, people have to park all the way down the road, almost to the picnic area." As he spoke he twisted around to the counter and pulled a pad of paper out of the stack of clutter. He grabbed a pencil too and began sketching as he spoke. "Even if he doesn't stay in the picnic area, he could creep all the way to the road to attack people and drag them back down the bridle path, one at a time. Nobody would think to look there at nighttime, and if anyone chases him toward the picnic tables, he can disappear."

He turned the paper toward me. It was a rough map of the area: a wide path in the foreground leading into a big circle, with the wiggly little bridle path on the other side. I studied it. "I don't know anything about tactics," I said slowly, touching the spot on Jesse's map where the wide path met the road. "But he could hide here, if there are bushes or shadows that can hide him, and then he's got a perfect trap. Some dumbass brings his girlfriend to the picnic area to see the romantic view, and then Remus attacks, trapping them in the picnic area." I traced the hypothetical dumbass's route on the paper while Jesse looked on, nodding approvingly.

"That's how I see it too," Jesse confirmed. "But we've got two advantages. One is the bargest, obviously. But the other advantage is that, from what I understand, there's no reason for Henry to know anything about a null."

I tilted my head, considering. He was right—the whole reason Henry had become a nova was because he'd been abandoned. He could theoretically connect me to suddenly feeling human again outside of Will's house, but he'd have no idea that I would force a change if he were in wolf form. There was no reason for him to know anything about the Old World. "Or about the bargest, for that matter. You're thinking we should trip the trap."

Jesse stood and held out his hand with a flourish. "Scarlett," he said dramatically, "I have a romantic view you should see."

I rolled my eyes. "Dumbass."

His smile faded. "We could use some backup with this, though. Is there anyone you think would help?"

I leaned back on my hands, considering. The vampires wouldn't get involved without Dashiell's permission and a damn good reason why they should care, and I wasn't sure I could provide either in time. The werewolves were out, obviously, because they'd be spending the full moon in the national park behind Will's. That left one avenue. I got out my phone.

"This is Kirsten," the witch said on the first ring. "What's up, Scarlett?"

"Hey," I began. "I'm looking for some help here." I explained the plan to her: that we take the bargest and bring it to where we thought the nova wolf would be attacking that night. "Can you and some of your witches help us out?" I asked hopefully. "Maybe just help us look for the nova wolf in the park, be on hand in case there's trouble?"

There was a long silence on the line. "Kirsten?" I asked uncertainly.

"I'm here." She sighed. "It's a good plan, Scarlett—bold, but good—but I don't think I can help you."

"What?" I said, surprised. Of the three Old World leaders, Kirsten is the only one I would peg as a team player. "Why not?"

"The Luparii," she explained. "Witches have heard half a millenium's worth of stories about Luparii boogeymen. I doubt you could find a single one of them willing to mess with their property."

I remembered what she'd said at the meeting, that the Luparii were like an ex-con relative you avoided. "What about you?" I asked. "You're not afraid, right?"

"It's not that," she said reluctantly. "I'd be willing to go up against them on my own, but everything I do can reflect back on the witches. If they find out a witch in LA crossed them, it's not just me they'll come after. It's all of us."

"Isn't there anything you can do?" I asked in a small voice. My plan had seemed solid only a few minutes ago, but now the thought of pissing off the Luparii was starting to scare me too.

"Perhaps . . . ," Kirsten said thoughtfully. "You think the nova wolf is going to camp out in a specific part of the park?"

"Yeah." I explained the path leading into the picnic area.

"Okay. That could work," she said to herself. To me, Kirsten began, "There is a minor hex we use sometimes for big gatherings, or if we're working a spell that has to be done in an area accessed by the public. The younger witches call it the Humans-Go-Home. It makes anyone with no ties to magic have a sudden, overwhelming desire to return home."

"So it's not just a clever name," I said, straight-faced. Beside me, Jesse snickered.

"No." Kirsten went on, "I can wait at the road, and once you and Detective Cruz are in the clearing, I can cast a Humans-Go-Home on the mouth of the pathway. It won't affect the werewolf, but anyone else should stay away from that spot."

"That'd be great," I said, trying to sound enthusiastic. It was a good idea, but I'd been hoping for . . . I don't know, a promise to storm the park in droves or something.

"Just remember, Scarlett, that when you get close to the spell it'll dissolve again, so you can't leave that area once you're in," she cautioned.

"Pee before we leave the house. Got it."

I hung up and explained the idea to Jesse, who was a fan. Before either of us could even get off the table, though, my phone began playing "Werewolves of London." I frowned. I had spoken to Will less than two hours ago. Picking up the phone again, I said, "Hey, Will."

"Scarlett," he said in a tight voice. I could hear noise from the bar behind him. "Describe the Luparii scout to me again." It was not a request.

"Uh . . ." I glanced at Jesse, then held my phone away from my face and put it on speaker. "She's maybe six feet tall, dark-blonde hair, slim."

Jesse added, "Hey, it's Cruz. Her name is Petra Corbett. She was wearing a black pantsuit when we saw her."

Will sighed heavily into the phone. “I was afraid you would say that.”

Jesse and I exchanged a glance. “Why?” I asked.

“Because she’s standing on the sidewalk in front of my bar.”

Chapter 44

"Of course she is," I said harshly. I really wanted to kick something. It couldn't just be okay for ten minutes, could it? "How the *fuck* did she get out of that bathroom?" And had she brought more than one black pantsuit, or was she wearing the one with the urine stains? Okay, that part maybe wasn't relevant.

Jesse shrugged and said, "She might have access to magic you don't know about, or she's got a handler or partner in LA. Or maybe she had scissors in the bathroom. It doesn't really matter at this point."

"I agree," Will said darkly. He sounded like he was barely controlling his temper.

"What is she doing?" I asked.

"Nothing. She's leaning against what I assume is her car, glaring at the door to Hair of the Dog. She knows I can't attack her in the middle of Pico Boulevard."

"She's going to follow you," Jesse said quietly, and I finally caught on. We'd taken the bargest away from Corbett, so she was simply going straight for Will. Either she'd try to kill him, or follow him to the pack.

"Why?" I asked. "What's she going to do against a whole pack of werewolves with no bargest?"

"She's still a witch, Scarlett. We have no idea what she's capable of on her own," Will said grimly. "And if she has access to a gun and a lot of silver bullets . . ."

"I thought these douchebags were all about the hunt," I complained. "That's gotta be cheating." I looked at Jesse. "Can you arrest her for loitering or something?"

Jesse considered it for a second and shook his head. "We'd have to leave her at a police station, and like Will said, we have no idea what she can do as a witch. She could hurt a lot of cops."

There was silence for a few minutes.

"We could just, like . . . kidnap her," I volunteered. "Jesse and I could come down and bring her into the bar. You could leave her in the back room or something."

"Because tying her up and leaving her worked so well last time," Jesse interjected. "We can't stay with her, Scarlett, we have to go after the nova."

"And we can't kill her either," Will sighed. "The Luparii in France would have kittens."

I wished I were in the driver's seat so I could pound my head against the steering wheel. "Well, shit. I have one other idea, but I have to check on a few things. Will, we need to call you back." I hung up the phone before either he or Jesse could respond.

Jesse looked at me, a little incredulous. "Tell me you have a plan," he stated.

"You know . . . I think I might. I don't like it, but it might be our best option."

On the surface it was simple enough: we needed to kill the nova wolf first, then go to Will's to deal with the pack. But we'd need a lot of outside help, and Jesse would have to make a few more moral compromises. I wasn't sure how he'd respond to that.

To my surprise, though, Jesse got on board almost immediately. "With one condition," he intoned. "When this is over, we'll finish that conversation I started."

The conversation about getting the hell out of LA and starting over somewhere else. I took a deep breath and nodded. "We'll finish it," I promised, meeting his eyes.

It took almost two more hours for us to get everything ready, which included updating Will and Kirsten and Jesse talking to Noah about what we needed. The last thing Jesse did before we left was check his gun, making sure the silver bullets were still loaded. Then he looked at me. "You ready?" he asked me, snapping it into his holster.

I shrugged. "As I'll ever be."

Impulsively, he stepped forward and wrapped me in his arms for a hug. "You're doing the right thing."

I wrapped my arms around his neck, breathing in his familiar scent. "No," I corrected. "I'm doing the best thing. Doesn't make it right. Now let's go before I come to my senses."

The sky was already beginning to darken when we left Jesse's parents' house at 4:30 with Shadow in tow. I don't know if she was just picking up on the tension in the air, or if she could actually sense the full moon, but she seemed to know something was happening—she was even more alert than before, her head up and her feet stepping lightly as her head swung from side to side looking for new dangers. By 4:45, Jesse was piloting my van up the winding road at Griffith Park. We only had fifteen minutes before the sun went down, which was when we figured Henry Remus would change and get in position. The moon was supposed to rise at 5:52 exactly, at which point any werewolves who hadn't already changed would be forced into it by magic.

We were counting on the fact that Henry Remus didn't know who we were or what I could do. If we were wrong about that, and he had had the foresight to, say, plant a gun somewhere in the park, we were screwed.

As soon as we passed the park gate, I closed my eyes and focused hard on my radius. Finding the edges of it was getting easier and easier; whatever had thrown off my inner equilibrium seemed to be finally wearing off now, and my senses were attuned. I could feel the bargest six feet behind me, curled politely on the floor of the van, waiting for orders. But there was nothing else Old World in my range, even when I extended it.

"Anything?" Jesse said quietly, trying not to startle me.

Shaking my head, I opened my eyes. "No, but he could be anywhere in the park at this point. If, you know, we're even right about this being the right place."

"We're right," Jesse said firmly. I couldn't tell if he really believed it or was just trying to reassure me, but I was grateful either way. "Do you want to drive around the park awhile, see if you can feel him?"

I considered the idea. "Nah," I said finally. "There are a ton of places to park here, and they're going to change any minute. When they do, they won't need to stick to the trails. Better to wait for him to come to us." *If that's even what he'll do*, I added in my head.

Jesse nodded. "I'll head toward the Observatory."

I didn't respond. Doubts about this plan were eroding whatever half-assed, caffeine-fueled confidence I'd had in it. We thought we could predict what Henry Remus would do, but that was based on . . . what? A place that his mother thought he may have remembered from his childhood? It was so tenuous. The guy could still be in any park in the city; hell, any open area, really.

My phone buzzed in my pocket, and I read the new text with a grateful sigh. "They're all set up at Will's," I said to Jesse. "She took the bait."

His shoulders relaxed a little. "Good," he said. "Then it's just the nova left."

When we reached Observatory Drive, I caught a quick, dim glimpse of the wide path Jesse had shown me in the photographs, before he drove right on past like we were going straight to the Observatory. There was a long line of cars parked on the side of the road already, and I spotted Kirsten's vehicle among them. I gave it a little wave, just in case she was still inside.

Jesse pulled the van over to park behind a big gray SUV with stickers of a little stick family decorating the back window. It was almost five. "Should we head for the scenic overlook," I asked, "or wait a bit first?"

"Let's go to the outlook," Jesse answered. "I'll take Shadow." We were counting on the bargest to be able to move swiftly where I couldn't, and to catch the nova wolf if it somehow managed to evade my radius.

He got out of the van, and a moment later the back door opened so Shadow could hop out. I turned in my seat to see her stretching her long limbs in the dying daylight. She yawned, displaying those terrifying fangs again.

"And here we go," I whispered.

Chapter 45

Jesse felt like they were so far out on a limb, he could no longer even see the tree trunk.

He bent his left arm so Scarlett could take it, and with the bargest's leash in his right hand, they started down the wide path toward the picnic area. The park was almost completely dark now, and although Jesse could make out a dim buzz of light and sound up the road next to the Observatory, the path itself was deserted. They were deep in the park now, well above the city, and soon the quiet began to unnerve him. With each step on the path, Jesse was half expecting the nova wolf to leap out of the shadowed hillside on his left, straight onto his shoulders, breaking his neck. Suddenly, Scarlett's plan was feeling more and more idiotic. What the hell was he doing out here? He had no idea what the bargest would do even if it *did* scent a werewolf. For all he knew, the stupid thing wouldn't move until he gave it a command in French. He glanced at Scarlett, who looked just as nervous. She gave him an encouraging nod, and they kept going. "Don't turn around," she whispered, "but I just saw Kirsten heading toward the path, so we shouldn't be getting any humans this way."

Step by step, the three of them crept forward on the wide path, until they finally reached the big circular picnic area. "Anything?" Jesse said quietly to Scarlett, who just shook her head. She reached down and scratched behind the bargest's ears, which Shadow accepted graciously. She'd been fairly calm since they'd left the condo, but this was the most focused and purposeful she'd been since they had first seen her. It was like finally releasing a fish back in the water. Shadow knew what they were doing, and she was in her element.

"Maybe we're too early?" Scarlett suggested. "It's only five; maybe he's waiting to change until the moon rises."

"Or maybe we're in the completely wrong part of the city," Jesse sighed.

"What do you want to do?" she asked, looking at him expectantly.

"I guess we wait."

They perched on top of a picnic table covered in red graffiti, legs resting on its benches—except for Scarlett's bad leg, which she'd stretched out along the table next to herself. The bargest, calmed by Scarlett's radius, lay curled up under the picnic table bench too. "At least he won't be able to see Shadow as well in the dark," Scarlett remarked. "So we don't have to worry about her size scaring him off."

"I guess so," Jesse said doubtfully. "But this close to you, does she have any chance of smelling the werewolf magic anyway?"

"Nah, but it's okay," she said, patting his arm. "I'm the perfect nova wolf trap. He tries to sneak up on us poor unsuspecting humans, and *bam*!" She snapped her fingers. "Suddenly he's just another naked crazy guy."

Jesse laughed. They looked out over the city lights in silence for a while with their backs to the wide path, enjoying the view. He was having a hard time gauging Scarlett's mood: she seemed sort of introspective and pensive, but maybe she was just trying to anticipate the nova's next move. His arm and shoulders touched Scarlett's, and he felt it when a shiver passed through her. "Cold?" he asked, putting his arm around her.

She nodded. "You know what the Native Americans call the full moon in January?" she asked idly.

"What?"

"Wolf Moon. True story." She turned her head and went still, looking at him in the dim light from the Observatory street and the city lights themselves. They each had a flashlight stashed in pockets, but had planned to leave them off for the moment in order to make themselves more enticing prey. Slowly, Scarlett raised the hand farthest from him, lifting it to his face. Her fingers were cool as she laid her palm flat against his cheek, cupping the side of his face from his eyebrow down to his mouth. Keeping his eyes on hers, Jesse turned his head very slightly so he could kiss her fingers.

Scarlett slid her fingers up into his hair, closing the distance between their mouths. She kissed him tentatively at first, then with increasing need. Jesse returned the kiss with enthusiasm. He still held the bargest's leash in his right hand, but his grip on it loosened as Scarlett's tongue dipped into his mouth.

After a few minutes, Scarlett pulled back, and her eyes were shining. "What was that?" Jesse said, half to himself, half to her.

"That . . . was a thank-you," she whispered.

"For what?"

"For the offer."

Jesse stared at her a beat before he understood. And then his heart dropped. "I take it you're not accepting," he said huskily.

"I . . . ," she began, but then with a single sharp tug and no sound at all, the bargest's leash was jerked out of his hand. Jesse yelped with pain as it was dragged off his wrist, and suddenly, the bargest was free, darting down the bridle path into the darkness.

"Shadow!" Scarlett shouted. Jesse tried the bargest's French name. But she had vanished.

"Did you feel someone?" he demanded, jumping off the bench.

"No, no! I don't understand why . . ." Scarlett's eyes moved back and forth frantically as she thought. "The smell!" she cried. "I'm a space in the smell!"

In a flash, Jesse understood. The nova wolf had no way of knowing what Scarlett was—but even before he reached her radius, he would notice that he couldn't smell her. The absence of proof was proof itself. The nova might not know *what* she was, but he would certainly know something was off.

Scarlett climbed down from the picnic bench like she was going to follow the bargest, but neither of them had any idea where it had gone. By unspoken agreement, they both froze, listening. There was a short, cut-off growl and the sound of bushy plants being trampled. Then silence. "Lights," Jesse said brusquely. They both dug out their flashlights and switched them on. It would make them an easy target to the nova wolf, Jesse knew, but they were an easy target anyway. They both flashed the beams around the mouth of the bridle path, but aside from some disturbed dirt, there was no sign of the bargest.

"Maybe she just went after a rabbit or something," Scarlett said anxiously.

Jesse shook his head. "She's too well trained to be distracted by a rabbit." He flashed his beam on Scarlett's stomach, so the edges of it would illuminate her face. She was looking doubtfully at the bridle path.

"That's really steep," she ventured. "I'm not sure I can make it down there with my knee. Or, if I *do* make it down there, I'm not sure I can make it back up."

"Wait here. I'll see what's going on, and if we really need you down there, you can slide down on your butt." She nodded. Scarlett looked so vulnerable, and he wanted to tell her to be careful or to go wait in the car. Then he reminded himself that she was far more protected from the nova wolf than he'd ever be.

Jesse held his flashlight with his left hand, using it to support his aching right arm as it held up his weapon. He picked his way down the steep rocky path, which wound around like an infinity knot before leading down into the depths of the park. There was a lot of brush along the path, ranging from knee-high tumbleweeds to wide, stubby trees as tall as Jesse. It was surprisingly dark and felt strangely claustrophobic, especially considering the size of the park. He was very aware of his breathing, which seemed painfully loud and obvious.

In front of him, somewhere behind the biggest tree he could see, Jesse heard a pained canine yelp and a series of scuffling sounds. He circled the tree as fast as he could, the flashlight bobbing wildly as he worked to keep his footing. "Where . . . ?" he breathed, and Jesse caught a brief glimpse of motion even as he moved the flashlight past it. He jerked the light back and saw what it had been: the bargest, frozen with its feet planted and its enormous jaws pinning the neck of a limp werewolf to the ground. The werewolf in its jaws was a deep cloudy gray, smaller than the ones he'd seen before. The werewolf wasn't moving, and at first he thought the nova was already dead. Jesse stepped closer, cautiously, and saw its chest heaving up and down. The acrid scent of urine stung his nostrils, and Jesse realized the nova wolf had wet itself.

It was a spooky tableau, mostly because both creatures were just staring at him now, silent and unmoving. It was the least dog-like thing either of them had done.

He swallowed, mind racing. Of course. Scarlett had said the Luparii would need to use the bargest, which meant they'd need to train it . . . which meant they'd need to teach it restraint. They were trained to kill werewolves *on command.*

It was waiting for his command.

Jesse did know the French words for "kill it," because his French teacher in high school had been afraid of spiders. But if he gave the command, he was killing a defenseless creature, one who had surrendered and posed no threat to him. It wasn't the same as shooting the nova wolf in a fight, and Jesse found himself unable to force the words out of his mouth.

Sensing his hesitation, the nova wolf reared up in a sudden burst of strength, trying to flip itself free, but the bargest let out a low growl and pressed down harder, suppressing the nova easily. The wolf yelped with pain again. *It has to be done*, Jesse reminded himself. He remembered Kate and Samantha and Ruanna, the women who'd done nothing to deserve the brutality that this monster had shown them. Jesse needed to get justice for those women. He took a deep breath and said, "*Tuez-le.*"

His words were drowned out by the sound of Scarlett screaming behind him.

Chapter 46

I stood just before the drop-off to the bridle trail, listening as hard as I could for sounds from below. I wanted to yell down to Jesse, make sure he was okay, but I was afraid to spook the nova wolf—or the bargest. What if I yelled at a crucial moment and distracted one of them? If Jesse was actually in danger, there'd be more noise, wouldn't there?

I was focused entirely on the bridle path area, feeling useless, with fear tightening the knots in my stomach. Then I suddenly realized that I was alone, and exposed, and injured, in the dark. It seemed as though Kirsten's Humans-Go-Home spell had turned the area into an isolated bubble, with just the nova wolf, Jesse, and me.

I heard a tiny noise behind me. I couldn't even identify it, it was so soft. A branch breaking? A scuffle in the dirt? But I turned around slowly, flashlight beam bouncing around the clearing. There was nothing there. In the distance, I saw car lights coming down from the Observatory, people leaving for the night, and I told myself I'd just heard a car sound.

And yet . . . something felt wrong. I moved the flashlight beam through the clearing one more time, intending to turn around and yell for Jesse when I was sure it was okay. On the second pass, though, I saw a bright flash of something under one of the picnic tables. Twin glowing spots, menacing in the shadows.

Eye shine. Like you see in wolves.

I kept the flashlight moving, trying to hide my discovery, but it was too late. The werewolf crept out from under the table, growling. It started to advance on me.

It was clearly expecting me to try to run, probably figuring I'd be easy prey with the cane. It looked momentarily confused, however, when I started limping straight for it. That confusion, of course, was increased exponentially when I finally took the last step needed to get it in my radius.

I've changed werewolves before, and they each react a little differently. Some, like Will, roll with the change. Some freeze, some even start shaking from the sudden absence of magic. The wolf in front of me, however, simply dropped, like a rock in a pond. I hurried closer, wanting to keep him in range, and stopped when I was four feet away, keeping the flashlight beam on the werewolf.

It was a him; that was obvious. He was naked, curled in the fetal position, shock on his face. I limped a couple of steps sideways so I could see his face—it was Henry Remus.

But if Remus was here . . . I opened my mouth to yell at Jesse, but something must have clicked in Remus's brain, because suddenly he had scrambled to his feet and was *diving* for me with mad fury on his face. He moved like humans *never* do: not trying to catch himself or keep his balance, not adjusting his movement for the moment we inevitably collided. He simply *hurled* himself at me, clumsy and desperate.

Under normal circumstances I could have dodged him easily, but even when I ignored the pain in my knee, I couldn't move fast enough. I stumbled backward and tripped on the leg of a nearby picnic table, starting my own fall even as Henry Remus barreled into me.

We hit the ground hard, and the back of my head rammed the packed dirt like I was trying to dig a frickin' hole with it. It wasn't exactly the same spot where I'd struck my head two weeks earlier, but it was damn close, and nausea and dizziness were suddenly tugging at my attention like impatient toddlers. My cane slid away in the dirt.

On top of me, Henry Remus had recovered and leaned upright, his foul breath on my face. "*You* again," he hissed from inches away. "What *are* you?" My flashlight had skittered away when we collided, but it pointed more or less toward my feet.

I really wanted to come out with something like "your worst nightmare," but I was busy remembering where my limbs were. Remus pushed himself off the ground and straddled me, grabbing my shoulders and shaking them. "What . . . are . . . you?" he whispered.

Instead of answering, I opened my mouth and screamed. It wasn't tactical or anything. It was just that I was so scrambled by vertigo that it was the only sound I felt capable of producing. I drew breath to scream again, and Henry Remus leaned down on me, his grimy hand smothering my mouth, his elbows touching the ground as he rested his naked weight on my upper body. I struggled then, but I might as well have been pushing against a downpour of rain. Finally I wrenched my mouth open just enough to bite down on the skin of his hand as hard as I could. It tasted horrible, but it worked.

"Ow!" Remus cried, sitting up without getting off me, cradling his hand to his chest. He gave me a wounded look. "Why did you do that?"

"Seriously?" I panted, sucking in air. I wiped at my mouth with the back of my sleeve. Ick.

There were footsteps behind me, and suddenly I heard the glorious sound of Jesse's gun as he took the safety off. "Police," Jesse said, his voice scary-calm. He began circling around us, trying to position himself to see my face. "Get off of her."

"What?" Remus said, looking suddenly baffled. He didn't move. "Why are you guys *doing* this to me?"

Jesse was close enough to see me now, and even in the darkness he and I exchanged a confused look. "Are you . . . *whining* at us?" Jesse said in disbelief.

Remus's face twitched distractedly. "I'm trying to do something great here," he protested. "Why can't you people see that?" He turned his head to glare down at me. "And *you* . . . why are you taking him away from me?"

"Taking who?" I asked, confused.

"Brother Wolf," Remus said reverentially. "He speaks to me. He wants me to kill, to eat, to fuck, to *create*." He leaned forward, giving me a look at his flashing eyes, filled with madness. I could feel his erection on my stomach, and I almost threw up on him. "Don't you see how that's bigger than you?" he whispered.

"Jesse?" I said nervously. I really, really wanted the crazy naked person to get off me now.

"Enough," Jesse barked at Remus. "Get off her. Slowly."

"You disappointment me," Remus whispered to me, like we were co-conspirators. He leaned forward to put his hands on the ground by my head, making like he was going to push off the ground and stand up. But then in a quick, scary motion, he tangled his fingers in my hair and rolled my body sideways as he swung a leg over me, forcing me in between himself and Jesse's gun. I cried out with pain as my hair and knee were wrenched. We were kneeling, and he very slowly forced me to my feet. It took every ounce of self-control I had left to keep from screaming at the pain.

Remus held me between him and Jesse, who looked anguished and uncertain. "Drop the gun and kick it away!" Remus sang gaily, delighted with the turn of events. Jesse didn't move, and Remus pulled his fingers out of my hair and grabbed my chin instead. The other arm wrapped around my shoulders and chest, pinning me to him. "I can break her neck," he mused to Jesse. "I mean, I'm pretty sure. Never actually broken a neck before. But how hard can it be?" I could hear the *interest* in his voice. Jesse must have too, because he dropped the gun. Before I could protest he had kicked it off into the darkness.

At least my hands were now free. I dug my right hand in my jacket pocket. Seeing the motion, Jesse tried to keep Remus talking. "And who's with you?" Jesse asked, his voice tense but steady. "Who's the gray wolf?"

Remus went alert, looking anxiously at Jesse. "That is our mate," he informed him, his hot breath on my neck. He took his free hand off my chin—it felt like he was leaving a greasy film behind—and wrapped it around my waist instead. I suddenly could feel his fingers worming under the waistband of my pants, pressing into my skin. It wasn't sexual, exactly, but intimate, like he was digging for warmth. Ick, ick, ick . . . I focused on breathing, trying not to panic. You can take a hundred showers when this is over, Scarlett.

"I picked her and Brother Wolf transformed her. She is ours now." I couldn't see Remus's face while I was being employed as his human shield, but I saw Jesse react to Remus's expression with revulsion. "Where is she?" Remus asked Jesse, plain curiosity in his voice, like he couldn't find one of his shoes. "Have you done something to her?" He sighed elaborately. "I hope not. We went through *such* trouble to make her. Most of the potentials were too weak." He tilted his head, as if listening to an inner voice. "Although that's true, number five tasted . . . interesting."

"Oh, yeah?" Jesse said casually. Very slowly, I started to ease the Taser out of my pocket.

"Oh, *yes*. But now we have our mate. Brother Wolf tells her what to do, and she must listen," Remus giggled, as though he hadn't heard Jesse at all. "We *own* her."

Holy shit, this guy was nuts. We'd miscalculated, thinking that it would be a while before he could control Lizzy Thompkins as her alpha. But Henry Remus wasn't a normal alpha werewolf; he was a sick, twisted imitation. And Lizzy was in thrall. "She's fine," Jesse said reassuringly, keeping his voice level. "She's hanging out on the path back there with a friend of mine."

Shadow. I'd almost forgotten about Shadow. I looked at Jesse questioningly, but he was focused on Remus, not wanting to give anything away.

I made a show of squirming, like I was uncomfortable, to cover up the movement it took to get the Taser in position with my thumb on the trigger. Remus gave me a little shake to keep me still. He was . . . ah, God, he was sniffing my hair.

Clumsily, as best I could, I reached my arm around and tasered the sick fuck on the hip.

That was what was supposed to happen, anyway. But I was dizzy from being shaken again, and instead of making a clear connection between his skin and the two electrodes on the Taser, I think maybe one electrode brushed against his skin briefly. It was enough to get Remus to let go of me and stumble back a few feet, but it didn't have nearly the effect it should have. I swayed from the dizziness.

Remus was already starting to step toward me again when Jesse yelled, "Scarlett, *down*!" I dropped as fast as I could. Jesse flew through the space where I had just been, and hit Remus in a flying tackle that felt very satisfying to watch, especially after he'd just pulled the same crap on me. "Get out of range," Jesse told me tersely, and I complied, scooting away from Remus on my hands and one knee. The full moon was high in the night sky, and as soon as he popped out of my radius Henry Remus began to change again. Jesse yelled something in French—later I learned that it was the word "release"—and suddenly, the bargest streaked into the picnic clearing like a flying demon dog from hell. I knew then that I had chosen the right name for her, because in the dark clearing she was nearly invisible, like smoke in the darkness. Jesse scrambled away from Remus, picking up one of the flashlights and pointing it at the nova werewolf.

I'd never seen anything like Shadow's attack. She was effortlessly fast, pouncing on Remus like a supernatural puppy on a squeaky toy. Remus was bigger, but in the few weeks that he'd been a werewolf, he hadn't actually had to face a single challenge. His half-developed fighting instincts weren't prepared for something that had been trained her whole life to kill him. The poor crazy bastard never had a chance. Shadow pinned him in an instant, and while he was still trying to squirm away, Jesse yelled, *"Tuez-le!"*

Shadow tore out his throat.

Remus fell back, panting shallowly as the skin reformed on his neck. As soon as it was more than translucent membranes, but before Remus could even take a full breath, Shadow reached down and ripped it off again, spitting the skin onto the ground next to Remus's head. Then she did it again. And again. He began to visibly weaken after the third time she ripped his throat out, and by the fifth, he was barely moving his legs anymore. Shadow kept going until his blood stopped pumping into the ground. There was a brief shimmer as his body changed, and then Henry Remus was lying there dead.

Shadow came over to me and sat down daintily, blood soaking her muzzle and front paws where she'd dug at the wound. Jesse and I both stared down at Remus's body, and then Jesse went over and nudged it with one toe. "What about DNA?" he asked me. "Will his be normal?"

I nodded. Werewolf magic, like most forms, depends on life to sustain it. When Remus had died, the magic had left him, evaporating back into wherever it had come from to begin with. "I don't know about bargest saliva, though. Maybe your pathologist friend could do something with those tests?"

"Mmm," Jesse said noncommittally.

"Where's . . . ," I began, but just then she came limping up from the bridle path, a tired-looking wolf with gray fur and bright blue eyes. Shadow stood, looking at Lizzy with a confused face like she'd just dropped out of the sky. I put a hand on her collar.

Bereft of her alpha, Lizzy came cringing into the clearing, weak and injured. I was pretty sure that not all of those injuries were physical. I motioned for Jesse to take Shadow's collar and he did, leading her a few feet behind me. Then I painfully knelt down on the ground and called, very softly, "Lizzy. Lizzy Thompkins."

The wolf's eyes flicked to me once, confused, and she stopped, her paws dancing nervously on the ground like she was ready to bolt. No one has ever been able to really explain to me how much of themselves the werewolves retain when they're not in human form, so I had no idea if any of this would work. "Lizzy, shh, it's okay," I said soothingly. "He's dead. And we know someone who can help you." I held out a hand. "If you could just come a little closer, I promise I won't hurt you."

Lizzy edged a tiny bit closer to me, and when nothing bad happened, a little closer still. I felt the bargest shifting restlessly behind me, but Jesse stroked her and murmured reassuringly. Finally Lizzy took the last step she needed to get into my radius, and flopped to the ground, human again. I thought she was going to stay there, but she kept moving, crawling closer and closer, until she reached me. She was older than I'd imagined, maybe in her early- or mid-thirties, a skinny mixed-race woman with dark hair that spilled down her back in matted snarls. Then Lizzy pulled herself half into my lap and collapsed there, sobbing.

I looked up at Jesse with surprise, but he just gave me a sad smile. Passing the bargest's leash from hand to hand, he took off his jacket and handed it to me. I draped it over her shoulders. When that was done, Jesse asked, "Phase two?"

I nodded, awkwardly patting Lizzy's shoulder. "Phase two."

Chapter 47

Jesse and Shadow took off for the van first, and I followed with Lizzy Thompkins gripping my free hand in both of hers. She still hadn't said a word, but she seemed to feel safer when she was touching me; maybe because I was female, or maybe just because I'd spoken to her first. I'm not a particularly touchy-feely person, but after what Lizzy had been through in the last two days, I was willing to deal with a little awkwardness if it gave her the tiniest bit of security. Our strange procession made its way toward the road, and I felt the little pop of the Humans-Go-Home spell dissolving as I got close to it.

Jesse put Shadow in the back of the van and grabbed a bag of supplies we'd prepared earlier. He dragged out his new gardening wagon, threw the bag in it, and hurried back to Henry Remus's body.

I led Lizzy around the van, to the side where we would be hidden from the street. As I helped her into a set of old sweats that I keep in the White Whale, I kept an eye on the pathway through the van's windows. When Lizzy was dressed, she clutched my left arm and we stood guard together, leaning against the van and gazing across the street to where the path connected to the road. A few cars rolled past us on their way home from the Observatory, but no one went near the path to the little picnic area. Maybe five minutes later Jesse was back, walking briskly with Henry Remus's corpse in the big garden wagon behind him. I held up a hand for him to stop, and then peered right and left, up and down, the road. No one in sight. I waved him on. He climbed into the van and stashed the body in the built-in freezer compartment in the very back. "Did you use the whole bag of dirt?" I asked Jesse, worried. If it hadn't been for my knee, I'd have gone back and made sure the crime scene was covered up to my satisfaction.

"Yes," he said shortly. "And I dumped out some water and ketchup and left the empty ketchup bottle. It'll look like picnic leftovers."

We got Lizzy settled just behind the passenger door, and Shadow moved over to hug the opposite wall of the van in response, as if she understood that Lizzy needed space. There was just enough room to squeeze the gardening wagon in sideways between them. As we pulled away from the park, I called Will on my cell phone. "It's done," I told him. "We're on the move."

After Will, I called Dashiell and gave him the same update. Then I dialed Noah, since Jesse was driving. He was just returning from a run. "Yeah, I got it," he said breathlessly. "Do you have any idea how hard it is to get authentic shit like that on a moment's notice?"

We spent the next two hours driving from one part of the city to another. We swung by Jesse's parents' house to pick up a bag from Noah, and then went back to Huntington Park. Then we went north, up to Pasadena, where Hayne met me on the back of Dashiell's property. "You sure you're okay with this?" Jesse asked me, as he followed Hayne's waving hand into a parking spot near a little detached garage.

I looked at Shadow, still curled in the back. It wasn't her fault she'd been turned into a weapon. But she wasn't mine. I couldn't decide her fate any more than I could decide the fate of Jesse's gun. "I have to be," I said simply.

Hayne walked up to my window, and I pushed the button to roll it down. "Hey," he said. "We've got a space all ready."

"I can take care of this," Jesse said to me, unbuckling his seat belt. But I shook my head.

"I'll stay by the van, for Lizzy. But I want to say good-bye."

We both got out, and Jesse got Shadow out of the back of the van. The bargest stepped out as gracefully as ever, still coated with drying blood. Hayne whistled, very unprofessionally. "That is one ugly dog," he said admiringly.

Jesse walked Shadow over to me, and I awkwardly crouched down and cupped her face with my hands, ignoring the blood on her muzzle. I pressed my forehead against hers for a moment. "You are a *good girl*," I said meaningfully. A couple of tears trickled from my eyes, but I just ignored them. I didn't care anymore. I gave Shadow a little scratch on the neck again. "Good girl. Go on."

When I looked up, Hayne's face had softened. He handed me a handkerchief, and I wiped off the blood on my hands.

"Burn this, please," I said as I handed it back.

He nodded. "No one's gonna mistreat her," Hayne said to me kindly. "We've got the biggest kennel on the planet set up for her, and Kirsten's gonna come over in a few hours to brainstorm about how to put her down. I promise you it'll be humane."

I nodded. I understood: the bargest was too unpredictable and too dangerous to be sent back to France, and if she stayed in LA she'd hunt the werewolves. Not to mention the fact that she barely passed for a dog. "Thank you, Hayne," I said, meaning it.

Jesse walked her all the way in to the garage, assuring me that it looked very nice in there and that Shadow had plenty of space before he got back behind the wheel. This felt like one of the longest nights of my life, but it wasn't even nine o'clock yet. We had more to do.

I turned in my seat to check on Lizzy. She had drifted off with her back against the passenger seat. "She's out," I told Jesse. "Let's go."

Chapter 48

We pulled into Will's driveway at nine thirty. I coaxed Lizzy out of the van, and the three of us made our way to the door. I tried the knob, but it was actually locked, for once. I rang the bell, in full view of the street.

The door was opened by twenty werewolves and one teenage girl, all of them wearing pajamas.

I stared, momentarily speechless. Will's jammies had little wolf pups all over them. Esmé was wearing a modest pink silk set with a matching robe. Even Lydia was there, dressed in simple baggy pajama pants and another ribbed tank top. And they were all packed together, as tightly crowded as I'd ever seen a group of people be.

It was probably the funniest goddamned thing I'd ever seen.

I couldn't help it; I broke into laughter. So did Jesse. Lizzy simply stared, but she'd been through a lot and maybe didn't see the humor. A young woman in a Hello Kitty sleep shirt, matching boxer shorts, and an oversized cardigan pushed to the front of the crowd, her ponytail bobbing a head lower than everyone else.

"Hey, Scarlett!" Corry chirped. She looked down at her own clothes. "Yeah, I guess we look a little funny, huh?"

At her shoulder, Will added. "Glad to see you guys made it. Come on in." He was obviously trying to sound laid-back and friendly, but there was too much tension and exhaustion in his voice for that.

"Backward march!" Corry called, and the werewolf pack began shuffling backward. It was clear they'd had some practice moving like this. "Where to, General?" she asked Will.

He shrugged. "Back to the den, I guess." To me, he said, "We can talk there."

Jesse and I followed the shuffling wolves through the house, with Lizzy in tow. The back living room in Will's house has a huge picture window that looks out over the park. It also has a television attached to one wall and lots of simple, very durable furniture, complete with extra blankets and throw pillows. When we got in there, Corry went into the middle of the room and the wolves spread out slightly around her. I could feel some of them entering my radius too, which was okay. There was a movie playing on the TV, and I laughed again when I recognized it: *Dog Soldiers*, arguably the best werewolf movie ever made.

The real werewolves went back to watching the movie, alternately jeering and cheering at the characters. Will, Jesse, and I stood in the doorway with Lizzy, speaking quietly so we wouldn't disturb them.

I started by making the introductions. "Will, this is Lizzy, the werewolf I was telling you about," I said. Lizzy's eyes widened at the word "werewolf," and she shied away a little so she was standing half-behind my shoulder. Will must have anticipated that she wouldn't want to shake hands, because he kept his in his pockets. "And Lizzy, this is Will," I said very gently. "He's the alpha in Los Angeles, and he's a good man."

She looked up at me quickly, a little startled, and then she whispered something I could barely make out. "Pleased to meet you." It was the first time I'd heard her voice.

"And I'm very pleased to meet you, Lizzy," Will said kindly, all trace of exhaustion now gone. "I hope you'll want to stay within the LA pack, but if there are too many bad memories here, I would be happy to help you find a pack in another city. I want you to feel at home with us, so anything you need, please let me know." He reached out *very* slowly, so she would see him coming, and patted her on the shoulder. Lizzy nodded, her back straightening just a little. She glanced at me nervously, and I nodded at her. *It's okay.*

"Can I use a phone?" she asked tentatively, shifting her weight from one foot to the other. "My family doesn't know where I am."

"Of *course*! It's important that you don't tell them about what you are, but you definitely want them to know you're okay," Will said amiably. "Let's do that right now. My cell's over there on the table. Help yourself." He pointed to a side table next to where the werewolves were all congregating, and I admired the move. He wanted her to wade into her new pack mates, and for them to accept her. Motivated by the phone, she began stepping through the crowd. Corry, in the center of the werewolf pack, glanced up and smiled at her as she passed, then went back to talking animatedly to Esmé.

Will watched them talk. "The pajamas were actually Corry's idea, you know," he said quietly. "Make it look like we were having a pajama party, to explain why we were all together. I don't know if she intended this or not, but it actually calmed a lot of my people down, to have something kind of silly going on." He looked at me. "She's pretty remarkable, isn't she?"

I smiled proudly. "Yes, she is," I replied. As if her ears were burning, Corry met my eyes. "Hi," she mouthed, grinning. "Hi, yourself," I said back. My gaze traveled past her and spotted Lydia, who was squashed in the corner of a couch, giving me the evil eye. No one was talking to her, or even looking at her. She sat there and scowled for a moment, then tapped her watch so only I could see it. Her message was clear: *the clock is ticking*. My skin went cold.

I'd almost forgotten. I had eight hours to produce Eli or she'd come after me. It might as well have been eight minutes. I shivered and turned back to the men.

"Have you seen any sign of her?" Jesse was saying to Will.

Will nodded. "It went just like Scarlett predicted. She followed me home, although I pretended I was trying to lose her. She parked across the street until sunset, and then she started sneaking around the outside of the house."

"Is she still out there?"

He shook his head. "She left about ten minutes before you guys got here." He frowned. "Since you guys stopped her today, I'm guessing she's going to come after you next. She'll want the bargest back, and she'll want to make you guys pay for humiliating her."

I looked at Jesse. "I thought we were very respectful. Except for the part where we made her pee herself."

He just looked at me blankly, uninterested in banter. "Scarlett," he said quietly. "Can we talk for a second?"

"Uh, sure," I said, taking a deep breath. The worst was over, and he wanted to finish our talk. I hadn't expected him to ask right away, but it made sense.

Will herded the outlying werewolves closer to Corry, and they all crowded together in front of the movie. Jesse and I went into the kitchen, where I could still see the group through the open doorway into the den.

Jesse's eyes searched my face. "At the picnic table, you thanked me like you weren't planning to take me up on my offer."

I nodded. "I'm not," I said simply.

"Why?" he demanded. Then, with an embarrassed smile at the harshness in his voice, he said, "Sorry. I just don't get it." He reached across the space between us and added softly, "I'm in love with you."

I nodded, hitching up my courage. "No," I said, as calmly as I could manage. "You're not." He began to respond, but I held up a hand. "I know, I know. You think you are. I believe that, Jesse. But you're not in love with *me*; you're in love with the version of me that you wish I was." I absently rubbed the fading burn on my wrist, from when I'd thrown Leah Rhodes's body into the furnace at the beginning of all this. "You think you're better than the things that I do, and you want me to be better than them too."

"So you think I'm, what, a *snob*," he said incredulously, "because I don't believe you should be destroying corpses?"

"I think . . ." I paused, trying to choose my words carefully. "I think that you were right when you said what I really wanted was control of my life. But if I leave LA with you, start somewhere new, that's not me getting control. That's just me giving it to someone else."

He stared at me, wounded. "I don't want to *control* you, Scarlett. I love you."

"How can you," I said very quietly, "when you don't really know me?"

He stepped all the way into my personal space, touching my cheek with one warm palm. "You're wrong," Jesse said gently. He smelled wonderful, and it took every second of growing up I had done recently to not throw my arms around him.

Instead, I sighed and took a step sideways, away from him. "Maybe I am. But then why do I *feel* so right?"

He stared at me for a long moment, hurt, and I felt anxiety and sorrow twist in my gut. Then Jesse shook his head in disbelief. "This is about Eli. You're pushing me away because of him."

"Eli's out of the picture," I corrected him. "He left LA."

"Then it's still about Olivia," he insisted. "You think you can't be happy because of what happened with her."

I gave him a sad smile. "No, Jesse. For once, this isn't about the psycho hose beast. This is just me."

He paced a few feet away from me, and then turned on his heel and came back. "Do you love me?" he demanded. I blinked, unsure of how to respond. "Do you?" he pressed.

"Yes," I said quietly. "I love you. But I don't trust you."

Jesse rocked back like I had hit him.

I could have kept talking. I could have explained that I trusted him to have my back, to keep me safe, but I didn't trust that he wouldn't wake up next to me in a week, a month, a year, and decide that I was a stranger. That I was tainted.

I could have talked and talked, but we would have always ended up back here, with that betrayed expression on his face. "I need to take a walk," he said abruptly.

"Jesse . . . ," I began.

He waved an arm to dismiss whatever I was about to say and marched off toward the front of the house.

I breathed in and out, slowly. And I let him go.

After our talk, the excitement finally began to wind down. I texted Dashiell with the go-ahead, and he arranged for an anonymous tip to be called in to the police station nearest the ugly wedding cake-condo. A few minutes after Petra Corbett returned from Will's house, the police knocked on her door and found her in the middle of packing her bags. They claimed that they'd received a report of a man screaming in pain, and an annoyed Petra invited them in to prove that the condo was empty. When the cops opened the door to the back bedroom, however, they found a very dead Henry Remus, stark naked, lying next to a big pile of creepy, macabre prop house items: jaws full of fangs, vicious claws, stone knives. They all had Remus's blood on them. There was also a bunch of Remus's blood and hair inside a huge wire cage, along with a totally illegal Taser.

Jesse had hated planting that evidence, but he'd agreed it was the only option we had left. None of those things had any fingerprints on them, of course, but later we learned that when they searched the front bedroom, the police found a lot of weirdo occult stuff: spell books and charms and creepy black candles. And *those* things were covered in Petra's DNA.

Personally, I enjoyed the irony of the Luparii scout getting arrested for the one murder we were sure she *hadn't* committed. Jesse saw it a little differently. "She wanted the nova wolf," he said righteously to Will. He wasn't meeting my eyes. "And she got him."

"If she hires a really good attorney and fights hard, that evidence may not stick," Will warned us.

I shrugged. "I bet they'll at least deport her ass, though."

An hour later, Jesse called the relevant LAPD station and confirmed that Petra had been officially booked for murder. The pack was free to go back into the park and change.

Which meant that Corry was done for the night. I was supposed to take her home after I'd walked the pack into the park, but Jesse pulled me aside and asked me if he could drive her home instead. "I'm ready to be done," he said plainly.

I flinched. "Jesse . . . ," I said, touching his arm.

He shook it off and started to walk toward the door. Then he paused. "You're wrong, you know," he said, turning to face me. He was so angry.

"About what?"

"I *do* know you," he said firmly. "These things you do—the things we did today—you push them out of your head. *Terrible* things." He stepped closer and added, not unkindly, "What happens when you can't run away from them anymore? What happens when everything you've seen catches up with you?"

I recoiled as though he'd slapped me. We stood there looking at each other for a moment, and then he stepped in and kissed me on the head. "The thing that scares me," he said very quietly, "is that by then, maybe you won't find them so terrible."

And he left, taking Corry with him.

Chapter 49

I didn't cry, although I wanted to. I was sure I had done the right thing, but watching Jesse walk away still felt suspiciously like giving up on my own future.

When they were gone, I extended my radius to keep the wolves human until we could get a little deeper in the park. "Everybody ready?" I called.

About half of them left their pj's at Will's house, unashamed, while the rest of them kept them on. We hiked into the woods, going very slowly in my honor. We were a strange procession: almost twenty people compromising a mixed bag of ages and races, gathered around a girl with a cane like they were my Secret Service detail. Will brought up the rear to make sure there weren't any stragglers who got out of my radius. Nobody spoke much on the way, but after a few minutes I became aware of a man sidling toward me. I took a deep breath, working to keep the concentration required to extend the radius, and looked closer at him.

He was African American, with snow-white hair, and he looked like he was in his mid-fifties. I recognized him right away. He had been on a flight from New York with me a couple of weeks earlier, and he'd sent me champagne out of gratitude for making him human on the long flight. "Hello, again," I said politely. "I didn't realize you were actually part of the LA pack."

"That's because we haven't been properly introduced," he said cheerfully, with a honeyed Georgia accent. He wore stately flannel pajamas in a navy blue that disappeared in the darkness. His movements were easy and fluid, which felt a little ironic given that he looked like a senior citizen and I was walking with a cane. "Deacon Crosley," he said, holding out his left hand so I wouldn't have to stop using my cane. "I'm a photographer."

"Scarlett Bernard," I replied, shaking his hand. "Wait, I've seen your name before. You took some of the pictures at Will's bar."

"I did."

"They're *beautiful*," I said honestly.

"Well, thank you, miss," he said, pleased. Then he added, "If you don't mind me saying, you sure look tired. Run hard and put away wet, as we used to say."

"Yes, sir. It's possible that I bit off more than I could chew today," I admitted.

Even in the dim light from my flashlight, I could see his eyes twinkle a little. "But you had to find that out for yourself, didn't you?"

Those words sparked something in my head, an idea I'd have to look at later. But at that moment, Will called from the back, "That's far enough, Scarlett."

I smiled at Crosley and stopped, closing my eyes and extending my circle as far as I could so that those who had waited to disrobe could get a little ways away for privacy. "Go ahead," Will said gently, and the werewolves at the front of the pack began to step forward, out of my radius.

I'd never actually seen the pack on full moon night before. I knew that during the rest of the month, changing into a werewolf is a painful process that can take as long as four or five minutes. On the full moon, though, the magic calls them quickly, and the change is smoother. I watched the first row step away and crouch, and there was a moment that looked like water running over rocks, a sort of shimmering of skin and muscle followed by sprouting fur. It's like watching something being born, I thought. Natural magic at its most terrifying.

Those wolves moved aside, stretching and shaking out their fur, and another group moved forward, and then another. Esmé turned out to be a lovely tan wolf that could have made a fortune shooting wildlife calendars. Miguel, the wall of muscle who had terrorized Molly almost a week earlier, was a muscular, rangy wolf with a dusting of black where most of the others had brown. Deacon Crosley was a grizzled gray wolf. He yawned once, displaying a mouthful of fangs that would make any predator proud.

They all trotted off into the darkness, deeper into the woods. I watched them go for a while, entranced. Before she'd gotten very far, Will called to Esmé, who paused and waited at the edge of my radius. Will walked Lizzy toward her, whispering something in a low, soothing voice. Lizzy nodded and took the last careful step away from me, and towards her life as a werewolf. I looked away, not wanting to watch her go through the change again. I can be cowardly like that. When I looked back, Lizzy was in her wolf form again, and Esmé was nuzzling her, nudging her, getting her to move. I found myself smiling.

Will came and stood beside me. "You did good work today," he said quietly.

"Bullshit," spat a voice behind us.

Will and I both turned. Lydia stood there, still dressed, the last werewolf beside Will to change. She looked very sane, but that was almost scarier than when she'd been twitchy. She was trembling with anger.

"What's wrong, Lydia?" Will said patiently.

"I think this . . . *person* . . . killed Anastasia," she growled, pointing at me. "You-all seem to be playing nice, pretending like everything's fine now. But Ana's *gone*." Her voice broke on that last word.

Confused, Will looked at me. "I thought—Scarlett?"

Fuck it. "It's true," I said, as calmly as I could manage. "Anastasia attacked me two nights ago. I think maybe she followed me home from your house." I pulled down the collar of my jacket, showing them the bruises. "She tried to kill me. I stabbed her in the heart."

Lydia let out a scream of anguish and dove for me, but Will stepped in front of her and held her back.

"Why?" Lydia screamed, her voice a raw gash on the night air. "Because she was on to you? Because she knew you have a cure?" I glanced around. The other werewolves had heard the commotion and returned, gathering in a loose circle just outside of my radius. Several of them pawed the air, agitated, but most stood silently, staring eerily at me.

"I don't have a cure," I said wildly. I could feel anguished tears threatening to spill over my cheeks. "Please believe me, I can't cure anyone!"

"Eli!" Lydia screamed. *"You cured Eli!"*

There was a sudden tug of magic on my radius, and then a familiar voice said, "Cured me of what?"

Lydia whirled around. And Eli stepped forward out of the darkness.

I felt the steady pulse of magic in my radius, and I stared at him with my mouth open. He was a werewolf again.

He was a werewolf again.

By my side, Will subtly put a hand under my elbow to steady me. Eli walked toward us until he was right in front of Lydia. He was nude, but unaffected by it. "Hey," he said to her. "Hi, Will. Scarlett." He was careful not to let his eyes linger on me. "I've been running around the forest looking for you guys for hours."

Lydia dropped to her knees. I couldn't see her face, but whatever Eli must have seen made him stride forward and kneel down to hug her.

"Where were you?" she cried, wrapping her arms around him.

"I had a family thing, back in New York," he said casually, patting her back. "I had to keep it quiet because . . . you know. It's a vampire town." I just kept staring at him, speechless. What an awesome cover story. Why hadn't I thought of that a week ago? "Sorry I couldn't say anything. What's all the fuss?"

Lydia sobbed into his neck, telling him about Ana's death.

I glanced at Will, who seemed to have adjusted to Eli's second change a lot faster than I had. Too fast, actually. I wheeled on him. *"You?"* I whispered. "You did this?"

He nodded. "Sorry I couldn't tell you," he murmured. "We weren't sure if it would work. I was afraid his body might reject it the second time, and he said if you knew, you'd try to stop it."

"I fucking . . . you're damn right I . . . ," I sputtered. He grinned at me. Then he moved toward Lydia and Eli.

"Come on, Lyddie, let's give these two a chance to talk. You'll run with me tonight, and when we get back, we'll talk about a memorial for Ana," he said soothingly. She nodded, still crying, and rose to her feet, allowing Will to lead her outside my radius for the change.

And then it was just Eli and me.

"Hi," he said softly, smiling up at me.

"No," I mumbled. I swayed once, and Eli barely had time to look alarmed before I fell, sideways, landing on my left. He scrambled across the ground toward me. By then I was shaking, and tears had come. "No," I wept. "No, no, no, this can't be happening."

"Shh," he whispered. "Shh, it's okay, I wanted to."

"You did *not*!" I wailed, trying to control my breathing. "You did *not*, and don't say that you did. You were happy . . ."

"I'm happy with you," he insisted. I started shaking my head, and he took my face between his hands, gently forcing me to look at him. "Listen, listen. That morning, I followed you and Lydia to the diner." I froze, my sobs hiccupping to a stop. "I heard what she said to you. I knew she would never give up until she saw me."

"I could have changed her," I hissed. "I could have fixed it somehow, or talked her out of it . . ."

"No, you couldn't," he contended. "You were right, I could never stay in LA unless I was a werewolf. And this is my home. You're my home," he said simply.

I stared at him through my tears. It was like the fucking "Gift of the Magi." I'd thought I was fixing his whole life by changing him into a human again, and so he tried to fix my whole life by changing himself back. I let out a half-hiccup, half-laugh. Men.

"I love you too, you moron," I said, smiling at Eli through my tears. "I can't believe you turned yourself into a werewolf just to be with me."

"Well, I was gonna buy flowers, but then I thought . . . ," he joked, and pulled me close. I threw my arms around him. "What do you say?" he said, returning the hug. "Can we do this for real?" I could hear the smile in his voice. "I mean, we can keep it quiet, if you want," he added. "If you're worried that—"

I pulled back just far enough to put my mouth over his. "No," I said after I kissed him. "No hiding. No pretending." I kissed him again. "Take me home."

Chapter 50

Eli and I spent the whole next day in bed at his Santa Monica apartment. We talked a lot, and watched a couple of movies, and Eli insisted on elevating my knee and putting ice on it at intervals. He'd been a paramedic in another life, and old habits really do die hard.

We ordered pizza for supper, and then I told Eli I needed to go back to Molly's for a few things. He offered to come with me, but I wanted to go by myself so I could clear the air with Molly. I needed her to know we could still be friends even though I was looking for another place to live.

The sun had been down for an hour when I hobbled down the outdoor stairs at his apartment and made my way toward my van.

Hayne was leaning against the driver's side door. "Scarlett," he said, grinning.

"*Teddy,*" I retorted. "You could have just come and knocked, you know."

Ignoring this, he stepped back and opened the car door. "He wants to see you."

"Now?" I complained. But I didn't really have a good reason to blow off my boss, aside from a slightly less than professional *but I don't wanna.*

Hayne nodded, unaffected by my whine. "Fine," I sighed.

Half an hour later, I stalked into Dashiell's office. Well, as much as one can stalk with a cane. I saw Dashiell behind his desk, staring at my approach with a completely unreadable expression. My steps faltered, however, when I entered the doorway and saw Will sitting in front of Dashiell's desk—with the bargest.

"Shadow," I said in surprise, feeling all of them in my radius. The bargest trotted over and pushed her nose into my hand, wagging her strange club tail. I petted her head, which I could do without needing to bend. I looked up at Will, puzzled. "What are you doing here? I thought you were going to put her down?"

"I was," Will grinned. "But we came to a different arrangement instead."

I hobbled over to the second visitor's chair in front of Dashiell's desk and sat down. "What arrangement?"

"We got off the phone just a little bit ago with someone who calls himself the head of the Luparii," Dashiell announced. Tiny smile. "He was suddenly interested in taking my calls, after his niece was arrested for an American murder."

"And?"

"And we made a deal," Will informed me. "Petra Corbett's going to plead guilty to murder and serve her time. And the Luparii won't return to Los Angeles, *ever*."

I looked from one to the other. "That seems like a *really* good deal," I said slowly.

Will shrugged. "I think he was more angry at Petra for letting a null and a human get the better of her than anything else." I could see him trying to keep a straight face, but he looked positively *delighted*.

"What's the catch?" I asked warily. There had to be a catch.

"We never take the bargest out of LA County, and we don't allow any witches to examine the spell that built her," Dashiell said evenly.

I thought that over. "That's why you can't kill her," I summed up. "Even if you found a way to do it. You have to keep her as leverage in case they renege."

"Exactly," Will said, smiling broadly like I was a star pupil. "And we know you love dogs, and you haven't been able to have one because you're around so much magic." He spread his arms, indicating the bargest. "It's a perfect fit."

I stared at him. I admit—my heart leapt at the thought of taking Shadow. She would be a lot of work, both because of her size and because we had no idea how socialized she was, really. But I loved her already.

On the other hand, I wasn't a child anymore, and I wasn't stupid. "Of course, it doesn't hurt that it keeps your werewolves in line too. If I have her, and I work for you, that makes her a tool in your toolbox, doesn't it? What better way to restore faith in you as a leader than a scary new weapon?"

Will's face hardened. "No," he allowed. "It doesn't hurt. But let's not forget how my pack became unstable in the first place."

I winced. Touché.

"So what do you say, Scarlett?" Dashiell asked pleasantly. "Is that arrangement acceptable?"

They looked at me, both a little smug, waiting for my response.

I patted Shadow one more time and sat up in my chair. "Guys, you've seen *The Wizard of Oz*, right?"

Looking confused, Will nodded, and Dashiell said a short, "Yes."

I had a moment of stark curiosity where I wanted to ask him if he'd been to the original theatrical run, but I managed to stay on topic. "At the end of the movie, Dorothy realizes that she had what she wanted all along—but she had to learn that for herself. And see, I always thought that was total bullshit. Why wouldn't Glinda just tell her that the shoes would take her home the minute they appeared on her feet? Why go through all of that, just to realize the value of what you had?" I looked Dashiell and Will in the eyes. "But I'm coming around on that."

Dashiell sat there motionless—vampires have all the time in the world, literally—but Will leaned forward. "What are you saying, Scarlett?" he asked impatiently.

"I'm saying that I have value," I said flatly. "And I know it now."

An amused glint appeared in Dashiell's eye. "You're asking for a raise?" he said disdainfully. "All right. I suppose we could increase your pay slightly."

"No. Well, yes, a raise would be nice, but that's not what I'm asking for," I replied. "You want me to keep hiding messes for you, fine. You want me to take in the bargest, fine. But I've put my life on the line for you three times in as many months, and I want to be a goddamned partner."

Even Dashiell's eyes widened at that, and I felt a little twist of satisfaction. "What exactly does that mean?" Will asked.

"No more cleaning lady," I said firmly. "When you make big decisions together, I want to be there. I want health insurance and a small team I can work with to make sure we don't have any oversights. Oh, and you're paying for my knee surgery," I added to Dashiell. "Call it a signing bonus."

Will stirred in his seat, but my eyes were on the vampire.

"We do not accept demands," he said coldly. "What's to stop me from killing your bright young brother instead?"

I'd been expecting that, and I forced myself to shrug, keeping my face as neutral as I could. "You could do that," I allowed. "It sure would show me who was boss. But if you touch Jack, if you send *anything* his way besides the occasional 'Keep up the good work, buddy,' you will never hear from me again," I said flatly. "You will lose me as an asset. I will go to another city and declare loyalty to another cardinal vampire, or maybe another alpha werewolf, and I will use everything you taught me for someone else's gain."

"We could kill you," Will pointed out, but in a neutral, "devil's advocate" kind of way. "And we've got Corry now."

"You could do that too." I shrugged again. "Why not? My life isn't worth much. But if anything happens to me, I have arranged for Corry to leave LA and offer loyalty to another city too. We *can* do this the hard way, guys," I said calmly. "Or we make a few adjustments, keep the peace, and you can let me help you."

Will and Dashiell exchanged an unreadable look. "Give us a moment," Dashiell said carelessly.

"Of course," I responded. "I'll take Shadow outside. But," I added boldly, "do me a favor and conference in Kirsten. She deserves a say in this too." And I limped out of the room, with as much dignity as I could manage.

Shadow went slowly out to the yard with me, being patient with my cane. She pooped on the cobblestone driveway, right in front of one of Dashiell's cars, and looked up at me guiltily. "Good girl," I told her.

When we got back inside, Dashiell looked grim. He pointed to the chair, and I braced myself for a smackdown, possibly physical. But he said, in a cold voice, "Fine. We agree to the partnership, the health insurance, and the bonus for your knee. But no team. Instead, you'll take Corry on as your official apprentice, and the two of you are a package deal."

I took a deep breath. It still felt wrong, making decisions for someone else. But Corry had asked to be a part of the Old World, and helping the werewolves last night had seemed almost . . . good for her. "She gets paid $10 an hour, and works nights and weekends only," I negotiated. "And when she turns eighteen, *she* gets to decide whether to keep working for you or not. If she says no, you let her go with your blessing."

Dashiell arched an eyebrow. "If we're going to pay her, you won't get a raise."

"I can live with that," I said firmly, looking him in the eye. "But if Corry's going to work for you, her mother needs to be able to know about the Old World."

And to my eternal surprise, Dashiell did something I'd never seen from him: he full-on *grinned* at me, a natural unguarded smile. If I hadn't known better, I'd say he was . . . *proud* of me. "Sounds like we have a deal," he said levelly.

And we did.

Epilogue

Tuesday. Moving day.

Shadow trotted at my heels as I limped around Molly's house collecting my things. There were a lot more of them than I remembered, and it was a little sad, having to tear my belongings away from their homes in the kitchen drawers and on the movie shelf. Molly had mysteriously procured a bunch of boxes from somewhere and left them out for me. I went around the house and filled them up, leaving them where they sat so Eli could come carry them out to his truck when he arrived in a few hours. I had hoped Molly herself would wake up to make an appearance, but although I kept popping into range of her, she never emerged from her room. I wasn't sure if I had fully burned that bridge, but it did seem to need some repair.

At ten thirty, the doorbell rang, and Shadow went into an immediate stalking pose. "No, Shadow," I cautioned. "First we see who it is, *then* we eat them." She tilted her head at me in a classic "I know you're trying to communicate, but I'm a dog" pose, and I laughed and limped toward the door.

I opened the door. It was Jesse. Wearing, of all things, an immaculate suit and tie. "Um, hey," I offered. "I didn't expect to see you." We hadn't spoken since the night of the full moon.

I realized, with a pang of sorrow, that I had missed him.

"It's Tuesday," Jesse reminded me, hands in his pockets. "I promised to take you to see the surgeon."

"Oh. Right," I said lamely. I'd forgotten the appointment. "I didn't think you were still gonna . . ."

Jesse shrugged. "I swore on my honor," he said simply. "And I'd like to keep whatever I have left."

I eyed his clothes. "Is this a particularly fancy doctor, or are you *also* planning to tell me about Jesus my Lord and Savior?"

He smoothed down the tie self-consciously. "I have an interview later today. Didn't know if I'd have time to stop and change." I opened my mouth to ask if the interview was for Homicide Special, but he gave me a tiny head shake and said, "Get your coat, we need to go."

I put Shadow in the megacrate Dashiell had sent me and got my jacket. When I returned to the door, Jesse was staring at the half-packed boxes. "I heard Eli was back. You moving in with him?" he asked, his voice detached.

"Just for a bit, until I can find a new place. One that allows *really* big dogs."

"Are you referring to Shadow or Eli?" he asked innocently.

I swatted him on the arm, and Jesse smiled faintly. "He really loves you, doesn't he?" There was sadness in his voice, and bitterness, and pain.

I looked up at him. "There are different kinds of love," I said quietly. "His is the kind I need right now."

Jesse nodded silently, stepping aside so I could make it through the doorway. I started to scoot past him, but impulsively stopped, brushing dust off on the back of my jeans. I met his eyes and held out my hand. "Friends?" I asked.

He shook my hand, a ghost of a smile on his beautiful face. "Partners, dummy," he corrected. "Come on, I'll race you to the car."

Acknowledgments

Hunter's Trail has been my most ambitious project to date, and it would never have come together without quite a few helping hands. Thank you to Tracy Tong, who didn't have to handle as many fashion questions this time around, but who did suggest that Griffith Park might be a good location for a showdown, and to the endlessly talented Elizabeth Kraft, who is as good at beta reading as she is at bookmark design (which is really, really good). And a big thank-you, as always, to my entire family—both the huge one I was born into, and the one I made for myself—for all your support, encouragement, and interest.

My deepest thanks also go to Dr. Adrian Treves from the University of Wisconsin, who was willing to entertain any number of my bizarre questions about wolves. His generosity made this book better, and any misrepresentations of real wolf behavior are my own creative decisions, and not a result of his excellent advice.

Thank you to the team at 47North, who were as patient and accommodating as ever, and a very special, quite enormous thank-you to my fellow 47North authors, whom I leaned on many times when I needed help or advice, or to just rant a little when I got stuck. You guys have truly made this process into a pleasure.

Speaking of social media, I also want to thank those of you who e-mailed, messaged, or tweeted me to ask about *Hunter's Trail* and tell me you like the series. You guys mean the world to me.

My thanks to the people who took time out of your lives to post reviews—good or bad—for the books, and to spread the word when you enjoyed them. Without you guys, I wouldn't be able to keep doing this. I am so honored that my books are in your lives.

For more information about me, adorable photos of the real-life Max, sound tracks for all three novels, and much more, please visit my website at www.MelissaFOlson.com.

About the Author

© Elizabeth Kraft, 2013

Melissa F. Olson was born and raised in Chippewa Falls, Wisconsin, and studied film and literature at the University of Southern California in Los Angeles. After graduation, and a brief stint bouncing around the Hollywood studio system, Melissa moved to Madison, Wisconsin, where she eventually acquired a master's degree from the University of Wisconsin–Milwaukee, a husband, a mortgage, two kids, and two comically oversized dogs—not at all in that order. She is the author of *Dead Spots*, *Trail of Dead*, and the short story "Sell-By Date."